LORD EDGINGTON INVESTIGATES **ABROAD**

BOOK 2

DEATH ON THE NIGHT TRAIN TO VERONA

A 1920s MYSTERY

BENEDICT BROWN

COPYRIGHT

This is a work of fiction. Names, characters, places, and incidents are either the product of the author's imagination or are used fictitiously. Any resemblance to actual persons, living or dead, is entirely coincidental.

Copyright © 2025 by Benedict Brown

All rights reserved. No part of this book may be reproduced or used in any manner without written permission of the copyright owner except for the use of quotations in a book review.

First edition September 2025

Cover design by **info@amapopico.com**

For my father, Kevin,
I hope you would have liked these books an awful lot.

LORD EDGINGTON'S GRAND TOUR

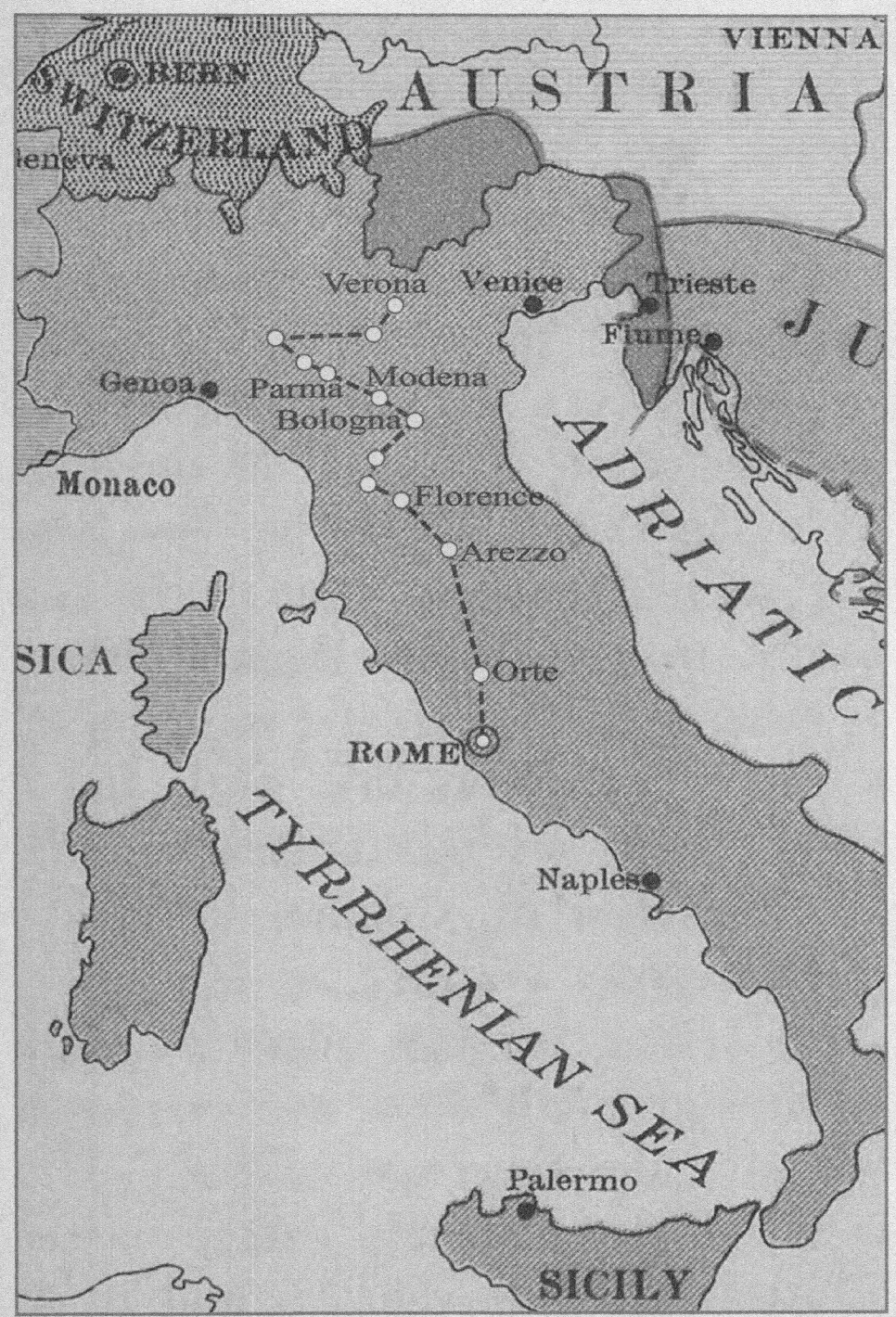

Rome to Verona

READER'S NOTE

This is the second mystery in the new *Lord Edgington Investigates Abroad* series, but it is spoiler free, and you don't have to have read any of my other books to enjoy it.

At the back, you'll find a list of any unusual or period words I've used. I've included translations of the foreign expressions in the book, though I think the majority of them are easy to understand in context. You'll also find a character list and chapters on my historical research and influences.

I hope you love it!

CHAPTER ONE

Rome, Italy, September 1929

I thought I would struggle to love Rome as much as the places we'd already visited in Italy. That was before I came to realise that the Eternal City is different from any other. You see, I would happily move to Florence tomorrow, but if someone were to tell me that I could never set foot in the Italian capital again, I fear my heart would break in two.

The three months we'd already spent in the country had proved that the world was not the place I'd previously imagined. It was wider, brighter and more complex. Italy felt as close to my home in England as Mars is to the moon, and every single thing there, from the manner in which people greeted one another to the way they dressed, and communicated, was distinct from what I knew. The food wasn't bad either.

I sometimes felt like an anthropologist studying the ways of a new civilisation, even though, in reality, *I* was the rare species. I stuck out in Rome like a chicken on holiday in a fox's den. The strangest thing was, though that, while I'd spent my whole life feeling out of place and self-conscious, not fitting in there made me feel more like myself. I jumped out of bed each morning, eager to explore every facet of Roman life. I drank coffee in piazzas, discussed art with cultured locals and even tried my hand at painting – I was, inevitably, almost as bad as my grandfather.

As I prepared to leave the city, I felt as if I had to say goodbye to an important part of me. It was almost as though, having built up a life for myself, I was now required to leave behind a foot or an arm or something imperceptible that I never knew existed. The one saving grace was that I had spent so much of my time in that romantic city thinking of a girl I'd briefly met, that I hoped our exit might soften the blow of losing her. The fact I was now due to travel to the home of Romeo and Juliet made this very unlikely.

Our servants had already left for Verona in the Alfa Romeo limousines that grandfather had purchased for their comfort, and we would take the train from the central station in the Piazza dei Cinquecento.

"Are you ready to go, Master Christopher?" our chauffeur asked as I looked up at the villa where we'd spent the last month.

"Not really, Todd," I answered quite honestly. "I'm going to miss our time here." I looked down at the River Tiber which ran past the front of the property. It glistened prettily in the afternoon sunshine. "I've had the most wonderful experience, and I was hoping that it would never come to an end."

"But best of all you didn't find any bodies!" he whispered in case his employer should happen to hear.

I smiled so much that it turned into a laugh. "Yes, it has been a few months now. I'm starting to believe that things have changed, and Grandfather and I won't get tangled up in a murder investigation any time soon."

Todd's face suddenly fell, and I knew just what he was thinking. "Dear me, Master Christopher—"

"Oh, no. I shouldn't have said anything!" Panic had entered my voice. "I've cursed my luck."

"There's no such thing as luck." The words carried over to me from the pillared porch of the neo-classical house, and there was my grandfather, hurrying down the stairs to us. "A man's destiny is his own, and don't let me catch you saying otherwise."

"Yes, Grandfather." I decided not to point out that another of the old sleuth's favourite maxims directly contradicted this one. He was in a good mood, and I didn't want to spoil it.

He came to stand next to his immense Bugatti motor car and, inflating his chest, looked up admiringly at our temporary home. This was all the time he'd set aside for reflection, and he immediately turned to climb aboard the stately black and white vehicle.

I allowed myself a few seconds longer, but then our dog came shooting past me, and I followed her into the car. Todd released the brake, and we rolled out of the driveway. For all his self-possession, I believe that even my grandfather looked a little nostalgic for the city we were about to leave. I might have said there was a mistiness to the old lord's eyes, but he turned to look out of the window and wouldn't say a word until we reached the station.

I took that time to enjoy the sights of Rome one last time. We followed the river for some distance before turning towards the majestic Colosseum to circle its ancient walls. I found the sight of it just as awe inspiring as the day we'd arrived, and I would happily have jumped from the vehicle to revisit it. I couldn't help imagining the chariot races to which it had once borne witness, though I did my best not to think of Christians being eaten by lions and men brawling to the death.

In mere minutes, the luxurious vehicle had crossed the city, and it was time to say goodbye to our factotum.

"I hope you have a trouble-free drive to Verona," I told Todd in a solemn tone, despite the fact we would only be parted for a day.

"He's coming with us." Grandfather explained as though this were the obvious arrangement.

"I beg your pardon?"

He looked a little concerned about me as his right-hand man helped a porter to unload our luggage. "You heard me. Todd is coming on the train with us. I've hired a local driver to transport the Bugatti north."

It took me a few seconds to make sense of what he was saying. "You bought an inordinately expensive car but prefer to take the train, and now you're paying someone to drive it to our destination so that your usual chauffeur can accompany us?"

He brought his hands together and smiled. "You see, Christopher. It wasn't so difficult to understand."

It was at this moment that a smartly dressed Italian driver popped up beside me with his gloved hand extended to collect the keys. With a softly issued, *"Prego,"* he entered the vehicle to set off through honking traffic.

"But…" Just as I had been doing for much of the last four years, I struggled to comprehend what my complicated mentor was thinking. "…why?"

He looked pensive for all of three seconds. "It's quite simple.

After the last time we travelled by train – a method of transportation I greatly prefer over long distances – I decided that I would never again embark on such a journey without sufficient staff to assist me."

There were any number of reasons to pick apart this bizarre statement. For one thing, our train trip from Britain to the Continent had been the very definition of comfortable, and at no point had we lacked for the attention of our attendants. There was no sense in reigniting that particular discussion, though, so I focused on another mystery.

"I can't understand why you don't simply employ Todd as your valet and leave someone else to deal with your many cars."

He shook his head even as he walked away from me. "There are few people I can trust to enter my inner circle, my boy. So unless you see yourself taking responsibility for the driving, we'll leave things as they are."

I'd tried driving a few times, and it did not suit me or the hedges into which I crashed.

"You make a very good point," I lied as I seized my travelling bag. Our golden retriever, Delilah, gave me a sympathetic look, and Todd took his master's remaining case so that the three of us could hurry after him.

"Come along, all of you," Grandfather commanded without turning round. "We have a train to catch."

My lofty forebear, Lord Edgington of Cranley Hall, was not the kind of person who arrived early for appointments. He lived his life with a five-minute margin of error. Such was his confidence, he felt that no traffic jam or roadblock could delay him, and he strode towards the immense iron and glass station with all the self-assuredness of a man who knew that the train would be there waiting for him when he reached the platform.

"Delayed?" he asked in Italian. I concede that he had picked up quite a lot of the language during our time in the country. "How can it be delayed?"

The stocky, dark-eyed station master pulled down his cap and changed to English in the hope it might appease his honourable guest. "My apology, Lord Edgington. I no know the reason. I assure that we do all we can for you."

Before he could say anything more, an incredibly neat man with bushy eyebrows and a matching beard stepped down from one of the waiting carriages and shot over to us at breakneck speed. He was not a tall gentleman, and the pace at which his short legs moved reminded me of a duck paddling beneath the water. He wore the livery of the *Compagnia dei Treni Notturni,* with its bright emblem picked out in silver brocade on his breast pocket, and I took him to be the conductor.

"Lord Edgington, Lord Edgington!" he called over eagerly, and I thought, *Here we go. Another of Grandfather's admirers.* "I can't apologise enough for the delay. My name is Georges Nagelmackers, and I will be your *chef de train* for your journey to Verona."

He bowed low and long, and I tried to build up an impression of the man based on the first moments of our acquaintance. He certainly wasn't British, not least for the politeness he'd shown which bordered on subservience. From the way he'd described his occupation, I could tell that he was a French speaker, though he didn't sound like any of the Francophones I'd met on my travels.

"Is that a Belgian accent I detect?" Grandfather hazarded. "You're from Brussels, if I'm not mistaken." The chance to show off his powers of deduction had apparently made him forget the inconvenience of having to wait for a train.

Returning to his full height to smile for a half-moment, Nagelmackers now bowed once more to show just how impressed he was. "I am indeed, Lord Edgington. You have quite the ear for accents."

In case, like me, you've lived your life under the impression that Belgium was some far-off land, I'd recently discovered that it shares a border with France and wasn't nearly so distant as I'd always (for some inexplicable reason) imagined.

"Now, about our train…" As Grandfather had won the man's respect, and perhaps his confidence, he evidently believed this was enough to solve the little matter of our delayed departure.

Sadly for us, he was mistaken, and M. Nagelmackers's expression turned contrite once more. "Yes, Lord Edgington, about your train… I am terribly sorry to inform you that the locomotive needed to operate the service to Verona has been delayed. It is quite out of my control, but I can assure you that…" He paused then, and I got the sense he was doing his best to be both honest and evasive at the same time. "… that it is on its way here and we shall leave forthwith." He extended his hand to gesture towards the waiting room door. "You will find more of your fellow travellers in the first-class salon."

Grandfather glanced ahead of us, and I thought he might object. Instead, he tipped his top hat to the helpful chap and moved in the direction we'd been pointed. Todd raised his eyebrows to me, and I could tell that he meant, *Things already aren't going as they were supposed to.*

I looked at the line of burgundy carriages and noticed that the second-class compartments already had people inside to await our departure. I only had a few seconds to inspect them, as I realised that I was standing alone and even Delilah had scampered off ahead of me.

The waiting room had an appropriately grand entrance with a fleur-de-lis pattern painted by hand on the translucent glass door. I found myself questioning what lay beyond it, but before a clear picture could form in my mind, the sound of an angry man's protestations carried out to us.

"I know that, you snivelling idiot. Now tell me what you're going to do about it, or I'll have your head!"

CHAPTER TWO

My grandfather threw the door open and veritably swooped into the room, his long grey morning coat catching the hot air of the afternoon. If whatever had preceded our arrival hadn't served to unsettle the men and women within that spacious salon, the famous detective's entrance certainly did.

A rather nondescript, sleepy-looking man instantly sat up straighter. The woman in a large, elaborate hat beside him began to fan herself far faster than was necessary, and the dapper fellow who had just been shouting at the porter froze where he stood.

"I suppose it can't be helped," he said in an accent that I might have been able to identify as German even if he hadn't added a brief "*Entschuldigung.*" He had presumably been holding the station employee by the collar, as he proceeded to brush off the man's clothes ineffectually. "Please let me know if you have any news."

Looking back at my grandfather, he seemingly decided that this gesture didn't go far enough and went poking in his pocket for a coin that he placed in the petite porter's hand.

The worker hurried off to whatever his next task was, and the German kept watching my grandfather. He had bright blue eyes that shone like candles, and a prominent brow that reminded me of the craggy overhang of an alpine mountain. I can normally construct some impression of a person's character and background from his appearance, but this tetchy figure was a mystery to me. I would have said that he was thirty-five, and his clothes were clearly well-tailored and expensive, but I was at a loss to say who he was or what he did in life.

"Lord Edgington," an American voice now spoke up. The woman with the flamboyant hat, which held a large display of wax fruit and silk flowers, stood to engage my grandfather in conversation. "My name is Sharlene Campbell, and this is my husband, James Joseph. Say hello to the man, James Joseph!"

She barked this last sentence at the slight, spectacled man sitting on the bench behind her, and he duly rose without raising his eyes.

"James Joseph Campbell, as my good wife just mentioned." He held out his hand and bowed his head.

I could tell from the way Grandfather sucked in his cheeks that he didn't know what to make of the pair of them. I could also tell that, although he would have liked to concentrate on the man who had first caught our attention, Mrs Campbell wouldn't allow any such thing.

"I am such an admirer of your work, your lordship: a true fanatic, you might say." She had a warm, treacly voice. I couldn't tell from whereabouts in America she hailed, as I'd only met one true American before (and another who turned out to be an imposter).

"I genuinely enjoy meeting my admirers." Grandfather pretended to be coy, and I was certain he hoped that the interruption had reached its conclusion. He wasn't the only one. Delilah walked to the corner, to curl up beneath the bench with a yawn, and I realised that we'd lost Todd at some point.

"Oh, you Brits. You all have such… what's the word I'm looking for, James Joseph?"

Her husband started then, as though he hadn't expected to be addressed. "I can't say, my sweet."

"Yes, you can, James Joseph. They all have such…"

"Bad teeth?" he cautiously replied. "I don't know, my darling. I really don't."

That impatient tone entered her voice again, and she thwacked her husband's legs with her closed fan. "Bad teeth indeed? I meant wit, James Joseph! Brits have such wit. Do you really think I would tell a marquess that he had bad teeth? Have I recently lost my mind?"

"Yes, my love …" He realised his mistake and quickly swallowed his words. "Or rather, no. You are quite the most *compos mentis* individual I know." He had a halo of curly hair but was quite bald on top and set about pulling on a clump of what was left in a gesture that was part self-punishment, part nervous tic.

The immensely tall, gaunt woman continued to address her hero as if she had not just publicly reprimanded her husband. "It is so nice to make your acquaintance, my lordship. We're here all the way from Savannah, Georgia, in the United States of America. Do you know it?"

Grandfather was unusually hesitant, and so I answered for him. "The United States?" I asked, as I found the question a little patronising.

The husband laughed at my inelegant reply, which I thought was a bit much. I had hoped that he would have recognised me as a fellow brow-beaten dimwit and shown some solidarity, but no.

"I meant Savannah," Mrs Campbell clarified, as if my mistake was quite understandable. It wasn't.

I'd long since learnt that coming across as an idiot had its benefits. For one thing, people were more likely to underestimate you, which was incredibly useful when investigating complicated crimes. And for another, my grandfather could no longer be certain whether I was putting on an act, or I really was as stupid as I sounded – which I'd say makes me something of a genius.

When the silence held between us for a little too long, Grandfather began to recite the relevant encyclopaedia entry, "Situated in the southern state of Georgia, Savannah was originally founded under grant from George II and would go on to be a royal colony and an important port on the Savannah river from which the city takes its name."

"So you *have* been there?" The lady beamed at him, but Grandfather could only look bemused as to why this conversation was taking place.

"Alas, no, madam. Or rather, I have only visited it within the pages of the books in my library." He spoke in a weary voice. "This is my first time travelling abroad."

"What a disappointment." This appeared to be her assessment not just of the outcome of her enquiry but the whole encounter as, with something of a grimace, she sat back down and pulled on her husband's sleeve to ensure that he would do the same.

Grandfather still looked puzzled as to why Mrs Campbell had felt the need to accost him.

As we crossed the room to an unoccupied bench in the far corner of the plushly appointed waiting room, it became clear that everyone present had been listening to our conversation. The man who had made such a fuss before we arrived was still staring at us, apparently horrified to see my grandfather there, but the others in the room were just as attentive.

There was a pale young woman with incredibly thick-lensed glasses who I decided must be a maid. I know that might sound like a feat of deductive brilliance on my part, but her petticoat and white gloves rather gave it away. She looked pensive as she watched us through thick glasses and sighed a little tragically as we passed. Perhaps it was because the first girl I ever loved was a maid, but I found her rather gorgeous. I noticed her soulful brown eyes, which were magnified by the thick lenses of her glasses, before getting distracted by a far showier character sitting opposite her.

The gentleman, and I use that word in a literal sense, sat very straight with both hands atop a silver cane that was almost an exact copy of my grandfather's. He wore a long summer cape of white silk, which immediately told me he was a wealthy sort. Beneath a feathered hat, his dark features suggested that he was Italian, but then I'd come to such conclusions before and been proved wrong. The swarthiest fellow I've ever met was a chap from south London with not a drop of Latin blood in him. In this case, the fact that we were in Italy made that outcome a good deal less likely.

We took our seats on the velvet-cushioned bench, and I noticed that there was a newspaper wedged into the seat behind me. Someone who had taken the previous train must have left it there, and I was happy to see it was in English. Unlike my grandfather's, my own Italian had come to a screeching halt somewhere around *Buongiorno!*

Before I could open my newly acquired edition of *The Paris Herald,* the German was up on his feet, thundering back and forth in front of his bench and issuing a low moan each time he turned. This elicited a response from a man in the corner whom I was yet to spy.

"Would you stop that?" I couldn't see his face, but he sat with his shoulders hunched and seemed like the type who did not wish to be noticed. From his voice I could tell he was British, and from his crabby tone, it was clear that he had a short fuse. "You may be of a nervous disposition, but there's no reason to impose your mood on the rest of us."

The handsome German opened his mouth before surely remembering he was in the presence of the world's most suspicious judge of character and throttling his response. Instead, he nodded solemnly to his challenger and returned to his seat.

The grumpy fellow, who had a pair of binoculars on his person, was partially obscured by the bank of benches in the middle of the room. Above it was a large, gold-framed clock with faces on three sides. Its loud tick-tick-ticking did nothing to soothe the nerves of this mismatched group of people – myself included. I doubted it was the lateness of our train that had lent the room this tension. From the glances exchanged, I felt sure that several of them knew one another.

I decided that, without standing to get a closer look, I had learnt all I could about them, and so I opened the *Herald* to see what had been happening in the world whilst we were bathing in culture in the Italian capital.

The headline on the front page said that the French Prime Minister, Aristide Briand, had proposed the formation of a United States of Europe, which sounded jolly interesting, though I doubted it would ever come to fruition. In Spain, it seemed they weren't so keen on the idea of a military dictatorship after all. Everyone, from students to businessmen and academics, was unhappy with their leader, Primo de Rivera, whereas, over the pond, the American stock market had reached new highs, despite the predictions of one particularly pessimistic scaremonger that it would soon plunge.

None of this would take my mind off the delayed train or the glare of the disgruntled German, and so I flicked a few pages through the paper to lighter affairs. There was an article on a forthcoming film about the sinking of the Titanic. Apparently, it would be the most expensive production of the year and would either be a great success or end up bankrupting the British studio that had made it. I didn't read about that for long though as, on the very next page, there was a photograph of the actress, Geraldine de la Forge.

When I was at school, my friends had all been besotted with the lovely Geraldine. People regularly described her as the most beautiful woman in the world and, while I'd recently met a young lady who could disprove this claim, I was happy to admit that the star of *A Place in Heaven* and *Love's Lonely Flame* was a graceful presence on the screen. I could also not deny that I'd seen every film she'd made, right back to *The Door with No Key.* So you can imagine how excited I was when I discovered that we were in the very same city at the very same time.

"Beloved Film Star Makes Verona Her New Home" went the headline, and the article continued on the following page. I noticed my grandfather was reading it as I did, though he always claimed to be above such trivial interests.

British actress Geraldine de la Forge is in Rome preparing for the production of her as yet untitled new film. The renowned beauty was seen at several famous landmarks around the city this week and even took a solo walk at sunset down the legendary Spanish Steps, where she was mobbed by lucky admirers. In a statement communicated to the Herald by her manager, Miss de la Forge revealed that she always feels at home in Italy and is greatly enjoying her time in the capital.

Details of the plot for her new film are scarce, but it is understood that Miss de la Forge and her director, Hansel Reinhardt, have been looking for a talented amateur to star alongside her in the tale of love and betrayal. While the story is set to be filmed in the newly established Via Veio Studios near Rome, it has not yet been announced whether it will be her first sound film or Miss de la Forge will continue her run of silent movies that have made her so popular across the world.

All this being said, it was not Rome to which her thoughts turned when searching for a new home. The film star is known to have purchased a house in the hills overlooking the northern city of Verona. The setting of Romeo and Juliet will soon have a new resident after Miss de la Forge travelled there two weeks ago to sign the deeds on the property.

Rumour has it that this sudden change of scenery – the actress previously made her home in London – came about after the end of her much-reported courtship by fellow actor Eddie Denkin. Denkin has recently been seen entertaining Miss de la Forge's American rival, the rising starlet Maxine Hammond, as they collaborate on a film in England.

When pressed on the circumstances that led to her rupture with Mr Denkin, Miss de la Forge would only say that her heart was full of love for Italy, and that it was sometimes hard to find space for anyone else. It is believed that she will spend her weekends in Verona, and the city's new night train to the capital will enable her to work in Rome from Monday to Friday.

On reading the last line, I felt a little woozy. It was Friday after all, and we were waiting for the night train to Verona, which could only mean…

"My goodness," the German complained with a clap of his hands.

"It's for her, isn't it. *Ach du meine Güte!*"

No one spoke in response, but there was some definite shuffling of bottoms in seats. My grandfather's keen eyes flicked over to the agitated man, who ran to look through the long white curtains which covered the nearest window.

"What did I tell you?" he asked everyone and no one before switching to German for a few words then back again. "There are journalists on the platform. They're waiting for her. They delayed the train for *her*."

He seemed to think this was something of a revelation and hurried to the door to peer out of it. To my surprise, I found myself magnetically moving over to see what he could see. As I arrived alongside him, the dashing German looked appraisingly in my direction and, apparently unimpressed by what he saw, turned back to stare at the platform.

I spotted a small group of Italians standing there smoking. A couple of them had Speed Graphic cameras in their hands, and I realised what the German had meant when he said that the train was waiting for someone. If the information in the newspaper article was accurate – or the journalists believed it to be so – they were there to see Geraldine de la Forge.

"This is typical of her," the man next to me muttered. "She is the most selfish woman on earth, and it doesn't surprise me in the least that she would put her own needs before those of a whole train of people."

He clearly had strong feelings for the person he was describing and, as I was eager to confirm my theory, I asked, "Is it the actress Miss de la Forge to whom you are referring? Is she to board the five fifty-five to Verona?"

He had to look twice at me then as I'd evidently exceeded his expectations – thus proving the advantage of appearing a dimwit, even for a short time.

"That's right, boy. The station master must have held back the engine as Geraldine isn't here yet." He pursed his lips for a moment and, evidently realising that this did not sound like a believable prospect, he added a little evidence to support his claim. "You see those?" He pointed to the connected carriages that were waiting at the closest platform. "They're full of second-class passengers. Good working people who wish for nothing more than to head home to see their families for the weekend. I'm sure that each of them has his own needs and priorities. Perhaps one of them is hurrying to see his *Freundin* back in Verona and intends to propose to her tomorrow night in the moonlight on the banks of the meandering river."

His eyes became a little misty as he unwound this story for me, but then his voice suddenly shot up, and he blinked away the fog. "She doesn't care about any of that!" His breathing was noticeably louder, and he took a few moments to calm down. "There is a locomotive somewhere nearby. The *chef de train* says it has been delayed, but I know that, at any moment, it will pull into this platform from whichever shed or siding where they have hidden it, and then the world's favourite actress, Geraldine de la Forge, she will arrive to occupy her first-class accommodation." His English was remarkably clear yet occasionally broken.

He held his hand out towards the platform without looking and, as if he'd planned the whole thing, I caught the sound of a chugging engine in the distance. A short time later, the locomotive he'd mentioned came into view. I was so impressed by his trick that I stepped through the door to get a better look. It was a large, black and red 4-6-2, and it was already emitting thick clouds of smoke.

As I emerged, the group of journalists dropped their cigarettes to the floor and stamped them out, chattering in Italian as they did so. Their cameras were raised and ready and, as the engine linked up with the waiting carriages, their voices rose.

"*Signorina!*" I heard one of them call. "It's true Mr Denkin leaves you?"

"Miss de la Forge!" another shouted. "What have you got to say to Maxine Hammond? How do you feel about what she did to you?"

I felt my grandfather's hand on my shoulder as an elegant young woman appeared. In a gold-buttoned blouse and matching salmon skirt that was so tight it acted as a hobble, she strutted majestically out of the ticket hall and on to the platform. Even though I couldn't see her face, and her blonde hair was tied up beneath her oversized pink hat, her style and presence were unmistakable. I'd rarely seen a person with such confidence. I could hear the click, clack, clicking of her heels on the platform even over the shouted voices that were soon augmented by a crowd of locals who appeared shortly after. They must have read about her in the paper, just as I and the insistent reporters had.

She stopped for no one and flatly ignored the questions that the press fired her way. I would have expected such intimate enquiries to have had an effect on her, but that enchanting figure continued walking to the train as if she hadn't heard a word. Less confident of himself was the tall man who followed at a quick pace three steps behind her. He was carrying a stack of boxes and bags, which were piled so precariously that I was certain they would fall to the ground. Everything about him spoke of hesitance and awkwardness as he peered around his burden and almost bumped into the nearest journalist.

I found the reaction of the waiting passengers particularly interesting. There were quite a few arranged on the platform smoking cigarettes or simply taking the air, and every last one of them was mesmerised by the unexpected appearance of that singular actress. It occurred to me that a similar scene would have played out had one of the ancient Roman gods descended from the sky to cast judgement or sow mischief.

Grandfather had left the waiting room to observe this spectacle, but he wasn't the only one. Our dog Delilah stretched her legs as she waited for the next stage of our journey, and the rich Italian, with his silk cape flowing, was there too. Holding himself like some great military leader, he breathed in admiringly as he watched the film star.

The lovely brown-haired maid from the waiting room was clearly flustered as she ran past us with small, careful steps, and I realised that her employer must be Miss de la Forge herself. This would prove to be the spark that my German companion needed and, on seeing the young woman pass, he raced towards the noisy pack. It was impressive how he infiltrated the melee so that, by the time the star actress had reached the first-class compartment on the train, he was right behind her.

"Geraldine!" I heard his voice rise over the hustle and bustle that was surely a regular accompaniment for her wherever she went.

She paused on the step up to the carriage and turned to look back. I noticed then how beautifully made up she was. It was not something that would usually occur to me, but perhaps the difference between the world's most beautiful woman and any regular beauty I had come across was merely presentation.

For a moment, she just froze there and peered down at the young man with a distant mien. It was not so much that she viewed him with contempt as that she disregarded him completely – as if she couldn't quite recall who the nobody before her actually was. The impression was undermined when she tipped back her head and I could make out the word "Hansel" on her downturned lips.

I couldn't see him in the crowd, of course, but I believe they exchanged a glance before Geraldine spun on her heel to disappear into the train.

CHAPTER THREE

"Come along, Christopher." My grandfather nudged me forward as I'd apparently been staring into space, even after the star in our midst had ceased shining. "There's no sense in loitering here now that the train is ready to leave. We must find our compartment."

Todd now appeared, and I must admit that, with all the excitement, I hadn't questioned what he'd been up to.

"I thought it better to leave the two of you to relax in the waiting room," he said rather clandestinely, and I got the definite impression that he'd been off around the station gaining potentially useful information or on some mission for his master. All of Grandfather's servants were trained in the ways of espionage and intelligence gathering, but Todd was his top man for a reason. Even in foreign countries, he excelled at gaining people's confidence, and I looked forward to learning whatever he'd discovered just as soon as we were settled in our compartment.

"We do have reserved seats, don't we?" I put to my grandfather as I bustled after him.

"Of course we do, Christopher." He continued that quick walk of his along the side of the stationary train towards the door we needed. "Were you expecting me to spend the journey in the restaurant?"

"It's not that. I just wondered why you were in such a hurry."

The journalists were still clustered in front of the door to the first-class carriage, but they parted to let the maid on to the train.

Grandfather nipped through after her, calling over his shoulder as he went. "I would have thought that was obvious."

It was not obvious. In all honesty, I hadn't a clue why he was so agitated, but he jumped on board with all the vigour of a pole-vaulter.

I motioned for Todd to climb up ahead of me, but being polite to a professional level meant that he could not accept this, and we wasted twenty seconds arguing over who should go first. As with most of the arguments in which I engage, I lost.

"This is nice," I said after a neatly dressed porter in a pillbox hat had ushered me past the steward's cubby hole to the first door off the narrow passage.

My compliment didn't go far enough for Grandfather's liking. "Nice, my boy?" He stood by the window looking mystified.

"It's very nice."

"It was only inaugurated a month ago and is said to rival the Orient Express for comfort. I believe it is therefore only right to use a more emphatic word than 'nice'."

"Then it's very, very—"

He somewhat despairingly smoothed his snow-white beard with both hands. "Tell me, Christopher, is Michaelangelo's David very, very nice? Is the Colosseum?"

I considered the question for a moment. "Yes. Yes, they are."

He huffed a little as he dropped onto the folded-out sofa, and I knew that he would give up trying to convince me.

I must make it clear that what I'd said about our accommodation for the night was true. It was really quite lovely. The whole place was decorated with walnut panelling and brass fixtures. There was a picturesque scene of a lake on the rounded door to the lavabo, picked out in contrasting shades of glossy wood, and, though I couldn't at first tell where we would be sleeping, I soon realised that there was an adjoining door through which one could access two single beds.

"'Nice' indeed!" Grandfather shook his head as I poked mine into the other compartment.

"And what about Todd?" I asked to get to grips with the arrangements for the night.

"He booked himself a compartment in second-class. I believe he is there now."

"And what about me?" our dog enquired with a tilt of the head.

Her master understood every word. "You, my dear Delilah, do not need your own compartment. You are a canine and can sleep wherever you wish."

She was apparently not in the mood for a long, drawn-out discussion and sat down beside him to go to sleep.

"Grandfather," I asked with reticence plain in my voice, "are you quite all right?"

"All right?" He laughed a little too loudly, which only made me more worried. "Why wouldn't I be?"

It was hard to put my finger on what was different about him as he is always a few notches above anyone else I know when it comes to eccentricity.

I tried to put it into words all the same. "You seem distracted... and over-excited... and perhaps a tiny bit—" I was glad that he interrupted me, as I doubt he would have enjoyed my calling him mad.

"Over-excited? Me?" His laughter rose in volume but was soon clipped short as he realised there was no sense in pretending. "Very well. I'll admit that I've been in a funk for some days."

"Oh, yes? I hadn't noticed..." This was so transparently untrue that I had to add, "...until now."

He stood to pace about, so I sat down to give him some space. Although the carriage was very (very) luxurious, it was not built for men of a perambulatory disposition like my grandfather. He took two steps towards the window, and then four back to reach the door. He repeated this a number of times as he sought to define his unusual mood.

"My first thought was that I miss the thrill of an investigation, but we've had so much to distract us since we left Montegufoni last month that I no longer believe that to be the problem. You see, it was always my dream to visit Rome. Of all the European capitals, it appealed to me most for its unique history and culture. I believe that it is the thought that I might never come back here that has left me ill at ease."

Grandfather had recently turned seventy-nine years old, so I wondered (but certainly didn't question aloud) whether it was his proximity to his ninth decade on the planet which made him feel this way.

He had paused to look at the tracks through the window but now went back to his pacing. "I'm nearly eighty years old," he said, and I was quietly amazed that I'd been able to determine the cause of his dolefulness for the first time in weeks. "My father barely made it to seventy, and I can't help feeling as if I'm living on time which does not rightfully belong to me."

Delilah had tired of her master stepping over her and shuffled back under the folding sofa to get some peace and quiet. I tried to formulate an answer that was just as discreet.

"Our journey is only just beginning, Grandfather." I paused then as it occurred to me that our normal roles in this scenario had been reversed. He had spent the last few years bolstering my confidence when I needed it, and I wasn't sure how to do the same for him. "We have so much still to anticipate."

He came to a stop in the middle of the room as the train whistle blew. "Yes, Christopher. You're right of course." His tone implied that he said this with, at best, grudging acceptance.

I climbed to my feet and moved around to look him in the eye. "I mean it, Grandfather. You're glum for the simple reason that we've had such an incredible time here. Well, if that is the case, just think what lies ahead."

His moustaches wavered dubiously, and I knew it would take more to convince him.

"If you're worried about your age, then you shouldn't be." It was hard to be so honest with a man around whom I had spent much of my life watching my words. "You have more vivacity than many people my age and younger."

He displayed a range of emotions, which quickly changed as he considered my point. I suppose my awareness of this shows just how well I had come to know him, as his expressions had once been quite unreadable to me.

"I have no need for unwarranted sympathy," he said, as though I had implied anything of the sort. "I'm merely concerned how I will feel when our time comes to return home. I'm eager to travel as widely as we can on the Continent and enjoy the adventures that each destination offers, but I worry about what awaits us back in Britain."

I was glad that he had only doubted his immortality for a minute or two before turning to another fear.

"Grandfather," I said with a laugh in my voice, as the very idea of his not making the most of wherever we visited was unthinkable, "you would be able to find adventure in a cupboard!"

"You may be right, my boy." He pulled back his shoulders as we'd both been taught at school – and he had taken to heart far more than I ever had. "I'll try my best to remain chipper."

"My goodness, you could even find adventure on this train."

We were both smiling now, but something that Todd had said came back to me, and I wondered what was in store for us as the carriage shook to signal the start of our journey. I heard doors slamming shut and a voice calling out on the platform as we started to move.

"Wait!" someone called. "*Aspettare!*"

I walked back to the corridor to see what was happening and stuck my head out of the lowered window just in time to see a man exiting the ticket hall with a large case under his arm. The train was already picking up speed, and I doubted he would manage to board it, especially as he was pursued by a companion. I couldn't see her face, as her long, wavy hair obscured her features, but she ran with just as much determination though at a slower pace.

"Come along, child!" the fellow said in English, looking back over his shoulder while struggling with his own case.

If I'd thought I could have been any help, I would have hopped from the train and taken their luggage, but I wouldn't have reached them in time and might well have been left behind myself.

I saw the look on the man's face as he slowed to throw his case ahead of him and then pulled himself up into the last carriage. As the train curled out of the station, he held his hand out to the girl following him and successfully pulled her on board with a shout of excitement.

Though they were too far away to hear or even see in any great detail, I sensed their excitement at catching the train. The door slammed behind them, and I wondered what their story was and whether I'd ever get to hear it.

CHAPTER FOUR

Before I could return to our compartment, I spotted someone peeking through the door from a little way along the corridor. It was open just long enough for me to realise it was the same man who had rebuked the German in the waiting room. Though I hadn't seen his face before, I'd previously noticed his dull brown suit and the binoculars he'd had around his neck, and he was still wearing both.

Something about the way he pulled his head inside when he saw me, made me wonder what he was hoping to see. He had closely trimmed stubble and quick black eyes. I can't say I liked the look of him, but then I've learnt to ignore such swift conclusions and try, as a general rule, to give people the benefit of the doubt. Perhaps afraid that I would think badly of him, he did not immediately close the door but offered a wave and a nod to acknowledge me.

As one door closed, another opened, and the German himself – Hansel, was it? – looked at the neighbouring compartments as if he could see through the solid wooden doors. He didn't even glance at me as he counted his way along the corridor and stopped at the fourth one from his own. He'd been quite calm until now, but he banged on the door with such vehemence that it shook the floor beneath me.

"Gerry, it's me, darling," he called. "It's Hansel. Do let me in, my dear. I know we've had our differences, but there's really no need to—"

He was interrupted by the sound of the latch being unlocked and the maid opening the door, but it was her mistress who responded.

"I have no wish to see you, so please leave me alone," came the voice from within the compartment, and the German raised himself up on tiptoes, and leant to one side to see the actress to whom he was so desperate to talk.

"Listen, my darling. Please listen. I bought this ticket so that we could discuss what went wrong. It's not my feelings that should worry you. Think of the film that we both dreamed of making. Think of *The Other Half of Her.*"

"We've been through this before, Hansel. I'm not interested in what you have to say. How can you fail to understand that?"

With her mistress having said her piece, the maid moved to close the door, but the German stuck his arm out to stop her. He winced as it shut on him, but he wouldn't give in.

"Miss de la Forge doesn't want to see you," the young woman said in a soft, cautious voice.

Hansel positively growled. "Now listen here. I know you haven't been around long, but Geraldine and I are close friends and colleagues too."

"I'm sorry, sir, but she's already—"

He talked right over her. "You're making a big mistake, *mein Schatz*. Don't be such a blasted fool."

The anger he'd displayed in the waiting room was apparent once more as he forced his shoulder through the gap and, with considerable strength, pushed the door wider. The look of vitriol and triumph that he wore as he invaded this private sanctum was enough to send me shooting along the corridor.

"Think what you're doing, man," I yelled before I got there, slightly surprised at the way my voice resonated along the passage. "The lady said she doesn't wish to speak to you. Where are your manners?"

As I reached him, I saw the matching expression of horror on the two women's faces. Geraldine had raised her hands to her breast to shelter herself from the attack she must have thought was imminent. The commotion had caused two of the other passengers to emerge from their assigned spaces. The man I was almost certain was an Italian aristocrat and the American woman's husband both made their presence felt. Perhaps it was their cold judgement, even more than my words, that gave Hansel pause.

In the corner of the small compartment, as far from him as she could get, Geraldine was still dressed in the elegant outfit she'd worn when she arrived at the station. Now that the danger had seemingly subsided, she looked truly disappointed in the man's behaviour. In turn, the German stared down at his hands, as though they had formed into fists without his knowledge, and he couldn't understand how.

"I'm sorry," he murmured to no one in particular and then, with a pleading look on his face, he glanced around the maid to her mistress. "Geraldine, forgive me. I meant you no harm." Even now, he couldn't let the chance to address her pass him by and kept talking. "You must admit that we left things in a terrible state. I only wish to do what's right, but you keep—"

"That's enough, sir," the maid said firmly, and she took the opportunity to close the door and lock it. In the moment before it shut, I saw a look of defiance in her eyes. Hansel had mentioned that she was only recently employed by the film star, but she was clearly dedicated to her work, just as Grandfather's staff are.

"*Entschuldigung, mein Herzchen!*" Hansel pressed his head against the door to call through to Geraldine, and the defeat that was plain on his face sent the other men back into their rooms.

I considered ushering him away, but he spun on the spot and marched along the corridor to his own compartment, one door from the end. The signs certainly weren't promising for a nice quiet train journey, and if this was only the beginning, with all the drama that had occurred, I had to question whether we would get any sleep when the sun set.

I went back to see my grandfather and found that Todd had popped up there when I wasn't looking. He had a habit of doing so and had even managed to bring his wicker drinks carrier, along with a cocktail shaker and a collection of glasses. I found this particularly impressive as I'd only seen him with one of my grandfather's cases, and I knew for a fact that it was packed full of grey suits!

"I took the liberty of mixing you a *spritz veneziano*," he told me as I sat down in the small dining area. "That is to say, an Italian aperitif originating in the region of Veneto, to which we are currently travelling. It includes sparkling water and a local bitter liqueur."

It came as no surprise that we should be served drinks so early in the evening. As my grandfather had often reminded me, on the Continent, the hour of the aperitif can fall at any time between lunch and dinner. Although Todd had been trying to instil a love of cocktails in me, with the heat of Rome and the upheaval of our trip, I would have preferred something easier on the palate.

There was a table that, just like the sofa, could be folded away against the wall. Grandfather was already occupying one of two dining chairs, and he looked most excited about the sparkling drink that had been placed before him.

"What was the cause of all that shouting?" he asked as I picked up my glass and was about to sip from it.

"The German man we saw earlier. His name's Hansel—"

"Hansel Reinhardt, the film director. Yes, I know who he is."

It took me approximately two and a half seconds – actually, that is fairly precise – to work out how he knew this. I'd read the German's name in the newspaper, just as my grandfather had. He was working on a film in Rome with Geraldine, but clearly something had turned sour between them.

"He was banging on the door to Miss de la Forge's compartment," I explained. "He demanded to talk to her, but she refused, and it took me, her maid and a couple of other passengers to make sure he left her alone."

"Well done, Christopher. That was very decent of you."

"Thank you," I replied, though I was more concerned about the women that Reinhardt had harassed than my own role in the affair. "He became very angry, and I was concerned that he might hurt someone."

Grandfather sat back in his seat and took the briefest of sips from his flute. "It is interesting that you should say that, as I've heard unpleasant things about the man."

This did surprise me for a number of reasons. First of all, Grandfather wasn't one to read gossipy stories in the newspaper. Second, I didn't realise that he was familiar with anyone significant in the world of films. He greatly preferred the theatre and, now that I think of it, third, I couldn't imagine the newspapers printing such vague rumours.

"Not the newspapers, my boy." He was quick to correct my unspoken thoughts. There had been a time when I was amazed by his ability to predict what was going on in my head – especially as I barely knew myself. But I was older now, and those days had passed. "I heard it first-hand from a friend I met in Rome while you were exploring the city. He had invested money in one of Reinhardt's films, and things didn't go to plan."

I finally drank a little of my ruby red drink. I knew my ingredients well enough now to detect traces of juniper and beetroot in the liqueur, and I could appreciate just how refreshing it was, but I generally prefer a sweeter treat. It was no champagne flip or apple bomb. I could drink those all day – though I've learnt my lesson and won't do that again.

"To be quite honest, Reinhardt looked as though he wanted to murder Miss de la Forge when he attempted to force his way into her room, so it's no great shock to learn that he's a rotter."

"What exactly did he say when he banged on the door? I heard a commotion but not the precise words that were used."

I was already casting my mind back a few minutes. "Well, he said he wanted to speak to her. I got the impression that the two know one another… intimately, I mean. He described them as friends and colleagues. Perhaps they were in love once, but—" I stopped myself then as I'd remembered something else. "Wait a moment, weren't they in Rome to make a film? From what we read, I thought they were still working on it."

"Yes, I understood the same thing. I suppose these creative types are subject to more violent switches of mood than normal people like you or me."

It struggled not to ask in what world he classed himself as normal, but I just about managed it.

"At one point, he seemed to calm down when the maid wouldn't let him pass, but then the actress said something that irked him, and he simply barged the door open again. It was frightening to watch, as he was very much larger than the two women, even if Miss de la Forge is comparatively tall."

"I doubt she is actually much taller than her maid or the porter at the station. She has very high heels on her shoes, but I'm sure she'd be quite normal height if you saw her without them."

I'd expect my grandfather to know about the burns left on a shooter's clothes after firing a pistol, or the correct way to stab a person to minimise the amount of blood expulsed. What I find more impressive, however, is his familiarity with matters that have no impact on his day-to-day life. His discussion of a film star's shoes came quite out of the blue, but his eye for detail, and awareness of what goes on in the world, shouldn't have surprised me.

"I once heard a rumour that the actress Alma Cavendish stands on a box beneath a long skirt as she's too short next to her leading men. I believe that there are a lot of such tricks and illusions in the world of cinema."

This just made me think, *She's only wearing tall shoes, Grandfather.*

That hardly makes her a charlatan.

"Did you find out why it was that Reinhardt so desperately wished to speak to his leading lady?" he asked when I'd started to think of other things.

"He mentioned the film they were making, but she had no desire to see him. The poor maid tried to protect her mistress, but it wasn't enough. If the three of them had been alone, I can only think that he would have had his way. Whatever trouble has arisen between them must have started recently if the article we read was correct. Even as he expressed his anger, he spoke to her in loving terms. He called her 'my darling' and other German phrases that I took to mean the same thing."

With one finger stretched along the line of his jaw, Grandfather sat without moving. I believe that he was considering the implications of what I'd told him when he suddenly became unfrozen – or should that be 'he melted'? – and chose to dismiss the whole discussion.

"We will have to keep an eye on the situation. Of course, a woman in Miss de la Forge's position learns to protect herself from unwanted attention, but it must have been unpleasant, nonetheless."

"That's true," I said for want of anything else that came to mind.

We sipped our cocktails and quietly reflected on our busy afternoon. The scenery outside the window had already changed, and the sun was low over what I had to assume were the foothills of the Apennine Mountains. It still felt like summer there, and the fields were scorched by months of strong sunshine. It would all change when the autumn rains returned to make Italy green again. I heard an incredible statistic that, over the course of a year, Rome gets a third more rain than London, but it was hard to imagine after the time I'd spent there. I couldn't count the number of grey days I'd witnessed in London, whereas our month in the Italian capital had been as dry as a bone.

For a while, the only noise in our carriage was the steady rhythm of the train's wheels on the tracks and Delilah's peaceful snoring. There was something soothing about the mix of sounds. I've always loved train travel and would happily never sit in a car again – especially if Grandfather's driving it. I felt quite content watching the world pass by, and the idea that we were heading towards new vistas, new cultures and (perhaps most importantly) new types of Italian food helped heal the wounds of my departure from Rome.

This comforting accompaniment worked its way deep into my brain, just as a lullaby can carry a tired infant to the realm of sleep, and I soon found myself nodding off. I don't know how long I slept, but neither my grandfather nor Todd chose to disturb me.

I eventually woke up with a start – and a stiff neck – to discover that I was alone in the compartment with a still comatose Delilah. It took me a moment to come back to the waking world, and I was about to change for dinner when I heard two people talking outside my door.

"I can't do it," the first said, and I was sure it was Miss de la Forge.

Her maid had a coarser, East-London accent. "I understand you i'n't comfortable, Miss, but don't you think it'll look strange if you don't go to dinner?"

"I don't care what people think of me. I'd prefer to stay in my room."

There was a pregnant pause as the maid considered her mistress's request. "Why don't you wait while I see if he's in there? Would that put your mind at ease? It's early yet. You'll prob'ly be fine."

"Do what you like. I'm tired of the whole affair. I should never have agreed to any of this." The actress sounded quite despondent, and I wondered what that terrible man had done to her. The world is a shameful place if a young woman can't travel home by train without being harassed.

"Very well, Miss."

I heard them walking away from one another, and I hurried to the door to push back the curtain and peer along the corridor.

"Actually, I've changed my mind," Geraldine said, and the stress or sorrow or whatever emotion was running through her was clearly overwhelming. She no longer sounded sure of herself. "You'll have to bring me something to eat. I won't leave my compartment again."

I saw her turn and saunter away, her pale pink skirt trailing behind her along the thick carpet.

CHAPTER FIVE

The maid must have been back with her mistress by the time I'd changed for dinner, as I didn't see her again. I walked out of our compartment with poor Geraldine's words ringing in my ears. I don't mind admitting that I'd felt great compassion for her character of Charlotte in the film *A Heart in Two Pieces,* and I couldn't bear the thought of her suffering.

I should probably have checked the time as, when I got to the first-class dining car, my grandfather was the only passenger there.

"I was trying to read, and Delilah's snoring is too noisy," he informed me as he raised Ernest Hemingway's *The Sun Also Rises* to explain his reasoning.

"Would you recommend it?"

"Not in the slightest." He set down the book with a sigh as I approached. "The author has no sense of style. His sentences are far too short, and I feel quite confident in saying that he's a flash in the pan who will soon be forgotten."

"Based on that recommendation, you must pass it on to me when you finish."

I smiled at him and explained what I'd overheard from our compartment before coming to dinner, but then the head waiter arrived. He was garbed in a white swallow-tailed coat and black bowtie. He bowed to me and clicked his fingers so that two of his colleagues, who had presumably been waiting for the signal in a nearby cupboard, stepped into the room to serve us. The first removed the cutlery and plates that were on our table – as they were apparently just for show – and the second put them all back again as their superior asked us what we would like to drink.

"A simple glass of water," I swiftly told him, as the cocktail had made me thirsty.

"And a measure of *Galliano*," Grandfather followed.

We waited for the men to retreat before saying anything more.

"You were right, of course," I admitted. "This really is the nicest train I've ever boarded." I looked about the dining compartment to take in the sunsets in the tile mosaics at each end of the carriage.

39

On every window there were intricately patterned curtains, and multi-coloured glass lampshades decorated each table.

"Would you expect anything less?"

The correct answer was, *Of course not,* but I didn't tell him that, and the waiters soon returned with our drinks. Their supervisor's sole job was to keep a watchful eye on them and make sure that they saw to our every need. He had a scowl on his face as though he expected his underlings to make a terrible mistake at any moment, though I'm pleased to report that the service was top-notch.

I was keen to discuss possible plans for our time in Verona, but before I could say the words *Juliet's House,* the first of our fellow diners arrived. James Joseph Campbell, the American traveller, appeared without his wife. He had a good Celtic name, but he apparently lacked the more formal manners that we are taught in Britain from an early age.

"I'm sorry about before," he said without a *Good evening,* or a *How do you do?* "My dearest Sharlene is a kind woman, but she's not the best at hiding her feelings."

"That's quite all right," Grandfather replied with an accepting smile, though I could tell he was once more bemused by the encounter.

Without being invited, Campbell now seized a seat from the table in front of ours and pulled it over to sit down in the aisle. This surely broke between seven and thirteen rules of etiquette and perhaps a minor law or two. I'm not normally the stuffy type, but I'd rarely seen such a rude display.

"The thing is – and I won't mince my words, gentlemen – she was greatly disappointed by the whole thing."

Grandfather did not reply but took a sip of his liqueur as our waiters tiptoed away.

"You see, my Sharlene is a woman of strong opinions and high ideals." His Southern accent was even stronger than his wife's, and he looked at us through large, sorrowful eyes. "There are few people in this world to whom she has dedicated such attention and, I might say, passion as you, Lord Edgington. So you can quite understand the sense of disillusionment she felt after meeting you."

"We understand entirely," I replied on my grandfather's behalf, not just because he was left speechless by the man's words, but as it is always amusing to rib the old genius.

"Thank you, young man. I appreciate that, and I obviously don't wish to blame you or your grandfather for my wife's reaction. Her expectations were clearly set too high. When Lord Edgington here was so terribly rude to her, there was only going to be one possible reaction."

This was the most enjoyable exchange to which I'd been party in a long time. The shocked look on Grandfather's face was worth framing.

He finally managed to muster a response, and that response was, "Rude?"

"I can't think of another word for it, but I'm open to suggestions. My dearest Sharlene struck up a pleasant conversation with you, 'the bloodhound of Scotland Yard' – the man who is a legend in his own lifetime and certainly in our home. And yet all you could do in response was look back blankly at her and parrot dry information about our very own city. Do you understand now why she was so disgusted by your behaviour?"

Grandfather at least managed to refrain from repeating the word "disgusted"!

"All that was required on your part, mister, was a touch of warmth and human decency. Sharlene has read everything she could about you. She has followed your adventures since you were mentioned in the American papers for the very first time forty years ago. She has the whole series of novelisations of your exploits."

I was surprised by this, as I had no idea that there were books published about my grandfather.

"Are you saying that someone has been getting rich off the back of the cases that Lord Edgington investigated as a police officer?" I asked in amazement.

"Not at all, young man." James Joseph paused, and it went on so long that I thought he might never reveal the truth. "The books focus on his retirement and the murders you have solved together."

I didn't know whether to be excited or appalled. Grandfather did, though for a very different reason from my own.

"I need to know why your wife was disgusted by my behaviour."

James Joseph looked away from us for a moment and, when

he turned back, there was a definite sneer on his face. I might even have said he looked disgusted by my grandfather's attitude, though we've already used that word rather a lot. "If you can't see that, Lord Edgington, then this conversation..." He paused for the length of time it took to rise from his chair and gaze down at us. "...is over."

With his part said, he stomped back along the aisle to the furthest table and would sit there glaring at us for some time.

"What did I do that was so offensive?" Grandfather was dumbfounded by the man's demeanour and looked at me in disbelief. "Tell me, Christopher. Do you know what I've done? I really can't comprehend it!"

I did my very best not to show how much this tickled me. It helped that, at this moment, there was a loud and unexpected screech of metal on metal. We entered a tunnel and were plunged into darkness as the electric lights overhead flickered off. Out into the blinding daylight we emerged once more, and I was about to address the essential topic of what we might eat for dinner, when, just a few seconds later, the wheels clangoured on the tracks and back we went into a much longer tunnel.

"I'm very sorry for this inconvenience, gentlemen," the *chef de train*, M. Nagelmackers appeared out of the darkness to apologise. I could only assume he had come from the second-class carriage further along the train... or he was an illusionist of some variety. The lights flickered on, and I could see his petite, friendly face quite clearly for a moment. "This train has only been in service a short time, and the engineers are yet to resolve some minor technical issues."

"I hope there are no problems with its ability to get us to our destination," Grandfather said in an ominous manner, as though he were waiting for the inevitable sound of the train veering off the tracks or the boiler exploding.

Nagelmackers raised his voice once more to speak over all that noise. "No, no, Lord Edgington. I can assure you that it runs like a dream."

The lights flashed brighter for a second before darkness returned and the smartly dressed Belgian laughed uncomfortably. By the time we left the tunnel, he had disappeared again. Two menus had appeared on our table at some point, so we were distracted for a few minutes with the really very difficult decision between beef fillet in '*giardiniere*' style, giant prawns cooked in a grapefruit and white wine sauce and *rombo chiodato con pistacchi* (whatever that is).

"It's turbot studded with pistachio nuts," Grandfather told me without looking up from the menu. I had a sneaking suspicion that he had caught my reflection in a spoon or perhaps a glass and had read my mind – or at least my beaten expression.

"Do you know what?" I asked, then quickly pressed on to avoid the inevitable withering reply. "As much as I adore Italy and everything about it, I'm looking forward to reaching France in a few months' time so that I can understand the menus better."

Far from tutting at me, he replied with an unexpected and affectionate smile. "Oh, Christopher. You do make me laugh."

Over at his table, James Joseph Campbell was still glaring, and I was curious what my grandfather made of the man. Before I could open my mouth this time, a waiter passed our table with a trolley loaded with bottles, glasses and a large silver cloche under which – I concluded – sat a meal for one of the guests in first class.

I had to wonder whether it was the actress in compartment number three who had ordered this, despite what I'd overheard her saying. It was just then that the maid in her sombre black uniform appeared in the doorway, and the waiter with the trolley stopped to let her squeeze through. She looked rather distressed, as though she had been reprimanded by her mistress for some reason and was holding back tears. I almost called out to her, but she hurried past before I could. Perhaps she was simply in a hurry to reach the second-class dining room. I saw that the clock had just struck seven, so her break for dinner must have begun.

"Things keep getting stranger," Grandfather whispered a few minutes later as Sharlene Campbell came bustling into the dining car with a crinoline dress that made her look like Little Bo-Peep. The skirts were so full that she had to turn to one side and walk crab-like down the aisle.

She'd had quite the smile on her face as she entered the carriage, but she lost it immediately on seeing my grandfather. It was hard to fathom how she could have been so offended by his mild frostiness. She nodded perfunctorily to me but paid no attention whatsoever to her supposed hero.

There was one more tunnel through which to pass, and it was the longest so far. The lights flickered on and off again, and I had come to understand that the screeching sound was dependent on speed and the curvature of the track. It was a short time after this that the dining car began to fill up with passengers decked out in their finest.

The Italian aristocrat was first. He marched into the room and, as he arrived, the waiters respectfully directed him to the table second closest to the door. They spoke in fast Italian that I didn't catch and wouldn't have been able to make any sense of if I had. With the gentleman's order taken, the waistcoated young man returned to the bar carriage to fetch the chosen drinks.

Hansel Reinhardt, Miss de la Forge's apparently spurned director, was the next to arrive, and he entered the room a great deal more furtively than the flamboyant Italian had. He'd changed since we last saw him and, just like myself and the other gentlemen, he was dressed in full evening attire. He was apparently not comfortable in his outfit as he kept adjusting the silk rose in his buttonhole and pulling at his tie as though it were choking him. When his hands were free from these tasks, he would stroke his clean-shaven cheeks one by one.

There was something very apprehensive about his behaviour. Perhaps he felt out of place in these refined surroundings, or maybe he was worried that we would think badly of him after his run-in with his star. Either way, he caught my attention, which was quite the opposite of what he wanted. Grandfather had his back to the man, but even he peered over his shoulder indiscreetly, and the chatter in the dining car died down a fraction.

For his part, Reinhardt waited for the now far busier waiters to seat him, and he looked relieved when they showed him to the free table furthest from us, just one away from the door to the first-class carriage. He sat down to study the menu as if it were *War and Peace* and he had a test on it in school the next morning – which may or may not be one of my recurring nightmares.

I had a feeling that, assuming Geraldine refrained from making an appearance, there was only one person left to join us. Sure enough, the fellow who'd peeked out at me from his compartment arrived in time to complete our party. The expression he wore this time couldn't have been more different from the quick, calculating one I'd spotted earlier. He had a gigantic grin that seemed to take up more space than it should, and his manner was so free and relaxed that I half expected him to go around the tables introducing himself.

He resisted this impulse but, as though he wished to avoid any undue suspicion, he did take the time to talk to my grandfather.

"Lord Edgington." His terrible smile showed that he had far too many teeth for his mouth. They were crooked and noticeably sharp. His voice, meanwhile, was at odds with this impression. He spoke in the practiced tones of a public speaker – not posh exactly but strong and clear.

"It's a true honour to dine alongside you. The name's Marvin Pelthorpe. I won't interrupt, but I couldn't resist telling you what an honour it is to…" He apparently remembered that he'd already imparted this message as he broke off what he was saying and nodded to us in turn.

With this done, and without waiting for a waiter to direct him, he sat down at the table next to ours. He poured himself a glass of water from the carafe and drank it down noisily. I must say, I'm glad that I'd sat in that spot, as I could see the whole dining room and everyone in it.

Despite the latest arrival's cheery disposition, there was something I found starkly repulsive about him. Perhaps it was his black eyes, which were set so deep into his skull that they almost disappeared entirely. Or maybe it was the sharp canines he displayed whenever that supposedly benign smile of his fired. Marvin Pelthorpe was a true beast; I was sure of it now and felt that *canis lupus* was the most likely identification.

When no one else appeared, and the waiters were busy darting about the place with small appetisers and bottles of champagne, I realised that there were eight sleeping compartments in the first-class section of the train and eight tables in the dining room. Judging by the people we'd seen boarding the train, this meant that two were empty.

The lack of anyone else joining us caused the Campbells at the other end of the carriage to discuss Geraldine's absence. As they were the only other table with more than one person, their conversation was quite clear, and it caused all three of the single men who were there to glance over at them. Grandfather broached the same topic.

"It's a real shame," he said, turning to scowl at Reinhardt for a moment. "I had hoped to speak to Miss de la Forge this evening. I wish to tell her that we are at her disposal should she require anything." He definitely raised his voice as he said this, so there was no question that he had chosen his words to intimidate the German. "I'd like to set her mind at ease that we will treat any further threats towards her as potentially criminal behaviour."

"Hear, hear!" said the Wolf through a mouthful of bread, and then he raised his voice to shout at the German. "I saw you, matey. I heard what you said to the young lady, and I do not approve one bit."

Reinhardt grabbed hold of his knife. I don't know if it was a conscious act, but it was certainly a hostile one. "Oh, yes? And you are clearly one who involves himself in other people's business? Eh, *Würstchen?*"

"Careful what you say, sir." Marvin Pelthorpe at least pretended to be scandalised. "Ladies and gentlemen, you heard what this foreign fellow just said to me. Now, I don't know what the word he said means, but I'm fairly certain that you could get locked up for such talk where I come from."

"I called you what you are! No one should be locked up for stating a fact."

The two men's eyes clicked onto one another's and, just like stags locking horns, there was a moment's pause before combat commenced in earnest. The Wolf reacted first, and though he wasn't particularly big, he was definitely bad. He seemed to grow a foot as he shot up from the table, and I expected one of his claws to go flying through the air to strike Reinhardt.

The German was only a split second behind him, but their tables were far enough apart that a few extra steps were required before the two men could clash. Quite gallantly if you ask me, James Joseph saw what was happening and dived forward to put himself between his wife and the flaring disagreement. I liked him rather more after that.

The two undoubtedly angriest passengers on the train met in the centre of the carriage and grabbed hold of one another's hands. They grappled like this for some time, and it was interesting just how well-matched they were physically. At one moment, Reinhardt seemed to have the upper hand, but then he lost his footing, and Pelthorpe pushed him backwards.

The tension in the room was building. The head waiter stepped closer in an attempt to reason with the antagonistic pair, but there was nothing he could do, and so it fell to my grandfather. The man of quiet action seized his amethyst-topped silver cane and had raised it above his head to strike the Wolf when a scream of terror travelled out to us from the neighbouring carriage and everyone there froze.

CHAPTER SIX

At first, I was glad that the violence had come to a stop, but this emotion was bundled with several others. I caught the look of fear in Mrs Campbell's eyes, and that same feeling swelled within me. Still, I couldn't suppress the curiosity that my grandfather has instilled in me, which ignites whenever we encounter some degree of danger.

The train continued its noisy journey along the track. The jickety-can, jickety-can of the wheels was a constant accompaniment, but a stillness had set in across the scene. Even the wrestlers a few feet away from me looked along the carriage to see what had brought about that blood-chilling cry and, within seconds, we would have the answer we sought.

It was only the flamboyant Italian aristocrat who had remained calm until this point, and he now pushed his chair back to walk placidly along the aisle in the direction of our compartments. Before he even reached the door, it came crashing open, and a steward appeared in his navy blue livery and peaked cap.

"Signor Nagelmackers," he practically yelled to the *chef de train,* who was always on hand when needed. "*Vieni presto! La signorina è morta.*"

CHAPTER SEVEN

Now, as we've already established, I had not picked up a great deal of Italian – and even their diverse menus confused me. But if there is one phrase that is almost impossible not to learn when spending any length of time with my grandfather it is *(Insert victim's name here) is dead.*

I knew from when we boarded the train that the only carriages beyond our own were for the workers and the locomotive itself. I also knew that, with Sharlene Campbell there with us and the maid somewhere in second class, the only *signorina* that the steward could mean was Geraldine de la Forge. The first thought that entered my head was to question how I was going to tell my friends that the young woman we'd adored on the silver screen had died, but then I took the far more pressing decision to push my grandfather past the fighters and find out what had happened for ourselves.

I glanced at the pair of them as I passed. Suddenly, they didn't look like two big, strong men. I saw them as spoilt children who should have known better than to start a fight in the first place. As we reached the door, the nattily dressed Italian gentleman moved out of our way, and this time when the Campbells looked at us, there was a sense of respect for my grandfather that had been absent before. Well, it was either that or a sign of their fear over what would happen next.

The distressed steward led us beyond the cubby hole where he had been sitting when I'd left. We walked past a small communal cloakroom and on to the corridor that ran alongside the eight compartments. The first belonged to my grandfather and me. I assumed that the next was empty, and the third door was the one that Hansel Reinhardt had attempted to smash off its hinges.

"She in there," the steward pointed, his finger shaking.

When we reached the threshold, the poor man gazed nervously into our faces in a way which told me that the last thing he wanted was to step inside that room again. I put my hand on his shoulder and, without a word, reassured him that this wouldn't be necessary.

The door was a few inches ajar and, even before my grandfather pushed it wider, I could see a definite sliver of silky pink fabric. Though the sun had yet to set, the lights were on inside the compartment, and they reflected off Geraldine de la Forge's blouse. Grandfather paused before stepping inside. It's that moment when everything changes which makes being a detective so hard. Until we saw the actress's lifeless face, I could hold on to the belief that the steward had been mistaken.

Despite the instantly recognisable blood on her blouse, I lunged forward to check her pulse. Her eyes were open and perfectly still, which is never a good sign. In my experience, when people pass out intoxicated or faint, their eyes tend to float off to the side of their vision: Geraldine was staring straight forward. Her head was positioned awkwardly, and she lay supine on the carpet between the day bed and the small table. I knew she had left us even before I placed my fingers on her limp wrist. The large red stain that covered her stomach told me that much.

I shook my head, and Grandfather looked away for a moment in horror or despair. I wouldn't allow myself any such luxury. I studied her corpse for signs of who was responsible for her death. There was an intensity to her glare that sent a cold shiver through me, but it was the sheer amount of blood that really brought her suffering home.

"That's odd," I said as I motioned to a smaller but perfectly round red stain much higher up than the wound that had presumably killed her. "She was stabbed in the stomach, wasn't she?"

"Well, the abdomen, yes." He knelt on the other side of the victim and pulled back the poor woman's blouse to reveal a smaller wound.

"The second cut is superficial," I muttered, taking my time to be sure of what I was saying. "She wasn't stabbed there, and there was no great gush of blood as you might expect from a wound so close to the heart."

"So the skin was removed after death." The expert beside me said this in a whisper, so as not to upset the steward, whom we could still hear out in the corridor. "That explains the lack of blood surging from her body and the relatively small stain on her blouse there."

All I managed to utter in reply was a broken, "But why?"

"Love, I suppose," Grandfather said without hesitation.

He reached up to the table, which still held a cup of tea and a biscuit from earlier in the journey. There was a navy-blue napkin with the crest of the railway company embroidered on it in silver thread. With this in hand, he pulled the blouse back once more and carefully patted away the sheen of thick red liquid to show this near-bloodless wound more clearly.

"It was fairly rudimentary work – we're certainly not looking for a surgeon or an artist – but I think it's clear what the killer intended."

As soon as he said this, I made out the definite shape of a heart carved into Geraldine's chest. "He took a piece of her," I thought aloud. "What terrible sort of human being would do such a thing?"

Grandfather said nothing, so I could only think that he found the answer too obvious to give. He spurred himself into life once more to check the woman's hands, presumably for evidence of a struggle. Geraldine's nails had the neat, rounded look of most young women's, and the skin on her fingers was still rather rosy considering the amount of blood she'd lost.

I caught the sound of the *chef de train* talking to his steward in the corridor. M. Nagelmackers knocked on the open door then let out a sigh that soon turned into a low moan of alarm as he took in the scene.

"Lord Edgington, I have no wish to interrupt," he said in that always precise English of his, "but I am at your disposal should you need anything."

"That's very good of you, monsieur." Grandfather didn't look up from his task.

I had assumed that this would be the sum total of the Belgian's involvement, but he gave a brief, cautious gasp before speaking again. "My apologies, Lord Edgington..." His voice wavered. "I must ask whether you have noticed the pieces of paper here on the floor?"

This got the old detective's attention. We both looked over our shoulders to see what the capable little man with the fuzzy eyebrows had found, but it would be my job to inspect the overlooked items. There were two of them on the carpet beside the door. I could see instantly that they had been penned by different hands, one inordinately precise and flamboyant – with twists and curls all over – and the other so messy that there were black smudges covering half the paper and the name *Geraldine* would have been quite difficult to read if I hadn't known to whose compartment it had been delivered. In our haste, we had walked right past them.

53

"What do you make of them?" Grandfather asked as I put on my cotton gloves that I should have donned upon first entering the room.

"They both use her first name," I explained. "That suggests some degree of familiarity with the victim."

"Or a perceived familiarity," he replied, as the Belgian continued loitering in the doorway, perhaps curious as to what we would find. "It's not uncommon for devotees of an artist, actor or composer to feel as if they are close friends for the simple reason that they appreciate the art the person in question produces."

I wondered whether he was thinking in particular of the other passengers we'd met, but I had opened the first folded note by now and began to read aloud from it. *"My dearest darling Geraldine, I'll come calling for you tonight. Yours, D."*

Grandfather smoothed his moustache with two fingers. "We've met no one with a name starting with D in first class. Am I mistaken, Monsieur Nagelmackers?"

The *chef de train* consulted his memory to be certain, then shook his head. "To my knowledge, there is no one whose Christian name begins with D, but I can consult the passenger list to be certain. Isn't it possible that it was left here by someone from another carriage?"

"It seems unlikely," I replied. "It must have been delivered after we boarded the train. Her maid would have seen it otherwise. Besides, it would have been impossible for anyone to come here without being seen by the steward or one of us in the dining car."

"Read the next note and then we can enquire whether the staff saw anything important," Grandfather suggested at least partly, I felt, to satiate Monsieur Nagelmackers's curiosity.

I bent once more and retrieved the second, far grimier piece of paper. It read, *"If you know what's in your best interest, you'll meet me at midnight in the bar carriage. N.M."*

We didn't even ask the question this time. We simply glanced at the train's conductor and awaited his response. "I'm afraid I am unfamiliar with anyone on board with those initials."

"What of your staff?" Grandfather asked with a troubled countenance.

"I know each of the workers on this train, from the engine driver to the boy who washes the dishes, and I can assure you that there are no Nino Maldinis or Nicolo Marchesis."

As I have already indicated, Nagelmackers was an exceptionally polite man, and he seemed to view this admission as a personal failing on his part. Rather than stay to find out more about the notes or hear Grandfather's initial suspicions, he backed towards the door.

"That being said, I will not rest until I have verified every fact. I beg permission to leave, Lord Edgington, but I will report to you directly with my findings."

"I have one last question," I said before he could go. "Is the door between this carriage and the one in front of it kept locked? If not, could you please ensure that there is no one towards the front of the train who could be responsible for this terrible crime."

Nagelmackers didn't respond with words, but nodded his head sadly, then gave one last look at the dead woman on the floor before stepping from the room. We would soon need to talk to the steward on duty, but first Grandfather finished his inspection of the scene of the crime.

"I believe the killer stood behind Miss de la Forge to stab her in the abdomen." He rose and glanced about the small, though luxurious compartment. "From the way the cushions are disarranged and looking at the blood that has soaked into the seat itself, I can see that her face was held against the day bed throughout the attack. That would have reduced the chance of anyone hearing her screams."

I felt a little silly then. "I assumed she was killed as we went through the tunnel and the wheels screeched. The first time it happened, we were alone in the dining car, but perhaps Miss de la Forge's maid was still with her then. However, the second time we entered a tunnel, it lasted much longer. None of our suspects except James Joseph Campbell had joined us. I assume the killer waited for the maid to leave and seized his chance. The noise was so deafening that it would have been the perfect moment to attack."

He looked a touch impressed. "You're quite right, my boy. Quite right. I should have realised as much myself. That's excellent work."

Over the years, his compliments have become more frequent and effusive, but I still enjoy them, just as I enjoy discovering that I am not as dim as I tend to think. That being said, it was Grandfather's turn to notice something significant that I had missed.

"She was a truly beautiful young woman," he began in a mournful voice. "And yet it is easy to see that famous women like Miss de la Forge depend on the coiffeurs and dressers whom they no doubt pay a healthy sum to retain. She certainly wasn't a natural blonde, and the waves in her hair probably took an hour each day to set. I wonder how many people understand that the actors they see at the cinema are not the characters they play in real life."

I'd been so distracted by the blood that had seeped into her clothes and the terrified expression she wore in her dying moments, I hadn't taken the time to consider her more general appearance. "I suppose that for stars of the silver screen, the overall effect is far more important than reality."

"Precisely. The supposedly unparalleled glamour of film stars is helped by bright lights and soft-focus lenses. Based on the skin that was cut from the victim's body, I can only think that the killer had a mania for such superficiality."

None of this made it any less heart-rending that an innocent woman had been murdered. A lump formed in my throat as Grandfather poked his head into the exquisitely tiled lavabo, and I prepared to leave.

"There's blood in the sink, and the hand towel is missing," he explained. "The killer must have washed his hands before heading out to dinner."

"What about the weapon? He would have needed an extremely sharp instrument to cut the skin off her." The very thought made me shudder.

Grandfather pointed towards the half-open window. "I imagine it's lying at the side of the tracks somewhere, along with the bloody towel. If the killer has any sense, he'll have thrown them into a thick bush or off a bridge, and they will be very difficult to find."

I was distracted by a myriad of possibilities, and an eerie hush fell between us until Grandfather decided to break it. "Come along, Christopher. We won't identify the killer by loitering here. But fear not, my boy, we will find the savage who did this before the journey is out."

CHAPTER EIGHT

We didn't have to go far to continue the investigation. Two steps out of Geraldine's compartment, the steward who had found the body was standing with his back to the wall of windows. He had his eyes closed, and I thought perhaps he was praying that he could erase what he'd seen minutes earlier.

"I'm sorry for her," he began, and he gently banged his head back against the glass as he spoke. "I'm so sorry this happen."

"We have no wish to upset you further," I began, hoping to reassure him in case my grandfather was in a brusque mode that evening. "But we must ask you some questions about what occurred before you found the body."

He winced at this final phrase, and Grandfather took his cue from me to soften his approach. "What is your name, young man?"

I hadn't originally thought of this burly, beardy fellow as being particularly young, but I could see now that he was not a great deal older than I was.

"My name is Domenico." Even this simple answer was difficult for him to produce, and he spoke as though his throat were dry.

I suddenly began to worry what it said about me that, on encountering my first body at the age of sixteen – or rather, watching my aunt die from poisoned champagne right before me – I had largely taken it in my stride.

"Very good, Domenico," the true detective continued. "Am I right in thinking that you were on duty in the conductor's seat, next to the door which gives access to the dining car?"

"You're correct, *signore*."

"Did you leave your post between the time I went to dinner and the last of our fellow passengers passing you?"

He thought for a moment. "No, I do not. I wait in my seat since departure. I always wait in my seat until seven o'clock when I go to prepare the compartments for their night time."

"Do you mean to say that you make the beds?" I thought I should check.

"That is exactly correct, *signore*. I fold the sofas into wall and pull out the beds for the night time." I'm not sure this greatly helped in our understanding of what had occurred, but at least we knew a little of his responsibilities on the train.

"And that was when you found Miss de la Forge's body?" Grandfather asked and was rewarded with a nod. "Had you already seen to the other compartments at that point?"

Each question weighed heavily on him. "I go to her after I see many of the passengers are at dinner. The carriage it is quiet, and my clock signals seven, so I do my work."

We really had a very clear understanding of what he was up to at seven o'clock by this point, and so Grandfather rephrased his previous question to find out what he really wished to know.

"Did you go directly to Miss de la Forge's compartment?"

This seemed a pertinent point, as her compartment was the third along the corridor, and it was not long past seven now.

"This is correct again, Lord Edgington. I remembered I don't see Miss Geraldine, so I knock on door to know if she wants me to prepare for night time." There was something rather charming about his phrasing in English, but then his face dropped, and I remembered just how much of an ordeal this was for him. "When there is no sound, I wonder if she sleeps, but I think it too quiet, so I open the door just a… how do you say it? A small bit – *una frazione?*"

"A fraction," Grandfather replied before I could give the wrong answer.

"Yes, a fraction. I open her door *a fraction* with key, and then I see…"

"You didn't step inside?" I asked to save him from his memory of that moment.

"No, I just look through door. It is horrible." He breathed out heavily, tipping his head back to look at the wooden ceiling of the corridor.

Grandfather took a moment to gather his thoughts. "From my understanding of events, the two Americans—"

"They are the Campbells," Domenico interrupted, and it was clear he was at least as well acquainted with the passenger list as we were.

"Yes, the Campbells, Miss de la Forge's maid, Hansel Reinhardt, the Italian gentleman…" He waited then to learn the name we were yet to hear.

"That is the Count Giovannelli."

"Yes, Count Giovannelli. He was the penultimate passenger to arrive in the dining car before the Englishman, Marvin Pelthorpe. As I was saying, my understanding is that they all left their compartments before you rose from your station to see to the beds. Is that correct?"

"Yes, you are correct, *signore*." For a moment, it seemed as if he had his emotions under control, but then something of a cry escaped his lips, and he held his hand to his head. "I am sorry. This is all… This is not normal for me."

"We understand," I said as softly as possible. "You're doing very well."

Grandfather was away with his thoughts for a moment. "I think that will be all for now. Thank you, Domenico."

"Thank you, *signore*, and you, Master Christopher." He bowed to each of us, and I wondered whether Todd had told him my name, or it was on M. Nagelmackers list. "I stay in my seat if you need anything."

Grandfather tipped his head in acknowledgment, and the steward walked back along the corridor, happy to escape the miasma of death.

"Is he telling the truth, Christopher?" my mentor surprised me by asking. I was normally the one who posed such simple questions after an interview, and I found that I was thrown by his enquiry.

"Oh… well, I haven't actually… Yes, I think he must be. He certainly seems very upset by what he discovered, and I inspected his clothes and hands carefully as he spoke and saw no traces of blood or scratches on his skin."

"I'm not asking whether he is the killer. I believe that to be quite unlikely. I wondered whether he was telling the truth." Grandfather retrieved his silver cane from where he'd left it against the wall, and he tapped it on the floor a few times while he awaited my answer.

"No," I replied with far more conviction than I might have expected. I proceeded to drop my voice to a whisper so that Domenico couldn't hear me. "Or rather, in the large part, yes, but it made no sense for him to have gone to Geraldine's compartment first or for him to have entered when he must have known she was inside."

He almost smiled then. "So why would that be?"

I turned for a moment to watch the twilit world pass us by. "Like so many of us, the steward was obviously an admirer of the beautiful young actress. He saw that the maid had departed and assumed that her mistress would be getting ready for dinner, so he knocked on the door in the hope that he would be able to talk to her."

"That is an innocent way of looking at his intentions, but I believe you're not far from the truth." As he cleared his throat politely, I tried to think of a more wicked interpretation and admittedly failed. "It would have been far more logical to start his work at one end of the corridor and move along to the other."

"Will this help us solve the case?" I dared ask as we moved back towards the dining car.

"No, but it is interesting to consider any hidden motivations and remember that even good ordinary people lie from time to time." We had reached the small wooden box where Domenico had returned to his watch. Grandfather paused before opening the door. "Are you ready to confront our suspects?"

"Never readier!" I said with my confidence still showing.

For his part, Grandfather frowned and did his very best not to remind me to speak in full sentences.

CHAPTER NINE

As much as one can enjoy anything when investigating a callous slaying, I do take some pleasure from the power my grandfather possesses over the potentially guilty men and women whom we will come to describe as suspects. At no time is this phenomenon so evident as when it calls for him to announce a death.

We walked into the dining car with no fanfare or warning. I closed the door behind us, and the long, narrow room instantly fell silent.

"Ladies and gentlemen, I have an announcement to make." Grandfather's deep, commanding voice resounded through the carriage, and everyone who heard it froze. Even Mrs Campbell turned see him.

"Was the steward right?" the German film director demanded. "Is somebody dead?" I could only think it was superstition on his part that he chose not to utter the name of his leading lady. Perhaps he felt that, if he didn't say it, the inevitable wouldn't come true.

Grandfather would normally have held them in suspense, but after a brief, tense pause, he put them out of their misery. "As you will most likely have understood from what the steward told us, a woman is dead." Fine, he kept them in their misery for just a little while longer. "The actress Geraldine de la Forge was murdered in her compartment in the last half hour."

I watched the Wolf, Marvin Pelthorpe, for his inevitable reaction, and it did not disappoint.

"You monster! How could you hurt her?" he yelled across the tables to the man he had evidently decided was the killer. I was amazed by just how crestfallen he looked, but he held in any insults and, when he spoke again, his voice was steely and cold. "You murdered an innocent woman."

To give the man his due, he made no attempt to attack Reinhardt as he had before we'd left. Instead, Pelthorpe gripped his table with both hands, and the sorrow on his face turned to rage. When he said nothing more, I turned to look at the German.

"You can't possibly think I had anything to do with…" he began, but I knew that he wouldn't be able to finish that sentence. "I would never have hurt Geraldine. I loved her more than I love my own self."

The expressions on the countenances of everyone else there told him that no one would give him the benefit of the doubt.

"We all heard you." Grandfather approached the spot where the tortured man sat. "My grandson was there in the corridor when you tried to break down Miss de la Forge's door, and the first person I will now interview is the maid who stopped you from attacking her mistress."

Reinhardt's voice rose in surprise just as he slumped in his chair. "But I had no intention of harming anyone." His eyes grew wider, and his panic was evident in every sound he made. "I merely wished to talk to Gerry. The last time we'd seen one another, we'd left things in a terrible—" He cut himself short, as he must have realised the implications of any argument they'd had.

The muscles in the man's face were strained, and his eyes darted about in search of someone who might believe him. For their part, the Campbells looked much as if we'd released a lion into the carriage. James Joseph once more moved closer to his wife in case she needed protecting.

The only person there who appeared calm was the Italian count. He had a crystal decanter of red wine and now proceeded to pour himself a large glass of the stuff. I found his inexpressive mien a little frightening. I'd rarely seen a person look so entirely unflustered by the news of a death, and as he sat quietly sipping his libation, I came to wonder whether this emotionless response was more suggestive of moral degeneracy than Hansel Reinhardt's fear or Pelthorpe's anger.

Grandfather kept his eyes on the German, but I believe he had taken in all that I had. Before he could decide what we should do next, Mr Campbell took a few steps along the aisle to share his own feelings on the matter.

"This is the easiest case you'll ever investigate, Edgington." He extended one skinny finger and pointed at the director. "Arrest that man. Lock him up in a cloakroom or the luggage van until we get to the next station and then let the police do their worst with him."

"Or just throw him from the train as we're passing over a canyon, and none of us will mention it again," the Wolf suggested. "His sort don't deserve to live, and if he gets up before a judge, he's just the kind to wriggle out of it. Mark my words, I know the type. He'll hire the best solicitor in Europe to defend him, and he'll avoid the hangman's noose just as sure as sure is sure."

Before Hansel Reinhardt could expire from the very idea of our railroading him (pun intended), my grandfather spoke to calm frayed nerves. "I don't think that will be necessary, thank you, Mr Pelthorpe." If anything, his voice was deeper than the aforementioned canyon. "I don't generally inform suspects in a murder investigation of my thinking on a case, but it strikes me as unlikely that Herr Reinhardt would be so foolish as to kill the woman he had expressly taken this train to see."

Pelthorpe hadn't abandoned his cause. "So you're the first to crumble, are you? A few tearful words from Fritz over there, and you reckon he's innocent. So much for the legendary Lord Edgington's hard-headed implacability. You've already given up the girdle!"

It was tempting to offer the coarse fellow a piece of my mind, but Grandfather responded before I could. "I've done no such thing, thank you. Even if Reinhardt here knew the victim better than the rest of you and was overheard conversing with her a short time before she was killed, he was the last person to leave the sleeping carriage."

"Exactly!" James Joseph interrupted. "He waited to commit the crime until there was no one there."

"I disagree." He paused to see whether they would grasp this argument. "It would take a special kind of madness to murder someone in such close confines without any other suspects around to take the blame, especially after the argument they'd had. There was every chance that someone would come along the corridor and catch him in the act. Even if he had ascertained that many of us were already here at dinner when the deed was done, there was no accounting for the movements of the staff."

This did nothing to silence Pelthorpe, whose very being seemed to curl up in revulsion as he glowered at the investigating officer. "Come off it. You're basically saying that he is too likely a suspect so wouldn't have murdered a woman with whom he was clearly obsessed. I'll have no truck with that."

I could bear it no longer. "Who are you, Pelthorpe?" I quite involuntarily took a step forward. "You have a lot of strong opinions about what happened, but you've yet to explain what you're doing here and what your relationship to Miss de la Forge actually was."

That same disparaging expression remained right where it was. "Relationship? What relationship? I didn't know the woman any more than you or the old man did. I'm on this train because I need to get to Verona, and that's it."

Although no one contradicted him directly, the atmosphere in the room changed, and I once more had the sense that these supposedly disparate folk had crossed paths before. I looked from person to person, and each of them appeared more frightened than they had just moments earlier. Even the count looked perturbed for the first time, and I couldn't make sense of it. Something in what Pelthorpe had just uttered had a greater impact on them than the news of Geraldine's death.

When I failed to extract what that might be, Grandfather spoke again. "Despite what I previously said, Herr Reinhardt, I believe it would be best for you to be kept under guard somewhere until my grandson and I have had adequate time to investigate the circumstances of your friend's death."

It had been a while since the director had looked at anyone. His gaze had dropped to the floor and even this announcement couldn't resurrect it. Something in his demeanour told me that he would not object to the plan, though this was no great result for him.

M. Nagelmackers appeared at the end of the carriage, and the competent *chef de train* seemed to know instinctively that his help would be required as he drew alongside our main suspect. A few tables away, the Italian count took another satisfied sip of his drink, and the Campbells looked terrified that they would be the next to die.

CHAPTER TEN

"Lord Edgington, I have confirmed what I told you earlier," the train conductor explained in a low voice so that our suspects couldn't overhear him. "The passenger list provided to me before we left Rome states that there is no one in the first-class carriage with a Christian name beginning with D. I could also find no one with the initials N.M. on board the train at all on this journey."

"I see." Grandfather was oddly passive for once, so I put a question to the nifty Belgian.

"And what of the carriages beyond ours?"

"I verified that, too." He closed his eyes and tipped his head a moment, as if thanking me for the work he'd done. "You see, we have two shifts here on the overnight service. The men who are not currently working are in their accommodation near the front of the train. All of them were together playing cards at the time that Miss de la Forge was murdered, and no one could have got past them without their seeing."

"Thank you, Georges." It was unlike my grandfather to be so informal, and I wondered why he wished to win the man's favour. "I appreciate your assistance, and I trust that you will assign your best steward to watch over Herr Reinhardt. It's for his sake as much as anyone else's. Feathers have clearly been ruffled."

"Of course, Lord Edgington, though it will not be long before we can stop at a station. At that point, the local police will surely take charge of the case."

Silence fell between the two men, and it was Grandfather's turn to be caught off guard. He cleared his throat but, when he spoke again, his caution was apparent. "M. Nagelmackers, I completely understand why you might think that necessary. If nothing else, protocol dictates that we should inform the police of a murder at the first possible opportunity, but I sincerely don't believe it is the best course of action."

The little man bothered his moustache with the side of one finger. "Please, Lord Edgington, I know your powers of investigation are second to no one's, but you must recognise the position in which I find myself."

65

Grandfather turned to me then. I was not used to seeing him so flurried. I'd known him to be glum and occasionally pessimistic before, I'd even witnessed him doubting his own abilities, but there was a certain desperation engraved on his face at this moment, and I felt I should make my own appeal to the man who had the power to end our investigation just as soon as it had begun.

"You know, M. Nagelmackers, my grandfather is not an arrogant man." I questioned for a moment whether this was true and added something of a caveat. "Certainly not when it comes to his work. He wishes only to find Miss de la Forge's killer, and the very best way to do that is to keep our suspects in one place and ensure that not a scrap of evidence can make it off the train unrecorded."

He gripped his tie ever-so-strongly and, for the first time in my life, I felt a little sorry for an inanimate piece of fabric. "I don't know what to say to you. I really don't. It is quite unorthodox to…"

"Think of it like this," I said when his words tailed off, and I felt he needed some more encouragement. "It's approximately two hundred and fifty kilometres from Rome to Florence." While my knowledge of the language had not improved, I had come to know the geography of Italy rather well.

"It's over three hundred," he corrected me, nonetheless. "This old track winds about through valleys and villages more than you can imagine."

"I stand corrected, but between here and Florence, there are few large cities. None of their police forces will be equipped to investigate a murder like this one. I'm not saying it's impossible for provincial officers to solve a crime, but most would lack the experience that a man like my grandfather has. So I'd like to suggest—"

He cut me off this time. "Very well, Mr Prentiss, the two of you have until our first scheduled stop after midnight. There police will be called when we pull into Florence, and the whole affair will be out of our hands."

His tone had hardened a little, and his usual subservient manner vanished. He nodded to us, but there was no warmth in him any more. It seemed that he regretted the result of our negotiations and would have preferred to stick to his original plan. He left without another word, and I felt rather pleased to have solved a problem when my mentor couldn't.

Judging by Grandfather's pale face and the look of shock that was printed across it, I could only conclude that he did not share my positivity.

"Just out of interest," I said as we opened the door that led from the dining car to the first-class bar, "what do you think the average speed of a train such as this one might be?"

He did not need long to calculate the answer. "Based on the winding route that M. Nagelmackers described and the timetable Todd obtained when he bought our tickets, it will be somewhere in the region of fifty kilometres an hour. Night services don't tend to push their locomotives to the limit."

Any optimism I had briefly enjoyed now left me. "Which means we have around five hours left to find the killer, and you've already revealed that you don't believe the obvious suspect is the likely one."

I thought he might reassure me that he had only said that to keep the man safe from the other suspects, but he chewed his lip for a moment and looked suitably worried. "That's right, Christopher, and I must tell you that I don't like our chances."

It was a rare moment at which I would have happily sat down with the strongest drink the barman there could offer. I could have whiled away an hour or two at the shiny tin bar with its baby grand piano, golden-bronze coasters and matching accoutrements. The problem was, we only had five hours remaining and could hardly waste two of them getting tipsy!

We left the bar behind us, passed the concealed kitchen and emerged in the second-class dining car. It was not nearly so opulent as the room in which we had come so close to eating. There was barely any marquetry to see on any of the walls for one thing. The glass lampshades on the tables were un-beaded, and the pattern on the carpets was rather ordinary, but it was perfectly comfortable by most standards. Another noticeable difference was just how busy it was. There were more tables squeezed into the same amount of space, and the gleeful chatter that welcomed us was something of a balm to me.

"Lord Edgington, Master Christopher," Todd called to us from halfway across the narrow dining room, "I didn't expect to see you in here."

He had risen to address us and now pointed to the two spare seats at his table. The fourth was occupied by a young lady dressed all in black.

"Good evening, m'lord," Geraldine de la Forge's maid sounded almost impressed as she looked up at the great man.

"Good evening. As it happens, it is you that we've come here to see."

I don't believe that my grandfather had been intending to sit down, but whatever alternatives passed through his brain were quickly dismissed, and he took the seat in front of hers. Todd is at least half as psychically gifted as his employer, and his worried expression suggested that that he could already tell that something terrible had happened. Perhaps to support his new friend, he sat down beside her. Although I would normally have loitered nearby, there wasn't nearly enough room in the aisle for that. To allow the waiters to do their jobs, I filled the final seat, and the discussion began in earnest.

"I'm sorry if it seems rude, Lord Edgington, sir," the maid began in a tentative voice. She was every bit the East Ender, and her London accent came through strongly, even as she showed her good manners. "But I can't imagine what you'd want doing with me."

"We wish to ask you about your mistress," he revealed in as friendly a manner as he possessed. "Can you tell us what state she was in when you left her?"

She screwed up her napkin on the table in front of her. "Has she complained about me, sir? I was only trying to look out for her. I swear I never meant to—"

"Now, now, my child." Grandfather curved his eyebrows in sympathy. "There's no need to worry. I only wish to know what happened in the minutes before you last left her compartment."

She looked at Todd then who encouraged her with a nod of the head. "You see… Well, there's no sense in mincing my words. Miss de la Forge was upset at me 'cos I tried to convince her to eat some dinner. She's not exactly the heartiest of young ladies, and I know how she gets when she misses a meal." I believe it was at this moment she realised how strange this conversation was. "Sorry, m'lord, but why've you come to ask this now?"

"There's no easy way to say it, my dear: your mistress has been murdered in her compartment."

It was Todd who sucked in a noisy breath in surprise just then. For her part, the young lady froze. Her eyes were the only things which showed any movement, as the pupils got noticeably larger behind her thick lenses.

"How is that possible? I was only wiv her half an hour ago."

"I'm sorry to bring this bad news, Miss…" Grandfather waited for her to fill in the blank.

"Buckthorn." The answer emerged as a little more than croak from the base of her throat, and she pulled her hands under the table as if she'd burnt them. "My name's Milly Buckthorn."

"Well, Miss Buckthorn, I truly am sorry to make you answer questions at this sad time, but there's no other option. Do you mind telling me whether you knew your employer well?"

She looked like a hunted pheasant just then, even though he'd opted for this nice soft question to ease her into the interview. What we really wanted to know was whether there'd been anyone in the corridor when she'd left her mistress moments before her death, but that would have been a tough beginning.

"I…" she looked at me for help or reassurance but would continue alone. "I've only been working for her this last week and a bit. She hired me to accompany her back and forth to Verona. Most people woulda flown, I suppose, but Miss Geraldine says she don't like planes."

"How did she come by your services?"

"Murdered?" She shook her head then and was quite dismayed. "How can it be?" Her tears had arrived, and Todd handed her the white linen napkin from the table.

"You should try to answer Lord Edgington's questions, Milly," he recommended. "It really is for the best."

"Right, yes. My services…" A small, sad moan escaped her, and it made her subsequent expression all the more tragic. "I put an advert in the *Continental Daily Mail*. I know it were a bit silly on my part. I'd rarely travelled outside the Yock Valley before, but you hear so much these days about rich ladies touring the Continent and what have you, so I decided I would advertise my services as an international lady's maid. I never thought that a film star would hire me. I'd been working as a dogsbody for a horrid old woman in Tatchester. It was beyond my dreams to leave my petty life behind and move to Italy, but a month after I placed that announcement, I was contacted by Miss Geraldine's manager. Two days later, they flew me to Rome."

I could see just how much this still meant to her. She looked out of the window, but I doubted that her eyes saw much of the dusky countryside beyond the glass. She was thinking of that fateful moment when she felt her luck had changed.

"Back to this evening," I said to push things forward, "you say that Miss de la Forge was alive when you left the sleeping carriage?"

"Yes..." She hesitated and straightened her head a little. "Well, I think so. Only... You see, I went to use the W.C. in the corridor after I left her compartment. Like I told you, she wasn't in a good mood, and she said some things I know she didn't mean, so I went to dry my eyes before dinner. She wasn't a bad mistress, you know. I just can't believe she's..."

"Do you know what time you left her compartment?" Grandfather asked in a firm, insistent tone. "That could be very important."

She glanced then at the clock that was hanging above the door through which we'd entered. "As it happens, I do. You see, I wasn't supposed to finish with her until seven, but she was so unkind that I walked off five minutes early. I felt guilty at the time, but there were no reasoning with her."

"And you didn't see anyone in the corridor before or after?" I put in now that we were getting down to brass tacks.

The tears kept flowing, and her voice was faint. "I... I don't think so. No, I'm sure there was no one."

"There's no need to be afraid, Milly," Todd reassured her, and he put one hand on her arm. "Lord Edgington only has to ask his questions, and then you'll be left alone."

He looked at his master then, as if to confirm that what he'd promised were true.

"That's right, Miss Buckthorn." Grandfather reached out to pat her hands, but they weren't there, so he tapped the table instead. "I would like to build a picture of the woman who died. We must know all we can about her."

"I'll try my best." Her emotions kept changing. One moment

70

she was sobbing, the next smiling awkwardly. I suppose that was a servant's lot. In most houses, a maid's feelings are deemed quite irrelevant. She could have lost a parent or even a child, and many employers would still expect her to go about her work without a hint of emotion. I'm happy to say that we aren't like that in my family, and Grandfather soon set her mind at ease.

"That is all I am asking. I wish you to remain calm, despite the terrible events of this evening. Maybe we can move on to discussing Herr Reinhardt?"

I could see the muscles in her arms become tense as she heard the German's name. "That man? Do you think he's to blame? He certainly caused Miss Geraldine some problems since I've known her. She was in a terrible state the whole week, and he was awful to us both this evening. I was afraid for my mistress."

"Do you know anything of the circumstances that led to their falling-out?"

She paused before summoning a response. "I can't say I do, sir. All I can tell you is that it was connected to the film they was supposed to make. She would come home from the studio in tears."

She attempted a smile again, and it made her thin cheeks a little rounder. It seems an odd fluke that one young woman should become famous the world over for her beauty and another, just as pretty in her own way, should spend her days in servitude. I suppose the circumstances into which we are born is generally the most significant factor in life. There's no way I'd have become a detective if it weren't for my grandfather. I'm sure that, if I'd had any other family, I would have been dismissed as a dunce for my clumsy tongue and slow wits.

"And what about the scene in the corridor?" I asked, as that was surely something she had experienced first-hand. "Why did Herr Reinhardt get so angry and force the door open?"

The memory of the assault on their compartment must have come back to her then as she looked at me differently. "Oh, that were you, weren't it, sir?" Her appreciative expression made me feel a little heroic. "It was awfully good of you to put yourself out like that. I don't like to think what would have happened if…"

She couldn't finish this sentence. I imagined that every time the knowledge of the murder recurred to her, she began to cry more.

Grandfather would most likely have offered her a handkerchief, but she was provided for in that department. He did not prompt her to speak this time. The hush that fell did that for him.

"You see, the director fellow, he wanted to speak to Miss Geraldine, but she weren't having it. I'd seen the effect what his presence had on her, and I tried to tell him how things stood." She came to a brief halt, then continued as though afraid I would ask the same question again. "I can't tell you what happened between 'em. What I do know is that my mistress couldn't even face dinner because of him."

"Yes, I overheard your discussion outside our compartment," I told her as a waiter came to offer us a menu. Sadly, Grandfather batted the man away. I know we only had a few hours, but he's never been one to give mealtimes their due respect. I could have eaten a horse. "You went to get her some food, is that correct?"

"Yes, sir. Miss Geraldine asked me to call for her dinner, so I did just that. I went to the dining car – the first-class one, I mean – and placed an order which was to be delivered to her compartment. But when I got back there, she said she had no appetite, and I was to cancel the food altogether. I tidied her clothes away, made sure she didn't want my company, and that was when she were short with me, so I left her to sleep."

Todd showed his sympathy with a milder tone of voice. "It sounds to me that you'd already had a difficult time this evening… and now this."

She stared down at her lap. "You know, I'd never seen her quite like that before. She wasn't a happy person – there's no doubt about it – but this evening when I tried to convince her to go to dinner, she actually seemed…"

"Afraid?" Grandfather suggested, and the word made poor Milly jump just a little.

"Worse. She looked like she had no hope left in the world. It were terrible to see." A sense of purpose came over her as she dabbed her eyes. "When I took the job, I imagined Miss Geraldine's life being a dream… I thought that my time serving her wouldn't be far off, neither. The truth is, she were the most tragic character I ever met. It's heartbreaking when you think of it."

"You seemed very loyal to Miss de la Forge when you fought off that man," I felt it only right to say, and she reflected on the compliment before replying.

"It was hard not to be, you know? From the very first moment we met, I could see she needed someone to look after her. And if you don't mind me saying, sir, I don't think that the people around her were looking out for her best interests."

It had seemed for a moment that her tears had dried, but her eyes now glistened once more. If it had been me, I would have wasted more time reassuring her that everything would be all right, but Grandfather was very much aware of the task we faced.

"Aside from Herr Reinhardt, does anyone else come to mind with whom Miss de la Forge shared a... shall we say *strained* relationship?"

I noticed a slight movement in her throat as she swallowed before answering. "I suppose there's that Eddie fellow. You know the one I mean. They starred in *The Price of Paradise* together." She became more animated then, and I could tell that she liked Geraldine's films just as much as I did. "That's the one where he plays a brilliant composer who is dying of some terrible disease. She's the nurse he falls in love with on the front line, only for them to lose one another in the chaos of the war and be reunited as he lies on his deathbed years later when she's assigned to look after him."

"I loved that film," I needlessly replied.

"I can't say I'm familiar with it," Grandfather admitted, whereas I'd seen it twice with my mother. "Although I believe you're referring to her former paramour, Eddie Denkin."

"That's him!" Milly seemed content to have helped us this much. "The papers say that he's seeing some new woman, but he kept calling at her apartment after I arrived. I had to be firm with him just like I was with the German fella. Their type lose their heads for pretty young ladies."

Grandfather gave no sign of being interested in what she'd revealed and changed the topic. "So you were an aficionado of film even before you worked for Miss de la Forge?"

Milly nodded before replying. "If that means I like films then, yes, sir. Who doesn't?"

The simple answer to this presumably rhetorical question was, *Lord Edgington*, but I refrained from providing it. I decided to mention something more important instead. "When we discovered the body, there were two notes pushed under the door of your mistress's compartment. Both told her to meet them tonight. Do you know of anyone with the initials D or N.M.?"

Milly sat back in her chair and leant against the headrest as she considered her answer. "Except for Mr Denkin, I really don't. Do you think they were sent by the killer?"

"One was rather friendly sounding, the other gruff and demanding."

The maid pursed her lips for a few seconds and, when they opened again, it was only to reiterate what she had already told us. "I'm afraid I can't help you. Remember that I only stayed with her in Rome for ten nights, and Miss Geraldine spent much of that time preparing her new film. When she was at home, she preferred to keep to herself. Other than her former beau and the director, I can't think of anyone who came to visit."

"Thank you, Miss Buckthorn," Grandfather bowed his head in a manner which told me that he was about to conclude the interview, but I had another question to put to her.

"Before we leave, I must ask what the last words Miss de la Forge spoke to you were."

Her reticence returned, and she glanced once more at her dainty hands. "I was prob'ly a bit too curt. You see, even though I'd only been with her a short time, we'd fallen into a funny old routine where I had to talk to her like a child to get her to do anything." She must have felt guilty as she tipped her head back and wouldn't look at us any longer. "I told her I thought she were spoilt and that she'd starve if she didn't eat anything."

"And what did she say?" My voice had fallen lower.

"She said... She said that it didn't matter what happened to her, but if I continued to be so interfering, she'd send me back to England. I didn't say another word after that. I left her right where she was, and now she's..."

This was another sentence that would go unfinished. She raised the napkin to her eyes, but the whole experience had become too much for her. She shot to her feet and would have hurried away, but Todd's seat was blocking her exit.

"Thank you so much for your honesty, Miss Buckthorn." Just

occasionally, Grandfather sounds like a very satisfied cat. This was one of those times.

Though the tears were now travelling over the soft hills of her cheeks, she did her best to remain polite until Todd had moved out of her way. "You're very welcome, Lord Edgington. You'll find me in compartment number twelve if you need anything more."

CHAPTER ELEVEN

"What did you make of all that?" Todd put to us as I stared at Milly's first course that had just been delivered to the table and would now go uneaten. "We were having a lovely conversation until we heard about Miss de la Forge. I could see she was sad, of course, but Milly seemed to cheer up when she told me about her life back in England. Then, as soon as I saw you, I was sure that would change."

"At least we weren't here to arrest her," I muttered, wondering whether *I* could be arrested for taking another person's food even if she didn't plan to eat it.

"Thank you, Christopher," Grandfather tutted. "That's a very helpful contribution."

Todd was apparently a touch disturbed by our intrusion and returned to his previous question. "What did you make of Miss Buckthorn, sir? Is she a suspect in the murder?"

For the five seconds before Grandfather replied, I could see the apprehension on Todd's face just as clearly as a headline in the newspaper. "We will have to confirm her credentials, of course, but I doubt it. For one thing, she had less time than the other suspects to commit the crime and make her way here. Furthermore, if she really did only meet her mistress the week before last, it seems unlikely that she would have built up so much animosity that she would wish to murder her."

"We can't rule out a financial motive," I said, still distracted by my wilful stomach and not thinking for a moment about Todd's feelings on the matter. "It's possible that she killed poor Geraldine to cover her swindling."

Grandfather had become quite short with me. "You're forgetting about the heart that the killer removed. Does that sound like the behaviour of a swindler?"

Todd ran his hand through his well-groomed hair. "The killer removed the woman's heart?" The shock in his voice was palpable, even as he lowered it to a whisper.

"Not quite." Grandfather looked about the restaurant to ensure that no one was listening, but after the initial stir his presence tends to

77

cause, the parties nearby had returned to their conversations.

The only exception was a man at the table next to ours. He had a very high forehead and looked a little familiar. He was alone, but presumably expecting a companion as a neat, leather-bound tome was sitting amongst the cutlery in the place opposite his. I couldn't see the title of the book, but I did realise that this was the fellow who had jumped onto the train as it was pulling out of the station.

"A piece of skin in the shape of a heart was removed from Miss de la Forge's body," Grandfather revealed in a suitably skullduggerous tone. "The obvious inference is that the killer held strong feelings for his victim. While this could be a ruse to put us off the scent, it is rather an extreme one."

I had nothing significant to add, though I had finally abandoned the daring scheme I had concocted to make off with the goat's cheese tartlet when Grandfather wasn't looking.

"It sounds to me that this fellow Reinhardt has a lot to answer for," Todd suggested in my stead. "The newsstands were full of stories about him and Miss de la Forge this week. There was a strong implication that their 'close working relationship' was more than just platonic."

"And yet, when they met on the platform in Rome, it was evident that she wanted nothing to do with him." I finally said something worth saying. "Their encounter on the train only reinforces that impression."

Grandfather clapped his hands together in consternation. "It's such a shame that the maid didn't know our victim better. We are forced to rely on what the papers have told us, and that's highly unlikely to be true. I would have liked to learn more about Miss de la Forge before we interview the suspects, but I suppose it can't be helped."

With this, he pushed his chair back, and Todd did the same.

"What can I do to help, Lord Edgington?" He was clearly motivated to get to the truth.

Grandfather cast his eyes back to the door through which we'd entered. "I think it's best that you stay here and try to see if anyone in this part of the train was a personal acquaintance of the dead actress. We will return if we need your help."

"Very good, Sir." He bowed, as he tends to, and we left him behind to eat his dinner, but not before Grandfather had whispered a few words in his ear.

I assumed he was interested in Todd's attachment to lovely Milly Buckthorn. I could just imagine Grandfather playing matchmaker to the pair of them. Perhaps by the end of the weekend, there would be a new maid in his employ – as though we didn't have enough staff accompanying us on our travels already.

If this were the case, I could sympathise somewhat with how Todd must have felt as Milly wandered away from us. I can't tell you the pain I felt on being wrenched apart from that savoury tartlet. By the time we got back to the first-class dining car, the suspects were finishing their desserts, and it stung me deeply to know that the killer would have enjoyed a full meal whilst I dealt with the consequences of his wicked deed.

"What did you say to Todd just now?" I asked when I was certain no one could hear us.

"I? Oh, that was nothing. I merely reassured him that I would find Miss de la Forge's killer. I don't know whether you've noticed, but the dear chap is most definitely an admirer of her work."

He came to a stop in the middle of the carriage and looked about at the Campbells, the count and that unsavoury man, Marvin Pelthorpe. In reply, they stopped sipping their coffee and spooning their *gelo di melone* into their mouths. What I would have given for just a small portion of those watermelon puddings! I was fairly certain that I caught a whiff of the cinnamon and honey that the dish contained, though I have been known to hallucinate when I go too long without food. And for that reason, I will now stop talking about it altogether.

Grandfather raised one hand momentously, much as if he were about to start a race. Rather than picking one of the suspects for our next interview, as I'd expected, he shook his head and continued on through the carriage. I couldn't exactly feel sorry for the group we left behind, as not one of them had endeared himself to me. Still, I often reflect on how lucky I am not to be a suspect in one of my grandfather's investigations. If I had to put up with all the schemes and stratagems he uses to set people off guard, I'd end up confessing to the crime to be done with them.

"Has anyone passed through here except your colleagues since we left?" I asked Domenico, who still looked a little green from his run-in with the dead body.

"No, sir," the steward replied directly, and I felt quite confident he was telling the truth. "I have been at my post the whole time, and my colleague Fabio is guarding Signor Reinhardt's compartment."

"Keep up the good work." It was my grandfather's job to say, and the man looked more cheerful than he had since we'd first met him.

"So we're going to interview Reinhardt?" It was my job to point out.

"It's the obvious next step. He's the only person here who has admitted to knowing Miss de la Forge personally."

I paused outside our door, not yet wanting to approach the second steward, whom we could see further along the corridor. "You mentioned that you had heard troubling reports about the man..." I realised that this wasn't a question and needed a moment to turn it into one. "Beyond what you mentioned about his films being a poor investment, do you have any specific reason to doubt his character?"

Grandfather hesitated, and I could see that he would need some time to pick the right words. "It's very hard to say, seeing as..." And then he needed a little longer. "Well, you know..."

"Do I?"

He gave an exasperated sigh. "The war, Christopher. We were at war with Germany a little over a decade ago."

"That is true," I replied, still not seeing what impact this had on Herr Reinhardt's value as a human being.

"And Herr Reinhardt is German."

"Also true... Hold on. Are you saying that you don't trust him just because of his nationality? If we had to doubt the worth of the people of every country with whom Britain has been at war, it would really only leave Luxembourg and a few Pacific Islands."

He raised one eyebrow dubiously, so I imagine there was a war or two I'd forgotten. "You're missing my point, Christopher, and I'd rather hoped you'd think better of me than that. What I'm saying is that it is hard to judge him based on second-hand reports because so many people are still prejudiced against our former foe. Look at the way Mr Pelthorpe reacted to him."

He'd made an interesting point, which I would otherwise have overlooked. "So what you're saying is that many people are Germanophobes, but not you?"

"That's exactly right, and I'm impressed that you knew such an obscure term." He put his hand on my shoulder and looked a little proud of me. I decided not to tell him that I thought I'd made it up myself. "Are you ready to interview our *windiger Geselle*?"

I'm certain that my complete ignorance of what this (presumably German) expression meant came through in my resultant blank look, but he still said, "That's the spirit, Christopher. Our *slippery customer* awaits."

CHAPTER TWELVE

The steward who had been put in charge of watching the director's compartment wasn't nearly so broad as Domenico, but he had a rather suspicious glare and treated us as though we were coming to break out the prisoner from his makeshift cell.

"We're here to speak to Herr Reinhardt," I believe Grandfather said. Well it was something along those lines, but as he spoke in Italian, I'm really only paraphrasing. "M. Nagelmackers has given us the run of the train to investigate Miss de la Forge's death. (I have a secret love of the biscuits my dog eats for dinner.)" Fine, he probably didn't say this last bit, but I can't say for certain it's not true.

Fabio said nothing but stepped aside to let us pass. He continued to watch us through narrowed eyes as we knocked on the door and entered.

"It's about time you came," Reinhardt said as soon as he saw us. His fear had been replaced by irritation. "What am I supposed to do here all alone, eh? Can anyone tell me that? I haven't even eaten my dinner."

I could sympathise with him on this one point at least.

Grandfather would not be fazed by such protests. "Thank you for allowing us to visit you. I can quite understand that you wish to go about your evening, which is all the more reason for you to tell us the absolute truth."

Reinhardt's sleeping compartment was not quite so luxurious as the double one Grandfather had reserved, but it was still very elegant. There was a hand-painted woodland scene on one wall, and the upholstery was in rich blue velvet.

The bed was folded away in the wall, and so there was plenty of space for him to throw his arms about in dismay as Grandfather took a seat at the small, mosaic-topped table. It had been a while since I'd had the chance to loiter anywhere, so I decided to do that in the doorway.

"If you're about to ask me whether I killed the woman I loved, you can save your breath."

"Ah, so you loved Miss de la Forge?" There was no little incredulity in the wily detective's voice. "It was only weeks ago that she was known to be courting her co-star Eddie Denkin."

"Precisely, your lordship," Reinhardt delivered a hefty dose of sarcasm with his response. "Weeks are a lifetime in matters of the heart. That cheat Denkin broke hers, and I was there to fix it."

"Until something went wrong, and she wanted nothing more to do with you." I had meant to whisper this sentence, but it came out at full volume.

The German stopped his gesticulating and fixed his gaze on me. "That was a mere misunderstanding. As I tried to make clear to Gerry, I loved her more than there are words in the *Deutsches Wörterbuch*."

I was tired of everyone using expressions that I didn't know in languages I didn't speak, and while I'm aware that I was on the Continent and I really should have studied harder at school, I was happy when Grandfather leant closer to explain, "The *Deutsches Wörterbuch* is the largest ever German dictionary. It was started by the Brothers Grimm. As it happens, they were as important to lexicography as they were to—"

He must have realised that this was not the time to discuss such matters, as he returned to the previous topic a little gingerly. "Did your beloved Geraldine reciprocate your feelings?"

Reinhardt seethed quietly for so long that I doubted he would answer. "Yes, I'd like to believe that she did."

I was already aware that the discussion was leaning towards the abstract. However, the next question Grandfather asked was far less subjective. "Tell us about your time with Miss de la Forge. When and where did you first meet?"

There was no real windowsill to speak of, but Reinhardt had perched on a just-protruding edge beneath the glass there. "After she made her first film…"

"*The Door with No Key*," I reminded him with great haste. I must confess that I do like mysteries.

"Yes, *The Door with No Key*. When she became famous, I sought her out for another film. She was luminous in that role, even as that oaf Cecil Sinclair strutted across the screen like a self-important pigeon who believed he was a peacock." I had yet to hear Reinhardt mention anyone he actually liked. "I begged her to act in *Love's Lonely Flame*, and it was the best move I could have made for my career. The woman is… Or rather, the dear woman *was* a great actress, and the real tragedy is that I will never get to see her in the next production we were to make together. It was a project of passion for her. She even helped write the scenario."

Grandfather turned around to communicate something to me then. It was easy to interpret his look, as I was thinking the very same thing. *The real tragedy was not a film that would never get made but the loss of a young woman who did not deserve to die.*

"Which is the reason you were in Rome together," I said, remembering the article I'd read that afternoon. "Isn't that right?"

There was something very proud about Hansel Reinhardt. He held his chin up higher than seemed natural and, on more than one occasion, I believe I caught him admiring his own reflection. He was certainly a handsome brute, but the fact he was so well aware of it made him far less likeable.

"I don't mind admitting that to be the case. *The Other Half of Her* was to be the photoplay she would be remembered for. Her magnum opus, if you will."

"Why were you making it in Italy rather than London, Hollywood or Berlin?" Grandfather hurried to ask this question, and I think he already knew the answer.

"Because it was far cheaper here. The pounds and dollars that my producers could offer me went further." The German apparently failed to see that this statement could be at odds with his previous one. Personally, I doubted that the film would be a masterpiece if the primary concern from the outset was how to cut corners. "It was to be the second film we made in Italy. *Echoes of the Ocean* was only just released."

"So you started working on the new production within the last couple of weeks," I said to keep us on track.

He replied with a fierce shake of the head. "No, we started work several months ago. A lot must happen before any cameras start rolling. I worked with the writer on the script – it was to be Geraldine's first talking picture, though we hadn't confirmed that to the press. Gerry herself was instrumental in shaping the plot and even gave me some notes on the dialogue. I believe that she was just as keen to make the film a success as I was."

"So you started *filming* this production a couple of weeks ago," I tried once more to get him to talk about the things we really needed to know.

"Not exactly." Like my grandfather, he was a stickler for exactitude. "We spent a long time looking for the perfect actress to take the supporting role. It is the story of two sisters who are separated when they are very young and meet again years later. Geraldine went to great effort to find the right person. If I'm being totally honest, I felt that she was afraid of being upstaged. Actors are very particular about their co-stars."

"Whom did you finally choose for the part?" Grandfather once more surprised me by being the slightest bit interested in the world of film.

"We never announced who would play Leisel to Geraldine's Greta." He looked through the window then, but it was so dark by now that he could only see his own reflection. "As it happens, Geraldine finally decided that Maxine Hammond would be the best choice."

"Her rival, Maxine Hammond?" I certainly didn't hide my surprise at this revelation. "The woman seen out and about with Eddie Denkin? Her former boyfriend Eddie Denkin, whom you recently revealed had broken her heart?" I must confess that I sounded like a bad actor in a convoluted play who is charged with reminding the audience of all that has already happened. If being a detective doesn't work out for me, I suppose I could always become a plumber or perhaps a librarian; the stage clearly isn't the place for me.

"That is correct. Maxine flew to Rome to audition for the part, just like the many actresses we met before we took a different approach to the character of Liesel. Maxine is a fine actress. Not up to the high standards of the immortal Geraldine de la Forge, but a fine actress, nonetheless."

The obvious next question was whether Geraldine knew of the upstart actress's dalliance with her beau when she chose her for the part, and that is exactly what Grandfather now asked.

"I really can't say," came Reinhardt's response. "I noticed no animosity between them, but then that was before the premiere of—" He stopped himself short, and it was patently patent that we'd found something he had no desire to share with us. "That was before all that nasty business came out in the washing."

"And before you fell in love with the dead woman," I once more muttered far too loudly, and our suspect could do nothing but shrug unapologetically.

I think it bears saying that, for all the anger and frustration he'd shown, we were yet to see any great sorrow from Hansel Reinhardt, which was very much at odds with his proclamations of love.

"It is hard to say when I first became enamoured of my sweet Geraldine. Perhaps it was the first time I saw her grace the screen, or maybe it was that night when our worlds collided and we kissed like lovers do."

I would like to give him the benefit of the doubt and accept that he spoke in clichés because English was not his first language, but I think the more likely explanation was that he was a hammy sort who loved the sound of his own voice and spent too long with his head in the movies.

"What happened at this premiere that you mentioned?" Lord Edgington never misses a trick.

Reinhardt squirmed, then settled into his answer. "Well, I don't suppose it has much bearing on her death, but that was when the situation between Eddie and Geraldine came to a head. They had a very public argument at the party for the release of *Echoes of the Ocean* and, a day or so later, after a long day working together, Gerry and I…"

"So your worlds collided, you fell in love, and you both lived happily ever after," Grandfather said to play the man at his own game.

"We both know that isn't what happened. There is no need to be…" He looked for the right word. "…*spöttisch!*"

"Facetious," Grandfather replied, as apparently his German is as good as his Italian… and his French… and probably his Spanish for all I know.

"*Dankeschön.*"

"*Bitteschön.*"

Without giving the man time to breathe, my mentor fired off another question. "What happened after that? After Eddie Denkin broke poor Geraldine's heart and you did what lovers do?"

Reinhardt's tie had a very slender knot with which he now fiddled. My father had taught me never to trust men with skinny neck ties, and while I generally ignore my father's more ludicrous advice, I had to wonder whether this was one rule I should follow.

"Geraldine discovered something about me which broke her heart all over again." He didn't just turn away this time. He spun all the way around so that he had his back to us. "She found out that I am married."

"You're married?" I was apparently still in bad-actor mode. "To whom?"

"To my wife, obviously." He glared at me over his shoulder, as though I couldn't work out this much myself. "We were very young when she fell pregnant, and getting married was the right thing to do."

"You have a child with her?" Yes, this was also delivered in the style of a character whose only task is to help advance the plot. I cursed myself for being so obliging.

"No, I have three. Inge is a very good wife, but family life is not compatible with the work of a great director. I do not go home to see them very often."

The self-proclaimed "great director" was nothing but a rotter in my book. The fact that he could have presented himself as an innocent party in all that had occurred only confirmed this impression.

For the moment at least, Grandfather wasn't concerned with the morality of the complicated affair that Reinhardt had described. "So your brief liaison came to an end when Geraldine discovered that you were already married and you would have no future together."

Standing side-on to his interrogator, the man pursed his lips for a few seconds before revealing anything more. "Not exactly. This led to us arguing, but then I made another mistake."

"Oh, yes?" It was impressive just how much nuance Grandfather could put into these two words. What he was really saying was, *Oh, how interesting! I didn't imagine for one moment that you would be at fault yet again. You really have surprised me!*

"When she became so upset that she wouldn't leave her room for days on end, I threatened to promote Maxine to the lead role over her."

"At which point she did get out of her bedroom, and she left the house and refused to see you again. Which is why you bought a ticket for this train, as it was the only way you could hope to win her back."

There was something strangely honest about the swine in front of us. While he had initially denied any wrongdoing, he had proceeded to outline a lengthy list of his misdeeds and even now gave us a fuller picture of his low character.

"Yes and no. The truth is that I had no intention of putting Maxine Hammond's name at the top of the poster for *The Other Half of Her*. It was a ploy to get Geraldine back to work. For the remainder of that week, she came to rehearsals and was perfectly professional, but she wouldn't talk to me in private. I tried one last time to pressure her into meeting me, and she stopped coming to the studio altogether."

"So your ploys went terribly wrong, and you came racing over here to beg her to return." Grandfather's whole manner, from the expression on his face to his tone and bearing, was critical, and I would only take the attack further.

"You didn't take this train because you loved her. You came because you were afraid that your film would fall apart. We know you'd had money trouble on previous projects. You were looking out for yourself, not the woman you supposedly adored."

"Both things are possible!" he snapped at me. "I'm sure I don't have to tell you just how intoxicating Gerry was. It's perfectly possible that I loved her *and* wanted to avoid losing any money."

I let Grandfather have another poke at him. "Then you went about it the wrong way. In the weeks before she died, the two men who were meant to care for her let her down, and then you came yelling onto the train to scare her half to death. What did you hope to achieve by forcing your way into her compartment like that?"

He looked somewhat scandalised by the question. "I wasn't planning to murder her, if that's what you think. If anything, her death has caused me more problems."

"How terrible for you." Grandfather really is the ice king of the cold retort.

"You don't like me, Lord Edgington, do you?"

He released a tentative huff in reply as he considered his answer. "The question of whether I like or dislike a murder suspect has rarely entered my mind. Over the years, I've become fond of a number of criminals and positively detested countless innocent men. The only thing that matters to me is who killed Geraldine de la Forge."

The director clearly hadn't listened to a word his accuser had just said as he responded with a sharp, "It's my race that bothers you, isn't it? You can't stand me because I'm German, so you're willing to push any charges my way and be done with it."

"Actually," I interrupted, "I made that same mistake earlier, but we cleared it up. Grandfather is definitely not a Germanophobe." I'd used this word correctly once that day, and I was determined to make the most of it.

"That's easy to say, but I've met a number of fusty old Englishers who still think it's 1914. If you are going about this investigation without a hint of bias, tell me why it is that I'm the one locked away in here when any one of the people in that dining room could be the killer? You're the worst kind of bigot, Edgington: the kind who won't admit what he is."

Grandfather had heard enough. Leaning on his amethyst-topped cane, as though he were as old as his passport insisted, he slowly rose to look the man in the eyes. "I locked you up in here for your own sake, Reinhardt. I thought you would prefer to be kept apart from the man out there who would happily rip you to pieces. As you clearly don't need any protection, I will tell the steward to go back to his duties."

"That's fine by me!" I can't say for certain why Reinhardt shouted this response. I can only think that the tone of his voice hadn't caught up with the sentiment of his words.

"And as for the reason you were the first person we interviewed in earnest, that is because, aside from her maid, none of the other suspects was well acquainted with the victim. Or is there something you know that we haven't yet discovered?"

Reinhardt clenched his jaw so that his cheeks became tense, and I could see from the look in his eyes that he would have liked to punch the old man in the face. To be fair to him, Grandfather was very good at inciting such emotions in people.

I'm pleased to say that no violence ensued, however, and after this brief standoff, I stepped aside to allow my companion to open the door.

"Come along, Christopher. There's nothing more to be done

here…" He paused as he put his hand on the brass handle. "…for the moment at least."

This was a perfectly dramatic moment to finish the interview, but I realised that there was something we hadn't discussed. Before trailing after my grandfather, I stopped in the doorway. "I don't suppose you sent Miss de la Forge a note this evening?"

Reinhardt looked back in confusion as Grandfather called my name from the corridor.

"You didn't happen to go by a pet name with her? *Droopy* perhaps? Or maybe *Nice Man?*"

"No, of course, I didn't." The German turned to stare off through the window.

"Wonderful. I thought I'd better check."

"Christopher, come along!" Grandfather called again, and I left Reinhardt to think over all that he'd done, or more likely just feel sorry for himself.

CHAPTER THIRTEEN

"He's not our man, is he?" I said quite confidently, once we'd dismissed the temporary guard and were alone in the corridor.

"Why do you say that?" Grandfather had a distant look in his eyes, and I was surprised he'd even heard me.

"Well, it's as he said. He couldn't make the film without Geraldine. He's bound to lose a lot of money now and, if your friend in Rome is to be believed, it doesn't sound as if he can afford too many failures."

"That is all quite true, but have you heard of the concept of lying?" He couldn't resist turning to me with a quizzical look just then. His eyebrows arranged themselves at diagonals, and he adopted a supercilious pout. I couldn't entirely blame him, but I could answer back.

"I have, as it happens. And have you heard of the concept of a good detective being able to know when a suspect is telling the truth?" I gave him a moment not to answer before presenting my evidence. "If anything, Reinhardt went out of his way to reveal all his failings. Had he wished to lie to us, he would surely have painted himself in a better light from the beginning. We know that he is an adulterer with a fierce temper. He abandoned his family and put the film he was making ahead of the happiness of a woman he claims to love. All in all I would say that, if he is lying to clear his name, he's done a thoroughly poor job of it."

All Grandfather would offer by way of response was, "Perhaps." He approached the neighbouring door and put one ear to it to listen.

"That's where Marvin Pelthorpe is staying. I doubt he's in there."

He nodded once as if to say, *I knew that,* then moved along the corridor in the direction of the dining car. "Of course," he said to return to our previous discussion, "it's also possible that he has presented us with a number of dastardly yet in no way illegal titbits in order to make us think that no rational person who had actually committed a crime would reveal such details."

"So he lied about certain irrelevant matters to make us think he wasn't lying about the most important one?" I reflected on this as I followed the old fox along the corridor. "How very clever."

"Or perhaps he really is a rotter who is quite innocent of the murder and merely wished to show that he wasn't hiding anything. It's difficult to tell which is more likely."

"With all the experience you've amassed, shouldn't you be able to do that very thing?"

He had reached the next compartment and stopped to look back at me. "Yes, I suppose I should."

He allowed himself a brief laugh and was about to knock on the door in front of him when there was a noise further along the corridor and someone pushed a dining tray, complete with silver cloche, out of the room next to ours.

"I knew it!" Grandfather exclaimed, and I swear that he came very close to running along the carpeted hallway to apprehend the phantom tray pusher.

I was about to ask him what he knew when I worked it out. Milly told us that she'd cancelled her mistress's dinner and yet, when we were sitting in the dining room before Geraldine's body was discovered, a waiter had taken a tray of food into the first-class carriage.

"You're not going anywhere!" Grandfather got to the door just before it closed and peered through it to see who the mystery man was.

"'Oo are you?" In case you can't tell from his accent, the mystery man was French.

"Lord Edgington."

"'Oo?"

I might have answered the question, so that Grandfather didn't have to sound vain, but I was choking on my laughter and couldn't produce any words.

"I'm a... Well, I'm a rather well-known detective."

"'Ow lovely for you, monsieur, and I am going to bed."

"Wait!" Grandfather put his hand on the doorframe and his foot against the jamb to ensure he couldn't shut us out. "We need to talk to you about a crime that has been committed this evening."

The Frenchman looked along the corridor in the direction of Domenico's seat, but he was hidden away in his cubby hole. "I was 'aving my dinner. I know nothing about zis crime."

"So I suppose you've never heard of Geraldine de la Forge."

He wrinkled up his face and shook his head. "I 'ave not. Though with a name like 'ers, I suppose you think I should. Believe it or not, we French do not all know one another."

"She's not actually French," I managed to inform him. "Now that I come to think of it, it's almost definitely a stage name. You see, she's a British actress. Well, she was."

He was a big man with a large black moustache that might well have been stolen from a walrus, and he stepped out of his compartment to confront us. "If you are suggesting zat I was in any way responsible for her giving up acting, I can tell you zat I 'ave never met ze woman."

It was Grandfather's turn to pretend he wasn't smiling. "You misunderstand, monsieur. She has not retired. She is dead."

"So you 'ave accosted me to discuss an actress who is no longer even alive? In that case, we should talk of ze greats." He seemed to have relaxed into the conversation and now leant back against the closed door. "What do you make of Sarah Bernhardt or 'Ortense Schneider? I was lucky enough to see both in ze theatre at different times in my life." He looked up dreamily at the ceiling and joined his hands so that his forefingers and thumbs were touching as he recalled those performances. "I genuinely believe zat no one has come close to zat level of artistry since. Zeir deaths were a great loss to the world of *le théâtre*."

I would have liked to explain which end of the stick he had got (it was certainly the wrong one), but I was too polite to change the topic. "As it happens, Miss de la Forge was a film actress."

He did not actually spit on the carpet, though he did mime this action. "Pah! Film? I 'ave no interest in ze cinema. It is for ze little people: ze fools and ze children."

"Yes, that's very interesting," Grandfather interrupted, possibly hoping that I wouldn't remember the similar statements he had made in the past. "But we didn't come for a discussion of the relative merits of certain thespians *or* the value of live performance over moving images. We need to ask whether you happened to hear anything at around seven o'clock this evening."

"Why, yes. I 'eard ze boy knocking on ze door with my dinner. I ordered it as soon as I got on ze train, even before ze locomotive arrived to pull us north."

I decided to summarise the position in which we now found ourselves. "So you didn't know the woman who was murdered. You didn't hear anything around the time she was killed, but you did enjoy your dinner?" This final point was unnecessary to mention, but I was painfully aware of my own hunger, and I think it's fair to say that my deductive abilities were not at their best.

"Zat is all true. I 'ad the most delicious mushroom soup, with a terrine of—"

It wasn't just because I couldn't bear hearing about the food I wasn't eating that I decided to interrupt him. His story was a little too convenient. "May I ask your name, sir?"

Looking quite intimidating as he towered over me – and I'm not particularly short – he answered in clipped syllables with his usual Gallic twang. "You may."

I let out a frustrated sigh as I've never been one for farces. "What is your—?"

"My name is Gerard Laroche."

"And what are you doing on this train, M. Laroche?"

He looked a little bemused by my question. "I am travelling to Verona. What are you doing on zis train?"

"I mean, what is your occupation? What brings you to Italy?"

"If zat is what you mean, you should 'ave said it." I thought he might make me repeat the questions, but he soon continued. "I am a salesman. I sell wine. I am 'ere in Italy to sell ze wine of Burgundy."

This seemed very suspicious to me. I knew for a fact that Italy had plenty of its own wine, and I couldn't see the sense in bringing more of it from France. We drink French wine in Britain because we barely grow any of our own, but why would the Italians need even more than they have? Before I could ask this no doubt short-sighted question, Grandfather took charge of the conversation.

"I assume you are a married man?"

Laroche looked disconcerted by the sudden change of tack, but he smoothed down his moustache and answered. "I am."

"Would you happen to have a photograph of your wife in your wallet?"

The man's dark eyebrows knitted together and, without responding, he slipped back inside his compartment.

"What are you doing?" I whispered rather loudly.

"I've never known a travelling salesman over the age of forty who wasn't married," Grandfather answered in a similar manner.

"And what does that prove?"

Before he could reply, M. Laroche had reappeared with the requested photograph. "Zis is my wife, Paulette. She is beautiful, is she not? And those are our children, Ludivine and Laurent."

Sure enough, he was holding a picture of his family standing in front of a large stone house, which I could only conclude was somewhere in the French countryside. M. Laroche himself was in the background with a hand on either child's shoulder and a proud look on his face.

"A lovely family, indeed," Grandfather confirmed when he had studied the image.

"You are too kind, Lord Edgington," the Frenchman exclaimed, closely mimicking his expression from the photograph. "It 'as been a pleasure to meet you, but I must get some rest. I do 'ope your actress friend overcomes 'er difficulties."

I was about to remind him that she was dead, when he nodded to us both and slipped back through the door. I felt we should impress upon him that a woman had been murdered in the room next to his, but Grandfather appeared most buoyed by the encounter and even whistled a few notes on his way back to our room.

"Did you see something significant in the photograph?" I asked as I was certain he had stumbled across something important.

"Yes, indeed. I saw his family in a typical French farmhouse."

"So what does that prove?"

"It proves he's almost certainly the person he claims to be."

I couldn't help feeling disappointed. "You know, there's nothing to say that he's not an obsessive follower of Miss de la Forge's."

He looked perplexed for a moment, as though he couldn't possibly imagine why I would think such a thing. To reinforce this interpretation, he said, "I can't possibly imagine why you would think such a thing. He's just a normal fellow making his way across the country to sell wine."

"Aside from the fact that you've taught me to suspect everyone we meet when there is a murderer on the loose, I doubted M. Laroche because not once, on any of our cases, have we come across a truly unconnected bystander."

"That can't be true."

"It is. Every time someone is murdered, the people in the vicinity invariably have a motive for wanting the victim dead. Be it money, love, greed or jealousy, there's always something to uncover."

"In which case, this is the exception to that rule. I see nothing in what that man told us to suggest he has ever even heard of Miss de la Forge. France has plenty of its own actors whom neither of us knows, and I doubt he would have that photo of his family if he were travelling in disguise."

"So he has no connection to Geraldine? He's just a normal man who had nothing to do with the crime?"

"Precisely."

I breathed in deeply and tried to make sense of this. "Honestly, Grandfather. I've never heard of anything so far-fetched in my life!"

CHAPTER FOURTEEN

We sat at the table in our compartment as my mentor mulled over a particular issue. I can't tell you what it was because he wouldn't say, but he looked troubled for a few minutes while I stroked dear Delilah, who was not enjoying being locked away in a small space one bit.

"I'll take you out to stretch your legs when we get to Florence," I told her as she gnawed on a rather juicy bone. I didn't admit that I was jealous, but I was.

For once, Grandfather chose not to pace about, so perhaps he was adjusting to our surroundings. He stared out of the window into the pure blackness of the Italian night, and I wondered whether it was remiss of me not to be tackling some thorny question. I didn't feel that we were any closer to identifying the killer yet, so that couldn't be his immediate concern. If anything, we kept dismissing people from the enquiry, so perhaps he was planning to catch the culprit through a process of elimination, which he himself has told me on a number of occasions rarely works.

I thought for a moment that big, hirsute M. Laroche was our main suspect after all, and that Grandfather had been testing me to see whether I'd cotton on to his subterfuge. There really hadn't been anything in what the Frenchman said to lead me to that conclusion. The only mark in his column was that he was the least likely person to have killed her, and such fellows often turned out to be guilty when my grandfather investigated crimes.

I was starting to wonder whether we'd somehow overlooked the maid's involvement, but I was also feeling lightheaded from lack of nourishment. I thought I might have to beg my grandfather for a break from our work when something wondrous occurred. There was a knock on the door, and three of my favourite people appeared.

"Master Christopher," Todd said as he entered, "your grandfather thought you might be hungry after you missed dinner."

I was so happy to hear this that I didn't even concern myself with what our servant Dorie or her trainee apprentice Timothy were doing on the train after Grandfather specifically told me they were driving to Verona.

"I'm overjoyed to see you all." I admit that I made no attempt to play down just how thrilled I was that they were there (with trays of food).

"You didn't think I'd forget about dinner, did you, boy?" Grandfather had returned to us from whichever mental plane he had previously been exploring.

"Cook prepared your favourite," our giant maid Dorie revealed as she whisked off a cloche to reveal not the steak and kidney pie I'd been anticipating but a plate of asparagus covered in fine slices of red chili in a French vinaigrette. "Well, it's probably someone's favourite." Even she looked disappointed in what she was carrying, but then young Timothy stepped forward.

"We got the dishes muddled, Dor," he revealed and there was my delicious pie. I was so excited, I could have cuddled it.

"I'll leave the final course in the kitchen until you're ready for dessert," Todd informed me as he ushered the others out of our room.

I could now enjoy the excitement of imagining what I might get to eat for afters. Knowing our cook, it could be anything from a Queen of Puddings, topped with strawberry jam and meringue, to a flummery made of sour cream.

"How on earth did you smuggle Cook aboard without my knowing?" I asked once I'd devoured half of the pie and asparagus and could finally think straight. "And how did they find space for her in the kitchen?" I was tempted to ask why he would have bothered doing any of this in the first place, but I'd long since given up on Grandfather fully explaining his attachment to his staff. If he announces tomorrow that he's in love with our cook and has spent the last four years finding excuses for them to be together, I'll say, *Fair enough. That makes a lot of sense.*

"Don't forget that M. Nagelmackers delayed our departure and even hid the locomotive to ensure that Miss de la Forge could board the train," he reminded me. "He is an exceptionally accommodating conductor to his most important passengers." This still didn't explain why he would sneak three extra members of staff aboard when everything on the train was provided for us, but he did make one point that I couldn't deny. "Aren't you glad that I brought them with me? You'd have had to make do with sandwiches this evening otherwise.

It's such a shame for a young man to miss the opportunity to dine well."

So, from what I could understand, he'd brought reinforcements on the off-chance that someone would be murdered and we'd end up missing the normal dinnertime. I could think of easier solutions to this problem, but then I had a sneaking suspicion that, for all his openness to new flavours and foreign cuisine, Grandfather liked to know that his favourite British dishes were always available. As I tucked into my pie, I could hardly blame him.

"It can't be an easy job conducting a train when you have so many demanding passengers on board," I said between mouthfuls. Even the asparagus didn't taste too bad. "Half of first class were furious at having to wait ten minutes, but poor M. Nagelmackers had to cater for his star passenger's whims. We still don't know why Geraldine turned up late."

Grandfather had stopped listening or at least made no sign of having heard me. I finished my plates in silence, and then Todd reappeared at just the right moment to bring me dessert. I was most relieved to discover there was nothing sour or odd about it. The delicious Sussex Pond Pudding had a gooey centre where the raisins, butter and sugar had caramelised together, so that, when I broke it open with my fork, the liquid formed a scrumptious moat around it. I would never again tease Grandfather for bringing Cook with us. I did wonder how she had made the cake, though, as it takes hours to prepare.

"I'm torn," he finally told me when I'd finished my meal and Dorie and Timothy had returned to collect the dishes. "I know there are suspects whom I should be interviewing, and I even feel that they are connected to the victim in ways that they have not disclosed, but I don't know how to break into them."

"'Ave you considered putting a cat among the pigeons, Lord Edgington, your worship?" This was not me mis-titling him, our immense maid. Dorie had been a skilful pickpocket (and arm-wrestler) in a previous life, and she knew a thing or two about crime.

Grandfather frowned at her comment, which, contrarily, often meant that he was interested in what someone had to say. "Did you have any specific idea in mind?"

Dear Dorie was not the kind to stand on ceremony – or realise that any such ceremony existed – and so she sat down on the fold-away sofa. "From what Todd told us, the likely suspect is unlikely to 'ave killed 'er, and the remaining folk 'ave not yet admitted knowing 'er."

She stopped at this point as if the rest of her thinking should be obvious. Rather than attempt to predict her next comment, I took this time to realise that both Frenchmen who speak English and the British working classes have a habit of dropping their Hs. This was unlikely to help us with our investigation, though it was a curious coincidence.

"That is accurate enough so far, Dorie," Grandfather prompted her. "Please go on."

"Well, all you need to do is make 'em think you're on to 'em, and then they'll all panic like flies." I had lived my whole life without knowing that flies were prone to anxiety, but then Dorie looks at the world in a way that is virtually unique.

Her unofficial apprentice had come around to her way of thinking. "That's a brilliant idea." Timothy was only sixteen. He'd started working as Grandfather's page boy two years earlier, and Dorie had made it her job to train him – despite everyone else's pleas to the contrary. "You should tell them all that you have an important piece of evidence that incriminates them and, if no one comes to see you in your compartment before ten o'clock, you'll hand it to the police."

He flicked the messy fringe from his eyes and looked proud of himself. I knew what it felt like to await the great Lord Edgington's judgement, and I didn't envy him.

Grandfather clearly couldn't decide how to react. On the one hand, he preferred subtler techniques, but he was loath to dash the young fellow's hopes. "I appreciate your suggestions. However, I adopted a similar approach on the way from the second-class dining car."

I tried to recall what he meant, just as Dorie asked, "What did you do?"

"I went in there," he continued a little hesitantly, as though he were trying to recall the details. "I stood in the middle of the carriage, and I raised one hand in the air to suggest that I was about to point at one of them."

No one responded, as it wasn't clear what he was hoping to impart with this revelation.

"You see, I wanted them to feel that any of them could be atop my list of suspects. I wanted them to fear the interview to which I would soon subject them."

"And then what did you do?" Timothy sounded mystified.

"I put my hand back down and walked from the carriage. I can assure you it's a tried-and-true technique."

I had never expected to see Timothy and Dorie looking sorry for the man whom *The Daily Chronicle* had described as 'Britain's foremost practitioner of the art of deduction', but that's what happened. Timothy looked at Dorie through his puppy-dog eyes, and Dorie looked back with her lips sucked into her mouth, afraid to say what she really thought.

It fell to me to take up the slack. "Perhaps you were a little too subtle, Grandfather. Have you considered trying something more direct?"

"Yes!" Timothy was suddenly animated. "You should go in there and repeat the speech you gave to the party in the first novel about you. You know the one. It was at home in Cranley during the spring ball. Someone had been murdered, and you strode to the centre of the dance floor and said, 'Now listen here! I know there's a killer in this room, and I pledge that I won't rest until I have you in handcuffs or I die trying.' I bet that put the wind up the culprit and everyone else there."

I was eager to hear more about the books that had been written about us, especially as I couldn't remember Grandfather making any such speech at the real spring ball all those years earlier.

He winced a little as he countered the boy's plan. "I doubt that those are the words I would have used, but I do see why it would unsettle a group of suspects." He ran the back of his hand across his beard for a moment or two before continuing. "Yes, that could be just what we need. The two of you can return to your compartment now, and I will see to it."

Dorie had never looked so proud of her young friend. As she rose from the sofa, I thought I noticed the sparkle of a tear in one eye, and she put her hand on Timothy's shoulder to direct him from the room. "Come along, little man. Our work here is done."

Grandfather beamed at them as they trundled out. They reappeared a moment later, as they'd forgotten to collect the dirty dishes for which they'd gone there in the first place, but their master was still smiling appreciatively at them.

"You're not going to do that, are you, Grandfather?" I asked once we were alone.

"No, of course I'm not. But their cheerful prattling did put me in mind of the next step we must take." He got to his feet and checked that his cravat was perfectly aligned with his waistcoat in the golden-framed mirror over the sofa. "I know the very person to whom we must talk."

He didn't look back at me but marched from our compartment with all the confidence for which he was known. I didn't mind. I'd eaten dinner, the case still felt comparatively solvable, and I'd enjoyed the light comic relief of an oblivious Frenchman and Cranley Hall's most entertaining double act. I followed him feeling really very content, but when we arrived back in the dining car, some people were missing.

Pelthorpe was sitting at the other end of the room, picking dirt from his nails with a sharp knife. The count was reading a book, but there was no sign of Mr and Mrs Campbell. What there was, though, was little Timothy, looking through the window of the door that gave onto the bar carriage. He was trying to be subtle, but his cheery expression was visible to anyone who happened to look in that direction.

I believe that Grandfather was about to turn around when he caught sight of the expectant fellow and couldn't disappoint him. "Now listen here," he began half-heartedly before warming to his task. "I know there's a killer in this room. And I promise – so help me, God – that I won't rest until I have you in handcuffs or one of us dies in the process."

He glared from Pelthorpe to Count Giovannelli and back, and I was glad not to be on the receiving end of his ire, even if he was only putting it on for the boy's appreciation. With the triumphant address concluded, Timothy held both fists up in celebration on the other side of the glass. I suppose that, to him, it was like seeing a film star acting out a scene, and it strengthened the idea that I really must ask Grandfather about the books in which we feature.

"You are both to stay here until I have the time to deal with you. Do I make myself clear?"

I must say that, whether it was Grandfather's plan or not, it turned out to be a good one. We'd seen little reaction from the mysterious count until now, but I swear that he shivered, though the air in the train was still warm.

For his part, that grimy individual Marvin Pelthorpe fell perfectly still and, though he wasn't the type to show his emotion, I was fairly sure that he was afraid of Lord Edgington. While I admittedly enjoy taking my grandfather to task for any hint of pomposity I detect in him, I can't deny that the legend he has built for himself serves a purpose. Nearly everyone (except for M. Laroche) has heard of the implacable sleuth, and criminals have every reason to fear what he can achieve.

Like a master who has instructed his dog to stay, he watched the two men for a few moments longer to see that they would follow his instructions and then turned back to the sleeping carriage. I listened at the door for a moment to see whether either of them would speak, but they stayed in their seats with their heads down.

"So it's the Campbells you wished to interview next?" I asked my grandfather once we'd passed the steward in his chair.

"No, but I do now. I didn't expressly forbid them from returning to their compartment, but I'm surprised they would do so."

He looked along the line of doors but, after the first few, he couldn't be sure whose was whose. I knew where most of the suspects were staying and decided that the Campbells must be in the double compartment at the far end that matched our own. I walked past my mentor to knock on that door and was immediately rewarded with a response.

"My wife is sleeping," James Joseph shouted back to me. "You can't come in."

Grandfather stepped past me to reason with the man. "Come along, Campbell. We're in the middle of a murder investigation."

"It will have to wait until the morning," he replied. "It can't be helped."

"It certainly can." Grandfather's voice grew in force and volume. "Unless you open this door in the next fifteen seconds, I will ask the steward to unlock it."

I was tempted to count backwards from fifteen, but I resisted. Instead, I listened as Campbell hurried about his compartment, muttering to himself as he did so. It did not sound like the response of an innocent man, and various possibilities ran through my head.

"Very well," Grandfather said when the time was up. "I will fetch Domenico." He had already turned and was about to walk away when I heard the lock unlatching, and then the door swung open.

"My Sharlene is a very deep sleeper," he insisted, even as he made way for us to pass. "There's nothing to say she'll wake up."

I could see just how critically my grandfather looked at the man as we entered the compartment that was an exact copy of our own in reverse. The door to the sleeping berths was to the right not the left, and the fold-down sofa where Mrs Campbell was sitting was on the left-hand wall.

"If she was so tired, why didn't you put her to bed?" I thought to ask as Grandfather inspected the sleeping woman.

"She fell asleep where she fell asleep," Campbell replied, standing back against the door as if whatever was happening had very little to do with him. It was already apparent that the opposite was true, and my grandfather's reply sent a jolt through the man.

"She's not responding." He turned to glare at him. "You drugged her, didn't you?"

CHAPTER FIFTEEN

While it had been evident that James Joseph Campbell was on edge as soon as we entered the compartment, the expression that now shaped his face was one of utmost panic.

"Why would you say a thing like that?" he responded in that deep, southern American voice of his, and his eyes shifted about the place so as not to look at either one of us.

Grandfather responded in the calm, matter-of-fact manner which typified his best work. "Well, for one thing, she is not in bed, as I have already mentioned. Had she decided to take a sleeping pill herself, she would most likely have lain down next door."

The man put his hand to the curly hair at the back of his head and ran his fingers through it in a nervous motion. "We came in here, and she sat down. She asked for her medicine, and I handed her what she needed. There's nothing more sinister to it than that."

I walked over to the half-drunk glass on the shelf just beside her and gave it a sniff. I don't actually have the capacity to smell medicine that has been dissolved in a potent libation, but he didn't know that. "If she had wished to take a sleeping draught, I doubt she would have put it in alcohol." To be quite honest, I couldn't even tell what alcohol it was. My grandfather's training has not yet covered olfactory investigation. "You slipped it into her drink, didn't you?"

Grandfather stopped what he was doing to study our suspect. He didn't need to say anything; his very presence there was enough to instil caution in the man, and I had to wonder whether that was why Campbell had decided to dope his wife.

"You're making a mountain out of something that really isn't a big deal," he said, and you know a man is ruffled when he can't complete a common proverb. "I would never… I mean to say, I didn't…"

"There's no sense denying it. We know what you did." As he spoke, Grandfather opened the woman's eyes to look for a reaction to the light. I suppose he was afraid that she wasn't just sleeping but poisoned.

"She needed to sleep," Campbell persisted. "She had a terrible night in Rome last night. It was too hot in our hotel, and the stress of everything that has happened this evening only made things worse. This medicine was prescribed by her doctor, and I've done nothing wrong by giving it to her."

"A moment ago you said she took it herself," I said to point out another contradiction. "Which was it?"

"I told you. I handed her the sleeping draught. She put it in her port and drank it down."

Grandfather was tapping Sharlene about the cheeks with an open palm, and she stirred for a moment and seemed to want to say something.

When her words finally came, they were barely comprehensible. "...if I did anything, not that I did because I loved her. I never did it though."

I tried to extract something from her mumbling that might be relevant to the case, but Grandfather gave no hint as to what any of this might mean. It was now clear that she wasn't going to wake up, though, and he turned to her husband with a look of steely concentration.

"Tell me the truth: did you put something in her drink because you didn't want her to tell us what you were doing on this train?"

Campbell fell back against the door as though he'd been shot through the chest. "You people. You think the worst of everyone, don't you? I've never known why my good, sweet Sharlene cares one iota for the likes of you. She's worth a thousand Lord Edgingtons and his bumbling grandson."

I took exception to the word bumbling.

Grandfather, meanwhile, was never afraid of insults. "I doubt that you've answered a single question with any degree of honesty since we've been in here. Now tell me why it is that you didn't want us to talk to her."

"There's nothing to tell. My poor wife was exhausted, so I decided to help her rest."

I looked at my grandfather, desperate to communicate the very obvious fact that the man had been caught in a lie. He didn't return my gaze but kept up the pressure on our suspect.

"Knowing that you were both suspects in a murder investigation, you decided to put your wife to sleep for the night, even though I had made it clear I would need to speak to you both."

"We don't know anything about Geraldine!" He clutched at his pale summer suit jacket as he said this. The desperation he now showed was in stark contrast to the picture I'd had when we'd first seen him. He hadn't seemed like the demonstrative type, but now he was almost in tears. "We can't help you find the killer. We wish only to be left alone."

I could see the tension in Grandfather's muscles as he stared unblinkingly at the sleeping woman's husband. It was a moment that offered two clear options. Either he could yell and push in the hope he might force some kind of confession, or he could calm things down and hope that the weight of guilt was so great that Campbell would tell us what we needed to know.

I suppose that he ultimately chose a middle ground. He stood back from Sharlene Campbell and smoothed his cravat as I had seen him do a short time earlier in our compartment. With this done, he waited for James Joseph to open the door. I got the impression that my grandfather wanted the last word this time, so I hurried past him out to the corridor, but lingered close by to hear what he would say.

"I'm sorry, Mr Campbell. As much as you would like me to tell you otherwise, we can't just ignore what you've done here. We will return to speak to you both before long, and we will bring smelling salts."

I couldn't see Campbell's reaction, but I saw Grandfather nod to the man as he swept past. Not for the first time that evening, I struggled not to burst out laughing.

"Smelling salts?" I said when the door had closed behind us and I was sure no one else would hear. "Was that the best Parthian shot you could conceive?"

"I can assure you, Christopher, that if we find strong enough smelling salts, they will do the trick. They are a potent tool when used correctly."

"Yes, but the only people I know who carry smelling salts are old ladies with a propensity for fainting. It was hardly the most dramatic finale to the emotional and intense confrontation we'd had."

"I'll have you know, my boy, that ammonium carbonate is used by more than just little old ladies." He paused then, as he must have realised that any further claims he could make would only strengthen my argument. "It can be included as a leavening agent for bread and certain cakes."

My smile had grown so wide that I didn't need to say anything more, but that didn't stop me. "Oh, Grandfather. You do make me laugh."

When he'd made a similar comment to me earlier in the day, I had felt rather proud of myself, but I doubt he shared my feelings on the matter.

He shook his head despairingly and returned us to safer ground. "What did you take from our run-in with Mr Campbell, the wife-drugger?"

I needed some time to consider my answer. "It's difficult to say, actually. I haven't been able to settle on a clear picture of the man since his wife introduced herself to us in Rome. He seems protective of her to the point of hostility, while at the same time being oddly deceitful in his behaviour. I was moved to see the way he looked after her when Pelthorpe and Reinhardt went at one another, but it's hardly the act of a loving husband to put her to sleep for the night to stop her talking."

"Hmmm…" I knew this sound well. It meant, *To be honest, Christopher, I'm not so sure that you're right.*

"What do you mean, *Hmmm?* How can this be a *Hmmm* moment? Is it ever a kind-hearted act to put a sleeping draught in a woman's port wine?"

"It might well be." He was back at his game of examining the doors along the corridor. I was used to him not paying attention to me when investigating a case, but it was even worse this time.

As I've already mentioned, there were eight sleeping compartments in the first-class carriage. The Campbells were nearest the locked door at the front of the train. Just along from them was Hansel Reinhardt, then Marvin Pelthorpe. After that, I believe there was an empty compartment, which was followed by Count Giovannelli's room, the dead woman's, the apparently insignificant Frenchman's and then our own.

From what I knew, Grandfather had mentally assigned all but two of the compartments to their occupants. He went once more to listen at the empty one and, when he heard nothing, rapped his knuckles on the wood panel, but there was no answer.

"We haven't heard of anyone else being here, and there was no one in the dining car at dinner," I pointed out, but before we could try the handle, Hansel Reinhardt's door opened behind us, and Hansel Reinhardt stepped out.

"I suppose you begrudge me going in search of a spot of dinner, eh?" He was terribly good at communicating how much he disliked a person by narrowing his eyes. I suppose he had learnt that from the actors with whom he'd worked in silent films.

I read an article which talked of famous stars' fear for their careers now that films are to have speaking, but I think it's a real art to be able to communicate so much without words. I doubt that the form will ever die out entirely. There will always be public demand for talkies and not-talkies, just as people still go to the theatre, even though they could stay at home and listen to the radio.

This admittedly inconsequential thought reminded me of poor Geraldine in her compartment. She would never be able to progress from the silent cinema that made her famous to the new world of sound. Perhaps she would have become the greatest actress of the talking era. Perhaps her dulcet tones would have been heard in every land from America to Zanzibar (if that is a real place and not somewhere they made up for a film).

My apologies, I appear to have got carried away with my thoughts. My point is that the director marched past us along the corridor to escape from our equally disapproving stares.

"Conceited man." Grandfather sighed, as if the whole affair was too much to stomach.

I considered suggesting that we accompany that "conceited man" to the dining car in case anyone were to wallop him, but then Grandfather really showed his frustration: he let out a soft groan. By his standards, this was nearly hysterical.

It is hard to know what to say at a time like that. *Have you lost your mind?* wouldn't have been a bad option, but I settled on the more sympathetic, "Are you quite all right, Grandfather?"

"No, I am not. I'm discouraged."

I really couldn't imagine how to deal with this situation. All I could think to say was, "Right... I see."

He leant against the open window so that his elbow stuck out towards the rapidly passing world. "It's not the murder itself – as bad as that may be. It's the feeling that we still don't have any understanding of how anything fits together. Each person we've spoken to is less tolerable than the last, and yet none of them seems to benefit from the woman's death."

It was normally my job to be blue and his job to pick me up again, but things were different this time. "We haven't been at it long."

"That may be, but we've only a few hours left. Perhaps I've been spoilt recently. When someone is killed in a family or even a village, it's easy to understand the interactions between the various players. But here on a train, all a suspect has to do is say that he never knew the victim, and there's nothing we can do to disprove it."

"But that's why you're so good," I told him without knowing what I might say next. "For example, I'm sure you noticed that James Joseph Campbell referred to Miss de la Forge as 'Geraldine'. I suppose that he might feel close to her because of her films, but I think it's more likely that he and his wife knew her in person." I suddenly remembered something from before the murder. "And they talked of her together during dinner. I'm sure that they were acquainted."

His right hand, which had briefly curled into a fist, now hung loosely at his side. He shrugged, as if to suggest he no longer knew anything for certain, and I realised that his demeanour really wasn't so different from when we'd boarded the train. As soon as this thought entered my head, I wished that there were something I could do to make him feel better. He had spent the last four years teaching and encouraging me. While it was true that he was prone to looking dismayed at some of my more ridiculous ideas, I could never have become the person I am without him.

I looked at my watch, which I'd put on upside down for some reason. "It's almost half-past nine. You still have time to find the killer, and I have no doubt that you will. Normally when I despair like this, you tell me to go back to the beginning, so that's what we should do."

He looked about us uncertainly. I imagine he was searching for a way to argue with me, but he couldn't think of one, so I continued.

"What do we know about Geraldine de la Forge?"

"Very little."

"Precisely!" I already regretted my last question, but it was too late to take it back. "Which means that there's still plenty to find out. You said that you're afraid of our suspects denying that they were acquainted with our victim, but you're Lord Edgington – 'the bloodhound of Scotland Yard'. You'll see through them in a second. Look at Campbell just now. He was shaking in fear that you'd realise what he was really up to, and you'll have just as much success with anyone else we have to interview."

He at least appeared open to the idea that things might not be so black as they seemed, so I kept talking.

"You knew instantly that M. Laroche in the compartment next to ours was a normal, honest fellow, and I bet there's someone else here who gives you the opposite impression." I put my hand on his shoulder, looked him in the eyes and prepared myself for a very long sentence indeed. "Maybe it's the Campbells or Count Giovannelli or Marvin Pelthorpe, or maybe things will fall into place and we'll discover that Reinhardt is to blame, but you have approximately a hundred and fifty minutes before the train pulls into the station and the Italian police take over this case, and I know that, if nothing else, you're not going to waste a single one of them."

I had pictured him erupting in jubilation. I really thought that my speech had been so uplifting that he would raise his hands to the heavens, much as young Timothy had a short time prior, but in the end, he just said, "I suppose it's worth a try," and traipsed off to the dining car.

CHAPTER SIXTEEN

When we passed Domenico – who had now been replaced by an elderly colleague – and went through the double doors into the neighbouring carriage, we found that there was only one suspect left there.

I had been curious about Count Giovannelli ever since I'd first seen him. It wasn't just his impressive outfit which, now that he had removed his cloak, I saw had military flourishes. I had to wonder whether he would turn out to be instrumental in the case or just another M. Laroche: a bystander who happened to end up in the right carriage at the wrong time.

As we passed his table, where he had been sitting for most of the evening, he watched us calmly. His decanter of red wine had been replenished at least once, and he raised his glass to us in a manner that I found faintly challenging. If he were the killer – and let's not forget, we didn't even know his Christian name at this point – he was perfectly placed to watch events unfolding around him and plan his response. Had he boarded that train in search of the actress? Had he gone there to kill her for... some reason, knowing that no one could link him to Geraldine de la Forge?

I've read frightful stories about men who become so obsessed with a woman that, when they can't have the object of their desire, they wish only to destroy her. Was that who the count was? Had we ignored this maniac in our midst because of Grandfather's insistence on finding a complex web of evidence that simply didn't exist?

Man gets on train. Man murders unconnected woman. Man gets off scot-free.

It's not the sort of detective novel that I'd wish to spend hours of my life reading, but that doesn't mean such a sad series of events could never come to pass.

Grandfather nodded to the man, and I could see that he was wondering the same thing. Perhaps he dismissed it as too pat, too simple. Or perhaps he stored it away neatly in the filing system in his head, where every possible solution to a case is kept. Either way, we continued on through the carriage past bored waiters who had nothing else to do but wait for the Italian to finish drinking and go off to bed.

We found Marvin Pelthorpe in the bar. His brown suit looked even tattier now that I could see it in all its... what's the opposite of *glory*? He was sipping an amber concoction in a tall glass, and the very air around him smelt of alcohol.

"Good evening, gents," he said with a trademark snarl, and his messy teeth emerged like the fangs of a vampire. "And what can I do for you on this fine night?"

He turned around to lean with both elbows against the bar. There was a steward on duty to serve us and, rather than answer this difficult question, Grandfather ordered himself a brandy and me an apple juice. Now, some people would have found this infantilising. After all, I'm a twenty-one-year-old man, and over the last few years I've developed a palate for food, wines and many types of alcohol that I would never have consumed before. That being said, Grandfather knows how much I appreciate a refreshing glass of apple juice, and I didn't mind one bit.

He'd made our quarry wait long enough, and his opening shot was so furious that it almost knocked me back a step or two. "You can start by telling us your real name and how you knew Geraldine de la Forge."

The men looked at one another, and it was clear that Pelthorpe was set off guard by my grandfather's bluntness. In response, however, he didn't melt at the thought of the drilling that he was about to receive; he tipped his drink down his throat and slammed the empty glass on the table.

"I don't know what you're talking about. The name is Marvin Pelthorpe, as you well know. I thought you were famed for your memory. Maybe it isn't what it used to be."

For a moment, I knew how Goldilocks felt looking into the wolf's jaws. Wait, no. That was Red Riding Hood. Please ignore me.

Grandfather was clearly probing the disreputable fellow to see what would happen. I could see from the way he leant towards him then away again that he was willing to test the boundaries of what Pelthorpe would accept, but he wasn't ready to push him too far.

"Very well. What is it you do, Mr Pelthorpe?"

He tapped the metal bar a few times to signal to the barman that he required another drink. "I don't go around killing young women, if that's what you're thinking."

Adapting his approach with every new comment that was made, like a chess player measuring up an opponent, Grandfather allowed himself a brief smile. "I would never have imagined any such thing."

Pelthorpe's lip twitched. "As it happens, I came into some money as a comparatively young man and have been fortunate enough not to have to work too hard ever since."

I hadn't questioned how old he was until he said this. He was one of those people who seem both as old as time and infinitely young. Perhaps he was fifty – he had faint lines around his eyes, but a full head of thick, black, though decidedly greasy hair – but if that were the case, I believe he'd been the same age for some time.

"I hear that happens to some people," Grandfather replied, which was presumably a joke at his own expense as his policeman's salary did not compare to the vast wealth of the estate he had inherited when his brother died.

The barman had finished pouring a measure of whisky into Pelthorpe's glass, and he accepted it without looking back. "You might say I've spent my time since then studying the human race." He brushed his nose with one knuckle, and I understood that even he knew this wasn't true. "I like to think of myself as a collector of people and moments."

I'd done my usual disappearing act and faded into the background as much as possible, so it was no surprise that he'd barely looked at me. I was as noticeable as plain white wallpaper, but something in what he said almost made me speak up. It occurred to me that he was doing the very same thing as my grandfather. This dark and distrustful man was testing Lord Edgington's limits – teasing him with allusions to potential wrongdoing. It was fascinating to watch.

"That sounds like an interesting existence. My life as a superintendent for the Metropolitan Police required similar skills. Did you ever consider becoming a detective yourself?"

He turned away, and I thought perhaps he'd heard something in the neighbouring carriage, but he looked straight back at his opponent. "Me, a detective? My moral code would never allow it."

Grandfather laughed at this and, instead of immediately asking another question, he held his brandy up to the light and swirled it around the glass. With this test passed, he sipped it and returned to the peculiar conversation.

"And why is Marvin Pelthorpe headed to Verona? Are you off to collect more people?"

"Not this time." The tip of his tongue poked through his lips and, just for a moment, the Wolf turned into a snake. "As it happens, I plan to do a spot of birdwatching."

"Oh, really?" Grandfather was awfully good at pretending to be interested in what our suspects had to say. I felt that every word Pelthorpe uttered was a lie, but the esteemed detective made it sound as though it was all quite fascinating to him.

"That's right. I'm travelling up to Verona to see what I can find there."

"What birds are you hoping to spot?" I asked because, although I'm truly abysmal at telling swans from egrets and buzzards from budgerigars – well, I think I could just about manage that one – I'd recently spent some time reading about the birds of Italy.

"Oh, you know. I've always loved bee-eaters. Rollers, too." Although his manner suggested this was a fabrication, he delivered each comment with such conviction that it was hard to know what was true. "But what I'd really like to spot is a pin-tailed sandgrouse. I believe they're very rare."

"I am something of an ornithologist myself," Grandfather sounded as if he were boasting, but for once I knew it was just an act. There are many things upon which he prides himself, but bird watching isn't one of them. "As is my grandson here. In fact, Christopher has developed a real eye for birds."

I performed a quick calculation, starting with the fact that I'd seen Pelthorpe with a pair of binoculars around his neck after we'd boarded the train, then moving on to the likelihood of seeing the various species he'd mentioned. I was almost disappointed to concede that the three birds could feasibly be found in the country.

"I doubt any of this can help you with your unsolved murder." Pelthorpe offered a mocking frown. "But it's been lovely talking."

I thought he might swallow down his drink and wander off, but it was clear that he considered this his territory now, and it was down to us to vacate it. I believe it was this, rather than his denials or prevaricating, that upset my grandfather as, in the very next moment, he re-adopted the tone in which he'd started the conversation.

"N.M. They're your true initials, aren't they? Now tell us why you wished to meet Geraldine at midnight tonight."

Pelthorpe actually looked a little shocked this time. I could tell that he wasn't the type to show his fear, but as the knowledge of what my grandfather had discovered worked its way into his brain, he held himself for a moment.

"I don't know any N.M.s I'm afraid. I knew a Michael Norman once, but never a Nicholas Matthew or a Nathan Miller."

Grandfather raised the intensity a notch higher. "You placed a note beneath the dead woman's door. If, as you claim, you didn't kill her yourself, you can at least tell us what you wanted from her."

"I don't know what you mean."

As Grandfather had warned me, the man could simply deny knowing anything about the crime or the people involved, and there was nothing we could do.

"Don't try me, Pelthorpe." A touch of fury had entered the sleuth's voice, and I was reminded of his anger in the corridor when our interviews had got us nowhere. "Tell me what I need to know or, as soon as we get to Florence, yours will be the name I share with the police."

"I thought you said my initials were N.M." The endlessly black eyes of the suspect seemed to hide within their dark sockets. "You haven't got anything on me, and you know it. If you had, we would have stopped this train already."

"Sandgrouse!" I yelled without realising I was about to say anything, and the two men turned to look at me. "Or rather... as you've already mentioned, the pin-tailed sandgrouse is an extremely rare bird in this part of the world. It transports water to its chicks as drops of moisture in its breast feathers."

Wrong detail, Christopher, I told myself. *Try to concentrate!*

I took a deep breath and started again. "They're so rare, in fact, that they are hardly ever seen in Italy, so this isn't the obvious place to find them."

I could see a change in the mysterious N.M. He rolled his shoulders as he answered, perhaps trying to egg himself on. "Which is why I

119

said I'd be very happy to see one on my trip north, along with the bee-eaters and the… the rollers and what have you."

I wouldn't be distracted and took a step closer to the bar as I listed off some significant and less significant facts about the bird. I'd like to have been more efficient, but I was recalling the text from my book and knew I'd get to the key part eventually. "The male and female pin-tailed sandgrouse can be told apart by the patches of black or white on their throats. They have long tail extensions which are particularly noticeable in flight and, as their name indicates, they make their homes in sandy areas, particularly at the edge of deserts or in dried-up lake beds."

Even Grandfather wore a concerned look by now, and Pelthorpe pointed at me. "What's wrong with him? Was he dropped on his head as a baby or something?"

"You're not listening, Mr Pelthorpe. I've just demonstrated that you're lying, but you know so little about birds that you didn't notice."

"Here, don't you be…" He cut himself short as his curiosity apparently got the better of his need to protect himself. "How did you prove anything?"

"If you wish to have even the faintest chance of seeing a pin-tailed sandgrouse, Verona is in the wrong direction."

CHAPTER SEVENTEEN

"I've heard about your games, Edgington," N.M. said when he couldn't think of a way to dig himself out of the sandy hole he was in. "You twist people's words and make them say things they don't mean. Now you've got the boy doing it."

"Not at all, Mr M. I had nothing to do with my grandson's methods. He proved that you are either a very poor birdwatcher or an outright liar, the latter of which I had already identified you as before we started talking. Now tell us why you left the dead woman that threatening note. It said, *If you know what's in your best interests, you'll meet me at midnight.* So why did you want to see her?"

The Wolf appeared quite flustered and refused to look at either of us. Perhaps he was afraid that we might hypnotise him into saying what he was really thinking.

"What do you know about Geraldine de la Forge's death?" I directed this question at him with such force that he had to retreat.

"You're maniacs, you are. I don't know what's got into you, but I'm an innocent man, and I don't have to put up with harassment." All the confident malice had drained from him, and he went stumbling backwards towards the second-class carriages. "I'll find somewhere to drink where I won't be tormented."

And with that, he turned on the balls of his feet and escaped through the door.

"I can't quite believe it," Grandfather said, and he had to wipe his brow with the handkerchief that was always so well arranged in the breast pocket of his long grey coat.

"Yes, we certainly had him on the ropes. It's a miracle that he managed to deliver a final retort."

"Not that, Christopher." He made his eyes wider to look at me. He'd seen me nearly every day for years, so I thought this an odd gesture.

"What *do* you mean then?"

"I can't believe that your knowledge of birdlife has finally come in useful on one of our cases. When we first started working together, you thought a wigeon was a species of large pigeon."

I decided not to tell him that I was yet to learn anything to the contrary.

"You once identified a crow that you spotted from your bedroom window as a possible great bustard, even though those immense and magnificent birds have been extinct in Britain since the eighteen hundreds."

"I said it could be a juvenile, actually."

He was laughing too much to hear.

"My point, Christopher, is that you have proved yet again just how much you have grown up over the last few years, and I can now solemnly tell you, without doubt or pretence, that you know far more than I ever will about the pin-tailed sandgrouse."

I must say that it felt good to be more knowledgeable than my mentor, even in this ever-so-minor field of study. I was already blushing from his praise, though, so I returned us to the pressing issue of the suspect we'd just scared away.

"Before we go any further, I must know how you worked out that it was Pelthorpe who put one of the messages under Geraldine's door. And how did you know he was N.M. and not the other one?"

"I didn't." Grandfather's moustaches had bunched together in what passes for a smile, but they now fell flat. "As we'd discussed, we were getting nowhere, so I guessed that the rather grubby handwriting belonged to the rather grubby man."

"You guessed?" I couldn't believe what I was hearing. "The unfaultable Lord Edgington, Britain's greatest living detective – according to a number of newspapers and more than a few of your friends – guessed?"

He pulled his shoulders back as he often does when I find fault. "Another way of phrasing it is that I examined the evidence available to us and decided that the disreputable-looking fellow with binoculars around his neck was not travelling in clothes fit for walking in the countryside and, therefore, might not be the person he wished us to believe."

"You guessed!" I said, standing back to admire him because the idea was such a pleasant one. "You threw caution to the wind and had a pop! I wholeheartedly approve, Grandfather, and I must congratulate you on this new, devil-may-care attitude."

He did not appreciate my praise. "It worked, didn't it? Pelthorpe really must be travelling under a false name, and I now have an inkling of what sort of person he is."

I can't say whether he planned to reveal this to me, as it was at this moment that Todd walked into the bar with M. Nagelmackers.

"I'm so sorry not to have told you before," the Belgian began. "It quite escaped my mind, but I should have thought."

"I'm sure there's nothing to worry about, monsieur," my grandfather said, directing the man to the nearest comfortable seat as he sounded overwrought.

"I've been telling him there's no need to apologise, sir," Todd informed us, "but he won't listen."

"What is it, man?" Lord Edgington looked the *chef de train* dead in the eye in the hope it might encourage him to answer.

"Miss de la Forge's manager. He has a room in the second-class sleeping carriage. I should have told you as soon as she died, but it slipped my mind with everything else that has been happening."

"Ah, I see. Well, the important thing is that we know now," Grandfather reassured him. "And while I've got you, we are in need of smelling salts if you can lay your hands on some. Leave them here at the bar. My grandson and I will find this manager you mentioned. There's nothing to say he knows anything about the crime."

"He's in compartment number eleven, three carriages along," Nagelmackers revealed, having finally calmed down a touch. "I really am sorry, sir."

Grandfather had already set off, and I had already set off after him. We worked our way past the kitchen to the second-class dining room, where Reinhardt and the fake Mr Pelthorpe were camped out with several tables between them. As there was no designated bar in that part of the train, the dining car had remained busy after dinner with people happily and obliviously drinking digestifs and playing card games as the waiters brought drinks from… somewhere. Every table was full, but there was no time to examine the assembled passengers as we had to press on to the compartments.

Number eleven was in the second of the two sleeping carriages. As Grandfather knocked on the door, I realised that Geraldine's maid Milly must be in one of the neighbouring rooms, but then the door swung open and there was no time to mention her.

"Have you seen what time it is?" the tall, angular fellow in an overly tight suit demanded of us. I instantly recognised him as the man I had seen carrying Geraldine's bags in the railway station. "I'm normally asleep at this hour!" He had a screechy sort of voice. I would say he was from the south-west of England, perhaps Devon, and the only other thing I can tell you is that he wasn't pleased to see us.

"Then it's lucky for you that you're not." Grandfather immediately silenced him with this comment, then waited for a moment before asking his first question. "We believe you work as Geraldine de la Forge's manager, is that right?"

He rolled his eyes and groaned. "I'd say 'manager' is something of an exaggeration. Dogsbody is closer to the truth. She tells me what to do and I do it, and she's normally not very happy with the results." He pushed his glasses up his nose. "I'm not saying she isn't a nice young lady, but two weeks ago when I started, and she told me that I couldn't possibly do a worse job than the last man she employed, I hoped for something a little more glamorous than carrying her bags around and feeding her dog."

Grandfather had clearly extracted something interesting from all this. "Are you saying that you had no experience when she hired you?"

"No, of course I didn't. I was in Rome on holiday. I'd always dreamed of going to Italy, and there I was in the City of Light. I had a lovely day seeing the sights and, in my hotel bar that night, I had just ordered a glass of wine when a beautiful young lady came to sit next to me. The poor lass was in tears, so I offered her a cigarette and a friendly ear."

He looked a little nostalgic but soon pressed on with the story. "She told me that she couldn't trust the people around her any more. Things had come to a head with her boyfriend. She'd got rid of her manager, too, and she was even in the process of changing her home. It was all very sad, and I told her that I wished I could make it right in some way, so she said—"

"Would you happen to know how to write statements for the press, book trains and carry bags?" I suggested.

"Not in so many words, and she tends to make travel arrangements herself, but that was basically it." He shook his head then, and I couldn't tell whether he wished to imply that he couldn't believe his luck or it had been a big mistake. "Anyway, I called my wife and told her I wasn't coming home—"

Grandfather looked horrified and had to interrupt. "You abandoned your wife for a job?"

Mr... actually we didn't know his name. Geraldine's manager looked at me as if we were now firm friends. "Would you listen to this one? Talk about a grim way of looking at the world. I didn't abandon my wife; I told her to pack a bag and join me in Rome. In some ways it's been the best two weeks of our lives, in others..." He didn't finish his sentence, but we already had a decent picture of what he'd endured.

"So then you can't tell us a great deal about Miss de la Forge's life in general?" Grandfather spoke a little gloomily once more. "You don't know, for example, what occurred between her and her former sweetheart Eddie Denkin?"

"Denkin? Oh, is that who she was courting? To be perfectly honest, I'd never heard of any of these actor types before I got to Italy. I'm more of a book person than a *cinema*-niac." He thought this play on words was ever-so-witty and had a good chortle.

"And you don't know anyone close to her with the initials N.M?" I added.

"Sorry, no. I can't help you. The only other person I met was her director. German fellow, he is. Can't say I warmed to him, but to each their own. He was always at Geraldine's house. They seemed to get on rather well... to begin with at least. Oh, and then there was her maid. Nice lass. Name of Milly. I think she's in the neighbouring compartment if you fancied interviewing her."

It suddenly dawned on me that he didn't know who we were.

"I say," he said, moving closer to speak in a whisper. "When you print the article in the newspaper, is there any chance I'll get a few quid for the trouble?"

"Undoubtedly," Grandfather replied, taking the man's hands in his to shake effusively. "We'll let you know when the day arrives."

The man was over the moon. "Oh, that's wonderful. Thank you so much. I'm sorry if I sounded a touch critical a moment ago. I've quickly discovered in my job that some journalists are an absolute pain, but you seem like bully sorts after all." He shook our hands, and we waited until he'd closed the door before passing judgement.

"Of all the people we've ever interviewed," I whispered, "I doubt that we've encountered such an uninformed witness."

"I quite agree." Grandfather put a hand on my shoulder as we navigated the train's ever-rocking corridors. "It's lucky that he's not a suspect or we'd have had to spend a lot longer talking to him."

CHAPTER EIGHTEEN

"So where does that leave us?" Grandfather asked.

The second-class dining car was clearly the place to be that night. A circle of gamblers had grouped together around a table, and there was a quartet of Americans singing an a cappella song in four-part harmony in the corner.

"Sweet Adeline (Sweet Adeline)" they sang ever-so-sweetly, and just as the first line came to an end, I lost sense of time and place.

All of a sudden, there was almost no one else in the carriage. I don't wish to imply that everyone saw my grandfather and decided to scarper – though, as it happens, Reinhardt had done that very thing. No, I mean that my sight was directed to one young lady who was sitting at the table where I'd noticed the man who'd run for the train. I saw that girl with her long brown ringlets of hair cascading from her head like springs from heaven – or a better simile that I will think of later – and my world shook.

You see, I'd crossed paths with her at the beginning of our trip abroad, and I'd thought of her every day since.

"My Adeline (My Adeline)" I heard the men sing as I approached her, but theirs were just disembodied voices and they might as well have been at home in America for all I cared. *The girl* was there before me! The girl whom I had spent the last months thinking I would never see again was there on the train, and I couldn't talk to her because we only had a couple of hours left to solve a murder.

"At night, dear heart (At night, dear heart)

For you I pine (For you I pine)," the song went, and my heart throbbed with anguish.

I was only a couple of feet away from her by this point, but she didn't look up at me because she was reading the book I'd seen across from (hopefully) her father when we'd been interviewing Milly Buckthorn.

I was so tempted to ask her what she was reading or whether she was going to Verona like us, but why would anyone want to be interrupted by a dull-witted chap with no discernible talents? Obviously, it would have been different if we hadn't had to find Geraldine's killer but—

"Christopher," my grandfather interrupted my thoughts, and the world came back to me for a moment. "I've just realised that I have a question to put to Miss de la Forge's maid. I'll meet you in the bar after."

He turned to go, and I realised that this was it. I approached her table knowing that this was my chance.

"In all my dreams (In all my dreams)
Your fair face beams (Your fair face beams)," the men continued, but I didn't notice what they were wearing or whether they were singing in tune.

My eyes were on the girl, and when the moment came for me to introduce myself, I realised that I wasn't nearly brave enough and continued walking straight past her.

"You're the flower of my heart,
Sweet Adeline (Sweet Adeline)."

Why destroy a perfectly good dream? If I'd sat down next to her and opened my mouth, the most terrible sounds would have come out. I would probably have compared her beauty to a tomato's or complimented her on how straight her spine was or something deeply unromantic like that.

Yes, it was definitely the right decision.

And yet, when I reached the end of the carriage, I felt as if I'd left an arm or perhaps a minor organ behind at her table. I mean it quite literally when I say that I had the physical sensation of being ripped in two. And so, as the audience around the dining car cheered and demanded another song, I walked back along the aisle to stand beside the table of the most enchanting woman I'd ever seen.

And I continued standing there because I didn't know what to say. All I could think was how lucky I was that she hadn't looked up and seen me gawping like a particularly unintelligent fish. But then she did look up. She looked at me from three feet away and her exquisite brown eyes made it hard for me to think. It was at this point I realised how hot it was so, to stop myself collapsing or running away (like the last time I'd seen her), I forced myself to say the only half decent sentence I'd learnt in Italian.

"Mi scusi, signorina, parla italiano?" I asked, and let me reiterate this, I asked it in Italian. You see, I'd learnt this phrase to help me

when exploring Rome, and it had taken several people saying *"Si,"* and then looking confused to realise I hadn't been asking whether they spoke English. I'd been demanding to know whether they spoke Italian. And even though my error had been pointed out to me, this was still the phrase that popped into my head.

"Non, je suis désolée. Je suis française," she responded in the gentlest, most musical voice that God has ever bestowed on a human being.

"Oh, so you're French." I took real comfort from this for some reason. "That's a relief."

She closed her book and looked up at me curiously. "Why? Do you speak French?"

"Ummm... no, not really. But I'm a lot worse at Italian. I can just about order off a French menu, and I haven't a clue what to say here. I normally just wave my hand about, point at a few dishes and try to look confident."

"So you must be British." It was hard to tell whether she considered this a good thing. "I've yet to meet a British man who has learnt much more than his own language." Her English was excellent, though she maintained her melodic French accent.

"And we struggle even with that," I quipped as, while we may not be particularly good at learning languages, we Brits excel at self-deprecation.

She laughed at me then, and it was like the sound of a heavenly host descending with good news about the economy or perhaps the promise of fine weather. The fact that I stood gaping, much as an art lover admires a classic painting, was irrelevant. She laughed at me, and I didn't feel like a complete fool. In fact, I felt as if I were back at home again.

"What's this boy doing here?" a voice said to break me from my reverie.

I turned to see the man I'd noticed earlier at the same table. He had a rather sharp, severe face and an American twang to his decidedly transatlantic voice. He clearly wasn't happy to see me and, when I didn't respond, he moved closer so that there was barely any distance between us.

"Well, boy? What do you want?"

I'd found it surprisingly easy to talk to the girl of whom I'd dreamed for months, but I was immediately tongue-tied now, and I began to back away.

"I..." I tried to answer him, but his glare grew more hostile, and my words died in my throat. "I... I'm sorry."

The young men in the corner started another song, and the warmth of the atmosphere only increased as people cheered and the gamblers cried out in a mix of joy and despair, but I had a terrible sense of unease around this strange fellow, with his pale face and patchy hair. He watched me all the way to the door, and it was just as I escaped from the dining car that I heard the screech of the wheels on the tracks, and the train began to brake unexpectedly. I was quite safe within the small chamber between carriages, but the sound of cries coming from the room I had just left was unbearable.

The force of the train's sudden braking had knocked people over, and others were hanging on for their lives. Steel scratched furiously against steel. The passengers' wailing only grew, and I put my hands out to brace myself for the inevitable lurch backwards when the train finally stopped.

CHAPTER NINETEEN

My first thought was for my grandfather who, despite his robust health for a man of his age, could still have broken a bone if he'd been walking down an open corridor. I looked back through the window into the second-class dining car, but the room was in an awful state. Two waiters and many of the people who had been sitting beside the aisle had fallen to the floor. In one instance, an extremely large German man, whom I'd heard singing along with the quartet, had landed on top of a young boy, who was now scrambling to get out from under him. Empty chairs had been tipped over by the force. Plates had smashed, and I doubt that there was a drop of drink left in any of the glasses.

But it was the shock and distress on display that were most painful to witness. There were people blocking the door, and I could only watch as they tried to make sense of this disastrous situation. There was audible relief that everyone had survived, but some cried out, perhaps nursing wounds or afraid for their loved ones. I did not get the impression that there was anything more serious than cuts and bruises, so I tried my best to look through the melee to where the girl had been sitting. She was too far away to see, and there was certainly no chance of my passing through the carriage, so there was only one thing for it.

With the train quite motionless and the sound of workers already shouting to one another from beside the tracks, I opened the door and climbed out. I saw people doing the same up and down the train. It was hard to make out faces in the dark, but I noticed a couple of the stewards and the first-class waiters who had served us. There was no sign of M. Nagelmackers or any of our suspects, but to my great surprise, I saw our dog Delilah jump down the steps from our carriage.

"Here, girl," I called to her, and she set off at speed to reach me. The train had come to a stop next to a vineyard. It was dark, but the light of the moon was bright enough for me to make out a scene that was familiar from our time driving around the Tuscan countryside.

I must say, it was a comfort to have our affectionate hound with me, but I was still worried about the others, so I ran along the side of the train to look for the spot where my (I think it's safe to say by this point) future wife had been sitting. She was standing by the window, so I could see her quite clearly, but she didn't turn around at first, and my heart was beating too fast for its own good. When she finally looked around at me, and her face illuminated with that exquisite smile, the world immediately felt brighter.

"I'll come back!" I mouthed in the hope she could understand. "I'll find you later. I promise."

Her cheeks rounded, and she waved down to me. Although I would have loved to ask her name or shown her in some way what she already meant to me, it was quite impossible. I could see that she was all right at least, and she watched me as I moved away.

With Delilah at my side, I ran to the next door and was about to climb aboard when I heard someone calling my name.

"Todd!" I shouted back from the step. "What's happened?"

"The brake cord was pulled." He was a carriage away from me and raised his voice to be heard over the hubbub of the train crew talking to one another. "I'm afraid that the killer might be trying to escape. If you see Lord Edgington, send him out to me."

I waved my hand to acknowledge that I'd heard and, once I was back on the train, looked through the door opposite in case anyone had got out that way. There was a steep, rocky hillside with nowhere to hide, but I made out the unmistakable and greatly contrasting silhouettes of our servants, Cook, Timothy and Dorie. They were already spread out along the tracks, presumably having had the same idea as Todd.

This reassured me somewhat, and I hurried on through the first sleeping carriage in search of my grandfather. There was no sign of him, and when I got to the maid's room, I knocked on her door.

"Are you quite all right, Milly?" I asked, as her safety was just as important as anyone else's.

"Yes, thank you, Mr Prentiss." She bowed her head demurely. "It's kind of you to ask, but I was lying down at the time the train stopped. I slid out o' the bed, but I i'n't hurt. Do you know what caused it?"

"Someone pulled the brake cord, but I don't know why. To tell the truth, I came down here to look for my grandfather. Have you seen him?"

She looked concerned. "He was here just a minute or so before the accident. Do you know where he was going after coming t' see me?"

I struggled to respond, as the idea of anything happening to him was too much to bear. "No, I can't say I do, but I'm sure I'll find him soon. Thank you for your time."

She gave a half curtsey and bowed her head again as she slipped back into the darkness of her room.

I looked up and down the corridor as I considered which way to go. I was certain he hadn't been in the dining car, and I was fairly sure he hadn't left the train so, unless he'd entered one of the sleeping berths, it was unlikely I'd missed him. With this decided, I kept walking.

I don't mind telling you that it had been a taxing five or ten minutes. First, the girl of my dreams popped up there on the train, then her travelling companion scared me away, before the train came to an urgent and unprogrammed stop, and I realised that my grandfather was missing.

I can't tell you how glad I was to find him at the end of the corridor. He was wrestling with the door into the next carriage.

"What are you doing?" I asked as I drew alongside him.

He had his shoulder up against the door and was pushing with all his might. "Someone turned the light off in the corridor as I was walking back to meet you. He tried to hide in the empty conductor's compartment, but I wouldn't let him. When I knocked on the door to demand answers, he pushed it violently open, and I fell over backwards. I must confess that I was a little disconcerted, and by the time I was on my feet again, he'd disappeared. I assumed he'd hidden in the second-class dining car, but there was no space to open the door, so I came back here."

"He might have slipped into a sleeping berth," I suggested, but Grandfather pooh-poohed the idea.

"Then why would this door be sealed? Help me to get it open."

I copied his pose and felt the force of whatever was blocking the door pushing back against us. "How can you be sure it's not locked?" I asked when it seemed that we would never manage it.

"I came to see what was here before speaking to Miss de la Forge's maid. It was open then."

With us both pushing, I felt the slightest movement. The door budged an inch or so, then all of a sudden, it burst wider, sending the two of us sprawling forwards.

"Well, that was undignified," Grandfather said as he picked himself up and brushed off his always spotless morning coat. I was still trying to extract myself from the mess of boxes that had been keeping the door closed. He had evidently sprawled with far more elegance than I could ever manage.

"It's the luggage van," I helpfully pointed out, though this was obvious to anyone with at least one working eye.

Speaking of which, Delilah had been close at my side until now but, presumably because she didn't like the look of that dark room, she realised she wasn't going to get any food, or there were more interesting things for her to do outside, she'd turned around and run back the way we'd come.

Grandfather didn't take the time to reply to my comment. He stood in the doorway searching for a light switch and, when he located it, turned his attention to the well-stocked carriage. From one end to the other, the space was filled with boxes, bags, trunks, chests and cases. I assume that they had previously been neatly organised but, except for those which were held in place by metal cages or nets hanging from the ceiling, many of the piles had tipped over when the train stopped.

"Is that a leg sticking out near the far door?" I'd caught sight of a piece of brown material with a noticeably leg-shaped filling.

"You're right." Grandfather moved with a little more urgency. "Whoever it belongs to isn't moving."

CHAPTER TWENTY

We had to move a fair few obstacles to clear a path, and some of them were so heavy that we had to work together once more. When we managed to reach the other end of the room, it reassured me somewhat that there was not just one leg sticking out from behind a stack of suitcases but a pair of them.

"It's that grubby fellow, isn't it?" I asked, because neither Marvin Pelthorpe nor Mr M suited the man now. "Could he be the person you followed in here?"

He crouched down to examine our suspect. "I really can't say. It was very dark, and I made out very little of his appearance. I'm a fool not to have turned a light on before trying to get him out of the cubby hole."

There was nothing more to say for the moment. I walked around to the other side of the motionless figure and studied his countenance as Grandfather took his pulse. His left eye was already swelling up from whatever had hit him there, but I had the definite impression that he was still alive.

"He'll be fine, I think," Grandfather said to confirm my baseless theory. His words served another purpose, too. They caused the grimy man laid out before us to stir.

"What did you do to me?" the fake Marvin Pelthorpe demanded, and his hand moved to the back of his head.

"It wasn't us, my good man." Lord Edgington really is the haughtiest fellow in Europe when it is required. He sounded posher than Queen Victoria just then. "I followed someone in here after I was knocked over. Do you know what happened?"

The Wolf threw Grandfather's hand off him and shuffled back a short distance to lean against the wall. "I do not. I was in here minding my own business when the light went off. The train had already stopped by then, and I suppose someone must have come in because, a minute later, I felt a fist to my face and something hard over the back of my head."

"Grandfather really should inspect your wounds," I told him, but he shifted away further. "He knows more about the human body than most doctors."

"And I bet he has the cold hands to match. No thank you, matey. I've had a lot worse than this before."

My mentor's keen gaze passed over the colourless character before asking another question. "What were you doing in here in the first place?"

The injured man wasn't the type to sit about rubbing his bruises. Using the boxes beside him for support, he pulled himself up to standing, then brushed off his coat. A short time earlier, my grandfather had gently removed a few unwelcome pieces of fluff with the back of his hand, whereas the Wolf bashed at his clothes as if he were beating a carpet.

"I was getting away from you two, wasn't I?" He gave a rather unappealing sniff – he did that a lot. "I was minding my own business in the plebs' dining car when you burst in, and I decided to keep moving. It might sound funny to your sort, but I don't greatly enjoy being around people who accuse me of murder."

The man really got under my skin, and I found myself spitting out a retort. "If you weren't such an out-and-out liar, we might not have accused you of anything!"

"Thank you, Christopher." Grandfather raised one hand to ensure that I wouldn't go any further. "Mr M here is free to go about his business."

He stood back to clear the path, and the Wolf looked confused. Hesitantly at first, he took a step forward and, when Grandfather did nothing to stop him, and there were apparently no more questions to be answered, his pace increased.

"Lovely talking to you as always, Superintendent Edgington." He turned around to wink at us, and I wondered whether he had known my grandfather in days gone by. In my experience, the only people who call him superintendent are former colleagues from the police and the men and women he once arrested.

"What an intolerable person," I declared when the door had shut behind him and we were happily alone.

"I can't say I disagree with your assessment, and we don't even know his name for certain, but his wounds looked genuine enough."

I kicked a box out of the way. It was heavier than it looked, and I hurt my toe. "That doesn't prove anything. Maybe Reinhardt came down here to give him a thwack after the run-in they had."

"That remains to be seen." Grandfather walked to the closest door to check whether it would open, and it did. He climbed down on the side of the vineyards, but I kept working my way back through the train, searching for whoever had given the Wolf what he deserved. All I could find were freight carriages and locked doors, so I disembarked and looked for Todd and my grandfather.

They were deep in colloquy beside the tracks. At M. Nagelmackers's request, stewards ran up and down in search of any problem with the train, along with the fireman from the locomotive itself and an engineer. The waiters and the elderly steward from the first-class carriage were checking on the passengers, and I saw through the wheels of the train that Cook, Timothy and Dorie were still on guard on the other side.

I approached in order to listen to Todd's report to his master.

"All in all, it would have been difficult for the killer to have escaped into the vineyard unless he had jumped off as soon as the train came to a halt, and I am happy to say I would have only been a few seconds behind him."

"That's excellent work. So there is still the possibility that it wasn't the killer who pulled the cord to stop the train." Grandfather often looked about as he calculated various possibilities. It was hard to know whether what he saw as he watched the stewards at work was relevant to his thought process or merely served as a helpful distraction. "Perhaps…"

He broke off what he was saying, and his eyes came to rest on the carriage where we had our berths.

"Has anyone checked on our suspects?" I asked, as I believed I'd caught some sense of what he was thinking. "Except for Pelthorpe or whatever his name is, do we actually know they're where we think they are?"

Delilah was the first to react. She ran off before I could, and it suddenly occurred to me that we'd closed the door when we'd last left her in our compartment. It was wonderful to watch her sprinting towards the first-class section of the train, though she continued on straight past it and apparently hadn't been listening to what we were saying after all.

As fast as I could, I followed her path beside the tracks and launched myself up the metal steps that gave access to Domenico's post.

"Have you been here the whole time since the train stopped?" My words came out at double speed. The steward looked discombobulated, so I repeated myself. "Tell me, Domenico, have you left your post at any time?"

He shook his head and searched for his words in English. "No, sir. I stay here like M. Nagelmackers instructs. I only leave my post when my colleague relieve me. I am back here since ten o'clock."

Perhaps it was due to my grandfather's obsession with grammar, but I had to remind myself not to correct his English.

"Very good. That makes things a lot easier."

I thanked him and moved along to our compartment. The door was open, as I'd expected after Delilah got out. Someone had clearly been in there, but why?

"I've just found Pelthorpe in the bar," Todd said, arriving alongside me from within the train. "But there's no one else in the first-class dining car. Shall I go back to second-class?"

There were seven other doors in front of me, and I was trying to work out what came next as I answered him. "No, I was in there just before the train stopped. I believe our other suspects are all here."

I had a map in my head of who was staying where, but in all the excitement, the names had become jumbled.

"Ah, young man," M. Laroche said as he opened his door and looked out at us. "Do you know what's 'appening? I doubt I'll be able to get back to sleep after all zis noise. I 'eard shouting before. Was zat you?"

"Not now, man," I said, moving along the corridor and presumably offending the Frenchman once more. "Stay in your compartment."

I heard him tut and issue a low complaint in his own language, but he did as instructed. The next door was to Geraldine's compartment, and then there were two more, one of which belonged to the count. What I couldn't decide was whether to try those doors or go straight to Reinhardt's, three further along. I don't suppose I was aware of it, but I'd been moving the whole time; sidling along the corridor ever-so-slowly in the hope the right answer would come to me.

When it didn't, I sped up to reach door number seven. I remembered

Reinhardt retreating there after he harassed poor Geraldine. I placed the flat of my hand on the brass plate for five seconds before entering. I burst through and there he was.

I must say that it is tiring to find bodies stretched out on the floor so often. This one looked as though he had been knocked over the head with a heavy glass vase, of which I'd seen the matching sibling in every other compartment. I didn't know how badly injured he was. I couldn't even say whether he was breathing., but I left Todd to examine his injuries as I ran two doors back down the corridor, and my grandfather arrived just in time for the finale.

"What have you—" he began to ask, but I raised a finger to my lips to silence him.

I counted backwards from three in my head, as if this would make our arrival any more surprising, but when I pushed the handle, it wouldn't open.

"You had better unlock your compartment this very moment," I said in my most authoritative and intimidating voice, which surprised me by sounding both authoritative and intimidating. "You've got ten seconds before we call the *chef de train,* and he comes to unlock it."

"Ten..." I decided that counting aloud might add a sense of urgency to the proceedings. "Nine..."

I was about to say the next number when the door swung open and a face appeared that I knew very well. "Eddie Denkin!"

"Hello there, my good fellows." The film star smiled back at me with all the charm one might expect from a man in his profession. "I'm surprised it took you so long."

CHAPTER TWENTY-ONE

"He's alive," Todd stuck his head out of Reinhardt's room to call. "It looks like a nasty concussion, but he's still with us."

"Thank you," his master replied in a doleful voice. Perhaps he was upset that someone kept putting our suspects to sleep. If it continued, there'd be no one left to interview. "Stay with him until I find someone who can assist you."

Todd nodded and moved back into Reinhardt's compartment. Between our retainer and a doctor with cold hands and a terrible bedside manner, it was obvious to whom I'd rather entrust the life of an injured man. If Todd knew as much about medicine as he did about cars, fishing, cricket, shooting, handicrafts and... well, almost any topic you care to mention, Reinhardt would be better in no time.

"What's happening out here?" Campbell called from the far end of the corridor, but a glare from Grandfather sent him packing.

"I think you should come with me," the forceful detective intoned as he turned back to Geraldine's former paramour. Wait, that's not clear enough: Geraldine's former paramour whom we'd just discovered. No, that still doesn't quite do it. I'm talking about Eddie Denkin.

Denkin had a truly immense figure that looked as though it had been carved from granite. His jaw was as square as a paving slab, and, just above it, his ever-present grin seemed to hover a half-inch in front of the rest of his face. It did not surprise me that he was one of the most famous men on the planet. He was almost as handsome as Geraldine had been.

As he followed my grandfather down the hallway, I decided to check that we'd accounted for all our suspects by knocking on the count's door. He took his time to appear and, when he did, he would only open it a crack to look out.

"Sì?" he demanded, and I felt that he had chosen to speak his own language to unsettle me.

"I just wanted to confirm that you weren't hurt when the train stopped."

"Too kind." The tone of his voice suggested quite the opposite, and it was clear that he did not appreciate the disturbance.

141

I'd barely spoken to the man, but I found him quite arrogant, and so rather than bowing and walking off, I said, "My grandfather will need to speak to you shortly, so don't go away."

I had hoped this might strike some fear into him, but apparently not.

"Where can I go? This is a train."

He closed the door on me, and as I walked back along the corridor, I found myself wishing that he would turn out to be the killer. Arrogant men in white silk capes and faux-military uniforms are guaranteed monsters in my book.

When I reached the doors to the next carriage, Grandfather was leaning out to talk to M. Nagelmackers. "Georges," he began in that overly familiar tone I'd heard him use before, "would you mind coming to discuss something?"

The *chef de train* was talking to the driver and looked surprised to be addressed, but he signalled his compliance and finished his conversation before coming over.

"What can I do for you, Lord Edgington?"

Grandfather didn't answer. He spun on his heel and walked into the dining car so that M. Nagelmackers had no option but to follow. Well, he could have run away yelling, *That detective fellow scares me! I'm better off out of here,* but that would have looked very odd indeed.

Eddie Denkin had already chosen a table and somehow found a waiter on duty from whom he'd requested a bottle of wine and four glasses. This was a new approach to getting through my grandfather's interrogation, and I felt it might just work.

"You're welcome to join me, Lord Edgington," he said as though we were his guests.

Grandfather was having none of it and stayed on his feet. This meant I had to reverse my usual strategy and sit at the table. It would have looked really very odd if we'd both remained standing. I allowed M. Nagelmackers to sit down before me and then took the chair beside him. The only problem now was that I'd grouped myself with a man who'd been hiding at the site of his former lover's murder and the *chef de train* who had neglected to tell us that said man was on board. I felt as if I were sitting with the naughty boys at school.

Grandfather opened his mouth to begin just as the Wolf stalked past us on his way back to his compartment. He had a wet napkin pressed to the bruise on his face but still stopped to point at Eddie Denkin. I could see that he would have liked to accuse the man of something, but he glanced at my grandfather and thought better of it. He hurried on then, and I imagine that he locked his door behind him when he reached his room.

Dorie was the next to interrupt. "Don't mind us, Lord Edgington, Your Highness." She had Delilah under one of her great strong arms and rushed past as quickly as she could to put the dog back where she was supposed to be.

Grandfather waited for a minute to check that there would be no more disturbances and was about to speak when Dorie reappeared from the sleeping carriage. "Sorry, Your Grace. I'll be outta yer way in a jiffy."

Grandfather was finally free to say what he'd been anticipating for some time. "We'll start with you, Nagelmackers!" He rarely looked quite so tetchy, and I could tell that he had taken up the role of headmaster to the three unruly pupils. "Am I right in thinking that you knew Mr Denkin was here all along?"

Eddie Denkin, who was even more charming now that we were sitting across a table from one another, poured the wine.

"Just a small measure. I have to keep my wits about me," I told him before he half-filled my glass and his eyes twinkled in my direction. "That's very kind."

"Sorry, Lord Edgington," Denkin said, clearing his throat in the internationally recognised sound of apology. "Please go on."

Grandfather had come to a stop beside the table and glared down at us before returning to his previous point. "Nagelmackers, did you or did you not know that Mr Denkin was in compartment number five?"

The Belgian pulled at his ever-so-tight collar and presumably wished he'd gone into another line of work. "Lord Edgington, let me first say that at no point this evening did I intentionally mislead you." These were the words of a practiced liar. "It was not that I wished to conceal Mr Denkin's presence…" He paused to wait for the film star to pour another glass and then thanked him with a nod that only served to irritate my grandfather more. "You see… I had facilitated his access to the train before anyone else boarded—"

"For a sizable tip, one assumes."

His fuzzy eyebrows rounded in sympathy for himself. "Now, now, Lord Edgington, please don't be so critical. In this job, such service is expected for special passengers. I was only doing what a hundred men before me have done."

Grandfather took two steps away from the table again before spinning around and directing another bark at Nagelmackers. "Stop feeling sorry for yourself and tell me what I need to know."

"Yes, sir. Very good, sir. It was not that I wished to hide his presence on the train from you, but when I consulted the passenger list, it quite escaped my mind that the *Pierre Mandalay* whom I'd included was really Mr Denkin."

Denkin raised his glass and smiled. I don't think I'd seen him look anything but cheerful since I'd found his compartment, which already suggested something that could undermine Nagelmackers's version of events.

"There's only one problem with that story, Georges," I told him, borrowing my grandfather's informality. "When we asked you to check the list for people with the same initials as on the notes we discovered, you said that no one in first-class had a Christian name beginning with D. I found this strange and concluded that you must have thought that Geraldine's surname began with that letter. However, as the first two words of *de la Forge* are considered lower case particles, and not part of the main surname, that is incorrect. Of course, being a native French speaker, you surely knew that."

My grandfather took a break from his quiet fury to stare at me in bewilderment. With his head to one side, left eyebrow raised, the right one surprisingly low, I believe he was thinking, *Who are you, Christopher? And what happened to the young boy who once thought that cyanide was a type of cough medicine?*

"Now, now, there is no need to be hasty," Nagelmackers continued his defence. "As I said, I did not set out to confuse or conceal, I merely…" The words got stuck in his throat, and he stared down at the table. As I watched him, his normally chipper, respectful demeanour became first clouded over, then stormy. "Oh, very well. What's the point of lying? I didn't tell you about this overly rich costermonger because he paid me plenty of money not to under any circumstances."

He released an exasperated cry that I believe he had kept locked away inside him for some years. "You don't know what this job is like, Lord Edgington. The company employed me for my refined accent more than anything else. I'm here to feign happiness as these spoilt little children cavort through my beautiful train, breaking things and never saying sorry. I am worse than a slave to them. I am a slave who says, 'Thank you for mistreating me!'"

There was a certain nobility in what he'd said, and he finished his short speech with his head held high.

His confessor, however, was unimpressed, "You should have said that from the beginning, and I'd have quite understood." Grandfather crossed his arms and released a weary breath. "I already knew you'd taken money from Miss de la Forge herself to delay the train, and I didn't think any less of you for it. Though may I suggest you look for another job if you hate it so much?"

Nagelmackers didn't reply. His anger was still evident, and he didn't want to say anything else. He swigged his wine and wouldn't look at any of us again for some time.

Grandfather turned his attention to the more important of the two men and the only one of them who could have killed poor Geraldine. "As for you, Denkin, you do realise that you're now at the top of my list when investigating your former love's murder?"

This finally rubbed the smug look off his face, but not for the reason I might have imagined. "I'm truly sorry you feel that way, but you're wrong in one respect." He looked up at the glass and gold starburst light on the ceiling, just as many film actors look away from the camera when delivering a romantic line. "I never stopped loving my Geraldine, and I certainly didn't kill her."

"Nonsense!" His interrogator moved back to the table and put his fists on it so that he could loom over the three of us. I don't know about Eddie Denkin, but I was most definitely intimidated. "You killed her because she left you for another man. It was one thing to replace her with a shiny new starlet, but you couldn't bear to see her with Reinhardt."

Denkin tipped his head back and laughed before realising that this sounded callous. "I'm truly sorry, old duck, but you're quacking up the wrong tree. I didn't lay a hand on Geraldine. And what's more, *I* left *her*, so where would the sense be in plotting my revenge?"

Grandfather pretended he hadn't heard a word and continued with his hypothesis. "And then, after she was dead, you decided to get your own back on your former director. You pulled the brake cord in your carriage and, when everyone was distracted, you sneaked from your compartment to look for him. That explains why our door was left open and Delilah escaped." Grandfather's voice was getting steadily louder as his ire grew. "When you found Reinhardt, you smashed a vase over the back of his head and went running to safety."

"Oh, please. You mustn't think so badly of me. I only opened the door to your compartment because your poor dog was whining and I felt sorry for her."

The imperious Lord Edgington raised one hand to point at the suspect, knowing he had the star just where he wanted him. "So you don't deny that you attacked a man in his own sleeping berth?"

Eddie leant back in his chair and grinned wider than ever. "I don't deny it for one moment. I gave that weasel just what he deserved."

CHAPTER TWENTY-TWO

"I beg your pardon?"

It was Grandfather's turn to clear his throat. Even Nagelmackers looked up at the man who had ever-so-casually admitted to an act of great violence.

"You heard me. I smashed that vase over Reinhardt's head. And if the truth be told, I planned to do a lot worse."

I wasn't used to seeing my grandfather lost for words, but that was what had happened. I also wasn't used to our suspects admitting to their crimes. It was oddly refreshing.

"So you planned to kill him?" Grandfather's confusion had reached its peak.

Denkin grimaced and ran his hand through his dark, pomaded hair. "Of course I did, but when I saw him sprawled out on the floor, he looked so pathetic I just didn't have it in me." He sighed a sorry sigh. "I suppose I might live to regret it, but it's done now."

"You smashed a vase over his head?" Grandfather was not coping with Denkin's unexpected honesty, so I nudged his foot with mine and took over the questioning.

"I believe what my grandfather is trying to understand is why you attacked your colleague?"

Denkin said nothing for a moment as he sipped his drink. He didn't lack confidence but perhaps needed to get his thoughts in order before incriminating himself. "It's simple enough. I've been in my compartment since an hour before departure. That was always my plan, you see. You don't know what it's like to be followed everywhere you go by hungry journalists after a scoop. Those people are worse than rats, so I came here early, spoke to the ever-so-helpful M. Nagelmackers, and accessed the carriage before it was connected to the rest of the train."

Nagelmackers winced, and Grandfather decided to let him off the hook.

"We no longer need you here," he said. "You can return to overseeing the efforts to search for whoever attacked Mr Pelthorpe."

The Belgian was back to his obsequious best. "Yes, Lord

Edgington. Of course, Lord Edgington, and I must thank you for your... discretion."

The detective didn't even glance at the scurrying man as he imparted a final message. "In future, however, I would recommend considering the limits of your loyalty. If it turns out that Mr Denkin is the murderer, and you enabled his crime, I may have to speak to you again."

Nagelmackers's large, innocent eyes seemed to grow in his head as he nodded and hurried away.

"As for you, Denkin—"

"As for me, I was in the middle of telling my story, so don't get ahead of yourself." People never speak to my grandfather like this, and I was amazed that his bluntness went unchallenged. "I stayed in my compartment all afternoon and into the evening. I did not go out when I heard that savage Reinhardt screaming at the woman he claimed to love."

He broke off then and nodded to me. "Good work on that score, old fellow." I couldn't help but enjoy his compliment, even as he continued. "I did not interfere with your investigation, but I did hear a lot of what went on. It took me some time to realise that it was Geraldine who had been murdered. I heard lots of running about of course, and I heard several angry exchanges. When I cottoned on to the fact that Reinhardt had been consigned to his room as the likely suspect, it all fell into place. There's no doubt in my mind that he killed her."

"So you're persisting with the idea that there is both a killer on this train and a smug stowaway who plotted to attack his love rival?" Grandfather made up for his earlier passivity with this truly cutting appraisal of the affair.

"The two things are not contradictory, Edgington." A little of Denkin's charm had faded, and his previously dreamy gaze had turned noticeably sharper. "It's the most natural thing in the world for a man to wish to punish a killer. Yes, I was the one who pulled the emergency cord. And I was the one who attacked Reinhardt, but I didn't lay a finger on Gerry. I would never have it in me."

"Said every unpunished wife-beater I've ever known," Grandfather snapped back at him, but I tried to keep the conversation on track.

"And yet you stayed in your compartment because you knew we would suspect you."

Denkin froze for all of three seconds. "I don't deny it. I knew how my concealment on the train would look but hoped that Nagelmackers would keep his end of the bargain. I planned to leave my compartment when the body had been removed, and we arrived at our destination. To be quite frank, I'm surprised she's still on here with us."

Unwilling to look at the arrogant actor, Grandfather turned away.

I picked up where he'd left off. "What did you hear from your compartment to convince you that Reinhardt is the killer?"

He licked his lips like a man who's about to smoke a cigarette. "I heard what you heard. I heard his rage as he begged her to let him into her room and, when her brave little maid denied him, I heard how he tried to break the door down. Anything that followed is irrelevant. We know who was in that state of mind and can work out the rest from there."

"I'm afraid that's not how it works." Grandfather had gone to perch on the table across the aisle, and he watched us from there like an owl on a fence post. "If we were to secure a conviction, we would need more than circumstantial evidence. While it is true that Hansel Reinhardt acted in a hostile manner, he did not issue any direct threats to the victim and was easily dissuaded from his action by my grandson, as you also will have heard."

I did a quick calculation and realised that Denkin's compartment was two doors up from Geraldine's and two doors down from Reinhardt's, so he would have been in the perfect place to hear what had occurred, especially if he'd been listening at the keyhole. He may even have spied the encounter through a gap in his curtained window.

"It's not just what happened on this train though," Denkin tried again. "There's something not quite right about the man. Whenever I've worked with him, it's as if he believes he owns his actors – as if he is the king and we are his subjects. He would scream and shout at poor Gerry until she was in tears. It amazes me that she continued to have anything to do with him after I…"

"After you swapped her for a dazzling new alternative." Grandfather was making no effort to hide how appalled he was by the situation. It was strange to see, as I am normally the sulky, sentimental one, and he is the master of his emotions.

"So that's why you don't like me, is it?" Denkin sounded alarmed that anyone could find him less than intoxicatingly charming. "I'll have you know that leaving Geraldine was one of the hardest things I've ever had to do."

It was Grandfather's turn to laugh. "Oh, I'm sure it was terrible for you. How did you ever recover?"

Denkin wasn't smiling any more. "You really don't understand, do you? I loved her deeply. That's why I kept trying to see her, but she knew the game. She knew I had to think of my career."

"Are you saying you left her for the sake of the attention you would get for courting another actress?" Grandfather's eyes focused on his target once more. "Isn't that the same attention you were just bemoaning?"

The actor wasn't ready to respond to this, so he continued with his justification. "No one could hold a candle to my Geraldine, but Maxine's star was rising, even as Geraldine's shone brightly. You have to understand that it's different for men and women in our business. I could have another twenty years of top billing, whereas she was already thirty. No matter how many people love her now, will they still feel the same in five years?" He asked this question with such open-hearted conviction that it was almost enough for me to overlook just how vile his thinking was. "I can't say that I love Maxine in the way I do Gerry. That's why I booked a ticket on this train to be alone with her for once. That's why I risked the others seeing me to slip the note from her dear, devoted Dennie under her door."

"Did you hear anything from inside the compartment when you did so?" I asked in as suspicious a tone as I could muster. I definitely still didn't trust the man.

"Not a peep."

"What time was that?"

Denkin looked up at the ceiling to recall what had happened. "I would say it was around a quarter-past seven. I knew people would be at dinner and made certain to wait a few minutes after I heard the occupants of the compartments on either side of me leave."

From my knowledge of who was where and when, this fitted with what we had learnt so far. Grandfather offered no response to his claims, and the room fell silent for some time. His expression was so censorious that I thought he might have heard enough altogether.

I wonder how long he'd have waited to say anything if Nagelmackers hadn't reappeared. "I'm sorry to interrupt you, Lord Edgington, but my staff are confident that no one has got on or off the train since we stopped. All passengers are accounted for, and there is no sign of any damage. I believe we can set off on our journey once more."

He nodded in reply, and the *chef de train* looked uncomfortable for a moment in the doorway. He wiped his presumably sweaty palms on his blue jacket and eventually backed away. I heard doors slamming shut up and down the train, and I believe I felt a slight jolt as the engine brake was released in preparation for our departure. Dorie reappeared, and she stood like a sentinel at the far end of the carriage from us. Perhaps it was the sight of the film star there that had told her just how serious the situation was, but she certainly added an extra frisson of menace as the train slowly chugged into motion once more.

"We have heard that you continued to see Miss de la Forge after the end of the affair."

"Gosh, really?" he seemed genuinely surprised by this small fact. "I didn't believe we had been observed. I'm normally a discreet sort of cove if you haven't noticed yet. Who saw us?"

"I would say that was beside the point." Grandfather maintained his stern tone. "But as it happens, it was Geraldine's maid."

"What about Geraldine herself?" I asked to return us to the previous topic. "How did she feel about being your *chère amie?*"

Denkin remained nonplussed, but he waved away whatever thought he'd had – much as if he'd been wafting away smoke from his cigarette. "I can't say she was too thrilled about it. I was away shooting a film with Maxine in Britain, but whenever I came back here, I would do all I could to convince her I was worthy of her time. The truth is, I was mad about her."

He sniffed in an amused manner, as if the woman we were discussing wasn't lying dead a short distance away. "Whenever we were in the same city, I'd have an uncontrollable, almost physical urge to seek her out. I told her all the sweet little nothings that I could to wear her down, and she normally gave in before long."

"So what changed?"

"Everything was different after the premiere." He shook his head and looked down at the table before an idea came to him. "Would either of you mind if I smoked?"

"Yes, we would," Grandfather answered. "What's this about a film premiere? Reinhardt mentioned it too, but he wouldn't tell us anything more."

Denkin suddenly shifted away from him and looked amazed. "You mean you don't know? You've been investigating all this time, and you don't know what went on that night?"

I recalled an unfinished comment that Reinhardt had made earlier in the evening, but I remained quiet and let Grandfather speak for the both of us.

"No, we don't." He was distinctly unamused by most of what the man had to say, but these words came out coated in disdain. I think he showed more tolerance for the Wolf than he did for Denkin, who wore his transgressions with apparent pride. "Tell us all about it."

Our suspect wasn't the typical vain, empty-headed thespian that we think of whenever the papers describe film stars of the day. He clearly had a brain and engaged it each time when answering. "I suppose it makes sense that none of the others would mention it considering… Well, I'll start at the beginning. Gerry and I had finished our last film together. *Echoes of the Ocean* was no masterpiece, and Reinhardt ended up losing a lot of money, but that wasn't our problem, and we treated the release just like any other. There was a grand party in Rome paid for by a wealthy American couple who are just about crazy for Gerry. Well, they're just about crazy, full stop, I'd say. Gerry's manager brought them in when it was clear that the film was a disaster, but they seem kind enough underneath."

Was he talking about the Campbells? It seemed rather likely.

"So, we all went to the cinema to bask in the glory of the overly sentimental, poorly plotted film we'd made, before the party began at the Palazzo Manfredi. I've been to some spectacular shindigs over the years, but with a view over the Roman skyline, and no expense spared, it was truly something special."

"That sounds lovely." Grandfather dryly outdid his previous extremely dry retort for dryness this time.

Denkin sat up straighter in his chair. "I'm telling you all this to explain why there were rooms with different themes in each. The great and good of the film world were out in force. There were politicians and sportsmen, and a particularly wealthy count lavished attention on Geraldine. My point is that we were split up between the ballroom, the African room – where topless tribesmen served us food that looked like it had just been hunted with spears – and a mock-up of a sweetshop which was dishing out luxuriously bright cocktails in place of pear drops and sherbet lemons. It was all very jolly, but Geraldine was in a foul mood.

"She'd barely looked at me at the premiere, even though we stood right next to one another for photographs and interviews, but at the party, she made certain to keep her distance. It got to the point at which I had drunk enough to go looking for her and, I swear, I wish to this day that I'd done no such thing."

"What was the matter with her?" If nothing else, I can be relied upon to give more important people a brief break from talking.

"I'm sure it will come as no surprise to hear that she was furious with me. She had been ever since I'd signed to star opposite Maxine. You know, before any rumours make it into the newspapers and journals of the movie world, they circulate through friends and enemies, and she had already heard that my interest in the young lady was more than just professional."

"So she confronted you?" I leant in closer despite myself. It's hard to say if it was down to the impact his account could have on the case or my inability to resist the shine of the people he mentioned.

"She did more than that; she floored me. Not physically, I must add, but when I asked her what the matter was, she didn't just attack me for spending time with lovely little Maxine, she told me that she'd chosen her as the co-star in her next film. We were there in public, and she announced it to the room."

His jaw hung open for a few moments, and he shook his head. "I couldn't believe it… I still can't. The woman was mad. I tried to reason with her, but she wouldn't listen to me. She was determined to work with Maxine. I couldn't believe that she would interfere in my life like that."

Grandfather gave a brief, cynical laugh, but Denkin was so self-absorbed that he didn't seem to hear.

"Is that all it was?" I asked, a little disappointed by what I was sure would turn out to be a wild and debauched tale. "You were surprised that no one else had mentioned the premiere, but it seems that the two of you were the only ones affected by the events of that night."

"I don't know if you're a film fanatic, little Edgington, but in the pictures I make, stories develop over time. You don't jump into the most exciting scene right at the beginning. The whole thing needs to come to a crescendo. It's the same with storytelling."

He huffed and searched in his jacket pocket for a pack of cigarettes, which he removed before remembering that Grandfather didn't want him to smoke around us and huffing again.

"Geraldine was inconsolable and didn't want to hear anything I said, so I told her things were finally over between us. I regretted it immediately, but she ran off home, and the rest of us tried to enjoy ourselves without her. That worked just swimmingly for a while. I can't tell you how many beautiful girls were there that night, and they all seemed to like me."

His grin became more crocodile-like, and I decided that he wasn't a very nice man at all.

"I began to question what I was doing wasting my time with a Brit and an American when there are Latin beauties under every stone you turn out here."

Grandfather had heard enough and snapped. "Would you stop it? You have no need to show what a morally delinquent person you are. We know just what to expect from you, so concentrate on the events of that night if you think they might go some way to explaining Miss de la Forge's death."

He clearly enjoyed scandalising us and raised his eyebrows teasingly before complying with the request. "Very well. As the party burned down, a man appeared whom I'd never seen before. He was there watching me in the Far-Eastern lounge as I danced with a simply exquisite Chinese woman. I caught sight of him again later as I drank my champagne from a goblet made of sculpted ice on the rooftop terrace overlooking the Colosseum, and when I went back down to look for my friends, I found him waiting for me on the stairs."

This was one of those fleeting moments when the subject of our interview looked less than sure of himself. "He was dressed up for the evening, of course; he would never have been allowed inside otherwise. But there was something seedy about him. He was unshaven, and his stubble sat on his chin like dirt. His eyes were small and black and, as they scraped over me, I felt as if I was being hunted."

"'I'm not in the mood to talk to admirers,' I told him when he stood in my way. 'I've had far too much to drink for that, and there's a young lady I haven't quite seduced yet.' But he wouldn't get out of my way and said, 'Oh, I think you're going to want to hear what I have to say, Mr Denkin. You'd better follow me.'"

Denkin paused then, and it all seemed too much for him. I don't know whether he was trying to make sense of his own thinking, or he was struggling to tell the story, but he crossed his legs under the table and waited a few seconds before continuing. "I really can't say why I went along with him. I suppose I hoped he was part of the entertainment. You know the sort of thing; a puzzle to solve or a charade of some variety that the organisers had laid on for us. When I got to the immense chamber on the ground floor, I saw that I was not the only guest he had fished.

"There was a circle of chairs set out in the middle of the marble floor. The American couple were there. The stiff, rather prickly husband stood behind his wife, his hand on her shoulder as though he were afraid she might escape. The Italian count, who had been at Geraldine's side for most of the night, was sitting with his eyes on the floor before him, and the select group was completed by my treasured director, Hansel Reinhardt.

"'What's going on here?' I asked them, still merry from the ten or so drinks I'd consumed. 'It's all very cloak and dagger, and I greatly approve.' But before any of them could answer, that revolting man shouted at me. 'You'll shut up and sit down if you know what's good for you,' and I knew that it wasn't a game we were playing – his acting was too good for that."

I was tempted to ask a question then, but I was immersed in the story and had no wish to hear my own voice.

He took his time studying the swirls in the shiny wooden tabletop, but then he suddenly started up again without prompting. "I could tell from the downturned eyes and grim expressions of the others in attendance that no one wanted to be there, but unlike them, I wasn't frightened. I kept looking at the parasite before us and asked him a question. 'Blackmail, is that your game?' I didn't bother waiting for an answer because I could see what was happening. No, I told him how things stood. 'There are only two things I've done in my life that wouldn't burnish my reputation, and I'm willing to bet you don't know either of them.' Then I gave him my most winning smile and walked calmly from the room."

Denkin put his hands to his lips as though he had a cigarette lit and ready to smoke. He was evidently very pleased with himself, but that was nothing new.

I couldn't say what he thought this story meant, but Grandfather appeared to know. "Can you tell us the name of the man who tried to blackmail you?"

"I'm afraid not." He paused for five long seconds, as though waiting for the title cards to flash up in the film of his life. "But he walked past us at this table around ten minutes ago."

CHAPTER TWENTY-THREE

"Did you know that the man with many or perhaps no names whatsoever was a blackmailer?" I asked my grandfather when we'd sent Denkin back to his room with instructions not to leave it.

"I had my suspicions. Not just from the things he said but his manner in general." This was an odd comment coming from him. He tended to rely on hard evidence rather than vague impressions of people, but perhaps he had known enough swindlers to say exactly how they looked.

I cast my mind back to the conversation we'd had with the Wolf in the first-class bar. "Something occurred to me when we spoke to him. I wondered if you'd known one another when you were in the police. It was the way he referred to you as Superintendent Edgington. It rang alarm bells for me."

"I know what you mean, but that solely proved he remembered me. I doubt I had any direct contact with him, though perhaps he was just a lad when we crossed paths and he looks quite different today. There's no doubt in my mind that he's some strain of criminal, and we know he was here in disguise."

Grandfather was clearly weighed down with thoughts and theories. He went walking back and forth along the aisle and didn't stop even when Cook, followed by young Timothy, appeared at the door with a trolley of appetisers. The train was in full motion by now, but she barely swayed, and she didn't put a foot wrong.

"Good evening, Lord Edgington, Master Christopher," Henrietta sang with all her usual cheer and warmth. "What an exciting one it has been. I didn't expect to be searching for criminals after I'd finished making dinner, but then nothing is ever off the table in this job."

Dorie and Timothy approached the trolley but, instead of serving their master as I might have expected, Dorie took two plates and helped herself to an assortment of pickled swede vol-au-vents, parmesan and fried liver balls, and *confiture de roquefort* toasts. Over the last few years, Henrietta had learnt to tame some of her wilder culinary impulses, but they occasionally burst through.

I decided that I wasn't hungry.

157

Todd appeared from the first-class sleeping carriage and was soon provided with a plate. Grandfather insisted that Cook join us, too. So in the end, I was the only one who wasn't eating.

"Shouldn't we interview the man we've recently identified as a criminal?" I dared suggest. "The time is still ticking on the case, you know, Grandfather."

"Yes, yes," he said, not looking at me as he heaped food on his plate. The great Lord Edgington is a Henrietta apologist and loves his cook's bizarre creations with a passion.

As I was clearly the only one taking our case seriously, I took up the task of walking up and down for no reason as I considered the various solutions that lay before us. "There is now the definite possibility that the Wolf killed Geraldine because she failed to pay when he tried to blackmail her."

"The Wolf?" Grandfather asked when he'd finished his mouthful. "Why do you call him that?"

I thought back to my first impression of our blackmailer. "I believe I identified something savage and predatory in his very core."

"Then that's a perfectly good name for him," Dorie asserted, but Grandfather had his reservations.

"It's fine, though I don't think it's fair to actual wolves. They would never stoop to blackmail."

Before this conversation could get any more absurd, I returned to my previous point. "He may be the killer, or he may be the spark that brought about Geraldine's death. We know that he holds information over the Campbells, Count Giovannelli and Hansel Reinhardt…"

"Who, you'll be glad to hear, has made a full recovery after his attack," Todd was quick to inform us. "One of the stewards had medical experience during the war and is staying with him, but the cut to his head isn't too deep."

"That's wonderful news," Grandfather said as he brushed crumbs from his hands, "unless he turns out to be the killer and then it's merely news."

I must confess that I was distracted at this moment by young Timothy's reaction to one of the blue cheese marmalade toasts. He seemed to like it at first, then his eyebrows arched, and I thought for a moment he might be feeling sick. Luckily for everyone, this was not the case, and he soon continued munching.

"What was I saying?" I asked as everyone nibbled and chomped.

It turned out that Cook was the only person who had been paying attention. "You were describing which of your suspects the Wolf had the ability to blackmail."

"That's it, Henrietta. Thank you. And bearing that in mind, it's possible Geraldine got caught in the middle. Perhaps one of the other suspects decided to put an end to the Wolf's games, and she suffered."

"Hmmm," Grandfather said in a manner which told me that, for the moment, he didn't plan to reveal anything more.

"Maybe the count sneaked out of his room when we were going through one of the tunnels and went into Geraldine's compartment by mistake. He may have been looking for the Wolf and only found the lamb, but Geraldine screamed when she saw the knife and so he had to kill her."

"Hmmm..." Grandfather replied, and this time I knew he would have more to say. "That might make sense, but surely after what happened with Reinhardt, Miss de la Forge would have kept her door firmly locked."

A couple of solutions entered my mind, though neither of them added up to much, and I had to accept his argument. "So we go back to the original hypothesis. Reinhardt is to blame. He convinced her to open, then killed Geraldine because she knew whatever the Wolf knows. And when the train came to an unexpected stop, he ran to kill his blackmailer but—" This time, I corrected myself. "No, that's just twaddle. Reinhardt was busy in his own compartment having a vase smashed over his head by Eddie Denkin when the Wolf was knocked out in the luggage van."

"The actor Eddie Denkin?" Cook asked with some alarm. "Surely he wouldn't do a thing like that. He's far too handsome."

"Hmmm..." Grandfather's doubt did not need explaining this time.

"I suppose you're right, Lord Edgington," she conceded. "Fine looks've never guaranteed good behaviour. And now that I think about it, Eddie Denkin does have something appealingly wicked about him. I'm rather excited that we're on the same train as one another." She made a sound then as if a shiver had travelled across her body. I really can't say what had got into her.

"However," her employer interrupted, "I do admit it is strange for the killer to risk detection by knocking out Marvin Pelthorpe or whatever you choose to call him. The blackmailer was avoiding us at the far end of the train, and you'd think that, if the killer was going to go out of his way like that, he'd have made sure to murder the man he was trying to silence."

"So maybe it wasn't the killer who knocked him out?" Todd suggested brightly. "Perhaps, just like Eddie Denkin with the German, someone thought Pelthorpe was to blame."

I was desperately trying to think of another solution and didn't pay enough attention. "Very well, then the Campbells are guilty because… Oh, botheration. I'm really just guessing. Aren't I?"

"It would seem that way." Grandfather was eating again, so little Timothy said this on his behalf and was rewarded with a nod for his trouble.

Minutes earlier, I had felt quite exuberant at the thought that we were creeping closer to the killer, but none of my theories had stuck. "So what options remain?"

Todd presented my grandfather with a napkin (which he presumably keeps tucked up his sleeve for just such moments), and Lord Edgington dabbed at his perfectly clean mouth before pushing his chair back and preparing to speak.

"Why did you skip so rapidly over the idea that the blackmailer is also the killer?"

I chose not to answer, partly because I didn't want to distract him but mainly because I didn't know what to say.

"Although the presence of a known criminal among the ranks of suspects does not automatically mean he is capable of such a violent offence, in this case, we know he wrote a threatening note to a woman who was murdered shortly after."

"If that's true, why didn't he remove it when he was in her compartment?" It's strange that I can sound clever like this when responding to my grandfather's ideas, but I still struggle to lead the conversation.

He was ready with an answer, nonetheless. "Perhaps he wasn't expecting her to be inside. She saw the note being inserted through the gap in the door, and so she opened it to see who was there. Rather than allow her to scream out, he forced his way in and stabbed her. However, removing the skin is the very last thing a professional blackmailer would do – it was an unnecessary complication that achieved nothing. Conversely, you could argue that is just the thing a professional blackmailer would do to mask his involvement – especially with its darkly romantic overtones."

This was all very interesting, but I decided to return to my previous point. "And why didn't he remove the note after he killed her?"

Grandfather doubted himself for at least a moment this time. "He forgot."

We both knew that this was an unsatisfying solution, and there was a hint of a smile on his lips as he spoke.

"Lord Edgington, sir," our former page boy Timothy began. We hadn't involved him in any of our investigations before, but he seemed keen enough. "If that's what you believe, then why don't you go to the blackmailer this very minute and put your allegations to him?"

Grandfather wasn't the only one who looked impressed by the young man's question. Four short years earlier, I had been a novice like him. I was naïve, impressionable and easily led. He, on the other hand, was yet to make any ridiculous predictions or present self-contradicting hypotheses. All that fun and diversion lay ahead of him.

"That is an excellent question, Timothy, but we are not quite ready." Although my grandfather had never found a hole from which he couldn't escape through clever deployment of blather and babble, he looked just as confounded by the case before us as I felt. It didn't last long. "One important element that Christopher overlooked is what the blackmailer knows about our suspects that could be damaging to them. Perhaps that will explain why someone murdered a beloved actress."

This was a very good point, and I immediately understood why he had felt calm enough to pause for something to eat. The way forward was far clearer than it had been a short time earlier.

"It's also worth mentioning that many in the first-class carriage denied knowing Geraldine. They also gave no indication that they were acquainted with the Wolf. I think it all comes back to that night in Rome when he winched up the sword of Damocles and left it dangling over their heads."

I don't think Dorie or Timothy understood this reference, but Todd and Cook were most interested in what I had to say, and Grandfather let me form the conclusions that he had pointed me towards.

"It's time to use the smelling salts," I said quite confidently. "Though actually, I'm a little peckish. Perhaps I will have one of those cheese balls after all."

CHAPTER TWENTY-FOUR

I think we can all agree that the real revelation of the night was not the presence of a blackmailer on the train or the fact that world-famous actor Eddie Denkin had been hiding on board the whole time. The sad reality of Geraldine de la Forge's tragic existence certainly raised my grandfather's eyebrows a twelfth of an inch or two, but that paled in comparison to my discovery that fried liver, when coated in enough cheese, can be just about edible. It came as quite a shock to me, I don't mind admitting.

"You see, my boy," Grandfather told me as we penetrated the first-class sleeping carriage and passed Domenico once more. "You're coming around to my way of thinking at last."

"Do you mean that you believe James Joseph Campbell is to blame for Geraldine's death, and he put his wife to sleep to ensure that she didn't incriminate him?"

He stopped walking in front of our compartment so as to express his confusion more clearly. "No, Christopher. We haven't found a clear motive for him to kill anyone. I'm talking about Cook's appetisers. Long you have doubted the deftness of her culinary creations, but I saw on your face how much you enjoyed them."

"Wonderful. Now that we've settled that matter, we can retire for the night." I opened the door beside me to drive my point home.

Grandfather pretended not to find this funny and, through the doorway, I noticed Delilah asleep on the floor. She'd had a good run around when the train stopped, and – judging by the way her legs were going like the clappers – she was now free to dream of more running around.

He ignored me and finally returned us to the important matter of an uncaught murderer. "Of course, we can't rule out the idea that Mr Campbell intentionally made an appearance in the restaurant and even approached our table in order to suggest he had nothing to do with the crime. His wife could have been the one to kill Miss de la Forge, and it would have been a good reason to sedate her if he feared that she might give the show away."

"I considered all that, but what we've subsequently learnt of the timing of Milly Buckthorn's departure could be significant." I paused in the hope that my observation might have impressed him. "She went to the cloakroom by our compartment before entering the dining car. During that time, Campbell could have murdered Geraldine and slipped past, making it look as though he had left before the murder occurred."

"You clever thing. You noticed that, did you?" He walked to the end of the corridor, and I strolled after him.

"We've been so busy with our other suspects that it took me a while to realise, but I'm sure he could have done it."

"It is time…" He paused to take the bottle of smelling salts that we'd taken from the bar out of his pocket. "…for answers."

He knocked and waited for the tense murmur from James Joseph that had greeted our previous visit to their compartment. Stepping past the thick wooden door, we were offered a similar, though not identical sight.

"Good evening, gentlemen," Sharlene said a little gingerly, and she sat up higher in her place beside the window.

I must admit, I was a little disappointed that we didn't get to use the smelling salts. James Joseph was looking sleepy, though, so perhaps we'd still get the chance.

"Ahh, madam. I see you're awake. Are you feeling any less drowsy than you previously were?" He eyed her husband as he said this, and I stood by the door because there was little space elsewhere.

"I woke her to show that we have nothing to hide." Her husband grumbled so that she didn't have to answer the question.

Mrs Campbell pointed her supposed hero to a chair at the table just in front of her while Mr Campbell propped himself up in the corner. As I had thought when I first met him, we had rather a lot in common. We were both largely unnecessary *âmes damnées* to grander, more commanding figures whose job it was to make all the important decisions. It wasn't the worst life imaginable, but I wondered how he felt about it.

"I understand you already came here once to talk to me," she said, as though she'd previously been busy with an important matter. "I apologise that I was not able to answer your questions, but I am quite recovered now."

"There is no need to apologise, madam. I am only happy that we will now have this opportunity to discuss the situation." The aristocrat and the woman who acted as if she were a member of the (entirely fictional) American royal family bowed to one another in an excessively polite gesture, which only made the atmosphere in the luxurious train compartment all the icier.

I'd been wondering how Grandfather would approach the interview, as it was not a typical encounter. Aside from the fact that we knew they'd lied to us, and husband had doped wife to avoid this very meeting, we had to contend with all the oddness that had occurred in our early discussions. I could see from the way Sharlene scrunched up her face between responses that she hadn't forgiven Lord Edgington for the perceived slight against her. For the moment, his splendid English manners were holding strong, though I couldn't imagine that being the case if she failed to answer his questions.

"Perhaps you should begin by telling us exactly who you are and why you came to Europe."

"Lord Edgington," James Joseph adopted a more conciliatory tone than he had previously employed. "Please don't think that everything we've said to you has been a lie. My wife is a good person through and through."

Grandfather tipped his head back as he looked at the man. "I appreciate that, Mr Campbell. And I am trying my very best to give you the benefit of the doubt but, considering the circumstances, that is really quite difficult."

James Joseph opened his mouth to reply, but his wife raised her hand before he could. "I told you when we met," she said, "we are from Savannah, Georgia. We have come to Europe for the first time to visit the homes of our ancestors. Between us, we have the blood of five different Old World countries in our veins. We grew up with tales of Britain and Germany, Ireland, Holland and Italy that made those ancient nations sound like lands from a fairytale."

"And you're already avoiding my questions." Grandfather had both hands on the top of his cane. Even as he maintained that excessively polite delivery, he leant forward in his chair to force his point.

"Sharlene's father owns large swathes of Georgia," James Joseph eventually answered when his wife couldn't or wouldn't. "One part of her family can trace its roots back to the First Families of Virginia, and the other helped establish Savannah as a thriving community."

"How impressive." It's a strange talent to be able to imply rudeness while maintaining crystal diction and a polite tone of voice, but it was one of Grandfather's many. "What I'm trying to determine is first, what your connection to the dead woman may be, and second, what a blackmailer could hold over you to make you so afraid."

If they hadn't been frightened before, they were now. James Joseph looked at Sharlene for the briefest of moments. It was far easier to know what he was thinking than it was with his wife. She barely flinched at this question, but I could still see the tension in her muscles and a certain flutter of the eyelashes that told me she was afraid of what the famous sleuth could extract from her.

"I have no idea what you mean, Lord Edgington." Sharlene turned away from him and stared at a point on the opposite wall beside the tiny lavabo.

"There's no sense in lying; I will see right through it. I no longer doubt that you had made the acquaintance of several of the other suspects before boarding this train, and yet, when I last spoke to you, you denied knowing even Miss de la Forge."

"We didn't know her well!" James Joseph tried once more, but Grandfather wouldn't listen to such bosh.

"Regardless of the depth of your relationship, it's still a lie. We have learnt from Eddie Denkin—"

"Eddie's here on the train?" Mr Campbell leant backwards against the wall as if this minor revelation had knocked him off his feet.

"We have learnt from Mr Denkin that you paid to host a lavish party in Rome after the premiere of his and Miss de la Forge's last film."

Sharlene suddenly turned back to look at Grandfather, and I felt that I finally understood something important about the behaviour of our suspects: they had been doing all they could to keep their secrets from us. Not just the Campbells, but Reinhardt, the count and perhaps even the Wolf himself. Of course, as I had learnt many times over, this did not mean that whatever they wished to conceal was connected to the murder.

"You are getting carried away now, Lord Edgington." Sharlene wrapped her skinny arms around herself as though afraid he would lash out. "I don't know what terrible theory you've formed, but I can see that your imagination has got the better of you."

We all knew this wasn't the case, but Grandfather wouldn't immediately disagree. He was happy to build up to whatever we'd gone there to discover and waited ten seconds to make the pair suffer before playing his trump card.

"My imagination doesn't come into this. I know that a man on this train calling himself Marvin Pelthorpe blackmailed you and three other suspects. On the night of the premiere, Denkin himself was unintimidated and walked away, saying that Pelthorpe couldn't know anything about him that he would be afraid of the wider public discovering. From what I have inferred, it was likely to have been the time he was spending in London with the actress Maxine Hammond that the blackmailer hoped to hold over him. Now I want to know why it was that you gave in to the blackmailer's demands."

Until now, Sharlene had resisted turning to her husband, but the pressure had become too much. She gripped the scarlet cushions on either side of her and, for the first time since we'd met them, I had the sense that she relied on her husband just as much as he did her.

"We'll wait until the police get here," James Joseph said without turning back to his interrogator. "We have nothing to hide, but we're only too familiar with how you work. My dear Sharlene likes to read me parts of the books she most enjoys, and I've heard all about the way you manipulate your suspects."

"Manipulate?" Now my grandfather sounded defensive.

"That's right." The man stepped forward and, finding some confidence after all, he glared at the detective. "You push forward your dim-witted grandson to make the killer think they will get away with their crime before swooping in to catch them out. You twist people's words and make them say things they don't even mean. Well, that won't work with us."

In the tick of a clock, he was irate – thumping his chest and shouting so loudly that it nearly deafened me. The louder he got, the more I thought, *Perhaps he really did snap and kill Geraldine!*

167

CHAPTER TWENTY-FIVE

"My grandson has a fine mind," was Grandfather's only response at first. I was too busy worrying that James Joseph was the killer to be offended. "And as for twisting people's words, I don't know exactly what it says about me in the books because I have never managed to read a whole one, but I would not use false evidence to convict someone."

Grandfather rarely looks at me in the middle of an interview, especially when the suspect is trying to turn the tables, but he did at this moment. We both knew what it meant. Perhaps the darkest secret he'd ever shared with me was about the time his own morals had been compromised, and it had haunted him ever since.

"I mean it sincerely when I say that I am not here to trick you into admitting something you haven't done, but an innocent woman whom you both knew has been murdered. Geraldine de la Forge didn't deserve to be stabbed to death in her compartment, and it certainly isn't right that the killer took a knife and cut a piece—"

"Please, no more!" Mrs Campbell suddenly shrieked.

So then I started to wonder, *Actually, was it her? Did she kill the woman she so adored and then cut off her skin as a memento?* And then I felt a bit sick, because that is an awfully dark scenario.

"I can't bear it. My nerves are not what they should be and..." She reached one hand out to take her husband's and pulled him a little closer to her. With his support, she seemed to find the strength she needed to continue. "I will answer your questions, but there are some things we simply can't tell you. I think it might kill me if I did."

James Joseph peered down at her with such tenderness that I felt a small pang of something approaching jealousy for the love they had.

"Very well, start by telling me about your first meeting with Geraldine. How did your paths initially cross?"

Another glance was exchanged as they silently decided who should answer the question. It came as no surprise that it would be Sharlene who finally spoke.

"I love her films," she said, and I was reminded of her apparently nonsensical rambling when we'd last been in their compartment. "I mean that I truly found her to be the most wonderful person who ever graced the silver screen." She spoke with all the enthusiasm of a child with a new passion for ponies. "Every character she played spoke deeply to me, and I found myself living my life as if I were Charlotte in *A Heart in Two Pieces.*"

"And she means that quite literally," James Joseph explained with an awkward smile.

I must say that they were unusual people. One moment, he sounded as though he wanted to kill us both and toss our bodies from the train for them to be eaten by passing… well, you get the idea. And the next he was cheery and polite. I suppose that the famous good manners of the Deep South that I'd read about in novels could explain such inconsistencies.

"I found myself intoxicated by the idea of what the real Geraldine's life must have been like. I longed to stroll through the streets of Rome or take an omnibus around London's beautiful squares. I dreamed of escaping the hum-drum reality of our existence."

This time, her husband just looked uncomfortable, and he rubbed his right shoe back and forth across the carpet beneath him.

"I don't think it's indiscreet to say that I had a real case of the doldrums. It was my dear James Joseph who landed upon the solution. Bless this man, for he truly is the greatest I have known." She reached across to place her free hand on top of his, and he cradled it for a moment. "He suggested that we turn our backs on Savannah, as much as we loved it, and move to Europe to save my spirits."

"If you had seen my Sharlene, you'd understand why I would suggest such a drastic course of action."

Grandfather adopted a sympathetic mien. "I do understand. Honestly, I truly see why you would have placed such importance on an actress. I believe that it makes us human to appreciate great artistic endeavours as we do. I have felt similarly enamoured of certain operas, novels and even paintings."

Had he been saying these exact words to me, a certain tone would have made it clear that films could not compare with the forms of art which he had mentioned. I wanted to believe that he had undergone a change of heart, but I thought it more likely that he was doing exactly what they'd previously suggested by lulling them into a false sense of security. That wily pup!

"Thank you, Lord Edgington. Thank you so much." She pulled her hand away to hold it to her chest, and I thought, *You poor thing! Keep your guard up!* "Perhaps it won't surprise you to hear that Geraldine wasn't the only brilliant Briton for whom I hold feelings of intense respect."

She was talking about him, of course. She had described herself as a 'fanatic' when we'd met her at the station, and she'd proved as much since.

"Anyway, we moved here to Europe," her husband said to help things along. "We came to live the life that my Sharlene had always wanted."

"That's right." She stared at the window as if she were watching a cinema screen showing her arrival on the Continent. "We came… *to Europe!* And oh, it was everything I dreamed it would be. If there is anywhere on earth like London, I certainly haven't found it. I walked in the footsteps of the great Lord Edgington…" She had to pause then as she was blushing so much. "I took tea with duchesses and attended the opera at Covent Garden."

"I enjoyed a round or two of golf, would you believe it?" James Joseph put in, which caused Sharlene to tut and reassert control over her story.

"The one thing missing was my dear Geraldine, and so we decided to move to the Italian capital, where she was making her last film."

"*Echoes of the Ocean*," I said, because I hadn't uttered a word since we got there, and I was still annoyed that he'd called me dim-witted. "I haven't had a chance to see it yet."

"Oh, you must! You really must. I can't say it's her finest work, but she imbued every character she ever played with such—" She stopped herself then as the words were cracked and fragile. "Please excuse me. I'm still getting used to the idea that Geraldine is dead. I just want to say that she was the finest actress of our generation, and when the dream of meeting her became a reality, I—"

Grandfather interrupted her this time. "And how did that chance come before you? If I may ask."

"We contacted her manager," Campbell explained. "I mean, her former manager. She let him go some weeks past. I can't tell you why."

"That's right." Whereas her husband had sounded a little stern and reflective, Sharlene continued with the same jubilant expressiveness with which she did most things. "We contacted Mr Mulgavaney, who subsequently helped us to speak to Geraldine's director, Hansel."

It did not go unnoticed that she referred to the German by his Christian name.

"He was most accommodating. All we had to do was to help him with his new film…"

"And the money for the premiere," James Joseph added.

"…and it gave us the opportunity to spend as much time as we wished with my beloved Geraldine." She was clearly still in awe of the fact that she had flown so close to her heroine. "We visited her in Rome, and then she came to stay with us for a weekend at the villa we were renting. We became firm friends, didn't we, James Joseph?"

"Yes, my darling." He was apparently now happy to contradict his previous position that they had hardly known the victim.

"We were like sisters! Oh, it was wonderful. Sometimes we would sit and talk for hours. We used to go out to dinner together with our gentlemen, though Mr Denkin was always too busy to stay long, and he had to fly often to London, of course."

There was an underlying story emerging that it was impossible for Sharlene to express directly, but it occasionally peeped out from behind her gushing enthusiasm.

"If Geraldine wasn't in the mood to spend time with us, dear Hansel would talk to her, and she would be as bright as sunshine again."

"For how long exactly did this continue?" I asked, trying to put the pieces together.

"I'd say around a month," he replied before his wife inevitably continued.

"And it was one of the happiest months of my life." She sighed almost ecstatically, and the idea I had formed that she was alarmingly innocent in her view of the world was only reinforced. Even then, a frown was about to cross her features as the story took a turn. "It wasn't her fault that things couldn't go on as they had been. I can't say what caused it, but Geraldine began to leave her apartment less. She barely set foot outside when she wasn't required to work. And I don't mind admitting that, when we did go to see her at the studio, she said some things which I found quite cruel."

"My Sharlene is a trusting woman," James Joseph decided we needed to know. "She wasn't made for that world, and I think Geraldine treated her unfairly."

"So let me be clear." Grandfather tapped his cane on the floor a few times before clarifying. "You paid two powerful men to gain access to a young woman whom you admired. You felt close to her – like sisters even – and the money you provided ensured that you could see her even when she wasn't eager to meet. Judging by the timeline you've suggested, when events in her personal life took a turn for the worse, she attempted to cut ties altogether. When you objected, she revealed what she really thought of you."

He had told the exact same story as Sharlene but judged the events from a particularly negative perspective. Cynicism is a skill which comes in handy for a detective and which, so far, I still lack.

"You've summed it up even better than I could." Such was Sharlene's naïveté, she did not realise what he had done. "After all I did for her, she tossed me out like a piece of garbage! I always treat others as they deserve to be treated, but such concepts are foreign to some."

James Joseph raised his hand to explain to his wife what she had failed to understand, but he had second thoughts and left it to my grandfather.

"I beg your pardon, madam, but you've quite missed my meaning. I'm saying that the way you behaved towards Geraldine was callous, presumptuous and overbearing. You had no right to the woman's friendship at a time when she was experiencing great sorrow. You paid for her company, and it seems that nothing she did would have been enough for you."

Sharlene held her hand to her chest, but this time it was out of shock, not appreciation. "James Joseph, he's doing it again! Why must he insist on being so honest?"

Even her husband could see that my grandfather's appraisal of the situation was fair, and his response was tentative at best. "Now, now, Lord Edgington, perhaps you could say things in a slightly less direct manner."

"Direct?" He laughed at this and decided to push her even more. "I suppose in the time that you considered Geraldine your friend you came to trust her with your deepest secrets. Am I far from the truth?"

To typify the girlishness she had shown that day, Sharlene blushed again. "I may have let her into my confidence from time to time. You know how we ladies like to talk."

"And did you happen to share with her the information that Marvin Pelthorpe used to extort money from you?"

Her coy expression disappeared, and her husband looked quite amazed by what he'd heard.

"How did you… Yes, that's exactly what happened."

"Then I believe we have discovered everything we need to know for now." I could see that Grandfather was relieved that the interview had finally finished.

"Well, bless my soul!" However much she had suffered my grandfather's bluntness, Sharlene was now distracted by something more important. "That little witch must have betrayed me. I should have known it."

"But why would she do that to us?" James Joseph demanded as I opened the door for Grandfather to escape.

"Is that really all you can say?" He could take it no more and snapped. "How can two people be so entirely self-obsessed? Instead of thinking only of yourselves, perhaps you might consider whether her betrayal, as you call it, could explain her death."

"What in heaven's name do you mean?" Sharlene was unnerved once more.

"I mean that Geraldine was surely tired of being a pawn in an unpleasant game, so she told your secrets to the blackmailer to serve you right. Now, if you'll excuse me, I still have to determine which of you murdered her."

CHAPTER TWENTY-SIX

Although it felt good to leave their compartment, we were on a train and, as had recently been pointed out to us, didn't have anywhere to go.

"This is it, my boy!" Grandfather very nearly roared once the Campbell's door was firmly closed behind us. "We're finally getting somewhere."

I'm sure I don't have to tell you that he proceeded to stride up and down that corridor in celebration as the excitement of our discovery rushed through him.

"I have some questions, Grandfather," I said, not to dampen the mood, but to confirm that we were on the right path after all. "First, isn't it the case that Reinhardt and Geraldine started courting after the film premiere?"

"Yes."

"So if she were the one who told the Wolf everyone's secrets, why would she then have spent time with one of the people she had betrayed?"

"Because…" He looked out into the ink-black darkness. There wasn't even a star visible on that side of the train. Whatever landscape we were then passing was as much a mystery to me as the identity of the killer.

"Because, as we've already seen, Geraldine has spent her career being used and controlled by people. After Denkin left her for a younger woman, perhaps she felt she needed Reinhardt's companionship, or maybe he forced her into it just as he manipulated her into feigning friendship with the Campbells. Bear in mind that the men to whom we've spoken today have put their own needs far ahead of any more generous instincts like kindness, loyalty and friendship."

"Yes, Denkin and Reinhardt are two peas in a pod, at least in terms of their loose morals and the lack of care they showed the woman they both claimed to love. Campbell has at least exhibited great affection for his wife."

"Precisely. So I don't believe the timing of when Denkin left Geraldine and Reinhardt picked her up for a while are relevant to the question of whether she shared their secrets with Pelthorpe."

"I thought we were calling him the Wolf?"

"Well, you are." Grandfather looked even more conflicted than when I'd suggested there was a chink in his argument. "But I've decided it sounds too childish. This is not a fairytale. Miss de la Forge would have made a wonderful Little Red Riding Hood, and I suppose Mrs Campbell could just about play the grandmother, but I wouldn't cast any of the men here as a noble woodcutter."

"I suppose there is some logic in what you say." I tried to remember my other questions. "It now makes sense why none of the suspects admitted to knowing one another. They were all together that night at the party. They saw the Wolf (sorry, I'm sticking with the name) and were worried about what he had discovered on them. Even before we arrived in the waiting room, Hansel (sorry, I'm mixing my fairytales now) was worked up and anxious. He knew that Geraldine was supposed to take the train, and he took his anger out on the station porter because he realised that the whole thing was a risky endeavour."

Grandfather went back to his pacing. "And yet they all got on the train even then. They could have abandoned their plans, but they didn't." He thought for a few seconds longer before saying something important. "We must also consider why they bought tickets in the first place. Obviously they knew Geraldine would be here – they could have learnt that in the newspaper as we did. Denkin said he couldn't resist her. Reinhardt needed to convince her to return to his film, but why did the others choose to come?"

An insane idea occurred to me then, and rather than keep it to myself, I decided it deserved airing. "You don't think…" I hesitated, nonetheless. "I mean, is it really too preposterous that they were working together?"

"Go on."

"I mean, if they were all angry with her – Reinhardt, the count and the Campbells because she told the Wolf their secrets, and Denkin because she wouldn't take him back – perhaps they decided to club together for a common cause. Perhaps they thought that, by collaborating, they could kill Geraldine and make the circumstances so complicated that even you wouldn't be able to untangle them."

"Christopher Prentiss," he began, and I was thrilled to think that I might have struck on something clever, "that is quite literally the least plausible scenario I have ever heard. You're suggesting that a group of people with differing motives and backgrounds would conspire to kill their enemy in the confined confines of a train of all places? A single person could have done it far more easily once Geraldine was in Verona and he wouldn't have run the risk of his accomplices giving anything away."

"I suppose it is highly unlikely."

He adopted a softer tone. "Besides, you're forgetting Pelthorpe himself. Why would he kill her if she was his informant?"

I didn't have an answer to this, so I asked another question. "Why did you go to see Geraldine's maid before Denkin pulled the brake?"

He replied in a distracted voice. "I had the idea that Miss de la Forge was murdered for some valuable in her possession. There have been a string of thefts on trains since we came to Europe. Don't forget that a lady was robbed of her jewels when we travelled from Calais to Florence. Well, my theory came to nought, as the maid told me that her mistress charged her with all of her valuables. So if that were the killer's motivation, he murdered the wrong woman."

"Did you ask Milly whether her mistress had any sentimental items with her when she died?"

"She says that, except for clothes and toiletries, the only things that the dead woman had in her compartment were her travelling papers and identification."

My brain whirred as I tried to make sense of all we had uncovered in the last hour, and the time continued to tick down. It was almost midnight. Taking in the time we had stopped, we'd be lucky if there was an hour left before we got to Florence.

"What else can we do, Grandfather? We'll be out of time before you know it." I was tempted to suggest that we go to the source of so much of the trouble we'd witnessed and talk to the Wolf himself, but he saw what I was thinking before I did.

"No, not Pelthorpe. He's the cleverest of the lot of them, and I'm not quite ready. There's still a man about whom we know nothing whatsoever. It may yet turn out that he is as innocent as our friend M. Laroche, but I'm rather keen on the idea that, after all we've done and every scrap of evidence we've brought to the surface, the mysterious Count Giovannelli could be the culprit."

177

CHAPTER TWENTY-SEVEN

It didn't surprise me one bit that the count was sitting in his compartment with a cigar in his mouth and a glass of red wine in his hand. He was the kind of man who could be sent to prison at the top of a cold, draughty tower and still find any number of luxuries about his cell.

"Gentlemen," he murmured through the smoke as we entered, "I feel this is the moment of talking."

He had a strong Italian accent, but he spoke slowly and clearly. I could tell from the way he phrased this, however, that he was translating directly from his own language. Many Europeans I'd met had apologised for not speaking better English, but not the count. He reminded me of Eddie Denkin in the way he sat so proudly in his chair and smiled throughout.

He was a handsome man. His hair was silvery grey, but his eyebrows retained their dark colouring. It gave him a somewhat devilish aspect, though he lacked the Wolf's hungry glare.

The bed in the compartment had not been pulled out from the wall, and so I decided to sit down on the sofa as Grandfather clearly didn't wish to lower himself to our suspect's level. Instead, he stood beside the table, making full use of his impressive height to loom over the man as he asked the first question.

"Who are you, Giovannelli?"

It was a simple enough point to answer, but the count raised the cigar in his hand as if to say, *I have wondered that very thing myself.*

"I know you knew Miss de la Forge, and you obviously took this train to be close to her, like seemingly every other passenger in this carriage."

I decided not to remind him of the Frenchman, who he continued to insist was there on business. However, now that I came to think of M. Laroche, what were the chances that only one person there would be unconnected to the dead actress? Perhaps the wine merchant in compartment number two was the real mastermind behind what had occurred. Perhaps he had been the conduit between Geraldine and the Wolf. Perhaps... actually, he'd hardly been out of his room, so probably not.

"I do not deny I know a beautiful woman. Never do I do this." He took a sip from his bulbous wineglass. It was far bigger than the standard glasses we'd used on the train, which suggested that he'd brought his own. This also told me that he was just as odd a chap as he seemed.

"So who are you?" Grandfather demanded once more, and the count sighed a world-weary sigh.

"My story is a long one. I have been many people and done so many things." He shook his head a little as though to communicate that he himself couldn't believe the diversity of his experiences. "I have been a soldier, a teacher, a maestro and a pupil. But most of all, me, I am a romantic."

Grandfather did not look impressed by any of this. "Is that a well-paid job?"

"Huh! I think nothing of money. I live my life for the thrill of existence."

I'm surprised that his questioner didn't roll his eyes at this point, which isn't to say he hid his feelings in any way. "That is a luxury of those born to great wealth. I know that I, too, fall into that advantageous category, but I have never taken it for granted. I joined the Metropolitan Police to show my parents that I could plough my furrow without touching their money."

The count tipped his head back and pursed his lips quizzically. "And what good did that bring you? You were happier? The women they love you more?"

I was torn between wanting to laugh at this strangely self-contented man and finding him a mite frightening. I couldn't remember another person who was so confident of his world-view.

Grandfather was happy to butt heads. "If you'd really like to know, it gave me a sense of worth that I don't believe someone with your priorities could appreciate. Too many people spend their lives questioning how they can get the most from the world when our fundamental aim as human beings should be to ask, how can I make this world a better place?"

The count waved his cigar around once more so that it gave off a neat circle of smoke, which soon disappeared. "Pah! You think that attitude is kind. You think you are…" He searched for his words in

Italian for a moment. "...*come Gesù... benefico...* You think you are *altruist!* But the good you do, it is selfish." He had become frustrated at not being able to express himself better, but then his words started to flow. "You can feel superior to wicked devils like me. You enjoy the adoration that the people they give you, just as I enjoy fine wine and caviar."

"Wonderful. Now we've established that I'm just as bad as you are, can you tell me why you're wicked?"

The count was greatly enjoying himself and took the time to appreciate his libation once more. "As I have told you, I have done so many things in my life. I am good and bad and everything in between."

Tired of the man's evasive answers, Grandfather moved away from the table to lean against the door as I had so many times that day. "Fine. Let's start again. What was your interest in Miss de la Forge?"

Giovannelli laughed this time. "I think you know the answer to your question. She was a beautiful woman. One of the most beautiful I have encountered in my life, and I have met many, many such specimens."

I have to say that he was living up to the cliché of the Latin lothario that actors like the departed Rudolph Valentino had done so much to popularise in the cinema. So it came as something of a surprise to hear what he said next... "In all my days, I have only met two women who are worthy of me. Two I did bless with my touch. The first is when I was a young boy growing up on my family estate in Tivoli. She was just a servant girl, but I loved her with every part of me."

"And the second was Geraldine de la Forge," Grandfather rightly guessed and drew a nod from the count.

"I see her films and travel to Roma to be near her. I achieve much in my life, but she would be my great triumph. The *Santo Graal* I have spent so long searching."

Even I, with my limited Italian and second-rate brain, could work out that he was referring to the Holy Grail.

"What did you do to win the woman you considered so far above all others?" I asked, slightly afraid of what the answer might be.

The count tapped the end of his cigar against the ashtray on the table and then left it there to smoulder. He gestured about with his empty hand as he spoke. "The first thing I did," he said, raising one finger, "was to commission a work of her in bronze by the great Italian sculptor Arturo Martini. It was based on a particular scene in Geraldine's finest film, *Love's Lonely Flame*. It showed her clutching her breast in anguish as her lover drowns before her eyes."

I couldn't imagine why anyone would want such a sculpture of herself and felt I had to ask, "Did you consider inviting her out to dinner instead?"

"Oh, he is humorous this boy. He plays the idiot to perfection!" He smiled affectionately, but I can't say I enjoyed his compliment. "But I could do nothing so simple to win my Geraldine." He was the third man that night to have claimed possession of the dead actress. "I shower her with jewels and gold, yes. I pay for the visit to *il Colosseo* for just us two, yes. But I believe that the way to a woman's heart – the best way to show the intensity of the fire which burns – is not through dinner in a restaurant. I sent that sculpture to her apartment in Roma without revealing who I was. Then I wait one whole month before knocking on her door and presenting myself."

He barely paused between sentences and, now that he had started his tale, moved the story along at a good pace. "I tell her that day. I say, 'I will marry you, Geraldine. I make this promise'."

"And how did she feel about that?" The low rumble of Grandfather's voice made it clear that he considered the count's approach to be vain and foolhardy.

Giovannelli didn't look too concerned. "I knew it would take time to win her. I visit every day, send more jewellery, send cars. I tell her that I will place her sculpture in the middle of the courtyard of my estate. I tell her that I will make her my countess and give her everything that she wishes to possess. I have opened my heart to her."

"And did you, by any chance, reveal your darkest secrets to convince her of your sincerity?"

He shot back in his chair, and his eyes immediately grew wider. "How do you know this, Lord Edgington? This is exactly what happened."

"Did not you worry," I was starting to sound like him, "that she was supposed to be in love with Eddie Denkin? Or that you were at least twenty years older than her?"

This was a kind estimate; there might well have been thirty years between them.

"Pah! That man Denkin! He had no love for my Geraldine. He kept her with him for the newspapers. He may even have liked her for her beauty. But he did not love *her*. If that were true, he would not go to this other woman – this *Americana* he sees in London."

I waited for Grandfather's reaction to this statement. A ripple of emotion travelled across his visage, and I knew that he had extracted something important. "You were the one who told her, weren't you? You paid some grimy fellow in London to follow Denkin around, and then you informed his sweetheart of his indiscretion."

"Not at all. I did not tell Geraldine a thing." The count looked indignant, and I wondered if we'd misjudged him. "I told the newspapers, and she read about it, but I said not one word to her directly. And for a short time afterwards, I believed I'd convinced her that she would be better off leaving Roma and the vermin who surround her and coming to live with me in the countryside."

"So what went wrong?" My voice came out in a whisper. I was far more intrigued by his curious narrative than I should have been.

"I cannot say. We walked beside the river Tevere. The moon was bright. The stars, they shine for us alone, and I looked into her soul and kissed her with great passion." I believe that he was already so nostalgic for that moment that his eyes began to glisten. "And then she pushed me away. I was not expecting it, and I fall to the ground. I looked up to see the fury in her eyes. I could tell that she was not simply upset, but that she hates me. My countryman, the great actor Rodolfo Pietro Filiberto Raffaello Guglielmi di Valentina d'Antonguella – you know him as Rudolph Valentino – once said, 'The women I love don't love me. The others don't matter.' And as far as I am concerned, no one else matters but her."

"And yet you've shown little distress at her passing," Grandfather observed, causing the man to raise his voice in disagreement for the first time.

"Externally, that is true. But inside me, that inferno it burns. No… I search for my words… It rages!"

"When did all of this happen? When did she reject you?" I was still trying to construct the chronology of events that had led to everyone boarding that train.

"Reject is such a nasty word. I never gave up believing that she can love me. I told her that I would give her half my worldly wealth if she would have me."

"You didn't answer the question."

He bowed his head in concession. "This is true. I apologise. The night we walked beside the river was just a few days before the party beside *il Colosseo* to celebrate her exquisite final film. She refused to see me all week, but I knew that we would be together again that night."

"And how did she treat you at the party?" Grandfather put one hand against the door to steady himself as the train jerked about.

"She was… not happy. She avoided me, even as I tried to plead with her to reconsider my offer."

"So you tried to buy her, and it turned out she wasn't for sale."

"You are a cynic, Lord Edgington. You know not what true love means. You see, I bought the ticket for this train as I know that Geraldine and I we will be alone together. I don't realise that every other person will have the same idea."

"How did you know she'd be on the train?"

"She sends me a telegram. She said she was sorry for all. That she knew I possessed good intentions and that she just need time alone to think. This is why she buys her house in Verona. I thought that, if I could talk to her away from the pressure of her ordinary life, we could find the connection that would unite us."

He spoke quite sincerely, but it occurred to me that his approach to women was similar to my grandfather's attitude towards luxurious cars. He simply had to possess the very best example going.

"Did you consider the possibility that she was not the one who wrote the telegram?"

The count swirled his wine around in his glass and shrugged. "I did not, but I do now."

"I see." There was a finality to the way Grandfather spoke these words. "In which case, I believe that you have given us the information we need. I must thank you for your apparent honesty. Truly, it is refreshing, and bearing that in mind, I have one last question for you." He pushed himself back off the wall and stood as straight as a rod. "We know about the man who blackmailed you and several of your fellow passengers. It does not surprise me that you did not come forward to tell me about him or your connection to Miss de la Forge, but I would like to know what it was that you paid to keep secret."

The count smiled again, but it was not quite so cheerful this time. There was a certain apprehension hiding behind it. "And why would I tell you this thing that cost me so much to hide?"

"You'll tell me for Geraldine's sake. You say you love her, then prove it. Tell me what I need to know, and I promise I will find her killer."

He hesitated for approximately five seconds. "And you will reveal it to no one outside this room."

"Of course, I won't." Grandfather moved a half step closer. "I'm not here for you."

"Very well." The count thought a little longer before nodding. "I mentioned the servant girl whom I loved when I was a boy. Well..." He beckoned my grandfather to approach, and I watched his lips moving as he whispered in his ear. I could hear nothing above the sound of the train. "You must believe me, Lord Edgington, I was in no way responsible, but if such rumours circulate, my life as it is will be over."

Grandfather straightened up but still looked perturbed. I was uncertain at first whether he was shaken by what he'd heard. "I understand, Count Giovannelli, and you must not fear that anyone will hear it from us."

I thought he might thank the man, or even shake his hand, but he just bowed, and I followed him from the compartment. Back in the corridor, I imagined that he would need some time to make sense of all we had heard, but I couldn't have been more wrong.

He tore along the passageway peering this way and that, evidently looking for one particular compartment before giving in and asking me. "Pelthorpe, where is he?"

I pointed to the door he'd just passed, and he hurried back towards me and grabbed the door handle without knocking. Luckily for us, it was unlocked.

"Tell us what you know about the count!" he barked at the man, who was standing at the window, smoking a cigarette.

The Wolf's bed had been pulled out from the wall, and the sheets were a mess. In the short time he'd been in there, he'd emptied the clothes from his suitcase all over the floor, and there was a pile of papers strewn across the small table. Even the shiny wooden panels that made up the walls looked a little dingier than in the other compartments we had entered.

"Why would I tell you anything?" the blackmailer replied ever-so-slowly, as though he took no small pleasure in making us wait.

"I'm not talking about the part you played in everything. I'm merely asking about Count Giovannelli. Tell us what you know about him."

"I repeat my previous question," he said, then made a meal of clearing his throat as the smoke from his cigarette curled around his lungs. "Why would I have any desire to help the likes of you?"

Grandfather conjured up an answer in the time it takes to say *Betty Botter bought some butter*. "Because if you didn't kill the woman in the room down the corridor from here, I imagine that you'll want to help me find the person who did, if only to protect yourself."

The Wolf showed his fangs as he considered this proposition. I found him a despicable character. I'd thought it when I first saw him, and he'd done nothing to change my opinion since, but he knew what was in his best interests.

"Ask your damned question."

It was Grandfather this time who paused before speaking. "I will come back before long to talk to you, but for now all I need you to confirm is what the count just told us. He said that, when he was a boy, he got a girl pregnant and she drowned herself. People in their village claimed that he was responsible, and so his wealthy father paid to hush it up. Did he tell you the same tale? And don't try denying that you know him because we're far past that point."

It seemed that he had already gone back on the promise he'd made a few minutes earlier, but then if this wasn't the reason the count was being blackmailed, he had lied to us and the deal was void.

The very fact that the Wolf showed so little surprise at the tale seemed to confirm its authenticity, but he still wouldn't admit it. "If I were to tell you…"

"Come along, man! I know exactly what you are. I know what you've done. Think about what will happen if I don't find the killer.

Even if you didn't do it, if you fail to help me now, I will make it my mission in life to see you prosecuted for your crimes. So tell me what you know."

The Wolf pulled down the large window to throw the end of his cigarette outside. As he did so, an unceasing gust of wind surged into the compartment, and the sound of the train screaming through a tunnel became louder.

"Now, now." He raised his hands to show that he was complying. "There's no need to talk like that." He needed a few more heavy breaths before he could say anything more. "Fine, that is what I heard about him."

Grandfather was backing towards the door before the sentence was complete. "And Geraldine was the one who told you. That's all I need to hear for now."

Something in what Grandfather had said made more of an impact on the suspect than either of us could have predicted. I'm not sure that my mentor noticed, but I did. When I left the room and closed the door behind me, the Wolf looked terrified.

187

CHAPTER TWENTY-EIGHT

"Will you tell me what you're thinking?" It had been some time since I'd felt so entirely lost on one of our cases. He was clearly some way ahead of me, and I wanted to feel that I was at least being dragged along on his coat-tails if nothing else.

Grandfather stood with his back to the window in the corridor. The floor beneath us creaked as the train cut through the darkness and we slowed to approach a bend.

"Why did you think it so important to ask him that one question?" I tried again when he didn't answer.

"To see whether Count Giovannelli was telling the truth of course. I had a strong conviction that he was. Whatever I might think of his treatment of Miss de la Forge, he certainly came across as honest."

I found this prospect puzzling. "Do you mean to say you were testing your own ability to spot a liar?"

"That's just it." He would clearly have preferred to reflect on the case than answer my questions, but he kept on all the same. "Every single one of our suspects has a reason to lie. With the exception of the count himself, each has attempted to evade questioning, and I was beginning to fear that my ability to spot the truth had faded."

"Well, excellent," I said, clapping my hands together in the hope I might encourage him. "And now that's been resolved, do we need to work out the other suspects' secrets? What do you think it was that the Campbells simply couldn't tell you?"

"I'd rather not speculate."

"You mean that it would be better to find out for certain?"

He turned back along the corridor. "No, I don't believe it's relevant. Whatever happened, I got the definite impression that it is buried in Sharlene's past. There does not appear to be a significant link between the Campbells' life in America and their time here. So we must concentrate on determining which of our suspects is the killer, instead of trying to fill in every insignificant gap. As it is, we have very little time left to achieve that."

He stopped in front of Geraldine's door and held his hand out without touching it. This suspension only lasted for a few seconds, but it spoke to the complexity of the case before us that he could be so frustrated – so deeply disconcerted by the puzzle we had to solve – that his usual ingrained confidence could have taken such a dent.

"Do you really want to go in there again?" I asked to offer him a way out.

"'Want' is a strong word, Christopher." And with that, he pushed the sliding door open, and I followed him inside.

I could have asked what we'd gone in there to find, but I decided against it. The notes were still where we'd left them. There were still traces of blood on the ceramic sink, which was partially hidden behind the cabinet doors, and Geraldine de la Forge was still very much dead. In the half moment before I stepped inside, I'm sure that some little voice in my brain said a silent prayer that she would not be, but there was no changing the past.

I rarely revisit corpses if I can help it – in fact, seeing them once isn't much fun. There's something even more final about the second time, though, and the sight of the lifeless film star that I had admired for so long sent a chill through me that was hard to bear.

If for no other reason than to be distracted from this sensation, I occupied myself looking for whatever there was to find. I found a silver cigarette case with the inscription, *From E.D. With all my love,* which was a lie if ever I'd heard one. There was a paperback of a Margery Allingham novel that I hadn't read. Sticking out from the edge was a half-written postcard with a photograph of the Pantheon. It was addressed to *Mum and Dad,* and said, *Rome really is a wonderful place. I know you'd just love it here.* But it broke off there as if Geraldine didn't know what else to say to convince her parents that everything in her life was just fine.

"The maid said that this is where we would find Miss de la Forge's papers," Grandfather inevitably explained, as I hadn't asked. "That's mainly why I came in here, but anything interesting that you find is worth mentioning."

I handed him the postcard, just in case, but he had a similar reaction to mine and put it back in the book for the police to inspect whenever we alighted in Florence. Instead of continuing to search without any thought, I stopped and looked around me. Sure enough, there was a small corner cabinet as you entered the room. The top drawer held some leaflets for the sights of the Italian capital and a train ticket from Calais to Rome, so Geraldine had recently taken the same journey we had a few months earlier. It was dated the twenty-fifth of August, so I could only assume she'd been to visit Denkin at around the time all the trouble between them started. The drawer below held the ticket for our train to Verona, and alongside it was her passport.

I held it above my head for Grandfather to take it from me as I continued rummaging. I shouldn't have bothered, as there was nothing more to find.

"Wonderful, my boy. This is the very thing." He tapped it on the palm of his hand and went over to the table to open it.

I gave up my search and joined him as he leafed through the pages. There were stamps from airports all over Italy, not to mention trips to London, a voyage to Morocco, and several stops in France. But that wasn't what seemed to interest my grandfather. He kept turning the pages at that same steady pace until he came to Geraldine's likeness, nationality and what have you.

"There we are then," he said in a rather relaxed manner, though personally I thought such a revelation deserved the dramatic tone of voice reserved for the end of important scenes in the theatre. "Her real name was Jemima Moorbank. As we said when we first came in here, very little about her was real."

As I looked at the photograph that showed a young Geraldine with her natural dark hair colour and a rather nervous expression on her face, I struggled to understand what he expected me to make of it. I thought perhaps she was passing herself off under a false identity but soon realised my mistake.

"It's quite common for actors to use a stage name, isn't it?" I said for my sake more than his.

"It is indeed, and we can't read too much into her decision to transform herself from plain Jemima Moorbank into the fabulous Geraldine de la Forge. I just wondered…" He bit his lip then and moved the passport into the light of the small, beaded table lamp. "Well, I half hoped that, as she'd chosen a French name, she had a European connection, but that doesn't seem to be the case."

He closed the document and went to return it to the drawer where I'd found it. I stayed where I was and looked at poor Jemima

Moorbank. We had spoken to all the people who were closest to her in Italy, and yet none of them appeared to know who she really was. It broke my heart to think of how she had been used by them and, as my grandfather cleared his throat to get my attention, I made a quiet commitment under my breath to remember the real person she had been and not just the star that her so-called fans, manager and director had forced her to become.

CHAPTER TWENTY-NINE

"Wait just one moment," I said when I felt I could speak more loudly again. "The European name you imagined: did you entertain the idea that our ignorant bystander, who just happened to book a compartment in the wrong carriage this weekend, could be involved in the murder?"

Grandfather decided to play the innocent – it was less skilful than my playing the idiot that the count had so celebrated. I could see right through him. "Christopher, I really don't know what you mean."

"You know just what I mean, you sneak. I'm talking about the Frenchman in compartment number two." He'd been so inconsequential that I'd almost forgotten his name. "M. Gerard Laroche, who you told me was categorically unconnected to any of this. You reconsidered his involvement, didn't you?"

"A fixed mind is never an asset, Christopher. Surely you know that." The old hound could get out of a sack tied with chains and sealed shut with bitumen. "And I will admit that the similarity between the names Gerard and Geraldine forced me to entertain the idea that she was his daughter. Now…" He pulled his pocket watch from his… well, his pocket, obviously. "It will be one o'clock before we know it. I just hope the driver is in no hurry to reach our first stop. We still have to talk to Reinhardt and Denkin."

He was surprisingly serene all of a sudden. Had he chanced upon a piece of evidence that I hadn't seen? Had he solved the case while I wasn't looking? It was very hard to say, but he strolled along that corridor with something of a spring in his step.

"Yes, my boy. Time is certainly ticking, so we'll have to find a way to speed things up." He stood in front of the Wolf's door and looked first one way along the passage and then the other. "In the circumstances, I think this might require me to employ my very best acting skills. Are you ready for what comes next?"

"I'm both excited and nervous about whatever you're going to do," I told him quite honestly.

"I'll take that as a yes."

He put his hand out to open the door before realising his mistake.

"Actually, which one belongs to Hansel Reinhardt? I really should have been paying more attention."

I directed him back along the corridor, and he nodded his thanks and walked brusquely into the director's compartment. "Come along, you fiend," he said in a fierce and forceful tone. "We know what you did, and we know why you did it."

Reinhardt was lying in his presumably self-made bed with a book in his hand that he very nearly launched into the air in fright. "What do you…? How could you…? You've got it all wrong."

"That's not what we heard from Eddie Denkin in compartment number six."

"Five," I corrected him, but he continued his act.

"He's been there the whole time, and he heard everything. That's why he came in here and attacked you. You're lucky you fell to the floor, and he had a change of heart, as he wanted to kill you for what you did to Geraldine."

Self-consciously or perhaps subconsciously, Reinhardt raised his hand to his bloodied head, which had been wrapped in gauze by the steward. "He was wrong, and so are you."

"Really, man, are you going to try that on me? We know about the blackmail. My grandson here can confirm everything I'm telling you."

He pointed to me then, but I wasn't expecting it. I've never been much of an actor. My tongue got all twisted and, whilst trying to sound both confident and intimidating, I muttered, "Yes… exactly. What he said!"

Luckily, Reinhardt was so scared of the former police superintendent, who now cast a shadow across his bed, that he didn't seem to notice my impression of a nervous seal.

"Stop making up stories and admit what happened!" Grandfather crossed his arms tetchily, and his silver cane glinted in the light.

Reinhardt glanced back and forth between us and, when he finally spoke, his voice was strained. "I have made mistakes in my life. I admit that. But I'm no killer. I promise that I'm no killer." He gripped the hair at the side of his head so hard that it hurt his wound, and he had to stop.

"Prove it," Grandfather said, which was only going to incite more panic.

"How can I prove it?" His voice had become breathy and desperate. "How can I possibly prove that I didn't murder a person when I was alone in my room around the time she was killed?"

"That's not what Denkin heard, is it, Christopher?"

This time, I decided that the best possible strategy was to stay silent but appear moody. I made my eyebrows waggle a bit and probably looked quite deranged.

"He says that he heard Geraldine utter your name shortly before she died."

Reinhardt dropped his hands to his lap pathetically, and I thought he was about to cry. "But… but that can't be. Or if she did say it, then she was talking *about* me, not *to* me."

"That sounds highly unlikely." Grandfather took a step back to allow this possibility to settle in his mind. "We'll talk to Denkin again to find out exactly how she said your name. In the meantime, you must think carefully about whether to continue down this path or confess at last."

Grandfather traumatised the man for just a little while longer with that piercing stare of his before striding from the compartment. I almost felt sorry for the German and would normally have tried to reassure him that everything would be fine, but I was fairly certain my grandfather wouldn't have wanted that.

"What *are* you doing?" I had to ask when we were alone in the corridor for perhaps the three hundredth time that night.

"What do you think I'm doing? I've returned to the suspect that everyone believed was responsible for the murder, and I'm applying pressure to see whether his story holds. I may have told some half-truths, but I feel that, were he to confess, it would be a fair result. We'll leave him for five minutes and by the time we return, he'll be so afraid of what we've learnt that he'll buckle."

"And this is a technique you've used before, is it?"

"Yes…" A slightly nervous expression came to his face for a few seconds. "…once."

"Did it work?"

"Well, it's hard to remember. It was an awfully long time ago."

My only real issue with this was that it didn't feel like something he would normally do. I must have frowned or perhaps looked gormless for too long, as he became defensive.

"Really, Christopher, you can be incredibly critical when the moment takes you."

I believe it was his own guilty conscience that forced this from him rather than anything I'd thought. Either way, he walked back to Eddie Denkin's compartment and knocked.

It occurred to me that, even though Denkin was just as likely a suspect as Reinhardt, and he'd concealed himself on the train, Grandfather did not treat the two men equally. Were we letting the actor off lightly even as we dragged his German rival over the coals?

"I need to know when you and Geraldine first met," Grandfather said without preliminaries.

Denkin had changed into a smoking jacket and looked very comfortable lying on his daybed surrounded by plump cushions. As soon as he saw us, his distinctive smile sprang to his lips, and he switched to his public mode.

"It's a pleasure to see you, too, my friends." That well-chiselled jaw of his jutted out as he smiled.

"I need to know when you first met Geraldine?" Grandfather sat in a cane chair at the small, round table by the window. It was the middle of the night, and I didn't blame him for taking the weight off his feet.

"We've known one another for ever. I had a minor role in her first film, and we never stopped palling around together after that. I knew she had something special about her right from the beginning, but neither of us could have imagined where we would end up."

His blithe expression did not change, so he either forgot that Geraldine had been stabbed to death, or he was so impressed by his own success that he could think of nothing else.

"Then what do you know about her life before she became an actress?"

This at least made Denkin swing his legs off the sofa and sit up. "You know, it's funny that you should ask that, as I never felt I knew the real Geraldine – and that wasn't even her name of course. She kept it a closely guarded secret, but she was really christened Jemima Moorbank."

"Yes, we know. We found her passport." This was my contribution to the discussion. I could now fade into the background.

"Well, she rarely let slip about her childhood or her home life. I know she moved around a lot, and she only saw her father intermittently. I believe her mother is still alive, too, but she never invited her folks to premieres, and there were no photographs of them in her house in London.

"Do you know what I think?" He leant closer to us then, perhaps to make us feel as if he were trusting us with some important information. "I've always thought that poor Jemima came from humble stock and didn't want anyone to know. I don't just mean working class. I mean climbing-out-of-a-slum-to-earn-a-crust-of-bread poor. The one person I can think of who may know more than me is her manager... or rather, the man who discovered her. Morris Mulgavaney was culled last month when Gerry got upset about the lengths he would go to obtain funding for her films."

He spoke as if all the terrible things that had piled up on top of the dead actress were minor inconveniences. From what I knew of her former manager, he had sold her as a commodity to the Campbells and presumably provided access to the amorous count as well. I think that was reason enough to look for a replacement.

"Don't misunderstand me," he hurried to explain. "He is a terrible person, but an excellent businessman, and he knows more about her than anyone."

"So you don't know where he discovered her?" Grandfather asked.

"I haven't the foggiest." Denkin reached for the jacket he'd previously been wearing, which was hanging on a hook beside him. He fished in one pocket for his cigarettes before presumably remembering that Grandfather preferred him not to smoke and putting them back again.

"Can you tell us anything more about her early life?" This question was almost a plea, and I could see how desperately my poor grandfather wanted to solve the case.

Denkin's smile finally faded. "I'm sorry, m'lord. I really can't. But don't worry. When we get to Verona, I'll put you in touch with Mulgavaney. He'll be able to tell you everything, just as long as you keep it quiet."

For a moment, I wondered whether it was not Geraldine who had shared our suspects' secrets with the Wolf but this Machiavellian impresario who had been pulling everyone's strings. Of course, the question of how she had crossed paths with the blackmailer still hadn't been answered. If Mulgavaney had used him to put pressure on Geraldine then perhaps... Half-formed ideas like this one kept popping in and out of my head, but none of them quite fitted.

Grandfather's chair shuddered across the carpet as he stood up, and he tipped the hat he had left back in his compartment to the film star. "Thank you, Mr Denkin. I appreciate your time."

He wandered calmly from the compartment and along the hall to Reinhardt's room once more. So it came as something of a shock to see his anger suddenly return.

"Denkin is perfectly confident on the matter," he yelled. "From the way Geraldine said your name, it was clear that you were there when she died. She wasn't referring to you as a third person. You were in the compartment with her, weren't you?"

Reinhardt had lost none of his fear in the time we were absent. "I've told you: I don't know anything about her death. What's more, I didn't hear her cry out." He waved one finger and seemed to think this was significant. "I mean, if she'd been killed before I left this carriage, I would surely have heard something."

"Yes, but you were the second to last person to enter the dining car at the time she was killed. We know that her maid left her room and twenty minutes later the steward found her dead. So there's no doubt about when she was murdered."

"But... but..." Reinhardt hopped out of bed to address the height imbalance. He was a tall man and could now look my grandfather in the eye, though his stripy pyjamas didn't do much to make him look tough. "You said it yourself. I was the second to last person to leave this carriage. So who was the last?"

Grandfather walked around the bed, presumably to give himself time to prepare his answer. "I believe you know that it was your blackmailer. And while I can't deny he's an unsavoury character, he showed what he thought of your mistreatment of the young lady even before we discovered her dead."

"No, you're wrong!" Reinhardt's hands were clasped tightly together, as if in supplication. "He did that because he knew she was dead. It's frankly ridiculous that you would consider anyone other than that criminal. The man is a reprobate. He took great pleasure in tormenting us over simple indiscretions that anyone could have committed."

The tables had now been turned, and it was hard to see how Grandfather would recover. Indeed, he did not immediately respond, and I hated to see him like that, so I said the first thing that entered my mind.

"I think you should look in the mirror before you criticise anyone else." This gave me time to think of something better to say. "You came pretty close to attacking Geraldine just minutes before she was murdered. The most obvious solution is not that a blackmailer suddenly decided to kill a woman for no clear reason, but that you were furious with her for abandoning your precious film. We know she was tired of your domineering influence. It's clear she was moving to Verona to escape from people like you."

"This is ridiculous. Geraldine was my muse. I might have applied some pressure to keep her working, but that's all in a director's job."

"You killed her, didn't you?" Grandfather tried for the last time that night.

Reinhardt was an expressive sort. He threw his hands in the air, and his face was bright red as he yelled, "I didn't touch her."

"You killed her because she'd had enough of you," I tried. "That's why she shared your secrets in the first place."

The level of his voice fell, but he still looked just as furious. "What is this... this *Blödsinn* that you speak." He was clearly so unnerved that he couldn't find his words in English and let out a long stream of German that was presumably very rude. "This nonsense! Why do you say these things?"

I remained calm as I explained something that he apparently hadn't deduced. "It was Geraldine who told Marvin Pelthorpe what you'd done."

"No... It's not possible. I refuse to believe that—" He broke off what he was saying and simply froze. He stayed like that for ten seconds before collapsing backwards against the wall.

"Tell us what she knew that could be so damaging to you," Grandfather demanded, and I could see that this was what the last ten minutes had been building towards. He'd wanted to break Hansel

Reinhardt in pieces, and he very nearly had.

When our suspect said nothing, I put my hand on Grandfather's arm to pull him gently away. "It's simple enough. We'll have to ask Pelthorpe what he knows."

Grandfather kept his eyes on Reinhardt as he nodded and moved away. The air in the room had turned cold, and it was not down to the cool breeze that came buffeting through the partially open window. The tension had chilled us all.

We left the compartment in silence, and there was something very mournful about our departure, until Grandfather closed the door softly behind us and gave a quiet laugh.

"Oh, that was perfect," he declared. "And you were wonderful, Christopher. It went just as I'd hoped. Now to finish this."

The Wolf's room was the next one along. We sauntered off to it, and it was only as Grandfather opened the door and stepped inside that his smile disappeared.

"Oh, for goodness' sake. Where has that mountebank gone?"

CHAPTER THIRTY

I followed him into the Wolf's compartment, fully expecting to find the wretched man in his W.C. but the doors were open and there was no one there.

"Christopher, the window." Grandfather pointed, and I stopped flapping about the place and took a deep breath.

"He may not have jumped," I said, willing this to be true. "He may be hiding somewhere."

The night air rushed about us, and Grandfather moved closer to the window to look through it. He stopped before he got there and turned back to me.

"He was facing a dark future." He pursed his lips, plainly upset by the idea that we had pushed a man to suicide. "He must have known that I would have had him arrested whether or not he was the killer."

"Don't be hard on yourself, Grandfather." I wouldn't allow him to think the worst. "He may still be on the train."

I left before he could convince me otherwise, running from the compartment and along the corridor in search of the steward.

"Master Christopher," Todd said when I went crashing straight into him. "What's the matter?"

"No time, Todd." I pushed past and arrived at the conductor's seat half out of breath from stress more than exertion. "Have you seen Mr Pelthorpe from compartment number six?"

Domenico looked as distressed as he had all evening but managed to produce a response. "I... No, Mr Prentiss. I do not see anyone since you pass here."

I spun on the spot as Todd caught up with me. "What's happened, Chrissy?"

There was no time to explain. I had to do something very stupid. I went to the external door and opened it a crack to make sure we weren't in a tunnel or passing by any signs before throwing it wide. The sound of the train's unceasing forward motion was deafening, and the contrast with the quiet carriage was so strong that I felt as if I had momentarily been transported to a different plane of existence.

There was a piece of metal over the steps which resembled the running plate on a car. I stepped onto it and leant around to get a view of the side of the train. This did little to help, so I swung myself back inside.

"Todd, you'll have to hold on to my arm for me to get a better view. He might still be out there."

Grandfather's ever-reliable factotum knew better than to ask unnecessary questions. He looped his right arm through a metal railing and held securely onto my left arm so that I could safely lean outside. Well, safety is a relative concept when engaged in such daredevilry. If I'd taken the time to consider what I was doing, I surely would have told myself not to be such a complete ass.

For right or wrong, I swung my body out into the pitch-black night. At first, I couldn't see anything but the glow of electric lights from the compartments that didn't have their curtains drawn. The first three were unilluminated, but just beneath Count Giovannelli's window I could make out a shape.

"Christopher," I thought I heard a voice call to me. It was presumably my imagination, as the train was too loud, but I could definitely see my grandfather's lips moving. He had stuck his head out of the Wolf's window and was trying to get my attention. He pointed down to the dark shape a compartment away from him and mouthed what I understood to be, "He's down there."

"What can you see, Master Christopher?" I could definitely hear this, as Todd was only just behind me.

"It's him. It's the Wolf." I couldn't remember whether I'd explained this nickname to him, but it wasn't the moment to worry about such things. "He's clinging to a small ledge at the bottom of the train. I think…" The train emerged from behind a long row of trees, and we were dowsed in moonlight. It was just strong enough to show me a route to the madman who had climbed out of his window. "Yes, I think I can get to him."

"Are you sure that's a good idea?"

I pretended not to hear him and took a tentative step onto the tiny ledge. It can't have been much more than half a foot wide, but there were places to grip with my hands higher up. The moment I moved clear of the doorway, a bush came up out of nowhere and nearly knocked me clean off the train.

Grandfather was waving his hands around like a drunken orchestra conductor until, all of a sudden, he wasn't. He pulled his head back inside, and I could concentrate on what I was doing.

My ears felt as though they were bleeding from the sound of the screeching, cranking, clattering wheels beneath me. The whistle of the train sounded, for whatever reason that normally happens, and I was about to pull my arm free from Todd when I saw a wooden post rear up at the side of the tracks and had to squash my body against the train to avoid it.

"Are you all right, Chrissy?" Todd demanded in a more insistent tone than before.

I hadn't noticed how heavily I was breathing until now. I was louder than the wheels. Louder than the wind in my ears or the trees we were whistling past. I couldn't speak, couldn't move. I clung on for my very life, but I could see the Wolf a few yards away, and I was fairly certain he could see me.

"Think what you're doing!" I called down to him, aware that my words were unlikely to get that far.

An understanding of just how narrow the ledge was came into focus in my mind, but it also gave me the awareness to be able to inch along it. I wanted to close my eyes and give into fate – or jump from the train and lie there in whatever state I might find myself. It was an almost peaceful sensation, but I couldn't let the Wolf die or potentially get away with murder, so I focused on my task. I was wondering how long it would take me to reach him at the rate of approximately three feet an hour when the window to Eddie Denkin's compartment lowered and two strong pairs of arms reached down to grab the idiot below.

"Thank goodness!" I literally yelled. "Pull me back, Todd. Pull me back!"

I felt like I'd travelled yards along the side of the carriage, but (humblingly, yet thankfully) I was still practically right by the door. I couldn't help thinking what a terrible irony it would be if I were to fall to my death trying to save a man who didn't deserve it in the first place and had already been rescued by someone else.

I'm very glad to say that didn't happen.

"What were you *thinking*?" Todd demanded. He rarely looked

surprised by our adventures, so I'd outdone myself on that score.

"What *were* you thinking?" Grandfather echoed as he appeared from around the sleeping compartments, and I braced myself against the reassuringly stable wall to breathe deeply.

"What was *I* thinking?" I replied with more than a hint of indignation. "I haven't the faintest idea!"

CHAPTER THIRTY-ONE

After a few seconds of Domenico leaning out of his little box to stare in sheer wonder at my stupidity, I found the composure I required to defend myself.

"I saw the Wolf out there, clinging to the side of the train and decided I would have to go out and convince him that he was making a mistake. It's the kind of thing that happens all the time in adventurous stories. I thought you'd approve, Todd."

My friend looked a little embarrassed for lending me the wrong kind of books, but his master was there to save him. "Don't blame anyone but yourself. If you'd fallen to your death, I would have had to explain to your mother that you were smashed to pieces at the side of an Italian railway because you'd got it into your head that you were the hero of an unrealistic novel."

This made me want to ask about the actual novels in which I featured and he'd never mentioned until that day, but he didn't let me say another word. "If you've finished your tomfoolery, it's time to talk to the man who caused all this trouble in the first place."

He turned to stomp off along the corridor.

"And if you think I was angry with my grandson just now," Grandfather was shouting at the Wolf as I got to Eddie Denkin's quarters, "then imagine how I feel about the man who caused him to do something so idiotic in the first place."

The windswept gentleman looked approximately as shaken as I still felt, though he now had to defend himself against various criminal allegations and I was at least spared that ordeal.

"Why would I care what you think?" The Wolf sounded more hard done by than when we'd last spoken to him.

"Were you going to kill yourself to get away from me?"

I should probably mention that Eddie Denkin was sitting enjoying this scene with a cigarette in his hand. He evidently believed it a safe assumption that Lord Edgington had too many other things on his mind to object – which showed how little he knew my grandfather.

"Please, Mr Denkin. I asked you to refrain from smoking."

The Wolf was crumpled up on the floor beside the window. He

looked like a pile of tatty old clothes that had been left for the rag and bone man to haul away.

"Suicide?" he finally responded. "Not likely, mate. I'm cleverer than that." He pointed at his head but offered no further evidence for his claim.

"So you were intending to hang from the side and jump off whenever the train slowed down?"

The Wolf clearly didn't want to admit that his exceptionally clever plan was actually quite obvious, so he huffed and turned away.

"We could arrive in Florence at any time now," Grandfather said, tossing the tails of his coat out so that he could walk in front of our suspect with a little more theatricality. "There's nothing to stop me telling the police that, while I haven't proved beyond any doubt who killed Geraldine de la Forge, I would not be surprised if the man with a criminal record going back at least to the Edwardian era – who was blackmailing several of the other suspects, including the dead woman – turned out to be the culprit."

He'd already looked disgruntled but now emitted a dissatisfied grunt. "Who says I was blackmailing Gerry?" I could have asked this myself, as it matched a thought I had formed then abandoned.

"So you don't deny the rest of the charges. How very interesting." Grandfather moved over to the sofa. Our most amused host Eddie Denkin had to shuffle along to make space, but they both looked comfortable there.

"You didn't answer my question. Who says that I was blackmailing Gerry?" Our suspect eyed Denkin as he spoke.

I saw what Grandfather wished to imply and did my best to support him. "How else could you have known enough about her associates to blackmail them if you weren't blackmailing her for the information?"

The Wolf sneered. "Oh, you're so clever."

"You can say what you like," my mentor continued with such serenity that the man before us no longer looked frightening to me, "but we're right, aren't we?"

Eddie Denkin clapped his hands in appreciation, whereas the Wolf just snarled.

"You discovered something that Geraldine wouldn't have wanted her public to know, and you came to Rome to use it against her. Was it her humble beginnings? I don't believe she'd ever disclosed anything of her past to the papers, and she is known for such refined roles that it wouldn't surprise me if she wished to forget the life she left behind."

"That's right, she was so ashamed of where she came from that all it took was a few words in her ear and she was mine to control. I'm sure you've heard what a wilting flower she was."

Grandfather wasn't put off by the cynicism that seeped out of the odious creature, and he rose to add to the allegations. "You forced her to give up her secrets, and when that wasn't enough, you booked a ticket on this train and sat in your compartment waiting for your chance to pounce. As soon as her maid had left and there was enough noise to cover her screams, you knocked on the door, presumably claiming to be an admirer in search of an autograph, and then you stabbed her when she turned to run from you."

There was something missing in what Grandfather was saying, and I think he knew it. It wasn't like him to present such a poorly sketched scenario to one of our suspects, so there had to be a reason.

"I would never do that!" the man practically exploded, spittle flying from his mouth as his eyes locked onto my grandfather's. As he shot up to his feet, he was just as enraged as we'd seen him when he'd confronted Reinhardt in the dining cart. "I would never have hurt her."

Grandfather didn't just stand his ground. He took a step closer to peer down his nose. "Why not?"

"Because he's her father," I said before anyone else could, and Eddie Denkin's jaw nearly fell off its hinge.

"No…" the actor whispered in disbelief. "No, he can't be. This is better than any film I've made." We all turned to stare at him, and he muttered a quiet apology. "I'm so sorry. Please continue." He pulled his legs up onto the sofa and waited for the remainder of the tale.

"N.M. must stand for Nigel or Nathan or Nicholas Moorbank," I said to offer at least a sliver of evidence. "The other suspects knew you as Marvin Pelthorpe, but you slipped a note under your daughter's door with your real initials on it because you believed she'd have to see you that way."

Mr Moorbank saw this as proof of his innocence. "That would be the note asking her to meet me at midnight, hours after I am supposed to have killed her."

"You're her father," Grandfather repeated my conclusion, but there wasn't a hint of astonishment in what he said. "I knew you cared deeply for Geraldine when you showed such anger towards Reinhardt in the dining car, even before we learnt that she was dead. When we found out her real name, it seemed we'd discovered the relationship between you. You are her father, and she contacted you when there was no one else left."

"That's right. I was her dad, and I've loved her since the day she was born. She couldn't love me back after all I'd done over the years, but she called me here and I came. I would have walked to the end of the earth and right off it if it meant we could spend one minute together, but after I managed to get a little revenge on the parasites who were leeching off her, she didn't want to see me any more."

This was the first time I realised that the Wolf really was human. His voice cracked for the briefest of moments. It was almost imperceptible, but I'm certain that I heard it. His head drooped, and even Eddie Denkin stopped smiling.

"What did you do with all their money?" he asked, which showed his priorities clearly enough.

"It wasn't about the money." The man of many names wasn't happy that we'd worked out his game and scrunched up his nose. "Gerry made me give everything away to some home for orphan kids or something. The fear I could instil in the people who'd hurt her was the reason she called me out here."

"So it's true," I said, realising that this fitted several of Grandfather's theories. "It's all true."

"I bought a ticket for this train because I thought I could be close to her one last time before I went home. I know I went about it in a terrible way – I should never have said what I did in that note, and I pray she didn't read it before she died – but all I wanted to do was sit in the bar with her and share a drink like when she was a nipper and I used to take her out to a Lyons' teashop every Saturday afternoon."

He directed this comment down at the floor, the emotion now plain in his voice. I can't say whether there were tears in his eyes, but it wouldn't have surprised me. The man had lost his little girl.

"I wanted one last chance to talk about the life we'd had together. If I could have any wish in the world right now, it wouldn't be to save myself from prison; it would be to have her back for even that short time."

Geraldine's father didn't look at us as he shambled out of the room. His shoulders were slumped, his back was crooked and, had I not known there was someone in the corridor waiting, I would have followed to be certain that he didn't try anything stupid, like climbing out of the window of a moving train.

CHAPTER THIRTY-TWO

Todd accompanied the wolf turned pup to his compartment, and I went with Grandfather to the bar.

"A large whisky, please, barman," I ordered glumly.

"And an apple juice for my grandson," Grandfather added with his usual generosity, but I had a correction to make.

"One large whisky and an apple juice with a large whisky inside it."

The barman nodded and got to work while we stood looking just as light and breezy as Mr Moorbank had.

"It's a disaster," Grandfather accurately declared. "We're no closer to identifying the killer than we were when Domenico found the body."

"Perhaps he killed her," I replied, just to have something to say. "Perhaps he was obsessed with Geraldine as an actress, and when she wouldn't speak to him, or he wanted something that she didn't want to give, he stabbed her."

"Then why would he have told us about the body? It would have been much better to wait for someone else to find her. And why would he have been carrying a knife, for that matter?"

This was a perfectly good rebuttal of my perfectly groundless accusation. "You're right of course, but there must be something obvious we're overlooking."

"Oh, I wouldn't say that." His drink had now been poured, and he held it up to enjoy the way the light shone through it, turning a patch of the silver bar a mellow brown colour. "We must now accept that we simply didn't have time to get to the truth."

Even as he said this, I felt the train begin to slow, and I had to conclude that we were approaching the first stop on our journey to Verona.

"I know you probably think I'm feeling sorry for myself, but it is better to be realistic," he continued. "We tried, and we failed, and it's time to come to terms with our limitations."

This apparently forgiving conclusion was followed by a sigh that told me he didn't believe a word of what he'd just said.

"There must be something we're missing," I repeated.

He turned to look at me. "Come along then. What is it? If you truly believe that we already know all we need to solve the case, what have we overlooked?"

I obviously couldn't answer this question, so I said, "Perhaps if we go through the suspects again, something will come to light."

His sip was more of a gulp this time, and I discovered that apple juice and whisky is a very fine combination indeed. Add a little honey, and it might even make a good cough mixture.

"What is the point, Christopher? As soon as we pull in at the station, one of the stewards will be sent to find a police officer and, before we know it, the whole train will be pulled apart by Italian constables eager to make a name for themselves as the men who solved a famous actress's murder when mediocre Lord Edgington failed to do so."

"Mediocre?" I replied in an anguished tone, as I'd rarely heard him use such language to describe his abilities. "Now you really are feeling sorry for yourself. Would you at least try?"

He considered this for a few moments, then denied my request before subsequently complying with my request. "No, I will not, because I've already done that very thing over and over in my head for the last six hours. As her most recent paramour and the man who tried to attack her shortly before she was killed, Reinhardt is the likely culprit. We never discovered with what piece of salacious information the man we previously knew as Marvin Pelthorpe…"

"Though some people were calling him the Wolf," I added one last time to see if I could get the name to stick.

Grandfather just talked over me. "…was blackmailing him. Of course, the information he had on the other suspects seemed to be mainly personal rather than criminal. Count Giovannelli, for example, was afraid of a youthful tragedy coming back to haunt him. Without solid proof of his involvement, it would be impossible to convict him of any crime decades after the incident. As for the Campbells, they have acted strangely ever since we met them, but the obvious explanation for this is that they are simply strange people."

He cleared his throat, had another gulp and then, as the alcohol had presumably not gone down so easily, he cleared his throat once again. "Take their reading matter, for example. I've never told you about the books that were based on our cases, as they are quite unreadable. The stories jump about all over the place. The characters change personalities as it suits the hack who wrote them. And, worst of all, in (metaphorically speaking) my book, the mysteries themselves have very little logic to them and are almost impossible to follow. I recall one moment in which I see someone with a red mark on his shoe and declare that he must have been to a particular beach in Greece, when, in reality, there are a thousand other reasons someone might have a red speck on his person."

He remembered one last flaw that he needed to describe. "Oh, and there is a lot of romantic piffle between me and a series of ravishing ladies, and then, from the time you're eighteen, between you and a series of ravishing *young* ladies. It's all quite nonsensical."

I actually liked the sound of having my pick of a selection of lovelies, but I wasn't about to tell him that. I'd been looking forward to hearing about the series of Lord-Edgington-inspired books but, now that he was discussing them, I found myself thinking of the case instead.

"I'm sorry, Grandfather, I am most eager to hear more about my literary counterpart, but what has any of this got to do with the Campbells?"

"They're strange!" he repeated as if this proved anything other than the fact that he shared that characteristic with the couple in question. "Anyone who tolerates such poor literature must be."

"You don't think that the source of their wealth had anything to do with the murder?" I asked, as I'd been quite sure when we'd heard their tale that Sharlene Campbell's obscenely rich father would turn out to be important.

"How would that have any relevance to Miss de la Forge?"

"I don't mean directly, but if the family had built their fortune on ill-gotten gains, and Geraldine discovered this, then—"

"I've already told you, Christopher. The details of why each person was blackmailed are of secondary importance. And besides, based on what we know of her, the information that Mrs Sharlene Campbell and her husband wish to keep secret is presumably connected to..." He looked for a euphemism. "...her 'wit-state'."

"I beg your pardon?"

"You know, her *mens sana,* or lack thereof."

I grimaced as I tried my level best to make sense of his overly vague euphemisms. "I'm afraid I haven't quite grasped your meaning there, Grandfather."

He groaned and tried to put me out of my misery. "I'm saying that at some point in her life she was touched in the upper storey." When I still looked puzzled, he kept going. "Her brain-wood needs trimming." He gave it one last try. "Oh, come along, Christopher, I'm saying she's as woolly as a flock of Southdown sheep. Why else would she move her whole life across the Atlantic and spend a small fortune just to traipse around after an actress?"

It was my turn to be polite. "She's clearly passionate about her interests." I decided not to point out that such a statement could also be made about him. While Mrs Campbell was an undeniably odd fish, there never was a more peculiar trout than my grandfather. "Imagine how that passion could have manifested itself. There's no doubt that Geraldine failed to live up to Sharlene's expectations. She thought they were friends until the betrayal. If her perfect image was shattered, and Sharlene really does have psychological fractures, the sudden change may have broken her."

It was difficult to talk of such problems without sounding belittling, but I did my best. "It does seem as though, of all the suspects, she was the most likely to snap without warning. We also know that her husband goes out of his way to support her fantasies. Look how the pair of them treated you simply because you were different from your character in those tawdry books… Of course, I still don't fully understand how they came into existence."

"There's no time for that now, Christopher," he replied, tapping his glass a few times with the edge of his finger, and I had a sense that I might never get to the bottom of that particular story. "While you have outlined a plausible case against them, in my experience, functioning individuals like Mrs Campbell rarely snap and murder those around them. It is a fable made up by scared people who don't understand the human brain."

So that told me.

"There's still the Frenchman, M. Laroche. We don't know enough to rule him out entirely. Perhaps he makes a habit of murdering women on trains. Or maybe his whole house is plastered with photographs of Geraldine and—"

"If we had more than an evening to investigate this case, all that would be swiftly discovered and he would surely have done all he could to hide his involvement. We must accept that he bought the right ticket for the wrong train and ended up an unwitting suspect. I believe he is a wine merchant and nothing more."

I still found it difficult to believe that there were murder investigations in which the person closest to the body at the time of the murder was not in any way connected to the victim.

"In which case Geraldine's maid, Milly Buckthorn, could have lied. Perhaps her mistress was already dead when she left the room."

"If that were the case, why would she have killed her? She has only been in Italy for a fortnight – which will be easy enough to confirm if we ask for her passport. We know that Geraldine fired her former maid and her manager too. She was clearly looking for a fresh start in life, so it seems unlikely that she would have upset her new staff so quickly that one of them would have turned murderous. Miss Buckthorn's past will be investigated by the police, and I feel quite certain that their enquiries will turn up very little indeed."

"Then Denkin could be our man?" I kept going, as his tone had made me worry that he would give up altogether. "It can't be denied that he, even more than the blackmailer who might reasonably have wanted to conceal his presence, went to great efforts to hide from us. Perhaps he believed he could kill Geraldine and go undetected for the duration of the journey. When we didn't stop at the first station after her body was found, he changed his plan. He decided that he couldn't stay in the compartment for ever, so he attacked Reinhardt to make it look as though the director were to blame."

He stared into his drink and said nothing for ten seconds. "Once again, my boy, you have conceived of a realistic and, dare I say, tantalising version of events. It is just the kind of eleventh-hour explanation that occurs on many of our cases and turns everything that came before it on its head."

"But this time..." I began so he didn't have to.

"This time, I don't think it's possible. For one thing, had he wished to avoid detection, his best bet would simply have been to go to bed once he'd killed his lover. We were only certain of his presence on the train because he left his compartment and attacked Herr Reinhardt. He also didn't come to tell us what he had done, and he did not make up the story – as I did when interviewing the German – that he had heard Miss de la Forge cry out her director's name before she was killed."

"But even more than that..."

"Yes, even more than that I don't believe that Denkin would have relied on such a plan because it required him to trust a stranger implicitly." He had come to life now, and his understanding of the case poured forth. "Just because he had given the man a handful of lira notes, that doesn't mean that the *chef de train* would refuse to testify against him. Nagelmackers kept his secret as long as he did because he was afraid of losing his job, but he was easily pressed into admitting his faux-pas. To be fair to the man, as soon as it was suggested that Denkin was involved in the murder, he made a clean breast of things."

"Bother, you're right." I crossed off the various suspects in my head and realised there was only one person still to discuss. "Which means that the last left on our list must be the killer."

"If only things were that simple." He smiled. "I know that you're joking, Christopher, and I appreciate your efforts to cheer me up."

I'm glad to tell you that I really had been joking and, unlike a few years earlier, I knew that you couldn't convict a person of murder based on the idea that you hadn't found evidence of anyone else's involvement. Such lax thinking and faulty logic had surely led to a great number of miscarriages of justice over the years, and I have to hope that most police forces are beyond such practices today. This did nothing to help us find the killer, though, and so I considered our final suspect more carefully.

"I know that you have already insisted that we put aside Mr N. Moorbank's—"

"You can continue to call him the Wolf if you prefer."

"Thank goodness! I really do think it suits him." I breathed out in relief and started again. "I know that the Wolf's criminal background isn't proof that he's a killer, just as a man who enjoys sewing is not automatically predisposed to knitting." I haven't a clue why this should be the comparison that popped into my mind. "But the fact is, the Wolf fits his name. He is an unsavoury fellow. He's bared his fangs on more than one occasion and, despite everything he said about loving his daughter, the note he left her was threatening. If the reason he wished to see her was merely a familial one, why would he blackmail her into coming?"

He let his recent sip of whisky refresh his palate as he considered my question. "There is something which I doubt is possible to appreciate until you become a parent yourself. I certainly didn't realise it when I was your age. It came to me after your Uncle Maitland was born and I held this incredibly complex and vulnerable creature in my hands. I knew then that the love we feel for our children is stronger than any other."

I considered this for a moment and didn't have to think long to know who I loved most in the world – perhaps after the girl in the second-class dining car. "I love my mother more than I can describe. She is the best person on earth as far as I'm concerned." *Father's not bad either*, I forgot to add.

"I agree wholeheartedly, because she is my daughter, and there is no question in my mind that I love her more than you ever will. Parents are programmed to do that, and children are conditioned to accept that their mother and father will die before they do. If it were the other way around, we'd spend half our lives in tears."

"So you're saying that the Wolf was telling the truth? He came all this way to help his daughter, who had long stopped having anything to do with the brute. And then, when he had done what she needed, she sent him packing. He bought the ticket for this train to be with her. He sent that note because he knew that it was the only way she might see him (and this tale is so tragic that it almost makes me cry)." I didn't actually say these last twelve words, but I was definitely thinking them.

"Precisely and, just like you, the thing that first told me how deeply he cared for Miss de la Forge was the anger he showed towards Reinhardt in the dining car. Despite his faults, and I can see there are many, he is her father, and he loves her. Of all the people we have suspected, I feel we can rule out his involvement."

I would normally have pointed out that he had broken one of his most important rules of detective work, but I knew he was right and that Geraldine's father was not the killer.

"Drink up, Chrissy." He put his free arm around my shoulder, and I was terribly glad to have him there with me. "We're almost at the station."

Silence fell. Well, the kind of silence you have on a rickety train ambling through the Italian night. The barman polished glasses, Grandfather's breathing had developed a slight whistle to it, as though he were sympathising with our hardworking locomotive, and the wheels turned on the tracks.

"I'm sorry," I said when it had gone on too long. "I refuse to believe that, with all the evidence we've amassed, we can't solve the puzzle together." I had a slug of drink and stepped back from the bar to list our major discoveries. "The notes, the skin cut from Geraldine's body, her passport with her real name, the evidence of her mistreatment, the revenge she enacted, her brief relationship with her director, the blood on the sink in her compartment…"

I came to a stop for a moment but soon continued. "…the article in the newspaper, which her manager must have shared, the way the Campbells were able to buy access to her, that party in Rome where everything came to a head, and the fact she cast her love rival to star alongside her: all of that and more must add up to something. It feels as if we're chasing a ghost, but she can't have just killed herself, so what's the solution?"

He didn't reply. I could have chattered on *ad infinitum*, and it would have done no good. He stood with his shoulders rounded, stroking his neatly trimmed snow-white beard and saying nothing. So I finally accepted that the time had come to admit defeat.

I sat on one of the plush, cretonne sofas and poured half my drink down my throat. It sent an instant buzz through me, and I wondered whether I should drink (well-disguised) alcohol more often. Sadly, whisky and apple juice would not be the inspiration I required to unlock the mystery that Geraldine de la Forge had left behind. I lounged in the comfy chair feeling angry to have failed so spectacularly, spoilt to travel on that luxurious train and really quite sleepy as it had gone one in the morning.

I would have happily dozed off, but the facts of the case kept circling my brain. The faces of the suspects flashed one by one before my eyes. As I'd told my grandfather, I was quite certain that there was a thread running through everything and, were we to pull it, the pieces would fall neatly into place. Or perhaps that was a terrible metaphor, and the real trouble was that there was something essential that we were missing. Yes, that must be it. A hazy understanding formed at the back of my really quite weary vision, and I was either about to fall asleep or solve the case when my grandfather spun around in his seat and said, "Christopher, have I ever told you that you're a genius?"

I was immediately wide awake. "It's possible, but I doubt I believed you."

"Well, there's no questioning it this time. You were right, my boy! I understand everything now."

CHAPTER THIRTY-THREE

And then, as the train slowed to a crawl, and we approached the station, something truly unexpected happened. For the first time since we'd been working together, Grandfather explained his theory in its entirety, not leaving out a single detail. He normally preferred to wait until he was on the point of confronting the culprit to reveal anything, but not this time. He was so happy to have finally got to the truth – with no end of help from me, I hasten to lie – that he told all.

I know the reason why he did it – I'm not entirely naïve, but it was still nice to feel that he trusted me enough to let me in on his plans. There was really only one thing left to do before we could tie everything together. We went to see Geraldine's maid to ask one final question.

Of course, this meant passing through the second-class dining car which, despite the earlier incident and a few sore heads, continued to be pleasantly rowdy. To my great joy, *the girl* was still there, too. She was sitting reading her book as her companion wrote a letter. I would have liked to speak to her, of course, but she didn't look up at me, and I didn't dare risk the ire of the man with whom she was travelling.

We carried on to the sleeping carriages, though I kept casting glances over my shoulder on the off-chance she might look up.

"I'm very sorry to bother you, Milly," I said quite sincerely when we arrived at compartment number twelve. She understandably looked quite slumberous, and I believe that we had woken her. "There's an important point with which we believe you can help us. We're about to arrive in Florence, and we suspect that we have solved your mistress's murder."

The young lady looked almost as astonished by this as she had at the news of Geraldine's death – which doesn't say a great deal about the faith she placed in us to do our jobs.

"Whatever I can do to help, I will," she replied with something of a curtsey, and she placed one pale, slender hand on the doorframe.

Grandfather remained silent, so I continued in my role. He often prefers me to take over interviewing duties for younger witnesses. "All we need to know is what made Geraldine late for the train tonight."

A conflicted smile graced her lips. "Oh, that's quite simple, sir.

Miss de la Forge, you see…" Milly was a polite young woman and hesitated over how to phrase her answer. "Well, she had a sudden change of heart about going away this weekend. She became quite distressed, and I thought we would have to cancel the whole thing. I managed to calm her down somewhat, and Mr Honeydew – that's Miss de la Forge's manager – well, he called the station to talk to the conductor, and he agreed to delay the train for their special passenger. I went ahead in a taxi, and she turned up half an hour later."

"That's just as we imagined," Grandfather replied in a solemn tone to match his expression.

"I reckon Mr Honeydew must have given the fellow a few bob for the trouble, though I can't be certain. He's in the next compartment along if you'd care to ask."

"I don't think that's necessary." Grandfather bowed in anticipation of the thanks he was about to give. "We appreciate your time. You can come to watch as I tell the suspects what really happened to your mistress, if you so wish."

She seemed to debate the possibility for a moment before replying with a firm shake of the head. "No, thank you, Lord Edgington. I'm afraid I find all this business a little ghoulish. It's truly terrible that my mistress was killed, but I will wish you good luck and good night."

I thanked her again, and she closed the door behind us. The information we had gone there to confirm made neither of us any happier, but at least we knew for certain now.

"It seems you were right, Grandfather," I told him, as we walked along the corridor to return to the first-class carriages. "What a very sad state of affairs. That poor tragic young lady," I muttered under my breath, but never did an utterance go unremarked when my grandfather was around.

"Isn't every murder we investigate tragic?"

"Yes, but just occasionally it turns out that the person or people who were killed were absolute rotters. I really don't think that was the case this time."

He offered a sad smile but had no words of reassurance. It is a wicked world in which we live – I already knew this, but it still surprises me whenever we learn of another injustice.

As we reached the bar, the train came to a complete stop, and I could hear passengers opening the doors to disembark.

"Lord Edgington." M. Nagelmackers waved his hand from the other end of the carriage. "I'm very sorry to tell you that I am now obliged to go in search of police officers to finish the investigation."

Grandfather looked a little maudlin. "I fully understand, Georges. You must do what you must do."

"I trust that you will keep all the suspects here until I return."

"We will indeed," he promised without even a twinkle in his eye.

Nagelmackers frowned stoically and turned to alight from the train. As soon as he was gone, we ran off to our carriage.

"Should we wake M. Laroche in compartment number two?" I asked just in case he was part of what had happened after all.

"No, Christopher, there will be no final surprise in this tale. M. Laroche really is a wine merchant on his way home to his family."

I still found this difficult to believe, but I accepted his decision. "Very well. Then I suppose I'll get the others."

I visited the compartments of the Campbells and Hansel Reinhardt, Count Giovannelli, Eddie Denkin and the Wolf. Todd came to guard the door as they assembled in our compartment.

"Well this will never do," Grandfather declared when the final suspects had squeezed in ahead of me. "There's no room."

The eight of us disembarked from the train with Dorie, Todd and Delilah there to keep us company, stand guard in case one of the suspects tried to get away and chew on a chair leg respectively. The platform of the Maria Antonia station was very nearly silent at that time of night. All the passengers who were leaving had gone, and the only sound was the quiet puffing of smoke from the chimney at the front of the train. Eddie Denkin did a good imitation of this with his cigarette, though more quietly and out of my grandfather's line of vision.

We walked across to the waiting room, and I'm sure I wasn't the only one to realise that the whole affair would end as it had begun. We had swapped the maid Milly Buckthorn for the film star Eddie Denkin, but the rest of our suspects were all there, just as they had been in Rome when we were awaiting the arrival of Geraldine de la Forge.

Once everyone was seated around the spacious hall that was lit

223

by an elaborate coloured glass lamp in the middle of the room, Lord Edgington stepped forward to do what he does best.

He took a moment to look at the suspects before launching into his tale. "And so, ladies and gentlemen, the story begins…"

CHAPTER THIRTY-FOUR

"I'm sure you all know that I have often found myself in this situation. I can assure you it is not through choice, and I have no special attachment to spending my free time around death, criminals or groups of nervous suspects." I'm not sure this was entirely true on my grandfather's part.

He paused his introduction to look from one face to the next. The Campbells were the only people without at least five yards between them. Sharlene sat on a bench, and James Joseph stood beside her with his hand on her shoulder. Neither of them moved and, in the dim room, they looked rather like statues, but at least I could see them clearly. The Wolf was sitting in the corner in the shadows, presumably not wishing to catch anyone's attention and perhaps still afraid of where he would end up once my grandfather had finished his telling.

"You all knew Geraldine de la Forge well. Some of you had come to Rome to be with her. She had worked alongside two of you, loved three of you, and befriended others, but I'm not certain that she felt any great affection for any of you at the time she died."

His delivery was so grave and his expression so haunted that it was not an easy story to endure. As I'd already told him, it was a melancholy case and, especially because I knew how it ended, every word he spoke made me sadder.

"I still do not know a great deal about her early life, but it seems she came from a troubled background." He didn't look towards the shadowy corner then, and I felt I knew why. "She certainly had a complicated relationship with her father, but she was the kind of person who fought for what she loved and somehow – against the odds we might say – she forged a career in films."

He was telling us what we all knew. With another group of suspects, I felt that someone would have interrupted him. We've encountered plenty of yelping loud-mouths over the years who couldn't resist sharing any stray thought that entered their heads, in the hope it might stop my grandfather from putting the blame on them.

"And one thing I can say quite honestly is that I haven't heard a single person criticise her skills as an actress. You may have had your disagreements with Geraldine, but I believe that every person in this room would agree that she deserved the fame and, indeed, the adoration she received. In a very real way, that made our job a great deal harder. My grandson Christopher and I had to answer a near unanswerable question: who would murder a film star everyone appeared to adore?"

He allowed this sentence to rattle around our brains for a short time, and it certainly had an impact on me. For a moment, I wondered whether I could have seen through all the confusion to the truth at the core of the case much faster if I'd been able to summarise our task like this. But then, there are plenty of talents my grandfather has that I am yet to acquire.

"I found myself ruling out suspects based on the idea that they had no clear reason to do Geraldine harm. Sharlene Campbell, for example…" He turned to the American woman, and her husband flinched at the sound of her name. "You clearly loved Miss de la Forge, didn't you?"

Her face lined with sadness, Sharlene nodded. "I did, Lord Edgington. I really did. She was my inspiration, and I travelled halfway across the world to meet her. It would have been enough to share the same air with her for even a minute, so the fact that we got to eat dinner together, watched films at the same cinema and went for walks in Rome like old friends is still hard for me to believe."

"And you supported your wife's obsessions, didn't you, Mr Campbell?" Grandfather had chosen this weighted term for a reason.

"I like to do what I can for Sharlene. I know you might doubt it based on what happened tonight, but I do."

"Oh yes, of course you do. Admittedly, you put a sleeping draught in her drink without telling her, but not because you were afraid she might incriminate you in some way, as I first considered. After all, it appeared you were in the dining car a few tables from us when the victim was slain. No, you put your wife to sleep to make sure she didn't say anything to implicate herself. It took me the whole night to decide whether you were afraid her obsession with Miss de la Forge would seem suspicious and you wished to avoid misunderstandings, or she really was the killer and you knew it."

"No, you've got it all wrong. That isn't what—"

Grandfather held his hand up to beg patience. "Don't worry, Mr Campbell. I know the truth now. I know that Sharlene was not the person who killed her idol. However, far from dissuading me from thinking such a terrible thing, your actions only reinforced the idea."

In that rather ceremonial manner that characterised her, Sharlene seemed to bow sitting down. "Thank you so much, Lord Edgington. I truly appreciate the kindness you have shown us both."

"Please don't misunderstand me, madam," Grandfather quickly told her when it was clear that their appraisal of the situation had diverged. "I am not suggesting that either of you is without fault. After all, you treated Miss de la Forge as a commodity that could be purchased. I believe that you paid her former manager for access, and that is why she parted ways with him around the time of the premiere of her latest film."

He didn't wait for confirmation. "No, madam, you are very much open to criticism as you considered your own happiness to be more important than that of the woman you have continuously claimed to admire. The woman you hounded – even going so far as to book tickets on our train in one last vain attempt to be close to her."

"But she wouldn't talk to me otherwise!" Her voice instantly took on a pleading tone. "You clearly don't understand how—"

"I think I do, Mrs Campbell. You told us yourself that there were days when she had no wish to see you until she was forced into doing so. As I quickly came to realise when we met, you have no interest in reality. You wished to fulfil a fantasy of friendship. You wanted a character from a film, not the real person. It's a deeply disturbing attitude to have towards another human being, and I find it quite repulsive."

He'd said too much for James Joseph to bear, and that devoted husband put his arm in front of his wife to protect her once more. "You've gone too far, Edgington. If you knew my Sharlene better, you'd see that she is a kind-hearted person, so we reject your accusations."

"And I respect you for doing so." The two men stared at one another across the room, and silence rushed into the space between them before my grandfather shooed it away. "I considered a number of scenarios in which you were the architect of Miss de la Forge's destruction before concluding that you were really only on that train to make the woman you love happy."

It seemed that James Joseph begrudgingly accepted this, even as Sharlene looked aghast. Grandfather would not soften his message as he moved on to the dead woman's director.

"Herr Reinhardt, I should probably tell you that I had a low opinion of you before this investigation began, and it has only sunk." He really was determined to put this odious bunch of people in their place. "You are dishonest, manipulative, selfish, unkind…"

"Self-deluding," I thought it only right to add.

"…conceited, adulterous and deeply unpleasant to be around. Before you accuse me of being bigoted again, this has nothing to do with your nationality and everything to do with your personality. I've seen you close to tears this evening, but only when you thought you might be blamed for the killing. And while you may have claimed to love Geraldine de la Forge – despite already being married at home in Germany – the truth is that you used her throughout your working and romantic relationship. She was little more than a bargaining chip to help you get your films made, especially after you owed your creditors money and had broken countless promises."

"How could you know that? I never discussed my financial difficulties with you." He sounded more vexed than sad now and jutted out his chin in Grandfather's direction to show his indignation.

"Let's say that I had a peek behind the curtain when I was back in Rome. The best I can say about you is that you haven't denied any of my criticisms. So maybe a lack of honesty is not one of your failings."

"Now, listen here, Edgington!" he said, to suggest he might finally have grown a spine. "I did love Geraldine, in my way—"

"I take it back. As my grandson has already pointed out, you have the capacity to lie even to yourself." Grandfather had been standing under the lamp in the centre of the room but now moved out of its beam. "You preyed on her as she emerged from a long-running courtship with her co-star. You saw your opportunity to swoop down on the poor woman when she was at her most vulnerable. And I know this was the case because she had already betrayed you to a blackmailer by that point and must have been desperate if she allowed you into her affections."

The reminder of Geraldine's machinations clearly rattled Reinhardt. He put his hand self-consciously to the bandage on his head, and Grandfather continued without interruption. "Even that wasn't enough for you. You may have been her last hope for comfort and companionship, but any loyalty you had to her was outweighed by her value as a successful actress. You blackmailed her into doing as you required and even threatened to fire her from the film into which she had poured so much of herself."

"You swine, Hansel." If Eddie Denkin is calling you a swine, then things must be bad. "I've always known you were a slimy cove, but I didn't think you'd stoop to those levels."

"Be careful, Mr Denkin," I warned him from the doorway through which we'd entered. I was standing there to keep an eye out for the police, though I assumed it would take them some time to arrive in any numbers at such a late hour.

"Why should I be careful?" Denkin was an excellent actor. For a moment, he truly sounded as naïve and unworldly as I am. "What have I done?"

"The phrase that you shouldn't throw stones in glass houses comes to mind."

"Reinhardt was the one who forced his way into Gerry's compartment and nearly attacked her!" I wouldn't have expected him to sound so hard done by.

"And you were the one who left Miss de la Forge for a younger actress, only to return to Italy on a number of occasions to persuade her to keep seeing you." My voice was surprisingly firm, my words direct. "You hid on this train before anyone else had boarded in the hope of catching her at a moment when she might accept your advances. By the standards of an even half-decent person, you are a lowlife, and I will never watch one of your films again."

I'm aware that this was a very small threat, but it was one I intended to carry out.

"Oh, please," he sneered, turning away from me only to meet eyes with the man who, I'm fairly certain, he did not realise was Geraldine's father. In response, the Wolf showed those ever-so-sharp canines.

"Keep your eyes to yourself," the blackmailer demanded, and in that moment, I had more respect for him than almost anyone else there. I'm sure it was misplaced, but that couldn't be helped.

"I'm going to have to agree with my young assistant," my grandfather intervened. "To use an appropriate term for your profession, Mr Denkin, you have failed to portray yourself in the best light. But you are not my first concern at this moment."

Grandfather turned on the spot, and I realised that there was one man I'd barely noticed. This was only right, as he had been lingering in the background throughout our investigation and had taken his time to come to the fore.

"Count Giovannelli," Grandfather began, "I'm sure you thought your intentions were noble. You believed that, by proposing to Miss de la Forge and offering her a life away from the leeches and charlatans with whom she surrounded herself…"

"My goodness!" Eddie spoke over him. "Was there anyone here who didn't attempt to steal my girlfriend away from me?" I would love to have taken him up on his use of the word "girlfriend" in this sentence, but Grandfather was still speaking.

"Count Giovannelli, you may have believed you were doing Geraldine a favour, but you still didn't love her for who she was. Much like Sharlene Campbell, you loved the person you'd seen at the cinema. You loved the idea of the moon-eyed romantic characters Geraldine played and so, having been a bachelor for decades, you tried to purchase this chimera and install her in your home."

For much of the evening, the count had seemed impervious to the events around him, but he looked quite dispirited as Grandfather cut through him with some of the sharpest words I heard that night.

"You may feel comfortable in your expensive clothes, with your fine wine and cigars, but everything we've discovered about you revealed a distinctly lonely individual. Even the information with which you were blackmailed was deeply tragic. From the sound of things, you've spent your life in love with a memory."

Though the man might have deserved some level of sympathy for this, Grandfather's voice was ice cold. "None of that can excuse the way you treated Geraldine. She meant little more to you than the bronze statue you commissioned of her, and it's hard to imagine you knew who she really was. And so, Count Giovanelli, my parting words to you are these: I hope you do find love one day and that feeling reveals just how callously you treated a woman who was killed in the prime of her life."

The great detective held his eyes on the man for a few seconds longer before turning his attention to the living film star.

"As for you, Mr Denkin, there are some things for which I cannot fault you," Grandfather said with a frown still on his lips. "You do seem to have known the victim very well – better than anyone else here, at least. And I believe you loved her in your own way, but you were just as thoughtless in your treatment of her as anyone else was. In some ways, that makes you worse than the others. You could have treasured her, as you had no doubt pledged to any number of times throughout your time together. Instead, you put your career before her well-being. You found another woman, even though you were so addicted to Miss de la Forge that you couldn't give her up entirely. You are, in plain English, a scoundrel."

Denkin's gaze was fixed on the door. I thought that incorrigible smile of his might blossom again, but it didn't happen. Perhaps the weight of his actions had finally taken its toll.

And where did this leave us? We'd gone through most of the suspects, and it felt for the moment as if we'd made no progress. There was still one person to address, though. Sitting in the dimmest part of the room was a man who had told us he was Geraldine's father. A known criminal who was almost too easy to pick as a killer. Grandfather looked over at the Wolf, and the scene appeared to freeze for a moment as the two men exchanged a glance.

The atmosphere became a little more crisp, too, as the other suspects considered what would happen next. I'm sure they had pegged the blackmailer as the only possible culprit. Perhaps they'd thought it all along and were afraid what he would do to them if they told us. Regardless of this, when Grandfather looked at the last suspect on our list, he smiled.

"There is only one person in this room who did a favour to Geraldine without asking for something in return. There is one person who rushed to be with her when she most needed him." He pointed across to her father but did not address him by name. "It would have made things easier if you'd told us who you really were and not claimed to have been attacked when, I can only assume, you fell over in the luggage van as the train stopped. That would explain your injuries, but I spent no small amount of time considering what the killer was doing at that end of the train and how he could have evaded us."

The figure in the darkness replied with an accepting nod, but he said not a word as Grandfather turned to look at the selfish, over-privileged bunch who had ruined Geraldine's life.

"As I hope I've made clear, the rest of you disgust me, and I don't use that word lightly. You are the epitome of egotism. You treated a vulnerable woman like a toy, never thinking once about her feelings. You pushed her so hard and for so long that she decided to give up the comfortable existence she had in order to start again. And when she tried to build herself a new life with a new home and staff around her, you wouldn't let her go.

"Geraldine de la Forge was in agony in the last week of her life, and I believe that many of you in this room were responsible." I thought he would tell them what we'd come there to reveal, but he held himself for a moment, much like a ballet dancer as he prepares to leap across the stage. "Christopher said something to me this evening which I had failed to consider. He said that it felt as if we were chasing a ghost, and I almost instantly knew that he was right. Ever since we discovered Miss de la Forge's body, I had the uncanny sensation that there was someone pulling our strings without anyone here realising."

He paused once more with such purpose and concentration that it almost felt as if he were continuing to lay out his theory. I knew what he was about to reveal, and I was still rapt and, indeed, wrapped up in everything he said.

"Geraldine's life was managed for her. She had no freedom, and several of you here ensured that her existence was a solitary one. That is why, shortly after we boarded the train, she was so miserable that she took a knife and cut a small piece of skin from her breast. She stemmed the blood flow to make it look as if the cut had happened post-mortem, and then dealt herself the mortal wound, casting the knife and the towel she had used from the window with her last drachm of strength before she died."

Sharlene Campbell inhaled loudly as the ramifications of this became clear. Denkin pulled his lips into his mouth, as if to hide that smile forever, and the count put his hand to his chest in solidarity with the woman who had died. In fact, it was only Geraldine's father who hid his emotions entirely. He turned his head away, and I could see nothing of his face in the gloomy spot he had chosen.

"Geraldine de la Forge made sure that you would be here. She placed a story in the international newspapers about her trip this weekend. She also sent a telegram to at least one of you to make sure that you would suffer for the way you all treated her. This investigation has been your punishment, and I don't think it goes far enough, but she saw no other escape."

He walked towards the doorway then. I believe he wished to show that he had no desire to think of them ever again, but when he reached me, he turned and delivered one last reprimand. "She brought you here to witness her self-destruction. And you must live with that for the rest of your lives."

CHAPTER THIRTY-FIVE

I made sure that none of the reprobates who had brought about an innocent woman's death could get away before the police spoke to them. That was the final part of the ordeal that Geraldine had designed. She knew that suspicion would fall on each of them, and it was no more than they deserved.

The *carabinieri* arrived before long, and Grandfather took the investigating officer aside to explain what had happened. I remained on the platform, guarding the door to the waiting room and, a few minutes later, the Wolf stuck his muzzle outside. When I didn't object, he emerged ponderously and came to stand next to me.

"I'm tired of all the nasty looks in there," he said as I enjoyed the relatively crisp air of the early morning. "I never properly introduced myself. The name's Naunton Moorbank."

My lifelong conditioning fired, and I held out my hand for him to shake. "Christopher Prentiss, and I truly am sorry for how you must be feeling. Geraldine was clearly a very special person, and I regret not having the opportunity to meet her properly."

"She was." He didn't speak for a moment but glanced along the platform. "You know, it's something of a relief that she didn't write to tell me that she would be going to Verona this weekend. I only read about her plans in the paper, so I don't suppose she expected me. She might not even have known I was on the train when she died."

He had a low, soulful voice just then, and I knew he was suffering. In the dim station light, his lupine features had receded, and he looked quite human.

"Run," I turned away from him to whisper.

"I beg your pardon?"

"I said, get away from here. When the police find out who you are, they'll arrest you for blackmail, but you were only doing what you did to help your daughter."

He let out a grim chuckle, but then I turned to him, and he could see I wasn't joking.

"You mean it, don't you? What about your grandfather?"

"He'd agree with me if he were here. He's given plenty of people second chances over the course of his career."

Naunton Moorbank looked up at me in something approaching amazement. "But I don't deserve it. My Gerry would never have been the person she was if it weren't for me. I'm to blame as much as anyone for—"

His voice broke, and I could see how much he regretted his actions. He'd lost his daughter, and underneath his bravado, he was in torment.

"Then use what's inside you at this very moment to become a better person. Think about how your victims felt when you stole from them. It's up to you to ensure you never again make someone feel the way you do now."

"You are a good man, Christopher Prentiss." He held out his hand again, and this time he looked me dead in the eyes as we shook. "I can't promise I'll be anything but the same rat I've been my whole life, but I will try my darndest. And in a year's time, I'll find some way to let you know what I make of myself."

"That is the very most that I can ask. Now run before the police catch you."

He still didn't look certain of my plan but nodded and slunk back into the shadows, as I imagine he'd been doing for decades. I heard a whispered, "Thank you," as he slipped around the façade of the building and out onto the road. I can't say for certain whether this was the best or worst thing I could have done, but I knew that Geraldine's father had a sentence to serve regardless of whatever the police might do.

With Grandfather directing them, the local officers inspected the train and, as soon as he re-emerged, I told him that the Wolf had bolted. He looked at me with a doubtful mien, then put one hand on my shoulder approvingly.

"Well done, my boy. I believe you made the right choice, and it's very unlikely that any of the other suspects will mention him." He stopped then, and I believe he was debating just what he would have done in the situation. "Yes, given the circumstances, that was the best option."

An inspector called for him then and, as I was finally off duty, there was somewhere I needed to be.

Delilah was busy following the Italian constables around the platform. Todd was standing guard beside the further sleeping compartments, and I dashed back along the train in his direction. The dining car was in something of a sorry state. There were empty bottles left on tables and a few of the singers had passed out on the chairs there, but most people had presumably gone to their compartments to get some rest or were only staying on the train until Florence.

My heart sank as soon as I saw the empty table where the girl and her companion had been. I felt very much as though someone had punched me in the heart. Well, in one way, I was relieved that I wouldn't have to endure an awkward conversation with that prickly man again, but this thought did little to ease my pain. I'd lost and then found someone incredible. I was certain when I'd seen her on the train that this was as close to fate as could be imagined. And now all that remained were two used glasses and an empty carafe of water, which the waiter fittingly cleared away as I arrived.

A brief surge of hope shot through me, and I ran to the door closest to the second-class sleeping berths. "Todd, did you happen to see a young lady with her father since we stopped here?"

He smiled his usual winning smile, perhaps thinking that this was what I wanted to hear as opposed to the diametric opposite. "That's right, sir. They got off shortly after we came into the station. My goodness, Master Christopher. That wasn't the girl you met the last time we were here in Florence, was it?"

The desolation on my face must have told him that this was not the news I wanted, as he looked disappointed on my behalf and wandered closer. "I'm so sorry. I didn't realise that—"

I raised my hand to show that I bore no hard feelings, but I didn't have the strength to say anything more. I wandered back inside the dining car, but all the excitement at solving the case had drained from me, and I collapsed in the chair where the girl's presumed father had sat. I tried to imagine that she was still there and spoke to me with just as much enthusiasm as she had earlier. I wanted to ask her more questions – to find out everything there was to know – but all I could hear, repeating over and over, were the few comments we'd already exchanged.

What did I actually know about this living dream other than that she wasn't Italian, was French, appeared to like classic literature, and was aware that most Brits are a disaster when it comes to foreign languages? I wondered for a short time whether I was just as bad as the group of vampires who had fed off Geraldine. Was it wrong to think myself in love with a girl after only speaking to her for a minute or two? Is love at first sight proof of how superficial a person I am?

I suppose that I only considered these things to distract from my anguish. Whether or not I was a fool to feel so blue, I had lost the girl for a second time, and I didn't even know her name.

"Ah, I see that not everything turned out as you had hoped," Grandfather said when he found me looking glum.

I don't know how long I'd been sitting there before he arrived, but I saw the body being carried out of the station and the police seemed to be finishing their work on the train. I'd even noticed our former suspects leaving the waiting room one by one, but time had no meaning to me anymore. I wasn't even upset that Grandfather knew exactly what I was thinking, or that I was such a simple creature he had understood my feelings for a girl to whom he'd never heard me speak. I was too busy being heartbroken for that.

I rested my forehead on the table and groaned.

"You know, Christopher, you must try not to be so melancholy. You've met this girl three times already; there's every chance you'll bump into her again."

I could just about see him by shifting my eyes in his direction. "Do you really believe that?"

"No, sorry, I'm afraid not." My grandfather is an exceptionally honest man. "I was trying to reassure you. Statistically, the chances of your crossing paths with the same unrelated person four times whilst travelling around a large continent are really very—"

I had to interrupt him. "Would you mind lying to me instead?"

"Of course not." He cleared his throat and, in a terribly overacted manner, tried to contradict his previous message. "You've already met three times, and there is every chance that *destiny* will bring the pair of you together again."

He sat down on the chair in front of me and awaited my reaction.

"Thank you." I continued staring at the table.

"I would tell you the story of how I met your grandmother, but I believe you have heard it many times and that such fairy tales will only make you groan again."

"Thank you," I repeated, and I genuinely wished there was

something he could say to encourage me, but that seemed impossible.

I could hear his clothes rustle somewhat as he changed position to look at me from a different perspective. "I have no way of making you feel better, but I think I may be able to distract you." He clapped his gloved hands together as though to build excitement. "I will allow you to ask me any questions you may have regarding the case we have just investigated."

I didn't react immediately. I didn't want him to know how appealing this was. "Hmm mmm…birdwatcher…mmm hmmm," I mumbled, then raised my head to say it more clearly. "Why did Naunton Moorbank come in disguise and even go so far as learning about birds in Italy to pass himself off as a birdwatcher?"

He needed a few seconds to consider this before amazing me by admitting, "I really can't say. He was certainly known to each of the other suspects. Perhaps he was afraid that there would be police on board the train, and he needed an excuse should anyone become suspicious – which is essentially what happened."

I sat back up, my brain now spinning with questions that I could put to him. "And what about Geraldine? Why did she cut the skin away?"

"That is also difficult to imagine, but I believe it speaks to her troubled frame of mind. Don't forget that she would have had to be quite disturbed to have completed her plan."

"I am in no doubt about that, Grandfather." I thought about what the dead woman had gone through and saw that my own troubles were paltry in comparison. I instantly realised that this was Grandfather's intention.

"To be frank, I believe that the heart-shaped piece of skin was cut from the body as a message to all those she would leave behind. She was saying that Reinhardt, the Campbells, the count and Eddie Denkin all wanted a piece of her, so that's what she gave them."

I didn't see why she would have thrown it out of the window if that was the case, but there were more discrepancies we were yet to resolve. "The other thing that stuck out to me was the fact that she pushed for Maxine Hammond to star opposite her in the film she and Reinhardt were intending to make."

"I would say that is self-explanatory," he claimed and, just in case this was true, I decided to share my thoughts on the matter.

"Do you mean that this was another way for her to extract a modicum of revenge and perhaps express her independence from Denkin after he mistreated her?"

"Precisely. I'm sure that smug fellow was frightened of the two women comparing notes on how he had treated them. I did at one point consider whether this was enough of a reason for him to kill her, but as Denkin proved when he ignored the threat of blackmail, he isn't the type to be ashamed of his actions."

I chewed my lip as I listened to him, and when I continued exploring the strange case in my mind, he spoke again.

"I have a question for you that has puzzled me for a long time." He put his fingers together to make the steeple of a church. "Why did all this take place so early in the evening?"

"What do you mean, Grandfather?"

"I mean, wouldn't it have made more sense to wait until everyone was asleep so that the body would be found in the morning? Someone might well have overheard and run to see what she had done."

"Yes, but the train was very noisy as we went through the tunnels. Geraldine clearly decided that it was the right moment."

His closed mouth moved from left to right and back as a complex argument raged in his head. "It's possible. However, I think it's more likely that she wanted to ensure that you and I would be the ones to investigate."

"How could she have…" I didn't finish this sentence as something significant occurred to me. "M. Nagelmackers. She may have spoken to him on the phone before the train left or even when she bought the tickets – her manager said that she made her own travel arrangements. As she was clearly hoping to attract all those various ghouls to haunt the neighbouring compartments, she would have needed to know there was space on the train. For a price, Nagelmackers would have been only too happy to tell her that the great Lord Edgington had already booked his ticket, and that, at the time, the majority of the remaining compartments were free."

"Yes, it could equally have been someone in the ticket office, of course. Nagelmackers isn't the only man in Europe who is open to bribery. There was one more possibility that occurred to me but—"

The train was pulling out of the station, and he cut this sentence short. "Listen to me going on at this hour. You must get some sleep." He frowned as he noticed something on the chair beside him and lifted it onto the table. "There you go, Christopher. If one thing is certain to take your mind off your troubles, it's your beloved Charles Dickens."

He pushed the blue, leather-bound tome across to me, and I could hardly believe what I was seeing.

"It can't be," I said, even as I spotted the gold-embossed words which read *Great Expectations*.

He wasn't listening any more and waved me away with a careless hand. "Goodnight, Christopher. It may have taken some time, but we did well tonight – you in particular."

I don't think I uttered a word in reply. I just stared at the book before me and tried to summon the courage to open it. I placed my hand on the cover, and a fizz of electrical charge passed through me. I must have held it there for ten seconds, but then I breathed in deeply and turned to the cover page.

There was nothing to find there. Well, there was. It said *Great Expectations by Charles Dickens,* and there was a pencil drawing of the hero of the book standing at a crossroads by way of a frontispiece. But there was no inscription as I'd been hoping, and when I briefly flicked through the book, the pages looked quite normal.

I wanted to scream, but that might have woken the sleeping singers in the corner, so I unleashed my frustration into my fist. My heart couldn't cope with all these curves and contradictions, though I was happy there was one final plot twist when I raised the hefty book above the table and a scrap of paper fell out.

Hello there, young Englishman,

I don't suppose you'll ever find this, but just in case you do, I thought I should let you know my name. I would like to have told you in person, but if you are ever in the Latin Quarter in Paris, and I'm not on a train somewhere else, perhaps I'll see you there.

Bon voyage, wherever you are going.

Kassara

CHAPTER THIRTY-SIX

I'm not sure I slept at all that night. My head was full of Kassara. To be quite honest, her name only added to the mystery that surrounded her as I was fairly confident it wasn't French or Italian, or any European nationality that I knew anything about.

I was so moved by my discovery, and now desperate to travel to Paris as soon as possible, that I barely thought of what the end of our journey would entail. I watched the sunrise through a crack in the curtains and was still awake some hours later when the time came to disembark.

"Are you ready?" Grandfather asked as we jumped onto the platform at Verona before the train had even stopped.

Todd had done the same thing from the second-class carriage, and I could only assume that Dorie, Cook and Timothy were close at hand. Delilah was tired of being on the train and immediately set about stretching her legs by dashing up and down the platform.

We stopped beside the ticket hall, and I did my shoelaces up because they were forever coming undone, no matter how many times I knotted the things.

"Ah, Miss Buckthorn." Grandfather took his hat off and smiled at the pretty young maid as I returned to full height. "I wondered if we might bump into you one last time."

"Good morning, Lord Edgington," Milly replied in her usual respectful tone, still dressed in her black uniform and with her dark brown hair tied in a bun on top of her head. "I trust you had a comfortable journey."

"We did indeed."

Grandfather came to a sudden halt. It was clear that he wanted to say something more, but instead of coming out with it, he simply stood looming over the young lady.

"I must be getting on," she finally told us with a half-smile. "I'm so sorry we met in such terrible circumstances, but I'm truly glad you solved the case." She nodded to us both and moved to go.

The persistent detective stepped forward to block her way. "Don't you wish to know how your mistress died?" He could be a real show-off when he didn't feel that he'd had enough praise.

She frowned as she replied. "I'm sorry, Lord Edgington. It's as I told you last night. I find your line of work gruesome. It's not for me."

"Ah, yes. I apologise." He looked away from her for a moment before continuing. "However, I was just wondering whether you have somewhere to stay here in Verona?"

She gave a gesture that was a mix between a shrug and a shake of the head. "I'm sorry, I don't see why—"

"Your life must be filled with uncertainty just now. You've come all this way to a foreign country and, within two weeks of your arrival, your employer is dead and you're out of a job. I can't tell you how much I sympathise."

"We both do," I added in a far more sincere tone than my grandfather's. "Still, you have Geraldine's valuables, don't you? We know that Count Giovannelli spoilt her with jewels and gifts, and they will surely fetch a pretty penny."

This was the moment that she realised the game was up. There was a faint flicker of her eyelids and, like a batsman deciding whether to hit a ball in cricket, she considered what to do next.

"They're not mine, sir. I'll look after them until I hear from Miss de la Forge's family, but I certainly won't gain from their sale."

"No, you certainly won't." Grandfather waved his hand in the direction of the ticket hall before gripping the leather valise that was under her arm.

A few seconds later, the officers whom the Florentine police had instructed to be there appeared beside us. Grandfather could have confronted the guilty party the night before, but we decided it would be rather wonderful to let her think she'd got away with her scheme. For their part, the police were happy to hand the work over to their Veronese colleagues.

"Officers," he said in Italian, "you are free to arrest this woman."

"What for?" she snapped in reply, refusing to let go of the bag. "For carrying the valuables that my mistress put in my care?"

"No, for murder." This is the kind of thing that a detective spends his career wishing to utter, and I can't deny that I enjoyed it.

"What do you mean?" She never broke character, even as she looked pleadingly at the policemen. I suppose she felt that was the safer option. "Who am I supposed to have killed?" Her voice was convincingly indignant.

Grandfather would answer her this time. "Yourself, in more ways than one."

"You killed the real Milly Buckthorn," I cut in because I'd got a little carried away, and the boldness of her act fired me on. "You killed the woman you paid to impersonate you. And you did so in order to make everyone think that you were dead, didn't you, Geraldine?"

It was mainly Grandfather's work that had got us here, so I shut my mouth once more and allowed him to speak. "We read in the newspaper that you were looking for an actress for the new film you were making. It seems it was the role of your sister, which was finally given to Maxine Hammond. I can only think that you advertised for women who looked like you, which is when you found the real Miss Buckthorn. What I don't know is whether you set out to execute this plan from the beginning or you were put in mind of it when you found someone who bore such a striking resemblance."

This was enough for the one of the Italian constables – who presumably had a good knowledge of both English and international film stars. He put a hand on her arm to ensure she couldn't get away as Grandfather continued.

"Did you offer the aspiring actress the job at the same time that you broke the sad news that she didn't have a part in your film? I'm sure you consoled her with the idea that she could still make good money by standing in for you at public events. The article also mentioned that Geraldine de la Forge was seen descending the Spanish Steps in Rome last week, and your admirers were in raptures to see you there. I suspect that you were testing out Milly's impersonation and your transformation into an unassuming, bespectacled maid. Was the story you told us about the dead woman's past actually true?"

Geraldine de la Forge pushed the glasses firmly up her nose but would not answer.

"You dyed the real Milly's hair, put her in high-heeled shoes, and changed her clothes to make her look more like a wealthy actress," I told her. "You even made sure her nails were perfectly manicured, just like yours. The exchange worked so well that your friends didn't recognise you. You sat in the waiting room in Rome, and no one there paid you any attention. Not Reinhardt, nor the count – two men who claimed to love you. But then, such conceited people rarely notice mere servants, and it was really no wonder that your plan worked so well… at the beginning, at least."

Grandfather didn't bother waiting for her not to respond this time. "We could never quite settle on any of the other suspects you'd enticed onto the train to distract from your involvement. I can only assume that you'd intended for everyone to see the fake Geraldine in the dining car before you killed her, but she refused to go. My grandson overheard her saying, 'I should never have agreed to any of this', which didn't alarm me at the time, but when it became increasingly difficult to find evidence of another person's involvement, I wondered what it could mean."

As this scene was playing out, many regular passengers had left the train and were collecting their luggage, oblivious to anything that had happened the night before. I almost envied them as I listened to my grandfather's summary of the crime.

"Milly Buckthorn couldn't take the pressure of pretending to be you. It was the reason you'd sought an escape from your life in the first place, so it's no wonder she should feel that way. She regretted agreeing to the plan and wouldn't do as you required, so rather than waiting until night, when it would have been easier to kill her without anyone noticing that something was amiss, you took the knife you had selected for that purpose and, as the train thundered through the tunnel and the lights flickered out, you cut the life from her."

Grandfather went whistling through the evidence and swiftly moved on to the next point. "You were driven by your anger. You felt that the people who had wronged you deserved to suffer and, had you not put your own life before that of another's, I might have felt some sympathy for you. Sadly, though, you believed that the only way to escape your dilemma, after various other plans went awry, was to make people think that you were dead, so poor Milly Buckthorn – a young woman who came to you in the hope of a better life – took your place."

I realised that there were still a few pieces of evidence he hadn't mentioned, and so I jumped in again. I must say that it felt right to share the task. "We assumed that the victim opened her locked compartment because the culprit was someone she loved, but the truth is that her killer was already in there with her. You were wearing gloves and a pinafore when you boarded the train, but not when we spoke to you in the dining car, so you must have removed them to hide the bloodstains. It took us some time to realise, Miss de la Forge, but we eventually saw you for the killer you really are."

I thought that she would deny it or try to convince the police that it was all a mistake, but Geraldine was tired of acting. "You may have discovered a few things about me, but that doesn't mean you know what my life was like." Her voice had changed. It was crisp yet mournful, without a hint of the East End brogue she'd previously adopted. "From my manager to my director and even people who claimed to care for me, I was nothing but a prop."

She began to sob then. Great tears gathered in the corner of her eyes to prepare themselves for the descent, and I realised it was the first *real* thing we'd seen of her that weekend. "I didn't want to hurt that silly girl. I promise I didn't, but when I saw everyone at the station and they looked straight through me, I knew that I could leave behind the nightmare in which I'd been caught."

I might have snorted just then as I listened to her petty defence. "You didn't want to hurt her, but you realised what good it would do you, so you cut open her stomach and sliced a piece of skin from her chest? I take it all back; you aren't so bad after all."

"Christopher…" She said my name as though she'd expected me to be kinder – as though she were not a compassionless killer. "Lord Edgington, please understand that I had no other choice. I really didn't. Without the hope of escape, I would have done something terrible."

She put her hands up to her tightly pinned hair and left them there as her situation came into focus.

"You did do something terrible," Grandfather insisted. "And nothing you say can excuse your actions."

"You're a monster," I whispered with great sincerity as I looked past her pretty exterior to what lay beneath. "You didn't just knock her unconscious or drop poison in her tea; you chose a knife, brought it aboard the train and sliced her open. You even mutilated the poor woman."

"Milly had a birthmark…" she began, but I believe that even she realised how evil her act was as her voice faltered. "That's the real reason I cut the skin from her breast. I knew that Eddie and Reinhardt would have noticed the difference, so I removed it. I would never have done anything so macabre otherwise." There was something abrupt about the way she finished this sentence, and I knew there was more she wasn't saying.

"Oh, please." Grandfather was unimpressed. "You can't describe what you did in pretty terms and hope we'll overlook your crimes."

The anger inside her had been bubbling up for some time, and she pulled her glasses off to throw them to the ground. "You're on the wrong side in all of this, Edgington. I'm the victim. I'm the one they used. How can you not see that?"

He ignored her question entirely. "I did wonder whether you flayed poor Milly to conceal something, but I'm certain that you cut off the skin in the shape of a heart to make it look as if one of your suitors were to blame. It might give you some succour to know that I let them believe you had killed yourself because of their mistreatment. They'll read about it in the papers before long, but I do concede that they deserved the punishment you designed for them."

Geraldine was shaking as the reality of her future became clear. I can't say I felt any guilt as I added a few final points. "We confirmed your identity when we came to your compartment in the middle of the night. I saw your delicate, well-manicured fingers that you couldn't disguise, and I forced myself to look at you as the film star I'd seen so often at the cinema. The questions we asked were largely irrelevant. I just wanted to see whether I recognised you once Grandfather had explained the solution to the crime. I'd mentioned to him that I felt we were chasing a ghost, and he unravelled the rest of your plan. It was all rather lucky really."

"The postcard that your victim had written home to her parents effectively confirmed my theory, though it took me long enough to realise," Grandfather now revealed, and this was news to me. "Not only was it written with all the excitement of a newcomer to Italy, you knew that your father was in the country and had no reason to write to him."

She opened her mouth to speak, but nothing more would come. Her lips trembled, and she was beautiful with brown hair or blonde, but it made no difference now. The officers had shackled her slender wrists, confiscated her bag, and were already pulling her away when Grandfather put his hand up to stop them.

"Miss de la Forge, I must tell you before you go that you are a great actress." He spoke most sincerely, and they halted their retreat. "You played your part to perfection."

She pulled at the handcuffs, but there was no escaping now, and the policeman pushed her towards the vestibule. Thanks to the sympathetic characters she played in her films, the world may have wished to believe that Geraldine de la Forge was a good person, but whoever she had been before that weekend disappeared with the slash of a knife.

And just as she reached the ticket hall, she stopped to glance back at me with all her sorrow apparent in those bewitching eyes. The officers waited for her to compose herself, and she looked just as pure and graceful as in any of the romantic roles she had played. But then, as we'd learnt only too well that weekend, appearances can be deceptive.

"Do you know what I think, Christopher?" Grandfather asked, placing one hand on my shoulder. "I think we should find somewhere selling breakfast. This is a region of fine cheeses, wines and cured meats, though if you prefer a ham sandwich and a glass of orange juice, I won't judge you… just this once."

"You know that I can't say no to a sandwich," I confessed. "But after that I'm fairly confident I'll need a nap."

Delilah had tired of running about and come to sit next to me, and Todd had brought a trolley loaded with our bags, so we moved off through the station and out to the street beyond in search of the two Alfa Romeos that had been sent ahead of us. Todd happily loaded one of the cars while Dorie, Cook and Timothy piled into the other.

"Do you feel any better?" I asked my grandfather as we waited. "I mean now that someone's been killed and— Sorry, I don't mean because of the dead body. I meant to say—"

"Yes, Christopher," he kindly interrupted. "I believe that the puzzle the case presented was just what I needed to frighten the black dog from my back."

"That's wonderful." I was genuinely relieved.

"And you're happy with your book?" He winked at me then, and

I looked down at the Dickens that had been tucked under my arm practically since I'd woken up that morning. He didn't require an answer but gestured towards the skyline before us. "Not to mention the city that we now have to explore."

"And all the food we get to try."

He laughed under his breath and ushered me towards the waiting automobile. "We will surely do that, Christopher. You have my word."

"Lord Edgington, I'm sorry if it's too much to ask," Todd interrupted a few minutes later as we drove across the river towards the historic centre of Verona, "but would you mind telling me exactly what happened on board the train? I wouldn't normally pester you for details, but I spent some time with the woman I thought was Milly Buckthorn, and I didn't imagine for one second that she was a fake."

Grandfather glanced across at me, and I wondered for a moment how he would answer this question.

"That's because Geraldine de la Forge really is an exceptional actress." He smoothed the creases from his waistcoat with the flat of his hand. "But it's a complicated tale, and I think that Christopher should be the one to tell it."

"Yes, of course," I responded in a mumbled, sleepy tone, but my head was heavy, and I was already nodding off. As the car rumbled along over the cobbled streets of the city, I believe I dreamt that I was a character in a Charles Dickens novel.

The End (For Now...)

Get another
LORD EDGINGTON ADVENTURE
absolutely **free**…

Download your free novella at
www.benedictbrown.net

"LORD EDGINGTON INVESTIGATES ABROAD"

The third full-length mystery will be available
November 2025.
Follow me on Amazon to find out when it goes on sale.

ABOUT THIS BOOK

I had the closest thing I've ever experienced to a heart attack when I got about halfway through writing this book and was suddenly terrified that I'd subconsciously stolen the plot. You see, I was fairly confident that I hadn't read Agatha Christie's *The Mystery of the Blue Train,* but I decided to do so once I'd settled on the details of my own story. I like reading Golden Age mysteries whilst writing as it helps with vocabulary and style, but I try to avoid being influenced by them, so wait until I'm sure of my narrative before beginning.

When I got to the murder in Christie's book, I was terrified that the twist at the end would turn out to be the same as mine. On top of that, both books feature a prominent role for a maid, a mysterious count, a murder on a train (obviously) and a stolen gem plot – which I then decided to cut in this book to avoid the similarities being any more striking. In the end, the resolution of the two books is different enough that I probably shouldn't have worried, but I place a lot of importance on not ripping off other authors' work, and so I had a very nervous night reading through the novel as fast as I could to find out – before getting a friend to read the Wikipedia summary and put me out of my misery when I was too slow. Had it been more similar, I would probably have sacrificed the final twist in this book and stuck with the *An Inspector Calls*-esque finale that precedes it.

I seriously considered that I'd read the book as a child – I hadn't – and internalised the plot. I've since checked on the TV version with David Suchet, in case I'd copied from that, but it was only made in 2006, I was on a memorable holiday when it was shown, and I definitely haven't seen it. So that was a relief, but I thought I should mention it here in case anyone wondered about the similarities. In short, I promise I'm not a plagiarist, but certain tropes and settings in detective fiction occur so commonly that one of my books was bound to cross over with the Queen of Crime's eventually.

Spoilers coming... As for the twist itself, I wonder if some people might find it unlikely, but I do know of two real-life cases of something similar happening. I may have mentioned before that, when I returned home from my first term at university, I went up to London for a Christmas fair with my family. My aunt came direct from work with a young man with long hair in a pony tail, a bushy beard and, importantly, no glasses. I waited for her to introduce me and, after thirty seconds, put my hand out to him, only to be told that this stranger was my brother Dominic. In the three months I'd been away, his hair had got a bit longer and he'd put it in a pony tail for the first time. He'd grown a beard, and got contacts. I was left stunned – but also wondered whether he was on the run from the police.

The other story happened to my friend's dad, Barry, when he was away at a conference. He had a problem with his eye but ventured down to the hotel bar for a drink and was amazed to see that George Michael and Paul McCartney were there. He waited until they'd gone before asking the barman about them. "It's not really them," he said. "There's a look-a-like convention on tonight." Barry had a good laugh, before Marilyn Monroe, John Lennon and several others appeared. A bit later, iconic Welsh entertainer Max Boyce came to buy a drink. "He's the best lookalike yet," Barry said, only for the barman to explain, "No, that really is Max Boyce. He's presenting the show."

And because Christie immortalised the train-set murder mystery with not just *The Mystery of the Blue Train,* but *Murder on the Orient Express, 4.50 from Paddington* and at least one short story, I wanted to try my hand at one of my own. I must say, it is not an easy endeavour. To keep the plot interesting, you need action, and because of the straight line in which everything is arranged on board a train, the detectives generally know where the suspects are at all times. This limited me to just one body, but I tried to get around the book being nothing but a long string of interviews by creating other types of action and distraction.

I like to have group scenes to establish character, but beyond the initial meeting in the waiting room, the dinner and the final revelation, I was limited in this respect. In most books, you need characters to have the ability to act and interact when the detective isn't there, but that simply wouldn't be realistic when someone has been murdered, and Lord Edgington has the ability to restrict the suspects to certain areas to save anyone else from being killed.

It's hard to keep things pacy under these circumstances, and it doesn't help that I couldn't even change the scenery very easily as the characters are trapped in a confined space and it's soon night time. The pulled emergency cord helped me to break away from the train and scatter the suspects, and I also enjoyed the movement between the contrasting worlds of first and second-class. Having Lord Edgington's beloved staff stashed away helped as well, and I hope I've packed the story full of enough twists and surprises to keep you turning the pages.

Of course, there was one action scene I included which runs more to parody than homage. I watched the original Hitchcock version of *The Lady Vanishes* recently and, having tried to create a somewhat realistic story, and at least abide by the common rules of train travel, I was amused by that film's scene in which our likeably English, folk-music-obsessed hero decides to climb between compartments on the outside of the train. It's clearly ridiculous, but a staple of the genre, and so I decided to put Chrissy in such a situation, which he ultimately doesn't really throw himself into.

It is a bit of a change for me not to be using a real place as a setting. I got to know the castle of Montegufoni, where the last book was set, so well that it required a shift of mentality for me to get used to an invented train on an invented route, even if both were based somewhat on reality. As far as I have discovered, there was no night train from Rome to Verona in the twenties, but the route was very much in use. The train system in Italy at the time was still heavily reliant on infrastructure that had been built some sixty years before and the route between Rome and Florence was famously slow and windy, as it avoided various mountains and went out of its way to take in particular towns. I think it's likely that you would have had to take at least two trains to get to Verona, but this is fiction, after all.

The Rome-Florence Trainline also followed this odd route because, back when it was first planned out at the end of the 1850s, Italy had yet to be unified. This meant there were political considerations as the trainline crossed, or in some cases skirted around, the separate kingdoms. In 1871, it took over nine and a half hours to cover the tortuous 372km route between these two major cities. Even today, half of the route is so curvy that trains can only go up to 100km an hour, and so I think the journey length, plus the further overnight leg to Verona, is fairly realistic in its timing.

The trains on the line were likely to have been pulled by 4-6-2 locomotives, which were ubiquitous at the time. The number referred to the arrangement of the wheels, with four small wheels at the front six massive ones under the boiler, and two smaller ones at the rear. In Italy, these engines were souped up at the end of the twenties with larger boilers and had a top recorded speed of ninety-three miles per hour. The world record for this type of train was achieved by father's (and thus my) favourite locomotive, the Mallard, in Britain in 1938 when it was clocked at 126 mph.

The name of the company that runs the service in this book, the *'Compagnia dei Treni Notturni'* or, the night train company, is fictitious. It is a reference to the ubiquitous *Compagnie Internationale des Wagons-Lits,* a French company that ran long-distance trains, including the Orient Express, across Europe and all the way to the Far East. They are often mentioned in 1920s detective and adventure fiction, and in real life it was on one of their trains that the 1918 armistice was signed. As it happens, I already knew this, as the place where it was signed is a twenty-minute drive from my wife's family home near Compiègne in northern France.

You can still visit the site today, and there's a very interesting museum along with a real *wagon* from the period, though it's only at the end of the tour that you discover it isn't actually the one on which Marshall Foch and various European representatives signed the armistice but an identical copy that once ran on the Orient Express. In fact, Hitler resented Germany's defeat so much that, when he took control of much of France in 1940, he returned the carriage to the same spot for the French to sign their own armistice. It is believed that the original carriage, which had belonged to Foch himself, was destroyed by the SS in 1945 to stop advancing American troops from reclaiming it.

As for the company, the *Compagnie Internationale des Wagons-Lits* was significant for allowing wealthy so-and-sos like Lord Edgington to enjoy luxurious and safe travel across Europe. It was formed back in 1871 by a Belgian called… let me check… Oh, yes, Georges Nagelmackers. His firm ran services which were pulled by local train companies, as they didn't own their own trains, but they did go on to open a string of high-class hotels for their passengers to enjoy. In the twenties, they had the monopoly on such services for a large swathe of Europe and, though the company's fortunes declined greatly with the onset of World War Two and tailed off even more in the seventies, it does still operate some services including (wait for it…) night trains in Italy!

When it came to the look of the carriages on my train in this book, I fell back on a couple of obvious sources. The first is the Orient Express itself, which continues to use Pullman-style carriages from the twenties and thirties. I didn't realise that there are now multiple services run by different companies under the name "Orient Express" but the one I looked at costs about £4,000 per night for short journeys, so I won't be taking up the offer any time soon. As for the look of the carriages, marquetry is the order of the day. Every other surface features glossy wooden designs in contrasting shades, and every luxurious piece of upholstery is heavily patterned. The Venice-Simplon Orient Express's bar carriage (#3674), complete with its own caviar menu, was only introduced in the 1980s, but offered an extra setting for a geographically limited book, so it came in handy.

I also used the Orient Express for information on sleeping carriages. There were definitely single and double-berth compartments in the twenties. While today you can have free-standing baths, and double beds in the most luxurious carriages, I believe that, back then, the compartments mainly had a small cupboard with a sink and perhaps a toilet. The sofas would have been turned into beds whilst the passengers were at dinner, which is what Domenico (named after my brother Dominic) tries to do in this book before hell breaks loose.

The second source of information for period carriages came from the exquisite Belmond trains that the company still runs today. They've had one of the carriages redesigned based on the ideas of one of my favourite film directors, Wes Anderson, and this is interesting as they have videos on their website which show how the incredible interiors are produced, so you get to see the phenomenal mosaics and marquetry being made.

I was uncertain about what order the carriages would be in, and I found it surprisingly difficult to locate the information despite delving into railway afficionado forums and consulting old documents, so I reached out to a man who I thought would know. My mum's cousin, who was an admiral in the British navy, is a true train nut and previously had an enormous model railway that filled his double garage. It was terrible timing on my part as Clive was in the middle of a family crisis, but he was very helpful and told me that the first-class carriages were likely to be somewhere around the middle of the train, where you feel the movement less, but ahead of the second-class ones. This made me happy as it was how I'd already planned out the book and meant I didn't have to rework anything.

Another important part of my research this time around involved finding out about the burgeoning film industry of the 1920s. Some of you may have noticed by now that I enjoy writing about actors. I suppose that the idea of someone who is skilled at imitating others fits well within the mystery genre as it offers the writer the chance to play with the question of who is being their authentic selves (or otherwise). I also did a lot of drama myself as a child, so it's a world I know something about. I have a really good twist worked out for another book featuring actors, but I think I'd better give you a break from them for a while, as they've featured in three Edgingtons, two Mariuses and an Izzy book.

I did enjoy reading about the European film industry as it was in the twenties and, though Italy was struggling at the time when compared to Britain and France, it would go on to achieve big things. In fact, Italy is the country that has won the Oscar for Best Foreign Language Film most often, along with receiving the most Palmes d'Or at Cannes. There are also many famous Italian-American directors including, one of my favourites, Frank Capra, who is often considered the personification of the strata-climbing American dream.

In the twenties, though, the Italian film industry was yet to bloom, despite the efforts of the *Unione Cinematografica Italiana*, which was created after the First World War to improve output. The organisation was formed through the collaboration of fourteen major Italian companies and would go on to focus on making historical epics. They would not be the last company to make the mistake of investing heavily in large-scale films that would not find a large public, and UCI went bust in 1926. A few years later, the company that replaced it, known as *Cines*, set up dedicated film studios in Rome, which get a mention in this book. *Cines* would find some success with the first Italian sound films and by making a genre of light comedy called *Telefoni Bianchi* (or White Telephone films) which copied the light, breezy style of Hollywood comedies of the day. The studio burnt down in 1935 and, two years later, the Italian dictator Benito Mussolini invested millions in order to save the film industry because he believed that "Cinema is the most powerful weapon". He commissioned the building of a grand new studio called *Cinecittà*, which remains the biggest film studio in Europe to this day.

Things didn't look too bright early on, as films made there were largely propaganda pieces approved by the Fascist government, before the studio was nearly bombed out of existence by the Allies during the war. However, after a three-year period during which it functioned as a refugee camp, *Cinecittà* was rebuilt and became so successful that Rome was known as 'Hollywood on the Tiber'. One of the first movies made there after the war was the MGM production *Quo Vadis*, which was a remake of the 1924 epic that had led the UCI to bankruptcy. Ironically, although the 1951 version was the most expensive film ever made at the time, it was a huge success and is said to have saved the American studio from collapse.

Since then, pretty much every famous director has made movies there. Not just Italian ones, like Fellini, Sergio Leone and Bertolucci, but British and Americans too, with films like *Ben Hur, Cleopatra, The English Patient,* and *Gangs of New York* right up to the Oscar-winning *Conclave,* which came out in 2024, all made at *Cinecittà*. So the idea of an Italian film studio having a major impact on the world of movies isn't far-fetched, and I have read of German-Italian co-productions at the time; however, it was more common in the twenties for films to be produced in the market they were aimed at. So, to sum up, I took a few liberties so that I could have an interestingly international cast of characters. And I have no regrets!

A last titbit before I move on is that perhaps the most famous Italian film export of the twentieth century was the Spaghetti Western. And perhaps the most famous Spaghetti Western was *The Good, the Bad and the Ugly,* which was produced not only at *Cinecittà* but also close to my home in Burgos in the north of Spain. You can still visit the sets from the cemetery scene and the (real) monastery beside the (fake) bridge which is blown up. In fact, it had to be blown up twice as the Spanish soldier in charge of the explosives mistook the cue to start filming for his prompt to push the lever. The cameras were destroyed, but no one was hurt, so the army rebuilt the substantial structure and took the shot a second time. Clint Eastwood was so tired of Sergio Leone's lax yet demanding way of making films that he demanded $250,000 plus two Ferraris and money on the back end to return for this third part in the trilogy. This was more than twenty times what he got for the first film. He did a lot better out of it than one of his co-stars. Eli Wallach almost died three times during filming when he drank acid, was dragged a mile by a frightened horse, and nearly got decapitated when filming on a train. Eastwood vowed never to work with Leone again, and he was true to his word.

Spaghetti Westerns were well known for having actors from different countries appearing alongside one another, often speaking their lines in their own languages, which would then be dubbed over depending on the market in which the film was shown. I had a sense of that juggling of nationalities in this book, and I didn't want to make any of them a stereotype. Sometimes this means not pushing accents and dialects too hard in my text, as otherwise dialogue can become a chore to read. The same is true for English dialects, as it's easy for a writer to get carried away. I hope I've struck a good balance here and not fallen in to cliché. Oh, fine, the way that Monsieur Laroche speaks is rather clichéd, but then he's a comedy character, and I am married to a French woman after all. Although I am a Brit living in Spain, I hear French at home more than any other language, so I think I can get away with gently poking fun at my-in-laws.

One final issue which I chose to explore in this plot is the idea of parasocial interaction, which was not deeply explored or perhaps even considered in the twenties, though you will definitely find examples of such behaviour when I talk about Rudolph Valentino a bit later. The term was thought up by sociologists in the 1950s to describe the relationship that forms between media personalities and their fans. This unusual bond can lead to a feeling of friendship developing on the fans' side, even though they may never have met the person in question.

At the heart of this book is the relationship between the actress Geraldine de la Forge and the people who adore her. The Campbells' approach to Geraldine is representative of this recognisably modern phenomenon and today, at a time when actors, authors, musicians and sports people are expected to present a public face through social media and online interaction, the line between fandom and obsession is an interesting one.

I would now like to say that 99.999 per cent of my interactions with my readers couldn't be nicer, and it wasn't that I chose to write about this topic because of any hesitation on my part to be open and accessible. I believe that one of the reasons I've been able to grow my readership is because I keep in regular contact through my newsletters and Facebook, and people are more willing to invest in a guy who writes sooooo many books when they can see I'm not all bad. That being said, I find the way that a small part of online fandom now expects their favourite singer, actor, podcast host or whoever to live up to their own personal expectations to be a really curious development. It's also a fascinating field of psychology to read about, and I found it curious to learn that similar behaviour is common in young children as they form attachments to sports stars, singers and even fictional characters – I'm looking at you, every five-year-old girl who dresses the whole time as Elsa from *Frozen*!

As a writer, the only experience I have of readers overstepping the normal social boundary between two people who don't really know one another is the one correspondent in ten thousand who writes to tell me everything that is bad and disappointing about my previous book. It's particularly odd because this particular person continues to read them and tell me how dreadful they are. Perhaps I'm simply not the author for him (or her, mentioning no names!).

I understand that my books won't be everyone's cup of tea, and I'm happy to hear constructive criticism, which is essential to improving as an author. However, I often see people in forums and on social media delivering critiques of their favourite personality which borders on the possessive or even abusive. Psychologically, I think it's fascinating to consider a character like Sharlene Campbell and her perspective that she in some way owns part of the actress she admires.

I must also reassure my North American readers that, while the Campbells are pretty awful, I do not think them representative of Americans in general. I feel especially guilty as they are named after some very nice readers of mine who won one of the Christmas competitions. To make up for it, I will make sure to include some far nicer countrymen in future books. Or perhaps I'm just saying that to make you think the next Americans I include are innocent when really they're the killers! We'll have to wait and see…

If you loved the story and have the time, please write a review at Amazon. Most books get one review per thousand readers so I would be infinitely appreciative if you could help me out.

THE MOST INTERESTING THINGS I DISCOVERED WHEN RESEARCHING THIS BOOK...

I should probably change the name of this chapter to *miscellaneous nonsense I stumbled across*, as I'm looking at the notes of all the things I researched and very much doubt there will be any kind of logical path through them, but here we go…

One thing that I'm very conscious of as I write is the approaching Wall Street crash of 1929. I'm not sure what impact it will have on these books, but I can hardly ignore it. For the moment, my characters are living in happy oblivion, though, as there are barely any rumblings of what will happen just weeks after this book is set. However, as Chrissy hilariously sneers at, there was already an economist pointing to what was coming at the beginning of September, seven weeks before Black Thursday. Roger Babson, who owned a company which analysed the financial markets, gave a speech to predict that "Sooner or later a crash is coming, and it may be terrific," which led to a three per cent fall in the stock market that same day. Still, plenty were happy to ignore him, and debt continued to mount. Most of you will know what happened next, but we'll wait for the next book to continue this story. Actually, the next one is set at Christmas, so you'll have to bear with me until the new year.

Staying with America, a friend of mine told me about how unique Savannah, Georgia is when I visited him in Seattle last year, and I enjoyed contrasting the two cities. Before then, the only place I'd been to in the States was New York, and I don't think I realised what large American cities were really like. I know it's often said that the car is king in the U.S.A., but I'm so used to towns in Europe being built around a largely pedestrianised or at least easily walkable centre, that I was amazed to find what looked to me to be three-lane highways cutting through nearly every block in downtown Seattle. I really enjoyed my trip there, but I wasn't expecting the city to look anything like it does.

Savannah on the other hand, was built more to resemble Old World settlements. Perhaps this isn't surprising seeing as the man who came up with the idea – and founded Georgia – was a blasted Brit! Lieutenant-General James Edward Oglethorpe was granted permission by George II to establish a new colony there. As well as being a soldier, Oglethorpe was a politician and social reformer who believed, like many would a hundred years later when it was still a social problem, that people jailed for their debts would be better served by being given opportunities out of prison. It was his work in this area which gave him the opportunity to sail to America and establish a new settlement built around the concepts of the enlightenment that inspired him. He believed that Savannah could be a more equal society, and that idea extended to the plan for the town itself.

The city is organised on an innovative grid system with residential and commercial blocks arranged around small parks, and the idea was that everything local people needed would be close at hand. The hope was that this carefully considered and sustainable use of the land could extend to neighbouring settlements and even across America. Oglethorpe spent years perfecting and promoting his ideas, and his impact is still felt in the city and other towns which it would go on to influence. I haven't been there, but I like the sound of it, and it reminds me a little of the nineteenth- century expansion of Barcelona which gives the upper part of the city (*L'Eixample*) its distinctive plan with hundreds of neat, octagonal blocks arranged around garden squares (which are now largely concrete courtyards with plenty of air conditioning outlets).

The plan's architect, Ildefons Cerdà was ahead of his time, just like Oglethorpe. He planned out a whole city thinking of the needs of its residents and including in his design allowances for heat, light, and ventilation, on top of concerns like access to shops, schools and hospitals. Not all of his recommendations were finally included in the plan, but if you've ever explored the streets around Passeig d'Gracia, Gran Vía and Avenida Diagonal, a near-seven-mile road which cuts right across the city, you'll know what an impact Cerdà had on what is often considered one of the most beautiful major cities in the world.

Sticking with European cities, I think it is a massively under-reported fact that London has less rainfall than Rome, and I will tell everyone I meet until this imbalance has been addressed. Of course, there is a major caveat to come, but on average Rome has almost 800mm of rain a year to London's 600mm. I don't need to point out that it's a third more! Admittedly, and this is definitely something I and most Londoners would like to change, the three months when Rome has less rain than the English capital are all in the summer. London has surprisingly consistent rainfall throughout the year in a range from 68mm in October, the wettest month, to 41mm in February, the driest. In fact, according to the data I'm looking at, spring in London is drier than our summer.

The problem in London is not the quantity so much as the number of days it rains. A conservative estimate puts the total days per year at 120 to Rome's 80. I love London and, with climate change, things are constantly shifting, but it would be nice to be able to plan a barbecue in the summer and not have to cook it inside! Anyway, the point is, London: not quite so rainy as you might think… but totally dry days are hard to come by.

My characters make it to Verona, though there won't be a book set there as, being almost wintertime, the next one will be somewhere snowy. I spent two weeks in Verona with my in-laws a couple of years back and we had a great time there, but (sorry anyone who loves it) I was left unmoved by la Casa di Giulietta. This former medieval inn is one of the main tourist attractions in the city and, in the nineteenth century, was erroneously connected to the Capulets of Shakespeare's Romeo and Juliet. What's funny is that, at the time, the house was in a terrible state and certainly didn't look very grand, so the authorities completely revamped the exterior wall, added Juliet's famous balcony, and plenty of pretty arched windows, and it's now a money-spinning tourist attraction.

In the seventies, they added a bronze statue of thirteen-year-old Juliet under the balcony. It has become the tradition for tourists to have photographs taken whilst cupping her breasts. I don't like to be negative, especially about countries that aren't my own, but this felt all wrong when I was there, and I did not queue for a photo. So many people have bothered the poor girl that, about ten years ago, the statue had to be replaced when the breast and arm began to crack as around five million people a year went to paw her.

Anyway, I'll stop being a grump and move on from one famous young lady to another. We all know the rhyme of Little Bo-Peep, but as I made a passing mention to it, I decided I'd better check on her history. The earliest record of the poem isn't as far back as I might have expected and only appears in print in 1805, though the term *Bo-peep* pre-existed it as another name for the peeking game we play with babies – known as *Peepo* in British English. Disturbingly, there was also the expression *to play bo-peep* which referred to the corporal punishment of being put in a pillory to have things thrown at you. It seems unlikely the writer of the nursery rhyme was thinking of this, though, and I like one interpretation which states that the sheep in the poem are an allegory for smugglers, and their tails, that they "bring" or "drag" behind them, are the loot they have stolen.

In a similar area, a curious thing occurred when I went looking for a tongue twister for Chrissy to reference. I searched for one in the British Newspaper Archive and found quite a few in use in the 1920s. "Betty Botter bought some butter", the one I ended up choosing, was written by Carolyn Wells who, it turns out, was a fellow mystery writer. She also wrote children's fiction and published 170 books in her lifetime, which rather puts my thirty-three and counting to shame – though to be fair, she probably didn't have to do too much online marketing for her books, as she died in 1942. The Betty Botter tongue twister was published in the wittily titled *The Jingle Book* in 1899, and the full poem runs to eleven difficult-to-read lines which I considered printing here to make my audiobook narrator have to say them, but I'm not that cruel.

Right, that's about as far as I'm going to get in terms of coherent segues. Here's a bunch of more unconnected stuff before I tell you a bit about the movies again and then finish with cakes and songs as always.

- I originally had Geraldine pull off her sunglasses as she boarded the train in a very movie-star-esque move, and I needed to check how common they were. Although, for the best part of a millennium, Innuits had made opaque glasses with slits to prevent snow blindness, and rich Venetians had tinted lenses to protect them from the glare of the sun on the water, it wasn't until the turn of the twentieth century that mass produced sunglasses appeared. And would you know it? Eye protection was particularly common among film stars in the 1920s. They presumably helped spread the trend as, by 1937, 20 million pairs were sold every year in the U.S.A.

- I was worried that brake cords hadn't been invented in 1929, but there was already a law obliging trains to have them way back in 1868. The first version of this simply rang a bell to tell the driver that there was a problem, but by the end of the century, automatic brakes had been introduced and the cord operated them directly. Phew.

- I wonder if this law was prompted by the Staplehurst rail crash, which happened three years earlier. Ten passengers died when the train approached a viaduct which was being repaired. The incident is mostly remembered today as who should be on board but… no, not Agatha Christie… the other one I always go on about… that's right: Charles Dickens! He was travelling with his possible mistress (or secret daughter, depending on who you believe) the actress Ellen Ternan. Dickens helped Ternan and her mother to safety and then went to the aid of the injured and dying. He was deeply disturbed by the incident and subsequently avoided trains as much as possible. He died five years to the day after the accident occurred.

- There is no direct equivalent of *count* in the English aristocracy, but the title is similar in status to an earl. No one really knows why the title isn't used, but some people have suggested that it might be due to it sounding not totally dissimilar from possibly the rudest word in the English language. We get the word *county* from count, which referred to the land overseen by an earl, but apparently that wasn't a problem. Over in Italy, meanwhile, you can't move for counts. These days, as in France, aristocratic ranks there have no legal status, but there are still famous people who go by their inherited title, and for a long time, counts held great influence. In the medieval era, they were the rulers of their regions, with the Count of Savoy being of particular importance. I really like the word for the sons of a count who are known as *contini*, or little counts. Do you think I can get away with calling my kids *scrittorini*? Perhaps they should write something first.

- Like Chrissy, I rather like birds, and I spent a while looking for an appropriate one to help him undermine the Wolf's disguise. As it happens, the pin-tailed sandgrouse has only been spotted a couple of times in Italy, but I liked its geographic specificity and the fact it takes water to its young using its feathers. I also considered using the Italian sparrow, as that is a bird which is found only in Italy. It's not so very different in appearance from the Spanish sparrow, which, ironically, is more common in other Mediterranean countries than the one from which it takes its name.

- What Chrissy says about there not being many countries that Britain hasn't gone to war with is true. Today, the only European countries that Britain hasn't been in some kind of battle against are Andorra, Monaco, Lichtenstein, Luxembourg, Vatican City and, debatably, Sweden. It seems to be accepted that, internationally, there are twenty-two countries that Britain hasn't clashed with, and a couple of those have some big asterisks next to them. There are 193 countries on earth, and we've fought 90% of them!

- In 1896, the British-supported Sultan of Zanzibar died, possibly because he was poisoned by his successor, a young firebrand of whom the British did not approve. As a result, the British navy bombed the sultan's palace, marking the start of the Anglo-Zanzibar War. It finished thirty-eight minutes later when the new sultan surrendered and was arrested. It is considered the shortest war in history.

- I needed to check whether passports in the 1920s already used photographs, and it turns out they became mandatory in 1915. At first, you could use any photograph of yourself and there are examples of Arthur Conan Doyle with his family and dogs, and the Archbishop of Canterbury in full robes and with his staff in hand. Shortly before that, you didn't even have to include a physical description of yourself as, eighty years earlier, the British decided that such a breach of privacy was degrading. Things changed with the outbreak of World War One and the fear of enemy imposters, though some people still objected. Traditionally, passports were a single piece of paper folded in two, but in 1920 the now familiar blue booklet came into use. My father always told me not to smile in passport photos, but it was only forbidden by law in 2004, though passports date way back to the fifteenth century. It is believed that Henry V introduced the first examples to help Brits identify themselves abroad, though the word passport didn't appear until over a century later.

And now to the world of cinema! When reading the newspaper, Chrissy mentions an upcoming movie which is based on the story of the Titanic. Released later in the year, the film *Atlantic* didn't get permission to use the name of the real ship, and the company that had owned it, White Star Line, threatened to sue. It was the most expensive British film of 1929, and some scenes were filmed on real liners from the day. There were different language variants filmed at the same time, including a German and French version with separate actors redoing the English parts. The grand finale involved a complicated reconstruction of the sinking of the boat with 'hundreds of tons of water' used, but it was cut as the makers were afraid of upsetting the families of those lost a mere seventeen years earlier.

It was the first sound film about the tragedy, but it was also released in a silent version for those who were weary of these newfangled talkies. A recent review claims that the actors were so aware of the momentousness of the event they were recreating that they spoke slowly and mournfully throughout. I looked at contemporary takes on it, and *Picturegoer* magazine from 1st January 1930 offers a very disparaging review. It calls the effects "graphic and grimly vivid" and complains about the director's use of the cast along with "unworthy" dialogue in which characters warn of not causing panic long past the point that everyone is panicking.

From a forgotten film to an unforgettable actor. As the Italian count in this book mentions him, I thought I should find out more about Rudolph Valentino. Incidentally, I'm not sure anyone really referred to him by his full name, but it was so long I couldn't resist. Valentino, later known to many as 'the Latin lover', arrived in America aged eighteen and spent his first year there doing odd jobs and even living on the streets in New York. He was a capable dancer and seems to have fallen into acting mainly to escape from the scandal he'd become wrapped up in, involving a Chilean heiress and her vengeful husband, whom she had shot dead. He made it to Hollywood, where his background as a dancer led to him trying out for bit parts in films. His roles grew, and he went on to star in 1921's *The Sheik,* in which he played the brooding romantic lead.

It's hard to exaggerate the impact he made in Hollywood. Fans went crazy for him, partly because of the exotic, outsider parts he played. However, it's interesting to note that Valentino himself fought back against the depiction of non-European characters being savages when he said, "People are not savages because they have dark skins. The Arabian civilization is one of the oldest in the world." In his short life, he often found himself in trouble, and he went on trial for bigamy after trying to marry a co-star less than a year after he'd divorced his previous wife.

He also went on strike against his studio as he felt he was being underpaid compared to many major stars. When the company counter-sued, it legally stopped him from acting and meant that he went looking for other work. This led to a highly successful dance tour, stopping in 88 cities across North America, before he was offered a new contract and returned to Hollywood. In a happy coincidence for him to do this, he turned down a role in *Quo Vadis,* a certain Italian flop that I mentioned in the previous chapter. However, Valentino was neither a savvy businessman nor great at choosing projects and starred in a string of disappointing films before making a sequel to his biggest hit in 1926.

The Son of the Sheik was a massive success, but Valentino died suddenly the month after it was released. He was only thirty-one, and his passing was so terrible to his fans that some killed themselves, others engaged in a riot and 100,000 of them turned out in New York for his funeral. **Big spoiler alert if you haven't read the rest of this book yet:** there were rumours that the body was not really his, which is where I got the idea for an important element in my plot. Valentino died of a previously unrecognised type of ulcer, which came to be known as "Valentino's syndrome". This is one of his minor claims to fame, but it goes to show just how much he achieved in the five or so years during which he was famous.

Though I found plenty of disparaging references to his swarthy foreignness in papers from the day, I also read the four-page tribute to him in *Picturegoer* magazine which was printed the month after he died, and it was clear how highly the journalist rated him as an actor and how analytical a person Valentino was when considering his own fame. He did not like being mobbed and thought poorly of the obsessive fans who fell at his feet. He said, "The character I portray on screen – the romantic, dashing hero I seem to be – is what the public are really interested in. They do not know me. How can they?" which is a very honest approach for the world's biggest star to take. He also said that "I would rather retire at the height of my fame than see it fading away," and he certainly can't be accused of that.

And because I'm never going to have a better reason, I'd like to talk about Valentino's countryman, the director Frank Capra, who had almost as incredible a life. Unlike the actor, however, Capra came from a very poor background. He moved to America aged just five, travelling across the Atlantic on a steamship in the most terrible cramped and unsanitary conditions, the memory of which would stay with him throughout his life. His family settled in L.A. and later, though he got a college degree in chemical engineering, he was unable to find steady work after he served in the First World War. Also like Valentino, he spent some time homeless, doing any jobs that would put money in his pocket.

In the end, it was a little white lie that got him into the film industry as he exaggerated his experience to get a job directing a silent film. This led to writing work and a bunch of miscellaneous jobs on set but, within a couple of years, he was directing full-length comedies. With the birth of sound films, Capra made a name for himself and Columbia, the small studio he would help turn into a major player with films like *It Happened One Night* and *Mr Deeds Goes to Town*. He won three Oscars and was nominated six times as best director, including for my all-time favourite film, *It's a Wonderful Life*. Which really isn't bad going for a poor immigrant who conned his way into the industry.

And now… food! I planned to use the menus from old trains for this book, but almost all that I could find were made up of French food, so I Italianised one and came up with some tweaks to what I found that suited the country through which the train is passing. *Gelo di melone,* for example, is a watermelon pudding with traces of cinnamon, pistachio and jasmine water. Many people assume it is of Arabic influence, and it may actually be connected to Eastern European immigrants who settled in Sicily. Some people add pieces of chocolate to imitate watermelon seeds in this starchy pudding.

As Cook is still with us, I did have to include a few British dishes, and the desserts I mentioned are some real classics. Queen of Puddings is a perfectly named dish, if you happen to like jam and meringue. It sounds like a cross between a cheesecake and a lemon meringue pie, as the base is made of baked milk, sugar and egg-soaked breadcrumbs, then there's a layer of jam with the soft meringue on top. There are similar recipes dating back to the seventeenth century, but it appears in newspapers by name in the 1870s and became widespread in the twentieth century. The British government even recommended it as a source of nutrition for sick children.

The word flummery is of Welsh origin and, rather unappetisingly, means something bland. As a dish, it started off as a sour oatmeal that was so inoffensive it was given to people with digestive problems. As a result, the word also came to mean inconsequential, empty chatter. The dessert developed into a starchy, milky pudding, but because of its ill fame, the word can still mean bland and unappealing food in general.

Chrissy was much better off with Sussex Pond Pudding, which I wish I had in front of me right now so that I could scoff it down. Like many such British dishes, it is first recorded in print in the late seventeenth century – which may say something about the development of publishing, rather than when our desserts were invented. Chrissy gives a better description than I can – he's the real expert – but the most important element to it is the way in which the butter and sugar inside the suet pastry caramelise so that, when you break it open, the gooey centre spills out like a chocolate coolant. It is also known as a *well pudding* or, if you add raisins, a black-eyed Susan. The inclusion of a whole lemon in the middle, which helps create its own sort of marmalade to add to the flavour, only came about in the late twentieth century, so Chrissy didn't get to taste it.

Just a few days before publishing this book, there was an article in the newspaper about ten traditional British desserts that people don't make so often any more. Coincidentally, all three that I have just mentioned were all in there, plus several others that have appeared in previous books. The writer concluded that most puddings are difficult to make and hard to execute well, which is why they have fallen out of favour. I don't think he's a brilliant dessert chef, so he didn't turn me off the idea of any of the dishes.

Righteo, that's enough mouth-watering. What about the music? I originally had a scene in the bar in which, rather than answering Edgington's questions, the Wolf walked over to the piano and started singing "That's My Baby". It was so incongruous that I axed it, but that song might turn up at another moment. Instead, we have an American barbershop quartet singing "Sweet Adeline". The song was written in 1903 by Richard Husch Gerard. Gerard wrote over 250 songs whilst making his way through medical school to be a dentist. He must have given up that career path as the obituary I found for him claims that he spent most of his life working as a manager at the General Post Office in Manhattan.

Two different versions of "Sweet Adeline" spent a total of seven weeks at number one in the States, but while its publisher would have made millions, Gerard only received a $3,000 fee. The music was by Harry Armstrong, and apparently the two began collaborating again just before Gerard died in 1948. Interestingly, JFK's grandfather, John F. Fitzgerald, who was a mayor and congressman, would sing the song as his theme tune at political rallies and performed it hundreds of times.

The song got me wondering about the barbershop genre as, while I've always assumed it had British roots, it is very much more common in the States than in Europe. I was half right, as there is talk of "barber's music" as far back as Samuel Pepys's time, but what that was like, beyond being some form of amateur pastime, is unclear. Barbershop as we know it today is more likely to have come out of black American culture, when small groups of men would sing a cappella in informal settings, as they were forbidden from entering concert venues at the time. This meant that black and white minstrels (or blackface performers) copied the style, and the genre reached a wider audience. The image we have of straw-boatered, candy-striped gentlemen was really only established in the 1940s when the Barbershop Harmony Society created singing competitions that were already harking back to an older tradition which – depending on which source you wish to believe – may not actually have existed. So now I know!

Well, folks. That's all we have time for today. I have another book to write, then another, then another. It's really lucky that I love my job. I genuinely don't have a clue what comes next in the story, but I'm eager to find out when I sit in front of my computer and the words (fingers crossed) appear on my screen.

ACKNOWLEDGEMENTS

I should definitely thank people who have helped me with foreign languages this time around. Lioba my dear friend, who is currently translating the Edgington books into German, is always very helpful when I WhatsApp her with questions. My daughter Amelie has a half-Italian classmate, and his father Fabio is a real star for the assistance he's given me. It's also handy having a couple of French people in the house to check my spelling! I must thank Admiral Clive Lewis for his help with train information, too. He will be the first person who receives a hard copy of this book.

Thank you, as always, to my kind and generous early readers, Bridget Hogg and the Martins. To Lisa Bjornstad, and Jayne Kirk for arduous close editing. And to my fellow writers who are always there for me, especially Catherine, Suzanne and Lucy.

And, of course, a massive thank you must go to my ARC team... Rebecca Brooks, Ferne Miller, Melinda Kimlinger, Emma James, Mindy Denkin, Namoi Lamont, Katharine Reibig, Linsey Neale, Terri Roller, Margaret Liddle, Lori Willis, Anja Peerdeman, Marion Davis, Sarah Turner, Sandra Hoff, Mary Nickell, Vanessa Rivington, Helena George, Anne Kavcic, Nancy Roberts, Pat Hathaway, Peggy Craddock, Cathleen Brickhouse, Susan Reddington, Sonya Elizabeth Richards, John Presler, Mary Harmon, Karen Quinn, Karen Alexander, Mindy Wygonik, Jacquie Erwin, Janet Rutherford, Ila Patlogan, Randy Hartselle, Carol Vani, June Techtow, M.P. Smith, Michele Kapugi, Helen K, Ed Enstrom and Keryn De Maria.

READ MORE LORD EDGINGTON MYSTERIES TODAY_

- **Murder at the Spring Ball**
- **Death From High Places** (free e-novella available exclusively at benedictbrown.net. Paperback and audiobook are available at Amazon)
- **A Body at a Boarding School**
- **Death on a Summer's Day**
- **The Mystery of Mistletoe Hall**
- **The Tangled Treasure Trail**
- **The Curious Case of the Templeton-Swifts**
- **The Crimes of Clearwell Castle**
- **A Novel Way to Kill** (novella available at Amazon)
- **The Snows of Weston Moor**
- **What the Vicar Saw**
- **Blood on the Banister**
- **A Killer in the Wings**
- **The Christmas Bell Mystery**
- **The Puzzle of Parham House**
- **Death at Silent Pool**
- **Murder in an Italian Castle**
- **Death on the Night Train to Verona**
- **The Alpine Chritmas Mystery** (November 2025)

Check out the complete Lord Edgington Collection at Amazon

The first sixteen Lord Edgington audiobooks, narrated by the actor George Blagden, are available now on all major audiobook platforms. There will be more coming soon.

THE "MURDER IN AN ITALIAN CASTLE" COCKTAIL

This may be the most popular drink I've ever mentioned on this page. When I moved to Spain in 2006, the Spritz was suddenly everywhere thanks to some savvy marketing from the Aperol brand, and its popularity has only grown since, with spritz bars popping up in a number of European cities.

As a cocktail, it is believed to have originated in the Veneto region at the end of the nineteenth century when foreign soldiers asked for a drop of water (or *spritzen* in German) in their drink as they found the local wines too strong. Jump forward forty years and the drink evolved, replacing wine with prosecco and the water with a carbonated alternative. Bitters were also added to the recipe and, depending on which you use, you have a different flavour and a different name. The one mentioned in the book is *spritz Veneziano*, which came from Venice and features the local Select aperitif. Coincidentally, it was given its name by the poet and soldier Gabriele D'Annunzio, who was mentioned in my last book and whose house I realised I'd visited. You could also use Aperol, which is from Padua, or Campari, from Novara.

The Aperol Spritz became popular internationally only in the last twenty years but is thought to have appeared in the fifties. The Select version came earlier, and while the exact year is a little vague, people in Venice were definitely drinking a cocktail called the *Spritz veneziano* with soda water, white wine and Select in the 1920s.

I personally prefer the modern recipe with prosecco for that extra fizz on hot summer days. So here's the *Spritz*...

> **3 parts Prosecco (sparkling white wine)**
>
> **2 parts bitter of your choice (Aperol may be easiest to find. Select is a little stronger and less sweet, whereas Campari is more bitter.)**
>
> **1 part of soda water.**

Mix together and then add ice and a slice of orange or whole olive.

You can get our official cocktail expert François Monti's brilliant book "101 Cocktails to Try Before you Die" at Amazon.

WORDS AND REFERENCES YOU MIGHT NOT KNOW

Compagnia dei Treni Notturni – the night train company, a reference to the *Compagnie internationale des Wagons-Lits* which was the dominant company running luxury trains at the time.

Chef de train – this is the French expression for a train conductor.

The Paris Herald / Continental Daily Mail – these were two prominent English-language newspapers on the Continent in the 1920s.

Hobble – this was a type of skirt which restricted a woman's freedom of moment in order to produce a more ladylike figure and walk. It was so ridiculous it became a bit of a joke.

Entschuldigung – sorry in German.

Ach du meine Güte - Oh my goodness!

Freundin – girlfriend.

Aspettare – wait!

Mein Schatz – my treasure (my darling).

Galliano – a type of Italian aperitif with vanilla and anise flavouring. It is an ingredient in the Harvey Wallbanger from 1969. In fact, that cocktail was specifically invented in order to promote the spirit in the US.

Würstchen – literally, little sausage, but as an insult, it means "squirt".

Canis lupus – the Latin binomial name for the grey wolf.

Vieni presto! La signorina è morta. – Come quickly! The young lady is dead.

Give up the girdle – to admit defeat.

Tin bar – I don't know how common these were, but there's a bar in the Chueca area of Madrid which opened in 1908 and has a very beautiful tin bar.

Skullduggerous – not a word, Chrissy! But it makes sense in context.

Windiger Geselle – Slippery customer (according to my friend Lioba who helped with the German translations).

Deutsches Wörterbuch – As Edgington explains, this is the largest dictionary in German, which was started by the Brothers Grimm but not finished in their lifetimes.

Photoplay – an old-fashioned word for a film. It was still in use in newspapers in the 1920s.

Came out in the washing – another way of saying that something will eventually come to light.

"Dankeschön." / "Bitteschön." – Thank you / You're welcome (in German).

Parthian shot – a synonym of parting shot. Parthians were an ancient people from what is now Iran who were known for their fighting skills on horseback.

Mi scusi, signorina, parla italiano? – Excuse me, miss. Do you speak Italian? (in Italian) This is a silly thing to ask, but my ex went around Germany asking people if they spoke German and she got some very funny looks when she subsequently changed to English.

Non, je suis désolée. Je suis française – No, I'm sorry. I'm French (in French).

Costermonger – a bit of a rotter. It literally means an apple seller, but Shakespeare turned it into an insult in *Henry IV Part 2*.

Chère amie – one's mistress, or I suppose… Wait, what's the word for a male lover outside of a relationship?

Like the clappers - a common expression I'm sure most of you will know meaning to go fast. What I hadn't realised was that the clappers in question were the dangling chime of a bell. Perhaps I am thick.

Give the show away – another expression for *give the game away*.

Âmes damnées – someone who is excessively devoted to another and will do anything for them.

Come Gesù… benefico – the count searches for the word selfless and says, "like Jesus…benevolent".

Santo Graal – Holy Grail.

Il Colosseo – the Colosseum

Blödsinn – nonsense (in German).

Mountebank – a swine, rotter, charlatan. Someone who pretends to be something they are not.

Wit-state' / mens sana / brain-wood / touched in the upper storey – these are all old-fashioned ways of referring to one's mental wellbeing.

Eleventh-hour – at the last minute. I mention it here because I hadn't realised (or I'd possibly forgotten) that it comes from the parable Jesus tells of the Labourers in the Vineyard in the Gospel of Matthew.

Cretonne – a type of strong, often expensive French fabric made of hemp with bold coloured patterns on it.

Drachm – 1/16th of an ounce.

Carabinieri – one of the Italian police forces.

The black dog on (someone's) back – a bad mood or depression. The OED tells me that Churchill described his low spirits in this way, but it had been around for at least a hundred years before he was born.

ABOUT ME

Writing has always been my passion. It was my favourite half-an-hour a week at primary school, and I started on my first, truly abysmal book as a teenager. So it wasn't a difficult decision to study literature at university which led to a master's in creative writing.

I'm a Welsh-Irish-Englishman originally from **South London** but now living with my French/Spanish wife and our two presumably quite confused young children in **Burgos**, a beautiful mediaeval city in the north of Spain. I write overlooking the Castilian countryside, trying not to be distracted by the vultures, eagles and red kites that fly past my window each day.

When Covid-19 hit in 2020, the language school where I worked as an English teacher closed down, and I became a full-time writer. I have three murder mystery series. My first was **"The Izzy Palmer Mysteries"** which is a more modern, zany take on the genre, and my newest is the 1920s set **"Marius Quin Mysteries"** which features a mystery writer as the main character – I wonder where I got that idea from.

I previously spent years focusing on kids' books and wrote everything from fairy tales to environmental dystopian fantasies, right through to issue-based teen fiction. My book **"The Princess and The Peach"** was long-listed for the Chicken House prize in The Times and an American producer even talked about adapting it into a film.

"Death on the Night Train to Verona" is the second novel in the "Lord Edgington Investigates Abroad" series. The next book will be out in November 2025. There's a novella from the previous series available free if you sign up to my **readers' club**. Should you wish to tell me what you think about Chrissy and his grandfather, my writing or the world at large, I'd love to hear from you, so feel free to get in touch via…

www.benedictbrown.net

THE IZZY PALMER MYSTERIES

If you're looking for a modern murder mystery series with just as many off-the-wall characters, try **"The Izzy Palmer Mysteries"** for your next whodunit fix.

Check out the complete Izzy Palmer Collection in ebook, paperback and Kindle Unlimited at Amazon.

THE MARIUS QUIN MYSTERIES

There's a new detective in town. Marius first appeared in the Lord Edgington novel **"A Killer in the Wings"**, and now he has his own series...

Check out the complete Marius Quin Collection in ebook, paperback and Kindle Unlimited at Amazon.

CHARACTER LIST

New Arrivals

Geraldine de la Forge – a beloved film actress and one of the most beautiful women of the silent film era (in this book at least).

Hansel Reinhardt – her German director.

Sharlene and James Joseph Campbell – an American couple in their fifties who are travelling around Europe.

Marvin Pelthorpe – a suspicious character who claims to be birdwatching in Italy. Named after the first Englishman my father-in-law ever met.

Count Giovanelli – a rich Italian aristocrat.

Eddie Denkin – Geraldine's co-star and ex-boyfriend.

Gerard Laroche – just some French wine seller… or is he?

Georges Nagelmackers – the Belgian train conductor or *chef de train*.

Milly Buckthorn – Geraldine's maid.

Domenico – the steward.

Mr Honeydew – Geraldine's manager. He doesn't really feature much.

The girl! – just some pretty girl Chrissy saw in Florence and on the boat from England. I doubt she'll be of any importance to the story.

The Regulars

Lord Edgington – former superintendent for the Metropolitan Police, nicknamed the Bloodhound of Scotland Yard. After his wife's death he retreated from the limelight for a decade and only returned to his sleuthing aged seventy-five with the help of his grandson assistant…

Christopher Prentiss – the no longer quite so naïve and chubby grandson, whose detective skills have come on a great deal since he left school.

Todd – chauffeur, cocktail mixer, factotum and general nice guy, Lord Edgington and Christopher both rely on him for different reasons.

Henrietta (Cook) – Lord Edgington's favourite person. Back home in Cranley Hall, she was the person to prepare his often unusual meals, and she continues her work as they travel.

Dorie – formerly a skilful pickpocket whom Lord Edgington arrested, she has gone straight and now faithfully serves the old marquess.

Timothy – the hall boy back home at Cranley Hall. I'll work out something important for him to do one day.

Made in the USA
Las Vegas, NV
04 October 2025

29106570R00173